# Grace and Gravity

# Grace and Gravity

## FICTION BY WASHINGTON AREA WOMEN

### Edited by Richard Peabody

Some of these stories and novel excerpts have been previously published: Melissa Hardin's "Close to Pink" first appeared in *Mass Ave Review* (Spring 1998); C. M. Mayo's "Manta Ray" first appeared in *Natural Bridge* (Spring 2002); Frances Park's "Walks Home in the Dark with Abby" appeared online in *USAToday.com's* "Open Book" series (Spring 2003); Mary Quattlebaum's "Suzuki" first appeared in *Washington Review* (1984); Myra Sklarew's "The Guardians of the First Estate" first appeared in *Like a Field Riddled by Ants* (Lost Roads Publishers, 1987); Mary Kay Zuraleff's "Hold Your Breath and Count to Ten" first appeared in *Membrane* (No. 1, 1995).

ISBN: 0-931181-18-6
First Edition
Published in the USA

*Special thanks to:* Christina Bartolomeo, Nita Congress, Lucinda Ebersole, Patricia Elam, Barbara Esstman, David Everett, Sunil Freeman, Patricia Griffith, Margaret Grosh, Donna Hemans, Karen J. Kovacs, and C. M. Mayo.

Paycock Press
3819 North 13th Street, Arlington, VA 22201
www.atticusbooks.com

*About the cover artist:* JODY MUSSOFF has been exhibiting her drawings for over twenty-five years and is represented in various museums and collections in the United States and abroad. More recently, she has been working in ceramics as well. She lives outside Washington, D.C.; her website is www.artworkphotographer.com/jodym/home.htm.

*In memory of six extraordinary Washington area women who passed too soon:*

*Eva Cassidy*

*Marion Clark*

*Susan Davis*

*Joyce Renwick*

*Mary Ann Suehle*

*Martha Tabor*

*Two forces rule the universe: light and gravity.*
—Simone Weil

# Contents

# Preface

## Richard Peabody

Assembling this exciting collection of laughter and pain has been the happiest and most gratifying experience of my literary career. Why didn't I think of this before? I love to work with women, I love stories, and I love my city. My initial idea was to assemble a book that emulated both Cris Mazza's and Lidia Yuknavitch's daring women's anthologies. I stated in my invitation that there would be no taboos, that I wasn't interested in "safe" stories, and that short-shorts were more desirable than longer pieces. I sent the invite to a select list of forty area women with book credits. I assumed they would explore all sorts of experiences—love, sex, death, murder, suicide, etc. Stories were not required to use the D.C. area as a setting, nor did they specifically have to feature a female point of view. I also wanted very much to print realism and magical realism side by side.

The thirty-two women who chose to participate are a who's who of Washington area fiction writers, all but four of whom have published one or more books. I frankly love the mix of voices. There are rising stars, venerable local names, those known primarily for their Young Adult books or their poetry volumes, and a handful of new kids on the block. The majority of the work is original to this collection, with only a few pieces being reprints.

Finally, what makes this volume feel groundbreaking to me is the freedom everyone has taken to create whatever they wished, freedom not easily found in the conservative America of 2004. I wanted the book to be a safe haven for area women to rant and rave and rock 'n' roll, to try something different, something dangerous, something that might not have found a home in the mainstream publishing world. The results hit universal chords, while being at turns funny, hip, heart-wrenching, sad, grim, and spiritual.

I'm grateful to all of the women involved, all of the women who write or have ever written in the Nation's Capital, and all of the women who are just beginning to find their writerly legs or wondering if there are other local writers worth reading. I'm grateful to Nita Congress for putting so much time and effort into the desktopping and design, to M. Scott Douglass for being a printer who actually understands small publishers and communicates intelligently with them, and to the Washington Chapter of the Women's National Book Association for being there to help float this baby out into the world.

R.P.

September 2004

Doreen Baingana

# Holy Shit! or Afterwards

DOREEN BAINGANA is a Ugandan writer whose short story collection, *Tropical Fish: Stories out of Entebbe*, is forthcoming in January 2005 (University of Massachusetts Press). She won the Washington Independent Writers Fiction Prize 2004 and the 2003
Associated Writing Programs Award in Short Fiction. She was
nominated for the Caine Prize in African Writing in 2004. Her
work has appeared in *Glimmer Train, Chelsea, African American
Review, Callaloo, The Sun, Crab Orchard Review, Meridian*, and
other journals. She has received a grant from the D.C. Commission on the Arts and Humanities, and scholarships to the Key
West Literary Seminar, the Bread Loaf Writers' Conference, and
the Anderson Center for the Arts. Baingana has an MFA from the
University of Maryland, College Park.

We walk out of his house one sunny morning in Kampala feeling all right. I am bursting with the happy-to-be-alive feeling that comes after a good night of lovemaking. Everything around me looks new; the clear morning sun just before it gears up for the midday heat, small birds twittering in the trees, a cute kid hiding shyly behind her mother's long skirt.

I hold my lover's hand as we walk down the street. I am old enough to have a lover, but the word still gives me guilty pleasure. For a night, at least, our bodies joined together and became one moving bulk with a joyous myriad of tentacles and orifices. After adult conversation at dinner, debate with fish stew, rice, and beer, I was on my back, legs spread wide and flailing in the air in that ridiculous position women, be they Supreme Court judges, little old ladies with funny hats and moustaches muttering to themselves on the bus, or our very own righteous mothers, end up in sooner or later. We are spread out like roast chicken and poked and prodded, and it is the most delicious thing there is.

My lover and I completely opened ourselves to each other; there were no secrets left. In bed, that is. He explored all sorts of places in and on me. Now he

*1*

knows me better than I do myself. In bed. We screamed and giggled and growled together. I felt we swam greedily in the exact same heat, tenderness, fury, waterfall, and languid fatigue.

Now we walk down a dusty road that leads to the main highway into the city center. The road, a typical African small-town scene, is lined with uneven wooden kiosks selling Ruwenzori bottled water, *chapati*, chewing gum, plastic cups, plates, and buckets in bright blue, green, red, and yellow, cell phone cards. Amid the stray dogs, old worn bicycles leaning on tree trunks, fast-spoken news coming from a radio somewhere, and old gray men sitting in the shade, is a lone thin brown cow. Its legs are stretched out, taut, straining to the point of tremors. I watch it. Even its face has a concentrated expression. Is it going to give birth? No, it's not swollen with pregnancy. I can't take my eyes off it. I tug at my lover's arm to slow him down. "Look, look!," I point as a bright pink thing pushes out of the cow's thin behind. The muscular-looking piece of flesh stretches, and out comes a dark army-green giant worm, out and down. It hangs mid-air for a moment, tentatively. Finally, now grown too long, it thwops down onto the roadside dust and spreads out into a flat steaming cake.

"Did you see that?"

My lover's face is an eloquent grimace of disgust. "You! Stop your bad manners."

I giggle as we walk on, but he will not follow wherever my senses take me. A cow shitting is not a beautiful and moving symbol of pure eros, not to him. For me, *that* is last night all over again. The naturalness and dirtiness and *honesty* of the physical. The cow's indecent, innocent pink protrusion and smelly loud plop of shit landing is the brazen badness, rudeness, sliminess of sex. Does he not see this, feel this? Wasn't he there? How can we be this different?

I had discovered and mapped his whole body. He gave it to me; I owned it. I deeply understood his mouth and cock. I have seen his face go tender. He has seen mine open-mouthed grotesque with sharp pleasure. But now, now, we are on the other side. Our clothes, deceivingly thin cotton shields, are back on. Coffee is speeding through our veins and brains, pushing us to the next thing, a crash landing.

I let go his arm. We go back to talking newspaper headlines, using words as steps to back away from each other, from ourselves. I look into his face and almost recognize the eyes of my lover. Almost. Where is he? Who was that lusty me? We move further and further away, like memory does from reality.

*Abby Bardi*

# *Away*

ABBY BARDI, born and raised in Chicago, has worked as a singing waitress in Washington, D.C., an English teacher in Japan and England, a performer on England's country-and-western circuit, and, most recently, as a professor at Prince George's Community College. Author of a column called "Sin of the Month" for *The Takoma Voice*, she is married with two children and lives in Ellicott City, Maryland. Her novel is *The Book of Fred*.

"I've been away," she said.

I couldn't tell who she was talking to. I looked at her out of the corner of my eye. Her look was wrong—not quite schizophrenic, not quite homeless. I tried to see into the shopping bag at her feet to check for clues: all I could see were a tattered newspaper and a jumbo pack of GE long-life light bulbs.

"How about you?" she asked.

I didn't know whether it would be better to answer or to pretend she hadn't spoken. The subway doors opened and closed with a whisper. "I've been here," I decided to say.

"And evidently," she continued, although I hadn't looked at her, "things have changed." I could feel her smile beaming onto my left cheek like heat.

I wheeled around sideways. "What medication are you on?" I asked, looking her over. She was a little closer to fifty than I was, with a sunburned face, light, stringy hair, and a big fat mouth that widened at me as if we'd just been introduced by a mutual friend.

"Oh, no," she said. "Oh, no. I'm not on medication. What about you?"

"Prozac," I said. "It used to be Thorazine. I used to do that Thorazine thing with the tongue. The lolling thing."

She nodded as if she understood.

"But everyone's on Prozac nowadays," I said.

She rummaged in her shopping bag, then pulled out a tiny spiral notebook and a Bic pen. "Spell it."

"P. R. O. Z. A. C."

"There are so many things I don't know." I could see her writing "Prozac?" in her notebook. "Things I need to know. I've been away."

"Of course," I said. It was suddenly clear to me. "You were kidnapped by aliens and taken to another planet."

"You're good," she said, smiling even more widely. "With some people it takes them longer."

"What was it like?" I asked, not wanting to pry, but curious.

"The usual, I guess."

"Like in the movies?"

"Kind of. Depends which movies you mean. Not at all like *Close Encounters.*"

"Like *Men in Black?*"

She gave me this eager look, like she wanted to understand but didn't.

"After your time," I guessed.

"Must've been." She smoothed her hair and glanced out the window. There was nothing to see; we were still underground. The train was beginning to slow.

"Is this your stop?" I asked.

"Oh, I'm going to the end of the line. I've never been there. I hear it's like a little country town, with stores and things."

"A country town? No, it's just a suburb. There are no country towns any-more. Except maybe in the country," I added for the sake of accuracy. "I'll ride with you. I'm just passing the time."

"Ah," she said, knowing all about me now, even knowing what my job had been and how many kids I lost custody of. Probably even knowing how I deco-rated my house, when I had one. I had been partial to valances. "It's warm in here," she said. "I like the way it's so quiet. For a train, I mean."

"Were the trains loud on Mars?" I asked.

She pursed her lips as if she was about to correct me and tell me that it wasn't Mars, that there was no life on Mars and everyone should know that. But then I could see that she knew that I knew. How could she tell? Because the biggest difference between us was that she had been away and I'd been here.

"They didn't have trains where I was. They had these things like bicycles, only they weren't really because they didn't have any wheels or pedals."

"How did they pedal if there were no pedals?"

"Well," she said kind of apologetically, "they didn't have legs."

"What did they have?"

"It's hard to explain. They didn't really have anything. They were kind of like lights."

"You mean like a thousand points of light?"

"No. Lights that hang from the ceiling. That's the closest I can come to describing them."

"They looked like chandeliers?"

"Yeah. Kind of."

There was nothing more to say on that subject, her look seemed to say, so I busied myself with studying the dirt under my fingernails. I knew my fingernails, in fact my hands in general, a lot better than the average person did.

"So," she said as the train rose into the light, "apparently George Bush is president again."

"It's a different one."

"Ah," she said. The train was whipping past rows of brick houses. Inside them, people were watching the news, eating dinner, arguing, having sex, yelling at their kids.

"It's funny," she said.

I knew what she was thinking. How time passes in such a weird way, especially when you are kidnapped by aliens and are gone a long time, and when you come back, at first it looks like the same place only funny, like when you first come out of the hospital and the sunlight hurts your eyes. You know your way around because the streets are the same streets some guy drew on a piece of paper two hundred years ago and then named each one as if it was his child. But things are different, as if someone has been in your house and slightly rearranged the furniture. It's like a weird odor: you smell that things are not the same, they only look the same. And she is thinking all right, being kidnapped by aliens was interesting, and she did have a few offers from some of the better supermarket aisle newspapers, but now she has a problem: time has let go of her. She's going to be pushing fifty for the next century, and while everyone else gets white-haired and walks with a stoop up and down the streets, up and down, she'll still be riding this subway with the same fresh face, this innocent look, wearing it like a sweater from her childhood. Since she has been riding around on bicycles with a bunch of chandeliers, she and time have parted company. She may as well be an alien herself, she is thinking, gliding silently along rubber rails.

I know she is thinking this. She doesn't have to tell me. "There are so many of us," I say as we reach the last stop.

## Jodi Bloom

# Fall

JODI BLOOM has published many short stories in journals here and abroad. Her most recent fictions can be seen on the wrists of ex-porn stars turned blues singers, famous romance novelists, heavy metal rocker wives, and by visiting www.so-charmed.com.

*E*unice sat on a high stool in Francine's kitchen, stirring the ice cubes in her cocktail glass around and around with her index finger. When it got too cold, she pulled the finger out and stuck it in her mouth, sucking the vodka off without even noticing that she hated the taste. Eunice couldn't remember having a drink in the middle of the afternoon in her life. In fact, this was her second drink and you could say Eunice was drunk.

Francine was talking, her voice droning like a pattern, a blurry buzz in the background. Not that it mattered what she was saying; it simply mattered that Eunice was sitting there, drink in hand, gazing into the lemon-lime printed wall-paper, smiling and nodding and sipping. She had arrived. It was what she had hoped for all summer—this glamorous, if drunken, moment. Eunice sat upright, bringing the room back into focus. She did not, after all her hard work, want to fall off her chair or something stupid like that.

Eunice giggled to herself. *In paradise there is no fall,* she thought. She giggled again. Francine looked at her sideways, cocking her head.

"Eunice?" she asked.

It was a poem Eunice had written in high school, one that her freshman English teacher thought was so good he had encouraged Eunice to write, write, write. "Keep a journal," he'd said, "write poems, stories. You're good; you've got a natural gift." He taught Eunice some special techniques for remembering her dreams which he said she could use for material later. He suggested she buy a miniature flashlight and a spiral-bound steno pad to keep by the bed.

Eunice couldn't, for the life of her, remember a single dream, but she wrote a few things down, an entry or two in her journal that began: *Dear Diary.* The entries were nothing special though. Really, they weren't very good at all, and the freshman English teacher quickly lost interest. "In Paradise There Is No Fall" became Eunice's one and only poem.

"I'm fine," Eunice answered, smiling at Francine. She was trying to stay with it—she didn't want to make any silly mistakes. "Mmm," she added, "I just love vodka."

"Yeah," Francine said, sipping her drink. "Vodka is heaven."

❧

Was it heaven or paradise that Eunice's husband Phil had promised when he first proposed the move from their cozy home in Ohio to the sunny Fort Lauderdale golf course community? Eunice tried hard to remember.

"Imagine, honey," he'd said, smiling in the handsome way that had won her over a number of times in the past. "No snow, no ice, just beautiful sunshine all the time. Like a picture postcard," Phil added. "Just wait 'til you see—it's paradise."

Or had he said heaven? Well, whatever. It wasn't really important anyway. Eunice admitted that she could certainly live without ever scraping the snow and ice off another car, without winter altogether, but unfortunately, she'd forgotten about fall. Eunice loved fall, didn't everyone? Why had she been so stupid? Here it was September, and Eunice craved the crispness of fall, a breeze of cool air, a crunchy walk through even a *few* dead maple leaves. But the Florida heat pressed on, and, with all that beautiful sunshine, dead leaves seemed like a whole lot to ask. Besides, she couldn't very well stand in the way of Phil's ship, the one he assured her (there was the handsome smile again) had finally, this time for sure, come in.

Phil's ship was a business deal. It would eventually run aground, become full of gaping holes, and, Eunice imagined, sink miserably to the bottom of the Atlantic Ocean, just a twenty-minute drive from the townhouse he'd acquired for Eunice and their small son in Fort Lauderdale. Why had she bought the scheme? Well, no matter. Here she was, relaxing in Francine Halpern's cool aqua townhouse.

❧

The air in the townhouse was chilled, like all of the indoor air in south Florida. And although the kitchen was a fun collage of bright yellows and acidy greens, Eunice had truly admired the heavenly shade of aqua, with its cooling effect, that coated the living room walls, the hallway, even the powder room, which Eunice had not really used. She'd gone in just to assess the decor.

She was already a little drunk, but Eunice had no trouble finding the powder room; Francine's townhouse was an exact replica of her own, except in reverse. So she walked right down the hallway, following the aqua walls, and, sure enough, there it was, to the left instead of the right. Inside the bathroom, which included a matching aquamarine rug and fuzz toilet seat cover, she ran the water and flushed, for effect.

Eunice decided then and there to completely redo her own townhouse, erasing the previous owner's hideous mauve and lavender decor forever. Maybe she would choose a nice blue, a pale sky blue; it would be similar to Francine's place, but still considered unique. She swirled the ice in her glass the way she'd seen Francine swirl hers, and banged back another gulp of the cold drink. She asked if she could see the bedroom (more decorating research), but Francine said no, it was an embarrassing wreck. "Maybe some other time," she offered, letting Eunice know there were to be other such nice afternoons spent together drinking and laughing.

⁓

Eunice had hated the townhouses at first; hers was such a terrible disappointment. Back in Ohio, Phil showed her photographs he had taken with their Instamatic, a pretty and sprawling suburban neighborhood, snapshots of big ranch houses dotting the edges of a perfectly manicured golf course.

"Look at this, honey," he said pointing to the beautiful modern homes. *They sure were lovely*, Eunice agreed. And each one with its own built-in pool! She'd take one of those pretty new houses any day.

"We'll buy one next January," Phil said, smoothing Eunice's hair with his hand when the last boxes were stacked in the tiny living room of the two-bedroom townhouse, at the remote southern tip of the golf course. You couldn't even *see* the golf course from the windows, Eunice noticed right away. You couldn't see it at all until you were back out on the main road.

But it wasn't completely without charm. Someone had designed the living room with a ceiling that went all the way up to the top, right where a room on the second floor would be. "A cathedral ceiling," Phil explained. Eunice wondered if she should start praying. Maybe she should pray that she would find space for all their junk; the townhouse was half the size of their old stone home back in Ohio.

"I thought your ship had come in," Eunice whispered. She imagined the great ship's anchor slowly lifting out of the silt of the ocean's floor—the massive structure beginning to sway and drift back out to sea as if to say, *only kidding, just docking at this port for a little visit.*

ᴦ

Besides the cathedral ceiling, the townhouse had other clever features. For example, one entire wall in the combination living room/dining room was covered
in big square mirror tiles. This was supposed to make the room look larger, Phil
had explained, but the tiles were not placed exactly flush, creating a fractured
effect that unnerved Eunice every time she walked by. Little Phil Jr. liked the tiles
and covered them with his greasy chubby handprints. *God help us if I run out of
Windex in this place*, Eunice thought.

She spent the first weeks doing some decorating, or rearranging, to be more
precise; she didn't have money for real decorating. When she had finished arranging and moving the furniture into every conceivable configuration, which took
about two weeks total, she spent another week exploring the mall down the
street, dragging Phil Jr. along by the hand.

Together, they tried the different foods at the twenty-stall food arcade: steak
fries and ice cream and slippery sesame noodles. They wandered through department stores and tiny specialty boutiques. They sat by the fountain and watched
the water spray up. "Another cathedral ceiling," Eunice remarked, looking way
up to the skylight that topped the mall's central atrium.

"What's round on the ends and high in the middle, O-hi-o," Eunice sang to
herself, wandering through the shopping center or yanking and shoving the sofa
back to the other side of her living room, where it definitely belonged. She was so
lonely those first weeks. She sighed and sat down. She missed her best friend back
home, Mary Lou, and other things. She missed her life.

Eunice tried writing a few letters. *Dearest Mary Lou*, she began, but it just
never went anywhere, so she gave up. I'll write later, Eunice decided, when there's
something to say. She hoped later would be soon.

ᴦ

Meanwhile she tried to get used to things, like the idea that she and Phil owned
what Phil called a share of the townhouse community swimming pool, with its
dozens of plastic chaise lounges. Phil paid monthly dues so that Eunice, and
whoever else, could sit and sun themselves, have a swim, or take advantage of the
clubhouse, which had a Ping-Pong table, three paddles, and no balls.

"You have to bring your own," Phil explained.

Eunice looked at him like he was crazy. Her husband was so *queer* sometimes.
She could just see herself and little Phil slamming Ping-Pong balls around the
dingy rec room.

During one of the mall expeditions, Eunice bought Phil Jr. a swimsuit, an adorable thing, tiny navy blue trunks with little white boats sailing across the fabric. The next morning Eunice put her suit on, a sleek one-piece black Jantzen racer that reminded her of something a lifeguard might wear, threw on an old shirt, packed up Phil Jr., and headed for the pool. *Maybe today will be the day my new life will start,* Eunice thought. But really, she wasn't all that optimistic.

The pool was crowded and noisy; school had let out for the summer. Groups of teenagers stood huddled and tense along the edges of the pool deck; some were asleep on chairs, occasionally opening a lazy eye to see what was going on. A radio blared. All of the lounge chairs were taken, and Eunice spread her towel on the hot concrete in the most out-of-the-way place she could find.

There were adults at the pool too, young women in their twenties, like Eunice, clustered in small groups, chatting or fanning themselves with fashion magazines. Every so often, they shifted their chairs, to maintain perfect alignment with the afternoon sun. The women seemed so glamorous and cool in their hot-colored bikini bathing suits. Eunice looked down at her old black racer and wished there were someplace to hide. She figured her bathing suit had to be ten years old, if it were a day. She yawned nervously and held Phil Jr.'s hand so tight he gave a little cry.

No one talked to Eunice or even looked at her. So she splashed around with Phil Jr. in the baby pool for awhile. Then she dried them off, went home, and took a roast out to thaw. Her new life had not started that day, that was for sure.

و

It took a week or two for Eunice to get up the nerve to go back to the pool. This time, Francine saw Eunice. Francine had actually noticed Eunice the first time, standing there in her old swimsuit, gripping her son's hand so hard her knuckles were white. But this time Eunice saw Francine seeing her—Francine, in the brightest bathing suit of all, a wild hot-pink bikini with a pattern of yellow daisies—Francine with her sandy blonde hair feathered back like Farrah Fawcett-Majors.

For a week, Eunice spied on Francine through her big round sunglasses. She peered at her over her magazines, watched the other women at the pool gathering around Francine, mimicking her easy style and laugh. It didn't take long for the idea to formulate: *Francine was the key to Eunice's new life in the Sunshine State.* Francine became Eunice's summer goal.

Really though, it hadn't been all that difficult. Eunice had a good eye for detail, and after saving up her allowance and scrimping just a little on groceries, she was able to purchase one of the pretty designer swimsuits and a shimmery pale pink shade of lipstick that everyone was wearing.

She spent another entire week's allowance on a haircut, without even feeling guilty. The salon at the mall, Rainbow, was not like any beauty shop Eunice had ever been to. It was more like a discotheque, with loud pumping music and a front desk lined in futuristic blue neon lights. A man with skinny hips and fluttery hands parted Eunice's long straight brown hair in the center, trimming bangs and at least five inches off the bottom.

"You look *fabulous*," he said to her, pulling her hair around to one side and whispering the words into her ear. Eunice could feel his breath; it made her uncomfortable. But she did, indeed, look fabulous—maybe a little like…Jaclyn Smith?

⁊

Then it just happened; her new life started and it wasn't even so remarkable. One day Eunice was smoothing Coppertone on her legs, Phil Jr. was waddling around somewhere, and when she looked up Francine was standing there. "Hi," Francine had said.

"Hi," Eunice answered, trying not to sound nervous.

"Um," Francine said, sticking her hand out toward Eunice. "I'm Francine Halpern."

Eunice was a little dumbfounded. She stuck her hand out and shook with Francine.

"Eunice," Eunice said. She forgot to add her last name.

Then Francine gracefully sat herself right down on the end of Eunice's chaise lounge, and you would have thought they'd been best friends forever, the way Francine started talking nonstop.

Eunice went home and told Phil, in a rush of excitement, about her new friend, trying to remember some of the things Francine had told her about herself and her life.

"We should get together with them sometime," Eunice said, meaning Francine and her husband, Larry. But somehow it never happened, and Eunice was just as happy to have her new friend to herself.

⁊

When fall arrived, the teenagers disappeared and Phil Jr. went along to first grade. Eunice dropped him off in the mornings, came home and changed, and headed straight for the pool to hang out with Francine and work on her dark beautiful tan. The sun stayed high and bright, the temperatures soaring into the nineties on some days. Palm trees loomed above, unwavering and defiantly green.

"This is incredible," Eunice said once to Francine, "this heat, I mean. It's September and everything."

"You'll get used to it," Francine said, looking up at Eunice from under her Christian Dior sunglasses, "we all did."

No one was actually from south Florida, Eunice discovered; the women at the pool had moved from places up north—where the arrival of fall was, of course, unquestionable—places like New York or Connecticut, anywhere and everywhere really. And now, here Eunice was, getting used to the relentless heat in Francine's cool aqua townhouse. She shivered—maybe she already *was* used to it. As a matter of fact, she was downright freezing cold.

Eunice stared drunkenly at Francine, keeping her in focus. It was like looking through a microscope: she could count Francine's streaky blonde hairs or even her eyelashes if she'd wanted to. Everything else was a blur. Eunice was wasted. But she felt she deserved this moment, as much as anyone did. She had given up one entire life, she surely deserved another.

"Is it chilly in here?" Eunice asked, crossing her arms into a little hug.

"Mmm. Feels alright to me," Francine said, but she walked over to the thermostat and fiddled around with it for what seemed to Eunice like an eternity.

*Now, what had they been talking about?* Eunice couldn't remember. Francine was saying something about a new Trans Am and Larry's overactive sex drive. It should have been interesting, Eunice thought; it seemed as though it probably was. She drifted in and out, and Francine did all, or most, of the talking.

Eunice hardly noticed when Francine slid her drink away from her and began mixing another tall one, her third. "Here, let me freshen that up," she'd said. Francine really seemed to be enjoying herself, clinking ice cubes into their glasses from the automatic icemaker on the front of the fridge and pouring the vodka and tonic like a real pro.

"We don't have an automatic icemaker," Eunice said, "that's super neat." *Super neat?* Eunice wondered if she sounded as dumb as she felt. She was totaled.

"Really?" Francine said. "You don't have one?"

Francine was drunk too. She looked like she was struggling to remember something. "Oh, yeah," she finally said, "we bought a new fridge when we first moved in. Because ours was a broken piece of shit. It melted a gallon of ice cream once which came running all out of the bottom, and this entire ant colony came out of nowhere and Larry had to massacre them with a can of Raid. It was kind of funny," she laughed.

Eunice laughed too, picturing Larry crawling around on the floor spraying up a storm in the tiny kitchen, dead ant carcasses and ice cream everywhere. Or was that Phil crawling around on the floor? She didn't even know what Larry looked like!

Eunice stood up. "I have to…," she started to say.

"Oh, go ahead," Francine said, waving Eunice toward the powder room.

ᨓ

Eunice wobbled down the hall. She wouldn't have to fake it this time, she smiled to herself sitting down. The little room was spinning, and Eunice bent over, hanging her head between her knees. She sat there for awhile. There was a knock on the door.

"Eunice?" Francine was calling, "You OK?"

Eunice snapped her head up.

"Oh. Oh," she said. "I'm alright. Just fine. I'll be right out."

She finished up and wandered back out to the kitchen, steadying herself against the wall. Francine had disappeared. Eunice frowned and stood staring at the things in the kitchen, the microwave, the pot holders hanging in a row above the stove. A sweat broke out on Eunice's forehead. That's strange, she thought, freezing one minute, broiling the next. It was suddenly hot as hell.

"In here," someone was calling from the living room. Was that Francine? The voice sounded thin, far away, and there was music. Eunice followed the sounds, turning the corner to the living room. Olivia Newton-John sang in the background, at least Eunice thought so. Things were pretty fuzzy. Francine was relaxing on the white slip-covered couch. "Have You Never Been Mellow?" blared out of the big stereo speakers.

ᨓ

All of Francine's furniture was white; chilly against the aqua walls, adding nicely, Eunice thought, to the overall cooling effect. Then why was it suddenly sweltering? Francine had taken off her bikini top. Two little triangles of hot pink fabric lay crumpled on the pretty white carpet. Francine's breasts were white compared to her tan arms and flat, tanned stomach.

"I think I turned the AC too low," she said, as if to explain her sudden half-nakedness. "It's hotter than hell in here."

Eunice looked away from Francine's pale breasts with their small brown nipples. When she turned her gaze back to Francine, nearly losing her balance in the process, the breasts were coming toward her. Then Eunice was kissing Francine, or Francine was kissing her, or something.

It was similar, Eunice thought, to kissing Phil, except Francine's tongue was smaller and pointy. She let Francine's pointy tongue flicker down her neck and around her body. She imagined butterflies dancing up and down her legs, her stomach, everywhere, their tiny legs crawling—beautiful fancy butterflies, and brown moths whose wings beat softly against her warm skin.

Francine was in front of Eunice and someone, Eunice was sure, was behind her. Whoever it was had untied her bathing suit top and had her breasts cupped in his hands. And weren't Francine's hands working their way up Eunice's thighs? Eunice turned around, confused. A large OK-looking man stood there, smiling.

"Who…," Eunice started to say.

"Larry," the man said.

"Oh," Eunice said. Then Larry's mouth was on her neck.

"Where…?" Eunice asked.

"Shh," Larry said, as if Eunice was being rude.

Eunice shushed and they did it for awhile, in positions Eunice had never even thought of, before she passed out from drunken exhaustion.

ॐ

Eunice woke up naked on Francine's white couch. Her mouth was dry and sandy, her head slamming. She thought at first that she was at her own townhouse, until she noticed the front window sat to left of the door, instead of the right. She watched a cloud drift past.

Then Eunice sat up with a start. Her bathing suit was on the floor, so she picked it up and put it on. Francine and Larry were gone. Eunice quickly let herself out of the quiet townhouse and walked a block and a half through the stifling heat to her own. The sunlight hurt. "Ouch," Eunice said, out loud, placing her hand on the top of her head. An Olivia Newton-John song was looping through her mind, a certain part of it playing and replaying.

She turned the key in her door and went inside and made coffee. Sitting down on a high stool in the kitchen she stared at the microwave and other appliances, the pot holders hanging in a row, just like Francine's.

The townhouse was freezing and Eunice went upstairs to get a sweater. She slid open the closet door and reached way to the back, where she had stashed her pretty wool sweaters in several cardboard closet organizers. One by one, Eunice yanked the sweaters out, tossing them behind her into a messy heap on the floor. The smell of mothballs filled the room and went straight up her nose. She gagged and coughed—sucking in big breaths that seemed to have no place to go.

"Not this one," Eunice said loudly, throwing a blue sweater over her shoulder. The gasps for air were threatening to become hiccups. "Not this one either," she shouted.

"Where are you?" Eunice yelled. Then she was crying.

Eunice yanked a few dozen sweaters out of the boxes in the closet before she found the one she was looking for, a red pullover with Christmas trees embroidered along the front in green metallic thread, and little white snowflakes dotting the sleeves. She pulled it on and sat down hard on the bed and cried for awhile. *Fall had been bad enough, what was Christmas going to be like in the Sunshine State?* Eunice thought about driving downtown and hopping on a train. She'd run away up North, like some tortured but passionate juvenile delinquent. Maybe she could get Mary Lou to join her. They would have a real Christmas somewhere with real snow and real god damned pine trees and everything. Maybe she would even take up writing poetry again.

The wool sweater was scratchy; it felt terrible against her skin. Eunice pulled it off, tossing it on the floor with the others and went downstairs to start dinner. She would leave the chicken marinating, she thought, while she went to pick up Phil Jr. from school.

*Susan Burgess-Lent*

# *Hackles*

SUSAN BURGESS-LENT is the author of two novels: *In the Border-lands* (Xlibris, 2000) and "The Slave Tour." Her short stories and essays have been published by *The World Press Institute*, *Wild Child Magazine*, *Breakaway Books*, and *Pictures and Stories*. She has also written a series of columns for *Videography* magazine. In 2002, she was awarded the top Individual Artist Grant for Fiction by the Maryland State Arts Council. Her second novel earned first place (Mainstream Fiction) in the 2004 Maryland Writers Association Novel Competition. She lives near Washington, D.C., with her husband and daughter. Her website is www.burgesslent.com.

Shadows muscled into the hut, lurking about the tools of her life: the fire stone, the metal wash bowl, the jerry can. It didn't matter, the coming darkness; she could feel her way now. It was better not to see what would only shatter her heart.

She had bathed and dried him. Now she guided the razor slowly along the soft curve of his head. People had always admired its perfect shape; like a piece of finely wrought pottery, they'd said. He'd kept his hair short, she knew, to accentuate this beauty.

Not long ago, he'd shaved snaking patterns from his forehead to the nape of his neck. With his black hair riven by pale gullies, his broad shoulders unbowed, he had looked like a warrior. The young women, working at their chores, had stared at him as he strode through the village and, when he had passed, turned back to their work with trembling lips. He'd smiled all that week and then, suddenly, shaved all his hair. Possessing such raw attraction at only fourteen had frightened him. He'd told her this, but she could see by the glint in his eyes that he was bewitched by female attention.

She cradled his head in her lap. Her hand sure and steady, she drew the blade against the last ebony curls, collecting them in her skirt as they fell. She would save these relics that carried his scent. When she had been young, she had pressed her face into the nest of his infant hair, fallen in love with the perfume of him. The baby sweetness turned inevitably to musk, and she had fretted over letting him go. He had resisted her entreaties to "Be Careful!" with a casual shrug, murmuring "Don't worry." Whenever he went out, she'd passed her hand, like a soft breeze, over his head, as if to conjure a spell of protection.

She now gazed at him until the blue moonlight cast half of his face into darkness, molding the fine arch of his brow, his high cheek. In pre-dawn hours she had stalked their compound, shaping her fear into a shield she hoped would fend off the violence swirling into their lives. She remembered when her boy and his best friend had been accosted by a group of men with pistols. Her boy had disarmed them with a clever mime of an injured lion. He had been lucky that night; the gang had been drunk enough to be distracted from their routine cruelties. The militia now roamed everywhere—they had stolen the night. She had wanted then to flee this place, to hide him, but she could think of no refuge.

Shifting slowly, she lowered his bald head to the mat. Her fingers, of their own accord, arranged his rough-skinned hands across his hairless chest, and set his head in a proud uptilt. She began to wrap the cloth around his calloused feet. When she had carried him on her back before he'd learned to walk, these had been virgin feet, soft and without blemish, untested against the dusty clay.

Moving rhythmically, she bound his ankles gently with the sun-bleached fabric. Eyes closed, she let her hands inspect his legs. They were scabbed and scarred from running in the bush. His passion for dance had rendered them firm and sleek, but they had not been able to save him in the end.

She lifted his hips, averting her eyes from the genitals that she had not seen since he had learned to put on his own pants. She wondered if he had known the sweet pleasure of loving a girl. He would not have spoken to her of such an epiphany.

She pulled the fabric taut over his flawless flat belly. His favorite food had been her fried sweet potatoes. He'd always eaten them greedily, stoking a fiery energy that had filled her with wonder. He had burned through his days with no ash of restraint.

Drawing the cloth over his smooth chest, she stopped to trace the edges of the small wound where the bullet had found entry. The hole gaped like an evil deformity. She covered it quickly. Her heart murmured that she would have bled for him—if that would have extinguished the blind hatred of his murderers.

His lips were cold and hard. She let her fingertips linger against his eyelids, shut now over once-merry brown eyes that had not seen fully the power of evil. She had cowered—when she should have made a public stand with those who'd lost sons and husbands. With a final strip of cloth, she covered his face and tucked the end tightly against his hairless temple.

Swaddled in white, the lifeless form of all she had loved seemed to fill the hut. She felt the tiny hairs on the back of her neck rise, rebelliously calling the lioness out.

*Sophy Burnham*

# *The Man Who Bought His Wife*

SOPHY BURNHAM, author of thirteen books, has distinguished herself internationally as a novelist, journalist, nonfiction writer, award-winning playwright, and spiritual teacher. Her works include three bestsellers, *A Book of Angels* (Ballantine Books, 2004), *Angel Letters* (Ballantine Books, 1991), and *The Art Crowd* (David McKay, 1973). Her book *For Writers Only* (Ballantine Books, 1996) (which is not only for writers) is about the artist and creativity. All of her writings have a spiritual context. Her latest novel is *The Treasure of Montségur* (HarperSan Francisco, 2003). She is now working on her sixth novel, which has a Biblical theme.

You might think this is a story about holding on, fear, and possessiveness, and if my mother were telling it she would mark the moral at the end. I'll tell you the moral now: that you always lose what you most desperately want; you lose what you hold onto tightest. She drilled it into me, this variant of the self-fulfilling prophecy. "*The coward dies many times before his death,*" she declaimed her Shakespeare, "*the brave man only once.*" I still hear her admonitions. The person afraid of poverty lives in perpetual want; the one who fears loss continually experiences abandonment. You grip your most precious possession in your fist, and one day you open your hand and find… it's vanished. Gone. If it was ever there. Live lightly, she would say. Give it all away.

I thought of this when I met the man who bought his wife. He told me his story. I almost cried aloud, I was so shocked. But I gave no advice, and, for a long time, that sat on my conscience. Was he asking me for help? Why did he pour out his pain to me, a stranger passing in a cheap motel? Or did he sense that, as a journalist, I would be interested in his tale?

I had flown into Miami on a long, transcontinental flight that arrived at seven a.m. on a balmy winter morning, my eyes burning from lack of sleep (thirty-six straight hours awake) and my body screaming from its need either to lie down or move—only to discover that an airline strike had stranded hundreds of travelers, who crushed and crowded at the ticket counters. There was no way for me to get back home.

I needed breakfast, time to think.

A taxi took me to the nearest motel. The name escapes me now—one of the orange ones, redolent with the smell of bacon and Clorox.

I was sitting, blousy and worn out, at my brown table in the orange dining room, and had just ordered coffee when the waitress approached.

"The gentleman in the corner," she said, "wants to know if you would join him for breakfast."

It was a line out of the movies.

"Who?"

She was as amused as I. She pointed to a table across the room, and there I saw a short, fat, balding man in a loud Hawaiian shirt. He caught my look and grinned and gave a perky wave of one fat paw. Since I'd peeked, I couldn't courteously refuse.

"Tell him I will not move to his table," I answered the waitress. "But he is welcome to join me at mine."

He jumped up immediately and made his way across the room to plump down opposite me, and then, in a gush of confession, bestowed the information that he came from California, was in Miami with his partner (who had not yet risen) on a business deal that was going to make a lot of money, and that he was a helluva businessman with aggressive interests. But he switched almost immediately to his passionate private life.

Have you noticed how often intimacies are told to strangers—to the seatmate on an airplane or bus, to the man at your elbow at a bar? I'm so accustomed to these confessions, usually from men, that my mother used to tease me. "Who did you meet on this trip?" she'd ask expectantly. Am I particularly open? Accessible? Once I had hardly sat down in the plane, was still buckling my seat belt in fact, when the man at the window to my left leaned forward—a middle-aged gentleman, with a professorial goatee. "I've just fallen in love with my fifteen-year-old niece," he blurted. "What should I do?"

He had been to visit his brother, whom he had not seen in years, and there he met for the first time his nubile, lovely, long-legged niece. He fell head over heels in love.

"What should I do?" he implored me. "I don't know what to do."

"Never go to California again," I answered. "Don't see her ever again."

He shot me an anguished look, and rocked back in his seat. He didn't speak again, except to murmur, perhaps four minutes later: "I don't think I can do that." And repeating to himself out the window: "I don't think I can do that."

Back to the man in the motel, who lifted both hands to his shoulders to let the waitress put down his eggs: he couldn't wait to unburden his private life to me. He had married young, he said, attacking his toast—and he'd thought happily, when suddenly after twelve years, with no warning, his wife had walked out. He did not come out and say it, but he left the strong impression that she'd run off with another man. He was incensed. They had no children, but he'd had to pay her *alimony*! And it wasn't *he* who'd wanted a divorce! *She* was the one who upset the applecart! Their marriage had been good! With each exclamation, the unfairness of the situation stabbed him anew, a thorn pushed into his fist.

But what was worse, he growled, leaning forward assertively, she had shattered the rest of his life.

At the time, he served as an elder in a fundamentalist church. The church had strict rules prohibiting divorce, and, when his wife walked out, it removed him forthwith from his position of elder—and never a question about whether he was the one responsible. Which was why he didn't believe in God anymore, he announced defiantly, falling into the common confusion between God and the religions we create.

"Let me tell you." He punched the air with one pudgy finger. "I always lived a decent life. I stood by all the rules. I raised money for my church—thousands of dollars. I worked hard. When the church stripped me of my rank, I walked. I'll never belong to a church again."

He paused at this point to mangle his eggs with a savage fork. The anger stood red in his face, and his eyes, when lifted again to mine, were hot with pain.

"Loneliness?" he said. "I wrote the book on loneliness. I've had my best friends turn against me. My wife walk out. But I won't go through it again." Now a cunning smile creased his lips. "My second wife won't ever leave me," he said. "I've seen to that."

"Oh really?" I said, curiosity popping up its head. "But how did you do that?" For I have noticed that nothing is set and settled in this world, unless you count the ceaseless cycle of birth, death, loss, and further replenishment; and this is especially true, I think, when it comes to human behavior: nothing fixed. I was openly inquisitive. "How could you keep your wife from leaving you?"

"You have to understand who she is," he explained. "Look, she's a whore. A common slut. She's nobody. She grew up in the gutter. She had nothin' when I met her. She came from nothin'. I come along. I'm a man of means. I got property. I got a great house. It's beautiful."

"And how does that prevent her from leaving if she wants?"

"When I married her, I made her sign a contract. It's a legal document, written by a lawyer. It lays out everything I own, and it says it's mine. It's all mine. And none of it belongs to her. It states the rules of the marriage. She can't interfere, f'r instance. I do what I want."

"What, have other women?" I asked, coming to the point.

"Sure. I'm only a man. I have my needs."

"So, then, can she have men as well?" I asked slowly. "It's an open relationship?"

With that question, I think I fell in his estimation. He shot me a searing look.

"Of course not. She's my wife." He was genuinely surprised. "The contract lays it all out. I give her a certain amount of money every week. I buy her food. I keep her in clothes. In return, she keeps herself looking good. She takes care of the house. She does her bit and doesn't ask any questions about what I do. She goes against my wishes, she loses her allowance. And if she leaves me—" he smiled and tipped his orange juice to me in a little toast—"she gets nothin'. Not a cent. It's all written in the contract that she signed. She walks out, she gets the clothes she came with, and that's it." He tipped back in his chair, triumphant. "She'll never dare to leave."

Appalled, I stared at him. "But now she can never say she loves you," I said—and stopped.

"What?"

"No, nothing." But I wanted to say more. I wanted to say, "You've just ensured your loneliness! Now you'll never know if she stays out of need or because she cares for you. You've lost it all. You'll never be able to hear her say she loves you." But I could not go on. I lay it to my being tired that tears pricked my eyes. I didn't know if they were for him or for his wife, or possibly for myself with my own strained relationships, and, to hide my distress, I stared out the green window at the softly waving palms, sipped my coffee, hunted in my handbag for a Kleenex—anything to keep my eyes from his.

Just when you think you have a hook on a thing, the fish wiggles out of your grasp. Hardly had I pegged and catalogued this man, possessed by fear of loss, when his business partner joined us. He was tall and thin with a dark moustache that wriggled when he smiled in greeting, like a caterpillar across his upper lip. He was the Jeff to plump little Mutt.

More burned coffee was ordered, more moist, undercooked toast and fried eggs and also jam in circular little tubs, one teaspoonful, and thimbleful of ersatz cream. By now, all I wanted was to sleep. My eyes were closing. I was incapable of making a decision, forming a plan of action. What was I to do? Go to the airport and stand in line, trying to catch a plane that day? Take a room in the motel and sleep? Money was one issue, but worse was my exhaustion—awake so long, I could not form a plan.

The two men were heading for the Everglades in a rented car. The trip would take four hours. Would I like to come along?

"Do you know what I would like to do?" I leveled with them. "I'd like to borrow your hotel room and go to sleep for a few hours until you return. I am so tired."

Immediately, my patron sprang to his apologetic feet.

"Of course you are. Thirty-six hours. Come with me." He grabbed my suitcase and shoulder bag and, pushing me ahead of him, struck out. I waved a hurried good-bye to the partner, who remained impassive, chewing his fried eggs solemnly. And now a new thought struck. The man was a self-confessed philanderer. What did it mean that he would let me sleep in his room? Did he think I was making him a proposition? Was he preparing an attack?

No time to ask. He snatched two sheets and pillowcases off a chambermaid's cart as we hurried to the room.

He made the bed himself, urging me to undress, take a shower, make myself comfortable. He wouldn't be a minute. He threw his dirty shirts and socks in his fine leather suitcases, tossed the used bed linens out the door, lined up his shoes (six pairs) against the wall, and then hurried to straighten up the john. He showed me the shower and how the faucets worked. He gave me soap from his own case and shoved his gold jewelry into a single heap on the marble counter, together with his toothpaste, brush, and shaving gear.

"My bathrobe's here behind the door. Feel free to use it."

My astonishment increased, but also my suspicion. If only I could pull my thoughts together. Perhaps he wasn't planning to assault me, but what if he went away and later let himself in while I lay helplessly asleep?

"OK." He looked about him, satisfied. "Look, just so you won't worry about someone walking in on you, here's the key. We'll be back around two p.m. We'll knock. That way you'll know no one's going to disturb you."

I was shamed by his sensitivity.

He hung the "Do Not Disturb" sign on the door handle, waggled his fingers at me, whispered good night, and softly closed the door.

I sat on the bed, bewildered at the man's behavior.

He had left a perfect stranger in his room with his $900 suits in the closet, his rings and bracelets on the bathroom sink, his leather suitcases crammed with clothes. We hadn't even exchanged names. I could have taken everything.

I dropped on the bed and slept.

Later that afternoon, he drove me to the airport and got me wait-listed on a plane before taking off himself for L.A.

And that would have been the end of our encounter, except for my occasional musings on his situation—and my mother's voice declaiming how you always lose what you're holding onto hardest. How sad that he would never believe she loved him! And should I have offered him advice—told him (as I'd been tempted) to release her from the contract? To let her go, because if she came back, he'd know she was really his? Did his wife leave him anyway? Or did she turn herself inside out cooking and cleaning for him, working to keep her side of the bargain? In my mind, I wrote numerous endings to his story, and then some two years later I ran into him again in one of those real-life coincidences that you couldn't put into a novel without your editor pointing you to the door.

This time I was not in Miami but Atlanta, hiking to the trains that move great crowds between vast terminals, and as we swelled and poured ourselves into the train and the doors shut, I found myself staring across the rocking car at a short, balding, portly man lugging a bulging black leather briefcase. Despite his stature, he wore a blue, double-breasted blazer with gold buttons, the kind of jacket a slender six-foot man can carry off but that looks ridiculous on a chubby five-foot-seven. He was a puffed-up pigeon, strong shoulders back and chest thrust forward, smugly pleased. I couldn't stop thinking that he looked familiar—that I'd seen him before—when turning (did he feel my gaze?), he caught my eye. Instantly I flung aside my glance, embarrassed, but to my surprise, he broke into a smile, and as the train pulled into the terminal and the crowd disembarked in a second wave that sent us boiling onto the reef of carpeted cement, he worked his way happily to my side.

"Hello! It's me. Do you remember me? Dave Ganz!"

I recognized his voice and immediately smiled back, immensely pleased to see him again. We were catching different flights, but we both had time for a cup of coffee before departure, and, as we drifted together to a Starbucks, we agreed that not only is it necessary these days to arrive at airports early, but sometimes such precaution carries benefits: imagine running into one another again! It must have been "meant." This time he would get my name and phone number and he would give me his.

He bought me tea and a biscotti, and for himself a double mocha almond latte. We stood at a little round table, hardly big enough for our two cups, and he opened up to me as if he'd never left off talking two years earlier. He still lived in L.A., he was still married to the same woman, and she did her bit as he expected or otherwise he wouldn't stand for it, and business was thriving—never better. He had twin nephews now, terrific boys, toddlers. Little demons both of them. Here's some pictures. They called him Uncle Dave. He was Uncle Dave to them, and it was too bad his wife couldn't have children, he'd have liked children, but no use crying over what can't be mended, and there were compensations. The twins were fun but tiring, and, in fact, he was always glad to see them leave.

"And are you happy then?" I asked him, curious at this whalespout of good news, when earlier he'd been so eager to exhume his anger for my examination.

"Happy? What's happy got to do with it?" he asked. "Life isn't meant to be happy. Life just is." But then he added, with his rejoicing and energetic attack, that he was coming to D.C. soon, and he'd bring his wife, and maybe we could get together when he came. He'd like to introduce her to a real lady. She could take classes from me in how to dress and talk. He'd tell her about meeting me. She'd be impressed that he knew a real published writer.

"But tell me," I asked, "I've always been curious—how was it that you just gave me your hotel room that morning? Didn't it ever cross your mind that I could steal your stuff? Or maybe you got out to the Everglades and had second thoughts?"

"Nah!"

"No?"

"Nah, not you. Listen, there's one thing I'm good at. I know people. I see someone, I know him right away."

"Or her."

"Or her, sure. Him. Her. You look at you, you know, you know?"

"And what do you see when you look at me?"

"Straight. You're straight. No pretenses, am I right? You get what you see. And you're thinking all the time. Stuff going through your head. Right? Am I right? Sure I'm right. You didn't even think to rip me off. How could you? You're a girl with class, grew up with class. "

I laughed. "Are you ever wrong?"

"Nah. Maybe once in a while. But not really never."

*What about your wife?* I wanted to ask, *What's happened with her, and does she love you? Tell you so?* But of course I held my tongue, and instead, as we were parting, I urged him to phone me when he came to Washington, assuring him I'd like to meet his wife.

"Two months," he said. "For cherry blossoms." We shook hands cordially, and parted for our separate planes, and, as I buckled my seat belt, I thought how I was actually looking forward to seeing him again, curious to meet the wife.

They came in early April, as he had promised, when the cherry blossoms were at their delicate pink peak, the trees just greening tenderly, and the streets jammed with the hesitant cars of tourists. I said I'd pick them up at Dulles Airport and drive them to the Jefferson Hotel. "Nothing but the best," he'd explained over the phone. "Friend of mine stayed there. He said it's great."

"It's not bad." I laughed.

His wife was surprisingly mild: a dyed redhead remarkable mostly for a soft, receding chin. She wore a beige knit suit, a powder blue scarf, and heels low enough to prevent her exceeding him in height. Her engagement ring flashed extravagantly, emeralds and diamonds setting off her scarlet nails, but next to his flashy exuberance, she seemed almost invisible. Yet what was curious: he fluttered round her.

"Do you see your bag?" he asked, and shot off to grab their suitcases from the baggage belt, then counted her cases, including the little, red leather, makeup case that she held by a strap on her wrist.

"Here, let me," he took the makeup kit from her. She did not demur. She had three suitcases in all, for just one week's visit, not counting her Kate Spade purse. I followed behind as Dave hailed a porter and covered the man with bags, herding us toward the exit. He held his wife's elbow with one paw; and she, accustomed to his bustling busyness, stood expectantly, waiting to be taken care of. I was stunned—not by her discreet looks, so different from the flashy burlesque dancer, the hard-eyed, gum-chewing streetwalker I'd imagined (with fuck-me heels and skirt to her upper thighs), but by his attentions. This was the woman he had bought! This was the woman he had vowed (eyes narrowing) would never leave him because he'd picked her out of the gutter and back she'd go if she made one wrong move. I led the way, puzzled by the two.

Apart from her murmured salutations on meeting me, I had yet to hear her voice. Was she so beaten down that she couldn't speak, the prototypical tamed shrew? Or was her voice so shrill and harsh that she didn't dare to use it—perhaps a common mountain twang that he'd ridiculed and bullied into silence? He bustled her through the door, then turned, waiting for the porter to catch up, fingers snapping impatiently.

"I'll bring the car around," I said. "Why don't you wait here."

She tucked in the scarf at her throat and dreamed.

"Good," he answered. I hurried off, feeling somehow that I ought to dogtrot, not keep him waiting—or her. I had hardly pulled up the car when he jerked open the door, and then he was peeling green bills off a heavy wad to pay the porter, lifting bags into the trunk, and guiding his wife to the front seat. He slammed her door, threw himself in the back, and once more became the man I'd met before; he leaned forward between our seats, commenting on everything as we passed: the highway flanked by office buildings and later the river, the fields of yellow daffodils, the Pentagon behind us, the Lincoln Memorial (because I drove them the long way round), and how he expected to go to the National Gallery the next day. Shirley liked art. They'd go see art. We had great art in Washington, D.C., and he wanted to see the Air and Space Museum too, but they might not have time. Shirley didn't like air so much. Oh, look at the cherry blossoms, d'y see the cherry blossoms, Shirley?

It was an unrelenting stream of commentary that left no space for any other voice. I dropped them at the Jefferson Hotel, agreeing to meet at 7:00 p.m. for dinner, and drove down M Street, grateful for a moment's silence, and musing on Shirley, who all that time had offered not one single word. She was the mystery of the duo, though it amused me how he hovered over her. His eyes trailed after her. His hands picked up her bags, and, if he'd been a dog, he would have run back and forth in front of her, a stick in his mouth, jumping and begging her to toss it for him, pet him, play. But who was she in their relationship?

I discovered it at dinner, and forgive me for taking so long in this story, but to make sense of it, you have to witness it the way I did, unfolding piece by piece and scene by scene. There was first the question of why I even bothered with the man. I owed him nothing. We had nothing in common. He didn't read serious books, attend the theater, or display an interest in philosophy. The fact is, I was curious about him in the same way that an ornithologist is curious to watch a mutant woodpecker pounding on a tree, or the way an ichthyologist observes the circling of a newly discovered coelacanth: something both familiar and extraordinarily strange.

We went to Asia Nora's, which I thought appropriately exotic but which also has good food. Shirley was dressed in a sleek black dress with rhinestones. In truth, she looked better than I. Moreover, she moved with none of the hard-edged, heel-clatter I had expected, but drifted, her "head in the clouds," as my mother would say; yet, as we walked down the brick steps from the sidewalk to the lower-level door, she looked back over her shoulder at the two of us behind, and the way she tilted her chin down toward her shoulder, her sidewise glance up at us from under her lashes, the curl of a beckoning, taut smile, startled me: What did it mean? This teasing look. Her glance was not so much inviting as…as smug, superior. She knew something I did not. The next moment, we were inside. The look had passed so fast I brushed it aside. We took our seats and opened menus, ordered drinks, and, for a time, all conversation was on the dinner, the ingredients, on organic versus regular food, and Dave's insistence that a good steak or lobster was good enough for him, none of this tofu natural nonsense. Shirley sipped her wine. She gazed around her with wide, unseeing eyes, though when she caught her reflection in the mirrored wall, she lifted one hand with interest to her hair. Was she bored? When she spoke, I discovered she had a decent voice, low pitched, no twang. But conversation was carried by her husband.

I didn't have a chance to talk to her alone until after dessert when Dave tossed his napkin on the table and excused himself for the restroom, and, just as I opened my mouth to offer some social courtesy about the restaurant, for example, or what shopping she might like to do in D.C.—though what I wanted to ask was *Where are you from?* or *What's your line of business?*—she turned on me.

"Now, we only got a few minutes, so you listen up," she said. I was so startled my mouth fell closed. I blinked.

"I know what you think of him. You're judging him. You think you're so hoity-toity better'n him. Don't think I don't see it. I know your type. But I won't have you making fun of him, you hear?"

"I wasn't—"

"I know what I see. I have intuitions. You think I'm a nobody, but I've been around. "

She stared me down.

"I'm sorry if I gave that impression."

"It's not an impression. Everything about you. Look how you act. La-di-da. You think you're so swell, well, let me tell you, you can't hold a candle to that man. There's nothing he wouldn't do for anyone—a total stranger, he'd give him the shirt off his back. He's not educated, OK, so he didn't go to your snotty, fancy schools. But he can run circles 'round those snobs. He's smart. And he's good. I won't have him ridiculed."

"Then why do you treat him so badly?" I shot back. I was irritated as much by her challenge as the truth of her charges against my snobbery. "Why don't you look at him? He's pleading with you for a glance, a touch, a soft word. I bet you've never told him that you love him. I bet —"

"No." She examined her fingernails. "I don't say those words."

"Well I think that's inexcusable. If you think so highly of him. He takes care of—"

"And you know why? You probably wouldn't understand with your high-n-mighty ideas, but I make him work for me, and that gives him everything he wants. Simple."

"What?" Her logic confused me.

"All you see is him falling over himself trying be helpful. Well, I see who he is, and he's the kind of guy needs to be helpful. He likes helping. Well, I'm giving him the chance to, which is more than just tossing out words. What good does it do for me to gush and go all googly over him? I love you, love you. You think he'd hear it? He'd be suspicious right away. But when he's doing something useful for me, he feels good. He feels good about himself. He feels good about me. That's what I do for him."

"By helping you?"

"By doing everything for me."

"And you?" I asked. "Are you satisfied with that?"

She tilted her head as before with that sidelong look that curled up from under her secretive lashes.

"Oh please. You think I'm stupid, don't you? You think I'm… Sure, I've been poor, and rich is better. But don't you get snotty with me, missy. You don't understand anything at all. I got a maid comes in once a week to clean the house. A girl comes in two-three nights to cook. I belong to a country club. In return I take care of his needs. He worships the ground I walk on, and I give him just enough crap every day, excuse my language, to keep him on his feet. Interested. You think he wouldn't be off with other women, if he didn't have nothing to work for? So I give him something to work at. Me. That gives him pleasure." She saw my face and tossed her head with annoyance. "You still don't get it, do you? You think I'm the one should be doing for him? Well, it doesn't work that way. The more he does for me, the more he likes me. The more I let him do for me, the more he adores me. And that's how it fucking, 'scuse my language, oughta be. And if I have interests on the side…" She shrugged. "But here he is."

She folded her two hands under her chin. "So tell me," she drawled. "Why is it you think you haven't ever married?"

*T P del Ninno*

# Shaking Loose the Pancake Hosts from Heaven

Some years ago, while living in Africa, T P DEL NINNO had a story to tell. *Banana Moon*, published by Power Press (2000), tracks the lives of an African landlady and an American homemaker in a rare penitent season when both Eid and Easter coincide. Del Ninno practices architecture in Alexandria, Virginia, and is finishing her new novel, "After Burgers."

*Thus do your wizards serve you*
*with whom you have toiled from your youth;*
*Each wanders his own way, with none to save you.*
—Isaiah 47:15

*S*atisfied, Eunice Marie Thorton peels the large green Post-it and taps it *into place, obscuring a square of the television screen. Rolling back into the couch, she pulls a larger, lined pad from the bottom of the laundry basket.*

The First Day of my new life. Today is another day and I have bad ideas. Things are piling up, laundry, bills, garbage, makes me want to strike a match if it wasn't for… Then, I saw the bible, collectin dust next to my wedding album, collectin dust, and it struck me. There is another way, a righteous way, a loving way. *Eunice slurps up the remaining pureed peas and mashed bananas in the half-empty baby jars.*

Wasn't Phil thoughtful for picking these up for me? Multi-colored, multi-sized Post-its. I know he's thinking it'll keep me organized while he's on the road. Been out a week now. She flips the page. These super sized ones are my favorites, plenty of space to save my ideas and thoughts. *She reaches for a smaller blue pad. The red flair scrawls, PICK UP MEDS. Her grip heavy on the armrest,*

*she leverages herself into a standing position, navigates the stairs, the blue tab sticks
to the fridge, the large lined Post-its behind the closet door.*

∽

> For what I fear overtakes me,
> and what I shrink from comes upon me.
> I have no peace, nor ease;
> I have no rest, for trouble comes!
> —Job 3:25–26

Job's grief pales against mine. My boy's fever swells in his eyes. He's cryin in his
crib, I'm feelin it in my bones, my heart. Cold baths, baby Tylenol, hair dryers,
singin songs, there's no consolin him. The Lord is tryin to take away my babies,
makin em sick, sending foster home people over, threatenin to take away my Kay
and my baby boy. Don't you see, it's only when Job himself is in pain that he
begins to doubt God's way, long after he loses his children.

> My flesh is clothed with worms and scabs,
> my skin cracks and festers.
> —Job 7:5

That's his own personal pain that turns his mind. Now I don't think he cared
for his kids like I do, didn't nurse them like I did; feel them move in his belly. The
boy's sick, they think I've been mistreatin Kay. I'll take action. *Eunice sniffles, her
handwriting becomes larger and larger on the pages, having to flip them faster. She
tosses the whole pad onto the growing mound in the closet, slams the door.*

∽

> For sighing comes more readily to me than food,
> and my groans well forth like water.
> —Job 3:24

Yesterday, after our boy must have been cryin for some time, I found myself
standin at the Great Falls Park Lookout. I'm not sure how I even got there, all I
felt was my cold iron grip on the steel railing. My hands were clutched and stiff.
I had no part of them, no control, I tried to unlock them.

Over and over I imagine the long fall through the air, my stomach tumblin
and giddy, the air on my face pushing tears out of the corners of my eyes. My
cartoon scream, loud at first, fading into a crashin splash, frightens the birds from
the trees. They circle over my crumpled body as it gently rolls downstream slippin
around the river's boulders. The boy's cries, mute in the enclosed car, had attracted some good soul.

Then, I pictured holdin the boy in my arms as we fell. His cryin stops, a curious look on his face, the delight of freefall. He would be lighter than I, float out of my arms, above me. A portal in the sky opens; we tumble onto the puffy popcorn clouds, serene and peaceful, together the two of us for eternity. My feet began to climb the railing, but my hands wouldn't release.

I hadn't walked away from the lookout. I found a park ranger standin beside me, his arm around me, asking me if I want to share a hot chocolate with him on this cold afternoon. He is a messenger from God, telling me today is not the day He's callin me home. He asks if the baby in the car is mine and can we all go together to the cafeteria. After warmin up, he insists that I call Phil, tell him to come and pick us up. Happens to be the day Phil's comin home. Long after the hot chocolates, his detached cab pulls up. He and the ranger speak in whispers, I couldn't hear. Phil was so silent. How could they have known what I was thinking

We drove straight to the emergency room at Fairfax Hospital, had our baby checked out. Must have had some type of infection to be cryin uncontrollably. I'm givin him pink syrup every six hours. The boy is sleepin now, Phil, too. Well, no wonder, it is four in the morning. I'd better lie back down for a while, I feel exhausted. *Eunice peels the notes from the pad, places them along with the others on the back of the closet door, butterflies in the dark.*

ॐ

I am feelin better. The boy's stopped cryin, Kay's been helpin me with the pink medicine. I've been watchin a show in the afternoons, called… Wait I'll get the *TV Guide*. It's called *The Waters of Life Ministry* with a wonderful man named Reverend Michael Ernest. I do believe the sun is coming into my life. This man is on a mission from Jesus to spread the word and the word is love. That is the truth. I've seen Billy Graham, and he's a powerful man, but Reverend Michael, so soft spoken, the love radiates from the screen. All those people lookin up to him. I feel like I just got out of the shower when the show is over, that good.

I went straight to my bedroom; put everythin of mine in a box, except for a few changes of clothes. There was a tear in my eye when I neatly folded my weddin dress and put it in the box. I felt a little blue about the prom dress, but no tears; it was green chiffon, after all. It's vanity to keep those things, I know. Of course I could never even try the weddin dress on, I have a different shape now than when I got married. But I was thinkin that maybe Kay could wear it some day. No hesitation I told myself. Without a second thought, I drove straight down to the Goodwill and handed over those boxes.

✂

*Because you felt secure in your wickedness,*
*and said, "No one sees me,"*
*Your wisdom and your knowledge led you astray*
*and you said to yourself "I and no one else!"*
*But upon you shall come evil*
*and you will not know how to predict:*
*Disaster shall befall you*
*which you cannot ally.*
*Suddenly there shall come upon you*
*ruin which you will not expect.*
—Isaiah 47:10–11

*Locking the puzzle in place, she sticks the piece on the last open portion of the TV.*

✂

Since my inspiration to rid myself of all my selfish baggage, I decided to clean out the children's excess material, and Phil's too. It's sinkin us, holdin us down. I did leave a couple changes of clothes and three pair of underwear each. Well, I had to leave a few more changes of clothes for the baby, he's growin so fast. I know they'll thank me for this, for my helpin them to be better people. They can understand that there are more deservin people than us. Keepin these Post-its, though. Got to.

✂

I have to say things are goin well. Phil came home and said how nice the house looks, so neat and picked up. I'm inspired; tomorrow I'm goin to give away all the dishes.

✂

Eatin on paper plates is so much easier, although somewhat costly. I find that I have extra time for my writin now that I'm not doin the dishes, that hot soapy water was chaffin my hands, anyways. Phil has been away drivin truck, he should be back tomorrow sometime, I think. The house really looks picked up now. No more of that materialistic baggage that holds us back. I gave the pillows away. We can't be too soft, we won't be prepared when Jesus calls us.

✂

Not a lucky day. Phil is back and very, very angry. He usually throws and breaks dishes when he's so worked up like this, but there weren't any to throw. So he just broke a couple pencils and yelled a lot. Kay hid under her bed and the baby cried and cried. Just terrible.

I couldn't hold back my tears anymore and when he saw how badly I felt, he regretted losin his temper. He drove down to the 7-Eleven and bought a couple sixpacks of beer and locked himself in the bathroom. I thought he'd be happy that I am so committed to doin the right thing.

᠔

Phil is out of the bathroom. Sleepin in the tub with all those empty cans has taken a toll on his good looks. He said that this was his house, too. He wanted to be asked before I gave another thing away. I told him that when he's gone like that, I have to make some decisions on my own, even if they're ones he doesn't agree with. I told him I was sorry about all his bowlin trophies and the huntin dog magazines, the radio. Keepin the television, though. It's our pathway to Reverend Michael.

I said "Let's go down to Goodwill and buy a few of those magazines back," thinkin that might make him feel better. He said he had a better idea and drove back to the 7-Eleven.

᠔

Everyone seems happier. Kay is doin well in school. The baby is not sick anymore. He's all rosy and pink. I haven't heard from Child Protective Services for days now, of course I'm not picking up the telephone or answering the door. Nonetheless, our lives are beginning to turn around. It's probably because of my good deeds.

I know that I shouldn't be bragging about them, even Michael warns us against this kind of vanity, but, heck, this is a diary, it's my business only. He's been askin us to give and give, well, I didn't hold back nothin, all our savins are now helping the spiritually starved heathens in other parts of the world. I got a good price for my weddin rings and my father's watch and gave that money, too. God's love is shinin on us. I hope Phil understands.

᠔

> *Everyone who drinks this water will be thirsty again.*
> *But whoever drinks the water I give him*
> *will never be thirsty again,*
> *No, the water I give shall become the fountain within him,*
> *leaping up to provide eternal life.*
> —John 4:15–16

It's not the actual water that we need, I've been trying to tell that to Phil. He's wondering what I'm doing, how could I be forgettin things on the stove, not even opening the mail. He found the closet where I've been storing the mail until I have time to sort through it all.

He was losing his temper again when Kay had called him to tell him there wasn't any water in the house. Seems like they had sent us some sort of notice a few months back. I'm sure it's in one of the closets. Anyways, Phil had to go down and stand in line to have the water reconnected, a small inconvenience. Phil should find time to read the bible with me, watch my show together.

The baby has some terrible diaper rash and he's crying about that. Poor dear innocent. I must change brands I think. Phil says I didn't change him for a couple whole days. Imagine. We figured it out, though, why he was cryin and all. I believe that the Lord will provide for us. We can't spend our entire lives worried about the physical nuisances of our everyday life. Unless we detach ourselves from all our minor burdens, we will never be called to dine with our Lord.

What can I say. He is just thinkin little…

I tell him, "The Lord is tryin us Phil. We can take our trials and still have faith. We can accept our crosses with smiles of gratitude." He says, "Change the baby's diaper." That's what I mean by thinkin little.

⌇

This afternoon Brother Michael told us that he has a website. I couldn't imagine that. I thought of someplace in Louisiana where giant frosty webs spread between the trees, webs of love, to catch the aimless sinners, inject them with the Word of Jesus.

Well, he explained how to talk to each other electronically through the computer, how the computer could bring our family together. If we don't have a computer in the house, there are many places to use them. I was inspired again. I made a few phone calls and found the Cyber Café within walking distance, can you believe that?

A nice little girl showed me how to find www.legacyusa.com and I saw photos of Brother Michael and his Ranch of Love, I read his prayers for the day and I could leave messages with other brothers and sisters. I felt so warm and happy, of course, the three hot chocolates with marshmallows probably helped. I was careful not to spill on the computer.

⌇

Things seem to be changin with Phil. I think he understands our new way of life. I know he's been trying to get a different route, to be closer to home. When he is on the road, he calls us, I don't know, every half-hour. He must be missin us so. Must be feelin the devil's pull tryin to break up our family. I told him the devil is manifestin himself as our mailman, bringing us more and more mail. (I've filled up another closet with those hateful correspondences.) I think it's best to keep this fact from Phil sounds like he's worried so.

ॐ

Last night I told everyone about the Cyber Café and how I learned to use the Internet. It is just like the card catalogue in the library. Phil, man, he was really impressed. I think I haven't seen him happier. He said I was really smart and on top of things to learn about the Internet. He said he was relieved, I can't imagine why. I told him to come down to the café with me, it's open all night. He says he'd like to do that sometime.

Kay says she's got computers on the Internet at the school's library and can show me some other things on the Internet, how to find other places. She says there's a whole different electronic world out there. That girl of mine is really growing up, she is always with her baby brother, now, changin him and bathin him. She helps me make dinner, sometimes makin it completely herself, and as always, she is so dear to her mother, giving me hugs and kisses. My life is really changin and I owe it all to Brother Michael. There's hope for us.

ॐ

I was on the Internet all day today, findin fellow believers and sharin our enthusiasm for the message of Brother Michael. I have my own mailbox. I get special privileges because of my support. I saw that I could also donate money through the computer with my Visa card. I sent that blessed prophet five hundred dollars. Funny, I felt like I was in Reno puttin money on the numbers. I got so excited, I gave him another five hundred, like I was doubling my bet that paradise will accept us with open arms, that the love of Jesus will shower upon us, like God's love waterin can. In fact, I gave that good man the limit on our card, two thousand five hundred dollars.

Listen, the best part was, I got a personal note back from Brother Michael, himself, thankin me for such overwhelming generosity, understandin that this might be a real sacrifice for the family, but this gift will be goin to some real needy people, spiritually needy.

I felt I couldn't tell Phil how happy I was about this. We just had our usual family dinner, talkin about Kay's day at school. I didn't let on to the notice I found in Phil's pocket yesterday. The check was pretty big, but the news was bad. Laid off. You tell me how they could have so many truckers.

☙

*False Messiahs and false prophets will appear,*
*performing signs and wonders so great as to mislead even the*
*   chosen.*
—Matthew 24:24

I know there are others out there. Other so called messengers of Jesus, trying to divide the flock, like a rabid sheepdog. I'm sure Brother Michael knows about them, too. You can find them on the Internet. Their messages are quite different, though. They are quite convinced the human race is vicious and doomed. They say that the ruined race of Adam is vile and corrupt, only deservin of condemnation.

In the afternoon, when I put the baby down for his nap, I slip out to the Cyber Café to read my mail, the prayers for the day. There is a young man who is always at the café, sittin next to me. I've been observin him out of the corner of my eye, because he looks so shifty, always lookin over his shoulder. He doesn't think twice about me, though. Well, I know exactly what he is doin, he has some number program running that gets credit card numbers from a site that uses credit cards. So, when he copies down the number, I do, too.

So, today, I was able to save who knows how many sinners and show them the way to Jesus. The money must have been flowin into the banks of Legacy, swellin the rivers, baptizin all heathens with the Word of God. I have opened the door to everlasting righteousness, actually rescued probably hundreds from eternal dam-nation, and to think that the vile currency of man's greed is able to do this.

Thoughts for the day.

☙

I have to say Phil is unusually calm, considerin we no longer have his paycheck. He hasn't told me this, though, he still keeps his truckin schedule, pretendin that everything is fine. I know it's fine, even without his job, we are blanketed in the loving warmth of Jesus.

He's been only kind and lovin with us, specially the children. I showed him the letter, finally, from the county, told him about the lady's visit and how we have to think about stayin together as a family. I can't lose my babies. I won't. I thought we might be able to run away, make a new life somewhere. I told him, look, we don't have so many things to move. He smiled at that and gave me a lovin hug.

Actually there have been a few letters. The one I found today was taped to the front door. That putrid defective soul had handwritten the amount of time she had spent knockin and the fact that the baby cried ceaselessly inside the house. Of course her knockin was probably what caused it. She is a merciless and self-absorbed peon of the devil. I think it's time to move closer to Legacy, work together with Brother Michael on his ranch.

God is tryin us.

I wrote to Brother Michael, askin him to make room for some new believers, we're comin home. I haven't heard from him. I know that he has many email addresses. He is probably busy thanking everyone for their donations to the mission. I'm sure he'll answer me soon. We don't have much time and I've told him so.

ॐ

No word from the man with the Word. I am beginnin to think that Brother Michael isn't who he claims to be. I've left hundreds of messages for him. I'm not sendin anymore money, either. Actually, the young man hasn't been at the café for a few days.

ॐ

Jesus, Jesus

ॐ

> *Thus do your wizards serve you*
> *with whom you have toiled from your youth;*
> *Each wanders his own way with none to save you.*
> —Isaiah 47:15

This morning I got in the car. I took my son and wrapped him warmly and drove to the Great Falls Lookout where I have often received inspiration. I seem to recall havin been there recently. We sat together on the park bench, the baby and me, for some time until he fell into a deep sleep.

Over and over I asked Jesus what to do. I was feelin misled. Brother Michael had lit such a fire in me and now the fire was burnin out of control. Brother Michael had snuck away like some kind of delinquent arsonist. A small voice, a girl child's voice, spoke to me. She said only a few words. Truth. Redemption. Family. What did this mean? What is the truth? Manipulated by the powerful words of the enemy, I realized how I had been deceived by the Waters of Life Ministry. How sophisticated was this demon who sowed his clever deception in the midst of believers. Help me, Jesus, help me Jesus. I must have spoken this out loud because I found a park ranger standin in front of me. The young man must have been freezin, his arms crossed and his hands tucked into his armpits. His face was the consistency of raw hamburger. He seemed to recognize me.

I accepted his offer of hot chocolate. The baby's cheeks were so cold. He asked if I wouldn't mind if he called my husband. He told me he had met him before but I didn't catch where. I was so happy to see Phil. When he came through the door of the cafeteria, it was like the first time we met.

The cafeteria was dark, the last school dance of our senior year. The city's lights twinkled through the large plate glass windows. The glass was sweating, so many perspirin kids, but it was cool on my back as I stood with Gina talkin about the boys. His tall lanky silhouette in the doorway. He had walked straight towards me. I'd seen him around, but I didn't even know his name.

Our first dance was...Average White Band I think. Then, that Elvis song, a slow dance and his voice was in my ear, soothin and sexy. His narrow hips nestled neatly into mine, rockin with the music. My body quivers with the memory. The song was over and we were standin still. He held my face in his hands, gently kissing it all over. I don't know what had gotten into him. Wasn't really like him to be so open. I think he'd been smokin some pot in the parking lot. He's a good man. We've had some good times together. Really good times.

‿

It's Phil with the plans now. I've turned him around. He's helpin me plan the banquet, decidin the menu, packin the tableware. The glory of the grace of Jesus fills our hearts. I'm so glad he's with me on this, we're readin the bible together. We don't need Brother Michael when we have each other. Oh I am so inspired. *Eunice sketches an idyllic banquet scene.* I've shown Phil how useful these Post-its can be and how busy and productive I've been writin and philosophizin. He's planning a winter campin trip we'll all take together. I don't know, somewhere in West Virginia. Don't think either of us has ever been winter campin. But that's how grace works, with trust and faith in meetin the challenges of new adventures! And that's just how Phil is.

‿

> *...And the hosts of heaven will be shaken loose.*
> —Matthew 24:29

Our new life together

It came to me in a dream. A dream of melting snow, of floating pancakes.

I am blind, being pushed along a crowded street. All the fingers and hands on my arms, my back, grippin and shovin. Colored nails, leavin impressions in my skin, scratchin my arms. I gasp for my breath. My sight gradually returns to me as the street turns into a snowy path, the crowd falls away. Pools of cool water pond on the path. The path is leading to a house. The house has a warm amber glow; I understand that it is my home although I swear I've never seen that house before. I walk up onto the porch and kind of pass right through the front door, without really openin it.

Banana pancakes hover in the room. They float shadowlessly above the table. The table is filled with happy people, so many I cannot see the end of it. Candles are burnin, crucifixes bleeding, and wine tremblin in the glasses. The room is gay. A man sits at the head of the table, a featureless face glowing phosphorescent green. The dinner revolves around him. There are few empty chairs.

A high chair. I see our baby clappin his hands and Kay kissin his cheeks. Phil raises his wineglass in a salute to me. Everyone cheers. I curtsy. I'm light, like the pancakes. Passing by a mirror, I see someone totally different; twenty pounds lighter a different face really.

An angel's voice. A clear and perfect soprano's voice. A chorus of angels join in. The children sit before me, all of them, lost babies included. We are a whole family again, happily singin with the angels. It is the banquet of Jesus. We are being called to eternal redemption at the banquet of Jesus.

మ

*The wicks died out long ago. Snow fills the crevices of the candelabra. The pancakes are frosted white, the apples capped with puffy white circles. The Rice Krispies box has a thick white top, a fresh white loaf. The snow forms in the shapes of the tableware it covers, exaggerating the swing of the forks, distorting the proportion of the spoons. The banquet, like an expensive plastic arrangement in a furniture showroom, emits no scent. Bon appetit!*

*Beyond the table lie a dozen tables mounded with snow. A dozen giant loaves of table-sized white bread seem to float above the snow-covered plain. The loaves encircle the sad picnic table, its red checker cloth suspended in mid-breeze. A man lies alongside one of the benches. The sheriff stands over him, poised with his right arm in the air. The swing and the strike.*

*"Wake up son,…son," shouts the sheriff. He removes his gloves and delivers a bare-handed slap.*

*The man sucks cold air into his lungs with the third blow. The sheriff grabs the lapels of his shirt, vigorously shaking him. "Is this your family, your wife and children?" His rancid coffee breath condenses in fine mocha droplets across Phil's face. Phil winces, anticipating the fourth swat, groaning.*

"You're in some serious trouble, buddy. I don't know if they're going to make it. We couldn't get pulses. Are you some kind of sick Jim Jones type?

The sheriff spreads his arms indicating the frozen buffet, the solid pitcher of raspberry Kool-Aid, the abstract bouquet of plastic tableware, the two-foot-high mound of banana pancakes. The spread is untouched, delicately preserved in the cold. Four paper cups half-filled with Kool-Aid, a still life of death.

Panning the banquet table, the state troopers taping off the scene, the receding ambulance, the cameraman turns a slow three-sixty, returns and holds the shot of two of the cups, one half-empty, the other tipped, spilling into the snow on the table like a strawberry snow cone. The lens absorbs the images of snow-frosted pancakes, the table set for four. The police cameras brightly flash, dazzling the dancing snowflakes.

*Lucinda Ebersole*

# Get Thee to Mount Pilate, Thelma Lou

LUCINDA EBERSOLE is the co-editor of several anthologies, including the infamous *Mondo Barbie* (St. Martin's Griffin, 1993) and
*Coming to Terms* (New Press, 1994). She is the author of numerous short stories, which have been published in *Yellow Silk*, *The
Crescent Review*, and *American Letters and Commentary*, among
others. She is the owner of Atticus Books, a virtual antiquarian
bookstore in Washington, D.C., where she lives. Her first novel,
*Death in Equality*, was published by St. Martin's Press in 1997.

"Why are there no queers on television?" Debra asked thumbing
through the *TV Guide*.

"Must everything in your life be so issue oriented?" I asked
in disgust. "You said we would grab some beer and pizza and watch TV. So far we
have analyzed the hiring practices of every major brewery in America before
grabbing a six-pack, we have driven to Pizza Hut instead of having Domino's
deliver because they once gave money to the pro-lifers, and now we're not watching TV because there are no queers on. Frankly, Debra, I don't think your therapy
is working."

"Well, I'm sick of it."

"Let's watch PBS. They have queers."

"When did you become such an expert? I spent an entire summer with you in
Rehoboth trying to teach you to pick out a dyke in a crowd. I got hit on all the
time and the only people you talked to were sixteen-year-old boys."

"Hey, one of those boys just sent me an invitation to his high school graduation and none of those women has sent you so much as a postcard. Besides, don't
you find it a stereotype to think that you can pick out a dyke in a crowd? I mean
it sounds like something one does to fleas."

"Well I can pick 'em out."

"What about Carol?"

"She is a dyke."

"Yes but you were never able to convince her husband of that small detail."

"Just wait, one day—"

"Let's watch *Dawson's Creek*. They have a new gay boy."

"One gay character and they make the national news. I want more than that, I want an entire city filled with queers, I want the straight character to be the odd girl. I want—"

"What about Mayberry?"

"Huh?"

"Mayberry, you know *The Andy Griffith Show*. They were all gay."

"No they weren't."

"Well, not all of them. Thelma Lou was straight and so was Opie. Every time I saw Thelma Lou on the screen I just wanted to yell, 'Hey, Thelma Lou, get a life, move to Mount Pilate, move to Raleigh, you'll never get any in Mayberry.'"

"How come," Debra asks, "you're insane, and I'm the one in therapy?"

"It's not my fault they were all queer."

"Were not."

"OK, name me one character in Mayberry who was married."

Debra pondered the question for a moment. "Otis," she replied.

"Did you ever see a Mrs. Otis? Why did he always sleep at the sheriff's office? Every morning that Andy showed up for work and Otis was sleeping over, did you notice that Barney was always there? And, I might add, he always seemed just a bit nervous when the sheriff walked in."

"Sheriff Taylor was married, married to Opie's mother."

"Did you ever see Opie's mother?"

"No, she was already dead."

"Yeah, sure, that's what they tell those little boys: 'Your mother's dead and you need to stay with me now.'"

"You're disgusting."

"Listen, Debra, don't you think it's just a little odd that Opie was the only child in Mayberry?"

Debra ponders this question even longer. "There were other children. I saw them. They just didn't have recurring roles."

"Right, they just showed up in Mayberry one day and then they vanished. Well I know where they are, Debra. Every last one of them is buried under Floyd's barbershop."

"Gross!"

"Didn't you ever wonder what was in that back room behind that curtain? He was so sleazy, sitting around all day reading magazines. And what kind of magazines were those that kept old Floyd so interested? I can't prove it, but I'm pretty sure that Floyd is the illegitimate brother of Jesse Helms."

"That's it. You've completely lost it."

"Even the bit characters were queer. What about Ernest T. Bass? He was the bitchiest queen in Mayberry."

"I suppose he was Andy's love toy."

"No, get real. He was Barney's other main love interest."

"That can't be right. They were always arguing."

"Of course they were. They never could decide who was the biggest queen, but underneath that combative exterior was a reservoir of passion. Andy and Ernest T. Bass, what a joke. Don't you remember the way Gomer looked at Andy? He would follow him anywhere and Andy knew it."

"OK," Debra says, "I'll give you that one. Gomer was gay on the show and in real life."

"That is not true. It was just a vicious rumor. I know, I'm from Sylacauga, too. There are not now, nor have there ever been, homosexuals in Sylacauga."

"No homosexuals in Sylacauga."

"None. It's a small town, someone would have told me."

"None."

"Well, no actual homosexuals, but I'd say in the last fifty years or so there have been several people through town who might be described as...unusually literary."

"I see."

"And how about Aunt Bee? Surely you know that Aunt Bee was the Natalie Barney of Mayberry. Don't you remember how Clara Edwards would sit beside Bee and hang on her every word? You could feel the heat rising right up under her clothes. And what about when Helen walked in. Clara would get into the worst snit, rightly so. Aunt Bee couldn't take her eyes off Helen. She thought about her even when she wasn't there. She'd be setting the table and talking to herself in that high-pitched voice rattling off the names of the dinner guests...Andy, Barney, Opie...Helen. Her voice would drop an entire octave every time she mentioned her name. I know it bothered Clara, but in the end I believe she was a pragmatist. She knew Bee was not the kind of woman who could be happy with just one lover."

"I don't know what bothers me more," Debra said, "the fact that I am still listening to this or the fact that you have given it so much thought. Do you have fantasies about this?"

"No, of course not. Well, maybe just one. I'm in my '52 red Chevy truck headed from Mount Pilate, only on the TV my truck is a stunning shade of gray…"

"Oh my God, I had to ask."

"Even before I get to the filling station, I can see Gomer waving. As I pull in, I roll down my window. 'Hey, Gomer.'

"'Shazzam, girl, I ain't seen you in a coon's age, but I'd know this truck anywhere. She's the brightest gray on the planet. Is she runnin' good?'

"'Yeah, great. I just drove her up from Sylacauga.'

"'Gooooly. I haven't been home in years.'

"'You haven't missed anything, it's pretty much the way you left it.'

"'Any homosexuals in town?'

"'No, Gomer, no homosexuals, but there is a new P. E. teacher and I hear tell she is unusually literary.'

"'Gooooly. You headed to see Aunt Bee?'

"'Yeah,' I say, ducking my head bashfully and blushing, though you probably won't notice it unless you have excellent contrast on your TV.

"'Yeah,' Gomer laughs and punches my arm. 'Andy and I had a romantic little dinner at the diner in Mount Pilate, and he said Aunt Bee couldn't wait to see you.'

"'Well then, I better get a move on. You know she gets mad if I'm late.' Gomer and I wave good-bye and, filled with anticipation, I head for Aunt Bee's. I always go in the back door because I know she'll be waiting in the kitchen. I climb out of the truck, and adjust my clothes. I want to look nice for her even though I know I won't be wearing them long. I look quite darling in my white T-shirt, short black pleated skirt exploding with gray, light-gray, and pale gray flowers, white socks, and Keds that match the same vibrant gray of my Chevy. I'm not wearing any underwear because with Aunt Bee there's really no point. I hope that she won't have noticed that I'm late, but when I get to the kitchen, she is waiting for me, hands on hips, spatula in hand.

"'You're late,' she says in that voice that sends shivers down my spine.

"She is a vision, her gray hair in a tight bun, a stark white poet's shirt flowing from her shoulders covering her ample bosom, jodhpurs that make her hips seem to go on forever, and tall black jackboots that I know she had Barney polish several times to get just the right shine. I fall into her arms and reach up, loosening her hair, and watch it cascade nearly to her hips. She lifts the back of my skirt and pops me with her still-hot spatula.

"'Ow.'

"'I've told you repeatedly not to be late. Now you run up to Opie's room and get naked.'

"'Yes, Aunt Bee.' I always do exactly what Aunt Bee tells me. As I push open the swinging door, I ask her, 'Where's Opie?'

"'Oh, I got him a sitter. He'll be gone all night.'

"In the dining room, I quickly turn around and push back into the kitchen, 'It's not Floyd, is it?'

"'Don't be silly, I'd never leave Opie with that pervert. Gomer's taking him to see *South Pacific* at the picture show in Raleigh and then they'll spend the night with Andy at his Raleigh love nest.'

"I run up the steps throwing clothes everywhere. Naked, I slip in between the fresh sheets that Aunt Bee has starched and ironed. I hear her coming up the stairs and when she enters the room, her entire body fills the door frame. She sets a plate of steaming cookies on the nightstand and reaches in, pulling out Opie's Hopalong Cassidy lasso. She gingerly ties my hands to the iron headboard. Roughly, she rips off the top sheet, which can only mean that Clara and Helen found out I was coming and neither one of them has slept with her this week. She climbs on top of me, the inside of her jackboots rubbing my legs. She lifts a hot cookie from the plate and lays it between my breasts. I grimace from the heat. Bee picks up the cookie and breaks it in half. I open my mouth, but she holds the hot, broken cookie over my breast. A single semi-sweet Nestle's chocolate chip begins to drip to my nipple, Aunt Bee leans over—"

"Stop. Stop right now," Debra yells.

"Don't you want to hear how it ends?"

"No, I don't. I don't want to ever think about it again. What if I start having wet dreams about Aunt Bee? What if I start having wet dreams about you and Aunt Bee? What will I tell my therapist? What will I tell my group? I'll have to lie to my group. No, I'll have to quit group."

"Don't you think you're overreacting just a little bit? You were the one who wanted more queers on TV."

"Real queers, not imagined in your sick mind."

"They are real. One simply has to learn to look more closely at the subtext. Much of literature and film has an entirely different meaning when one delves into the subtextual message. I think it was Derrida who said—"

"Stop, I can't take anymore. I don't want to know anymore, let's not ever mention it again."

"Fine. I'm more than happy to comply with your 'don't ask, don't tell' sitcom policy. One point of clarification. Does this mean we can or cannot watch *Melrose Place?*"

Debra goes to the kitchen for more beer and then slouches back in her chair. Her voice is softer, less strident, "I just wanted to see more queers on TV."

"Debra," I lean in and ask softly, "Have you ever watched *Gillligan's Island?*"

*Barbara Esstman*

# *Uses for the Word "Fuck"*

## A NOVELINI

BARBARA ESSTMAN is the co-editor of *A More Perfect Union* (St. Martin's Press, 1999) and author of numerous short stories and two novels, *The Other Anna* (Harcourt, 1993) and *Night Ride Home* (Harcourt, 1997), that were both adapted for television by Hallmark Productions. A National Endowment for the Arts, Virginia Center for the Creative Arts, and Maryland State Arts Council fellow, she teaches at the Writer's Center in Bethesda, Maryland.

### I. THE NATURE OF THE BEASTS

Let me preface this by saying that my sister and I grew up with swear words as taboos. If our mother broke a goblet, sliced open her finger, or was otherwise surprised by misfortune, she would on rare occasions say "damn" and then apologize for days. But she was dedicated to raising her daughters in a proper environment and seeing us grow into ladies like her who never upset anyone. We weren't allowed to see *South Pacific* until we were well into high school because of the gratuitous use of "damn," and we never, ever, heard any of the other Forbidden Words in her house. Our careful rearing had its effect on me, but go figure. It also produced my sister Sara whose three favorite words are "fuck," "shit," and "asshole," in that order.

Especially fuck. She adores everything about it. How it feels solid in her mouth and can be either spit out with force or said softly in awe or used to underscore the humor of a situation. How it can be both a noun and a verb—several, in fact—to fuck, to fuck over, to fuck it, to be fucked. And then of course, there's "fucking," the ever-popular gerund with its almost limitless possibilities. But most of all she likes fuck because, in her opinion, there's no more efficient way for a woman to be heard by a recalcitrant listener than to preface her statement with some form of it.

Fuck is mandatory, she contends, as a clear signal of unsubmissive posture. For all the advances of feminism, which have made it possible for women to be responsible for everything they used to be in charge of *and* to hold full-time jobs besides, we're still ignored, we're still dismissed, and if we don't verbally kick people in the shins before we speak at crucial moments, they don't really listen.

She has a rather substantial list of examples, the most frequently cited being her X-husband, who for years when she told him she was unhappy used to pat her hand and tell her that she'd feel better after her period. Others include my mother's termite inspector who tried to dismiss a wall that was being visibly eaten, a dinner date who insisted that Sara be dessert, and a doctor who diagnosed her menopausal insomnia as female hysteria. She swears that she calmly explained the empirical evidence from several different points of view, and that she didn't start emphasizing her points with "fuck" until after the complete failure of rational discourse.

I cringe when she goes off like this. On those rare occasions when I need to make a serious point, I say "frigging." Sara shakes her head in amazement. "It's just a word," she says. "What are you afraid of?"

I'm not sure.

"Aren't you angry?"

I should be, I suppose. I was the less favored, less talented child, firmly entrenched in the fat middle of every bell-shaped curve, while Sara lived consistently in the ninety-ninth percentile. She was president of her classes, captain of her field hockey teams, a National Merit semifinalist, and the fantasy girl of choice for many males in a two-county area. She's *the* only person I know who remembers high school as fun, and as far as our parents were concerned, she was as an exceptionally gifted, beloved, and virtual only child. One would have thought that her successes would have made her grateful and cooperative. But the more she achieved, the more pissed off she became about what went along with that achievement for a girl.

"Just because Spartacus was a good gladiator didn't negate the reasons for his rebellion," she's told me.

"What are you talking about?" I asked.

"Just because someone throws you a bone that you earned in the first place doesn't mean that you owe them your life."

"You're not making any sense."

"Oh, fuck, Ellen. Why don't you get this?"

I don't know. Sara started using "fuck" at the preppy girls' high school we attended. Our mother sent us there to become educated ladies with good manners, and, to be fair, many of us went through a brief adolescent stage of rebellion when we delighted in the daring use of "damn" and "hell," more commonly referred to as h-e-double-hockey-sticks. But Sara explains her use of fuck as a holistic response to Mercy Academy's repressive regime. She said the only place where you could find better mind control techniques was in a Chinese Communist POW camp, and "fuck" became her mantra against brainwashing.

OK, so we had rules of silence and were required to curtsey to the nuns. OK, so every week started with a general assembly when the entire school filed up one by one before our principal who read aloud our names, followed by a list of our offenses from the previous week. And yeah, besides this forced and public confession, we were punished not only for what we did wrong but also for not doing enough good. Really. Nuns took us aside to berate us if we didn't use our fifteen minutes of daily free time to pray in the chapel, collect alms for the missions, or otherwise volunteer to make the world a better place. If this didn't jump-start our charitable instincts, they became more stringent about noticing transgressions to be read at the Monday morning gatherings, and even the reluctantly submissive eventually capitulated.

But you could just *look* at Sara standing before the Reverend Mother and know she was thinking, "Fuck this." Not that she could change the system. But she loved to take on the nuns in the classroom and point out their inaccuracies and contradictions by using the reasoning and logic they'd taught her. She was proud of how many infractions of the rules she could rack up every week. The Brown Noses thought of her as the Antichrist and prayed for her soul. But to every girl who wanted to fight back and didn't dare, she was frigging Joan of Arc. Me? I was Sara Griffin's little sister, and I try to think of high school as happening so long ago as not to count.

But Sara contends that what we learned there was intended to be a lifelong pattern of self-sacrifice and emotional *hari-kari*. She says I only have to look around to see women our age who are afraid to open their mouths and who think of themselves as never having done enough for others. She says I only have to listen to how many females preface their comments with "I'm sorry" and who answer any request with "yes."

"The phrase they really need to learn is 'fuck it,'" she says. "Say it, Ellen. Fuck. It."

I can't. Which brings me back to our mother, Ruth Hobson Griffin. AKA Ruthless Ruth. She is relentlessly polite, humble, cheerful, and self-effacing. She generously sees to others and never troubles them in return. She has raised deference to an art form, except with her daughters. With us, she expects to exercise the control she's given up in all other parts of her life by insisting on our obedience. At least I obey. I say, "Yes, Mother." Sara says, "Ma, you've lost your fucking mind." Mother says, "Sara! Why can't you speak nicely like your sister?"

Since our father died four years ago, we've taken over our mother's care and feeding, though neither Sara nor I needed anything extra on our schedules. We both work full time. She has three college-aged boys, and I have two teenaged girls. I have a husband, and she's alone, which gives us extra work of opposite sorts, but extra all the same. We maintain our households near our mother's and did not have the foresight to move to another state or country.

Mother lives by herself, but her extra requirements run the gamut from commanding us to call every Sunday afternoon, even if we've just had dinner with her the evening before, to appearing coffin-side at every funeral in town, even if we'd never met the deceased. After she remarks on how natural the corpse looks, she likes to drag us around to meet the grieving family and other mourners. She beams as if she's presenting the Crown Princess Anastasia and one of the other sisters, the names of whom no one remembers, and she obviously believes that our mere presence is the universal antidote to sorrow. I smile tightly and feel like a steer in the county fair show ring. Ten minutes later, Sara will burst out onto the lawn of the funeral parlor and say a little too loudly, "Fuck, Mom, he didn't look *natural*, he looked *dead*."

But still, Sara reminds me whenever she needs to remind herself that our mother has been a good mother in spite of her recent and annoying neediness. She dedicated herself to our care, education, and well-being. She gave us her best, however illogical and sometimes superficial that was, and realistically, that's all we can ask of someone who loved us with all her heart. "Can't expect cows to fly," my sister says. "Can't make a silk purse out of a sow's ear."

All this is true in Sara's case, but our mother more often looks at me as if I'm a soufflé that's fallen and she can't figure out what went wrong. I can't either, which is maybe why I don't want to chance doing anything else to disappoint her. But Sara is clearer on the line of demarcation between what should be rendered unto Mother and what should be rendered unto us as our very own. We owe Mother care but not a pound of flesh, she contends. In the years since our father died, she's called on most Sundays as directed; she's attended thirty percent of the funerals; she drives Mom to doctors' appointments, DAR meetings, and bridge clubs if she can't get a ride; and she makes sure that she always has necessities. I never worry about Mom's daily care; it's Sara's part of the bargain. She fills the cupboards before they're bare, dispenses the pills, takes Mother shopping, changes the light bulbs, makes small repairs around the house, and keeps the cleaning crew and yardman in line.

We formed a quite orderly routine: on Mondays Sara blasted in and got Mom situated for the week; on Tuesdays my mother called to ask why I couldn't be more like my sister; and by Wednesdays I'd convinced myself that her insult was fair trade for not having to actually be near her. I'd say that for a family that was the equivalent of a thoroughbred, a mule, and a goat harnessed together, we were bumping forward rather well with minimal damage to the goat.

## II. THE OSTENSIBLE PROBLEM

That is, except concerning issues involving the Eternal Cousin, the EC being our mother's last living blood relative except us. The family tree on our maternal side had not reproduced well. Over the decades its many childless branches had withered and died off, each last survivor at the end of each defunct twig being cared for by whomever was remaining, until by the time Sara and I were middle-aged, only our mother and the Eternal Cousin remained of that once huge clan. After each death throughout the lengthy decimation of the family, the closest, able-bodied relation—usually our mother by virtue of her being the youngest of them all—moved into the house or apartment of the deceased for several weeks to clean it out for sale and dispose of the belongings.

This was not a task taken on lightly. Without exception, the family members were packrats with a preternatural capacity to horde, store, and keep whatever they might later have need for. In their minds, this included such varied treasures as grocery receipts from the Depression, unused ration coupons from WWII, and every aluminum pot pie container, Styrofoam meat tray, and glass jar they'd ever removed sustenance from. Not to mention that when one relative died, the keeper possessions were distributed to next of kin, so the arduousness of the cleanings increased geometrically with each passing, until by the time we got to the Eternal Cousin, her condo was filled with the remains of at least 3.5 households: hers, her mother's, her sister's, and her half of another cousin's that she'd divided with our mother ten years before.

To compound the problem, the Eternal Cousin had been senile for years. After our father died, Mother required someone to accompany her on her quarterly visits, and since Sara was always teaching a class she couldn't cancel, I always had to take off work to chauffeur. This was my portion of our sister act: the occasional concentrated and grueling journey traded for Sara's lower-intensity but more constant ministrations. Mother loved these trips. They gave her purpose and frequent opportunity to tell me that I was driving too fast, needed a haircut, and was putting on weight. I always started out with the fantasy that she and I were bonding. I always ended wanting to drop Mother off at a rest stop.

But how to handle the EC was a genuine problem. She refused to bathe, wash her hair, launder her clothes, or clean the apartment. She ate one small hamburger patty for every meal, breakfast included, and if she dropped a skillet of grease, she left it there to congeal until the kitchen floor was an archipelago of petrified fat. Rather than walk to the toilet during the night, she peed on the floor next to her bed, or *in* it during the winter when it was too cold to get up. The carpet was worn to the jute, the plaster streaked with soot, and, frankly, the EC reeked to the heavens. But whenever Mother suggested the reintroduction of hygiene, the cousin turned hostile as a feral dog, and Mother returned from these sojourns upset to the point of tears.

After listening each time to the litany of horrors, Sara would shake her head. "She's a bag lady with a condo, Ma. It's past time to put her in a nursing home."

"Oh, I couldn't do that," our mother said.

"Then let her enjoy her squalor."

"Oh, I can't do that either."

"If it's upsetting for you, I can find a good home and move her."

"Oh, I couldn't ask you to do that."

"I'm offering. I volunteer."

"No, I can't do that."

They would run through the options several times, and then Sara, who gets impatient with fence-sitting, hesitation, or indecision of any sort, would have enough.

"Ma, fish or cut bait. Shit or get off the pot. Do it or fuck it."

After establishing that stasis would be maintained, she'd refuse to listen until after the next visit, and only then to check if there'd miraculously been a new development. I just stood by during these debates. If Sara couldn't budge her, no sense me flinging myself against the castle wall or scaling that cliff at Gallipoli. But in the interims Mom called me once a week to agonize over the plight of the EC. I learned to switch the phone to speaker, empty or load the dishwasher, do the *New York Times* crossword, or fold the girls' laundry while I was listening. At appropriate junctures, I said "um" and accepted this penance—I'm not sure for what—as my lot. Or maybe I thought I could accrue enough points to become approved. Or worse, sometimes I caught myself imagining we were having a real mother-daughter conversation and that she'd called me for some reason other than my sister wouldn't talk with her.

But anyhow, after a long illness that involved coma, feeding tubes, and my mother's blatant disregard for the EC's Living Will, the EC finally managed to die in spite of everything. She was ninety-seven, and our mother at eighty-five couldn't possibly empty this last dwelling by herself. Sara and I knew that. We were braced for it. In fact, we'd been in training all our lives to take over this family duty. While growing up, we'd gone four times to Iowa to empty the houses of the dead (grandmother's, great-grandmother's, and two great-aunts', in that order), twice to Omaha (our mother's second and third cousins', respectively), and once to Evanston (to help the EC with her sister's house). As kids, we rode the Wabash and slept in a lower Pullman bunk there and back, our mother on the outside, Sara between her and the window, our dolls in the shoe hammock, and me at their feet. When we got older, Mother drove but wouldn't let us near the wheel—she said we'd wreck and strand us in Quincy or Keokuk. But at each house, Mom sorted and packed and pitched while Sara and I rummaged through the closets, drawers, and cupboards we'd not been allowed to touch, let alone pillage, while the owners were still alive. We draped ourselves in their pearls, decided which set of china we wanted to inherit when we got married, and sniggered at the girth and style of their underwear.

Conveniently for me, the EC passed on immediately before Sara's semester break, and she for once had no excuse to skip EC Duty. When Mom announced that she needed us to drive her to the burial and clean out the condo, Sara said, "Shit, Ma. The only time we go anywhere together is when someone croaks."

I felt an evil satisfaction that Sara was stuck with going, even as I was relieved that she'd be there as a DMZ. I was sometimes caught in this crossfire of feeling, similar to how I felt when I put down my copy of *Martha Stewart Living* to watch her indictment for insider trading. I love my sister, but truthfully, I use her, too. Point Sara at a problem and she's there like an arrow, and if she's there, I don't have to be. I'm grateful for her competence, but like everyone, I like to see the mighty fallen.

The next day, Sara picked me up first.

"Don't let her run over you."

"She's my mother. She's old. You want me to hit her?"

"You know what I mean. You let her push you around, and then afterwards you get pissed for being pushed."

"I don't get pissed; you get pissed."

"You just won't admit that you're pissed, and then to prove it, you let her do anything."

"She doesn't criticize you the way she does me."

"Of course she does. The difference is that I don't believe her, and the question is, why do you?"

I hate when Sara keeps on like a terrier after a rabbit, bringing up issues I don't want to think about. I've accepted my fate and just want her to leave me alone.

I said I didn't know what to do about Mother, and Sara told me that I did. She used the analogy of those long car trips our parents took us on as kids. The back seat of our Pontiac had a pull-down armrest in the center that divided my territory from hers. But of course she would slide her pinkie just slightly over the line or wedge her elbow next to mine or prop her leg so that her foot violated my air space. Then she would either whistle and look out the window or, worse, stare at me and grin until I screamed, "Stop looking at me! It's not fair! You're touching my side."

To be fair, I did the same to her, and the heated border disputes could go on seemingly for hours until Dad threatened to stop the car and Mother said that we were giving her a migraine. Sara pointed out that backing Mother off wasn't dissimilar to those long-ago battles. I pointed out if I got too much of an advantage then, she used to bend my middle finger back or give me Indian Rope Burn until I cried. If I'd been particularly uppity, she'd wait until we got to the motel, pin me to the ground, and sit on my stomach until one of our parents noticed and told her to get up.

"That wasn't exactly positive reinforcement," I told her.

Sara gave one good shake of her head.

"Well, you're grown up now, and she's getting too old to fight back."

So after the four-hour car trip, which lasted five and a half hours because Mom needed to stop several times, we arrived in Evanston, got our luggage in, and unlocked the door of the condo. Mother hurried past us to the bathroom, and Sara stood in the middle of the living room filled with couches that listed, chairs with bellies that dragged on the floor, and tables afflicted with leprosy. Plaster had fallen, wallpaper had peeled, and the windows were so dirty that the light in the room was the same silty gray as an unclean aquarium.

"Fuuu-uck," she said, softly and in awe. "For once she wasn't exaggerating."

She hadn't been here since we were in high school, and I led her through a preliminary reconnoiter, opening closets crammed with papers and magazines, cupboards filled with dishes stacked haphazardly, and bureaus stuffed with everything from Victorian evening bags to used tissues. When Mother emerged from the loo, she found Sara, ever compulsive and efficient. On the bed she'd laid a stack of the EC's dresses, all with food stains down their bosoms, and was rummaging amongst the shoe boxes and articles stored at the rear of the bedroom closet.

"What are you doing, dear?" our mother asked.

"Clearing this stuff out," Sara said, her voice muffled.

"Oh, I'm not quite ready to do that."

Sara emerged and put her hand on her hip.

"I thought that's why we came."

Mother looked around, distressed.

"I can't do that, not when we haven't even buried her yet."

So we watched TV all evening, though the picture was snowy, and Sara paced. The next morning, with the temperature in the twenties and the wind coming off the lake, we stood with the EC's pastor, two younger members of her DAR chapter, the funeral director, and a guy with a backhoe as she was laid in the last grave of the large family plot. As we were walking back to the limo, Sara put her arm around Mother, pulled her close, and said, "Poor old girl. Outlived almost everyone she knew." And then, "I bet I can get some packing boxes from that grocery down the street."

When we got back to the apartment, she went into the bedroom to change. Mother lowered herself into one of the derelict chairs and sat for the longest time smiling.

"I have such good memories of this place."

She told me how during the Depression she lived with the EC's parents and worked as a secretary in the Loop so that she could send money home to her parents after their bank failed. How after work she met the EC and her sister at the World's Fair or went with them to dance to the music of Wayne King's band. How they once all stood in a line six blocks long to see Dillinger's body laid out in state.

"Your father and I used to bring you girls here to this apartment when you were little. We visited and went to nice restaurants and took you to the Shedd and the Field. Oh, Sara loved the fish and animals. Remember?"

My only clear memories were of being spanked in the Walnut Room of Marshall Field's for refusing to sit on my chair straight and of being nose-to-tusk with a stuffed walrus. But I was beginning to feel weirdly nostalgic when Mother asked, "Now, where has Sara gone?"

We found her dressed in sweats and an extra large T-shirt, hauling boxes out of the EC's closet. When Mother insisted that we wait to do that on our next trip, Sara wiped the back of her hand against her cheek and left a smudge of dirt.

"Ma," she said. "I've got two more days off before I start cutting into personal leave without pay."

As if that explained everything, she bent back into the closet, just her butt jutting out.

"I don't want to rush into this," Mom said.

"Kay hasn't lived here for a year," I ventured. "You haven't exactly rushed."

In fact, she'd been torturously slow. While the EC was in her lengthy coma, Mom had had me drive her here twice on the pretense of putting the condo up for sale. But once we arrived, she'd insisted that Kay might recover and move back, though I pointed out that was highly unlikely for someone in a vegetative state. Now I couldn't believe that after the death of her excuse, Mother was still going to prolong our agony.

Just then Sara backed out of the closet with a rifle, slammed the bolt with a definitive *cha-chu*, and swung around to face us. Mom and I both stepped back.

"Wow, look. Must've belonged to Kay's husband in WWI. His helmet's in there, too."

"Is that loaded?" I asked.

"Not since the Armistice." She pulled the bolt out to show me.

"Oh, Sara, put that back. You shouldn't touch Kay's things."

Sara raised the rifle, squinted down the sights, and took aim at our mother.

"Ma, you had me take off work, leave my family, and drive two hundred miles to clean this place out. So that's fucking what I'm fucking going to do." Mother looked startled and Sara took a step forward. "You understand, Ma?" Laughing, she took another step. "Ma, don't make me shoot you. What would we tell your bridge club?"

Mother giggled, and Sara lowered the barrel. I laughed, too, uplifted by the catharsis of this little psychodrama. She propped the gun by the bed, picked up a stack of photo albums from the floor, and shoved them in my arms. "Here, you two check these and see if they're anyone we know."

"I don't want you to throw anything away," Mother warned.

Sara held up a pillowcase so ancient that it hung in shreds. She rolled her eyes.

"Well, all right. You can pitch that."

I took Mom into the living room and sat with her on the couch, the cushions sagging so that we kept sliding towards each other.

"Don't let her throw anything else away," she whispered.

"I won't," I lied.

I opened an album full of photos from some long-ago vacation—women in cloche hats lined up in front of St. Mark's, St. Peter's, Notre Dame, and apparently every other church in Europe. Mother said it was the tour the EC's sister had gone on after her divorce in 1931. Happily, she started looking for her in the lineups and had me get a pen to mark an X on the sister's skirt in each one so that Sara and I could find her. I squirmed. I chafed. Our mother had conned us and apparently would keep conning us to bring her here as long as she could work the Helpless Mother/Good Daughter angle. I would have to keep driving her to

Evanston with the same regularity that Sisyphus pushed his rock and Prometheus lost his liver.

### III. THE HEART OF THE MATTER

Just as I was ratcheting my dismay and resentment to a cosmic level, Sara answered the phone in the bedroom. I heard her say fuck, and next she was calling, "Ellen! Come quick."

Pulling on her jeans, she ordered me to repack her suitcase. Some gorilla of a TKE had tackled her youngest kid during the fraternity intramural basketball finals. Shattered wrist, pins, surgery. She was taking a cab to O'Hare. Don't worry. Explain to Mother. Call later. Kiss-kiss.

"What do I do?"

"Get her to let us clean out this place!" she called over her shoulder as she flew down the hall.

I was indignant that she'd not only deserted me but given me an impossible task besides. Mother stood at the living room window and watched Sara get into the taxi.

"Do you think she'll be all right?"

"Her kid's the one who broke his wrist."

But she didn't seem to hear me, and the next morning when I got up, she was dressed in her good suit and waiting for me on the couch. I felt like Poland about to be invaded.

"I want to go downtown today," she said.

"Sara said we should clean."

"We'll do that next time."

"There can't be too many next times."

"We'll do it later."

She looked away from me. I know it's not right to want to shake, slap, or spank one's mother. But I wanted to yank her up, drag her to Kay's room, and not let her out until we'd emptied it. I was explaining why we needed to get this done and pleading with her to cooperate when she snuck a look at me as if gauging how far she was from winning, and I pictured myself locked forever in this apartment for no good reason and at her mercy. I started crying and told her that I couldn't just keep leaving my husband and kids and taking off from work to drive her up here whenever she didn't have anything better to do. I was getting worn out and had too much else to take care of. It was selfish of her to keep manipulating us for no good reason. Just. Fucking. Selfish.

For the first time in my life, I'd said fuck with meaning. For a nanosecond I felt as if I'd just finished an exhilarating run. Mother's mouth formed an "O" and

then she squeezed her eyes shut. For several seconds her whole body went rigid
and then seemed to fold in on itself, the way crumpled paper breaks inward when
it starts to burn. She covered her face with her hands and shook with the sound of
her crying trapped inside.

I was speechless, first, over what I'd done, and second, that she'd gone down
with the first good swing I'd ever taken. Seeing her give up was more upsetting
than having her dig in. That at least was familiar. This I didn't know what to do
about. I put my arms around her and felt her light as bird wings. She leaned her
head against my shoulder and kept saying sorry, sorry, sorry. She didn't mean to
make me angry. She'd never seen me angry. She knew that we'd have to let the
condo go soon and that she would never come back to Chicago. She wanted to
see the old places and take the El, the way she used to go to work in the Loop or
with us shopping at Carson Pirie Scott. She'd had such happy times in this city.

But how wrong of her to put such a burden on me. She had no idea that I was
so upset—I'd never said anything before. But it was so lonely with everyone
dying, and she liked that I came with her. She wanted to show me those places
she remembered so that I'd remember, too.

So I was holding my mother and thinking, "Fuck, fuck, fuck, how did humans
get so fucked up with one another?" I hadn't a clue.

"What do you want, Mom?"

"Will you take me downtown?"

Then because this was a request and not an order, I got dressed, she pinned
her jewelry in her bra so no one could steal it, and we headed down the block to
the El. She marched along in that wind-up way she has, even though the wind
was so bitter that it took my breath away. We rode the train past tenement porches
hung with laundry and the Aragon Ballroom where Wayne King had played. She
talked about working at Wiebolt's where she bought macaroni and cheese lunches
for twenty-five cents and a piece of apple pie on payday. At Marshall Field's she
bought a navy suit and I a flowy skirt made out of scarves, both of them too
expensive. In the Walnut Room we ate cream cheese and brown bread finger
sandwiches and laughed over how I kept going limp and sliding under the table
the day she'd spanked me.

I asked where she wanted to go next. She said she'd like to see the Palmer
House where she and Dad had honeymooned the week before Pearl Harbor and
where they'd often taken Sara and me to stay as kids. I said that we should spend
the night. She said that would be too expensive. I said we could splurge. She said
we had to get back and start working on the condo. Besides, she just wanted to
see the lobby again. She didn't need to stay.

We came through the revolving doors of polished brass and down the marble gallery lined with shops smelling of perfumes and tobaccos. I had some dim sense of wearing Mary Jane's and a short, plaid skirt and being carried with my bare legs against the rough wool of my father's overcoat.

"I've been here."

"Your father liked to bring you, just you and him, and let you pick out a souvenir. He loved to spoil you, you know."

I must've known but hadn't remembered.

"Should we buy you a keepsake?"

I gestured to a Coach shop.

"Oh, no. I just want to sit in the lobby."

So for the next two and a half hours we did just that. The room was huge and highly baroque, all gilt and marble with a pastoral scene painted across the cavernous ceiling. Cherubs clustered around lords and ladies who danced and courted. Below, the elegant women in gloves and hats and men in double-breasted suits of Mother's day had been replaced by tourists in jeans and sports jerseys, loaded down with backpacks and towing suitcases on wheels. But she sat brightly with her hands in her lap, watching the main entrance as if my father would return any minute.

I asked her about her honeymoon, and she told me that they'd had a lovely wedding followed by a wonderful three days here. The next week the war started. I said, "Oh," and after that we didn't talk much. I was thinking that the next death, the next house to clean out, would be hers. I was trying to make some sense of this when she said something I didn't hear.

"What?"

"I said thank you."

She patted my forearm.

I hesitated and patted her back.

"You're welcome."

"I'm glad Sara had to leave. She can be…" Mother looked me directly in the eye, "…such a bitch."

She had that bright but wary look I'd seen on my daughters' faces whenever they'd chanced a move into adult territory without permission and were ready to admit it. For a few seconds I couldn't wrap my mind around what she'd done. Then I burst out laughing, and Mother smiled as if she was enormously pleased.

"Fuck Sara," I whispered.

Mother giggled.

"Fuck Sara," she whispered back.

We watched the tourists check in and out for another twenty minutes until she said that she was ready to go. I helped her on with her coat and took her arm as we crossed the wide, marble floor. As she was picking her way up the steps, I looked back once more at the vault of ceiling painted with putti romping among the clouds. A whole alternative universe was up there beyond our reach, where the weather was warm and the light was golden. The nymphs and ladies smiled down over the messy scene below them, and I smiled back. Then a new and curious thought came. Like my mother, I would probably never come here again.

But we'd gotten here. For an afternoon, at least. For the moment, fuck the rest.

*Ivy Goodman*

# At Home, after a Brief Illness

IVY GOODMAN is the author of two collections of short stories, *A Chapter from Her Upbringing* (Carnegie Mellon University Press, 2001) and *Heart Failure* (University of Iowa Press, 1983). She lives in Ellicott City, Maryland.

Lila shifted on the chaise longue, and the room lurched in the small mirror on her lap. A corner of the crown molding was reflected vertically, like a picture frame, and there was the tilted chest with its parallel drawers, and then, as she bent forward, she thought she saw a premonition of herself in cameo, looking out of the grave. Her jawline hung with folds of skin; striations thickened under one sidelong staring eye. Who was that? When she leaned back in her chair, moving her knees in turn, dissolving her lap, the mirror, like the cast-off desideratum in a child's sickbed, fell and rattled on the floor but did not break.

She was cold, always cold, even with her knit turban cap, her sweater, her jersey pants, her robe, the comforter, and the afghan tucked about her. She woke and slept and woke again in gnarled postures, seeking her own bodily warmth.

The lights were on, the window glass dark. She felt a draft from the French doors. It wasn't Gil out there, was it? "Gil?" She remembered that earlier she had told him "Don't," a single word that held all the others she was too weak to say: Don't let in more cold. Don't scrape that awful shovel against the wood. Don't fret about the heavy snow. What if all the balcony needs to collapse is your added weight? Don't do chores while I'm lying here, damn it! Gil, don't go out there and fall!

But if he had gone out, he had come back in. She realized that rhythmic sound, like the same footstep cracking over and over through a crust of snow, was really Gil snoring in the next room. He had the bedroom, she the sitting room that adjoined. The sitting room in the master suite, like one of those hotel luxuries that people are persuaded to want in their own houses, was the built-in sick room she hadn't known she had. But nowadays even hospitals, like resorts, competed with amenities. At her last discharge, Gil had rented her a special bed, which stood nearby, unused. She preferred the chaise, made up with sheets. The track lights, like the half-light in intensive care, allowed people to keep watch and her to doze, if she could. At seven o'clock, her aide had left for the night because Gil was home.

He was asleep. She was cold. Had someone unlatched the French doors? "Who's there? Who is it?"

Nights earlier, she had woken to a figure standing over her. In her sleep she had been made to regress and lose all hope of cure, though she had already lost that hope. It was like an obsessive dream of being robbed. Was that a pal beside her, looking on? They gave out pals at the hospital, but she had sent hers back. Before the dream had entirely dispersed, she had found herself awake, still alive, in a state of mortal calm. She was no longer frightened then, but she fully expected to find someone next to her. Now, seeing the girl, she thought, is this a girl? Or a table lamp, like the other night?

"Are you a pal?"

"You ask if I'm your friend?"

"No."

How could Lila explain? Had this girl ever grieved for strangers on occasion, in certain moods, driving a familiar route along the cemetery fence and recognizing that every monument stood for a human being, turning the newspaper page to the notices of death and feeling an unexpected gravity one morning? When Lila was first diagnosed, there her file had lain on the pal's desk. It made no difference that Lila was still alive; her pal had been the first stranger to mourn Lila's life.

Those had been the days of telling people and people taking pity on her. She had needed pity then. Making those calls was like collecting debts or selling goods or services by phone, and yet she gave something gratis in return: Whether a baby, a child, a young person, the middle-aged, or the old, it was always news when someone was about to die, and Lila died with every call. People were so good then. She supposed their terror and pity would rebound at her death, when friends and acquaintances would briefly look after Gil before they also tired of him. She remembered setting down the phone on one of those afternoons, and immediately it had rung. A stranger spoke her name: *"Lila, I'm your pal."*

The pal had arranged to meet her in the cancer center atrium, a space filled with light, as if with hope, but where devastation was heightened on the skin. The pal was Lila's age, fifty-seven; she had volunteered this on the phone. It had been five years since her treatment, five that appeared to have worn on her like ten. Nonetheless she had lived. As some people get God, she had Life and saw herself linked to every living thing. She rushed forward, her gray hair and wan skin slightly moist, as if she had been hurrying for some time. *"That traffic out there, Lila! Did you have traffic?" "No, I have cancer." "Oh, Lila!"*

Lila had wanted to take back her name. The pal could not know her; the pal diminished her, misperceived her. But didn't Lila herself get to know most individuals by crushing them in her hand? Those few she cherished, as long as she cherished them, she held safely cupped. She was at the center of her life—and who is not?—but her cosmology was no bigger, really, than the size of her palm.

And yet, meeting the pal, Lila didn't feel her usual contempt for the shabby of dress, or the superiority toward the gray-haired from someone whose own hair was dyed. Instead she was afraid. Because the pal did know, she must have known that Lila wanted to live as desperately as herself.

Lila had wondered then if someone who had outlasted the disease brought good luck or ill. Could a person catch luck, or if luck fell like heads or tails, wouldn't her odds improve if she were paired with a dying pal? And yet the pal did not look well. Her complexion was as khaki as her clothes. Live or die, who could say? Surely they both could live? But Lila had always hated seeing another woman in possession—of anything—until she'd secured a far finer version of her own.

She opened her eyes. Had she been sleeping? Had someone called her name? She touched her hand to her bald, turbaned head. Time was circular, in the hours sitting in the chaise, and the shivering cold brought her back to *now*.

A girl stood over her. "Your pal is like a son or daughter, part of you?" the girl asked.

"No. A pal means rotten news."

Pals were humorous, above all; they laughed, they wept and hugged, they persevered, they inspired, and all the living pals went to the dead pals' funerals. Lila had not liked or wanted her pal. The pal returned to the Office of the Pals, to phone somebody else.

But who was this red-haired girl?

She was not a girl but a young woman, and she reminded Lila of herself, as we all resemble one another in some earlier state, as the fetal face evolves out of a head shaped like a lima bean. But the same countenance—eyes, nose, mouth— that was a death mask on the woman in the chaise was beautiful on the girl.

"I'm Lila."

"I'm Natalie."

She had an extraordinary lustrous white skin, and Lila wondered how she cared for it. Soaps? Creams? From what elixir—animal, vegetable, or mineral—did the creams come? Snow? When the girl stepped closer, snow fell off her shoes.

"Did you shut those French doors? They're hard to latch."

"Yes, I latched them."

Something about the girl's voice was not quite right, as if she had learned to speak from books or tapes and not on her mother's lap. It was a voice without regional distinction, like a foreign actress speaking "American" or like the American English accents of Russians in the days of the Cold War. When Lila was young, she had been terrified by a TV news show in which Russian schoolchildren at their desks spoke an English like hers, though far more fluent and correct. Why had memory exhumed this? Because Russians, disguised among us, disguised to harm us—like Martians—had made her fear dying when she was eight years old?

"Who are you?"

"I told you. Natalie."

"Why are you here?"

"To be with you."

"You mean they sent you from the staffing agency? But my husband's here. You're not needed, and he won't pay. You'd better leave."

"Lila, Lila," the girl said, teasing Lila with her name, in the manner of the nursing staff. "Lila, I thought you were rich!"

"The phone's over there. Why don't you call a cab?"

"I didn't come by cab."

"On second thought, we will pay you. Just send a bill."

The aides, as Lila knew them, were lackadaisical or efficient. They sat and napped or bustled and nosed about; they didn't just observe, like this girl, as if considering their power, or the relation of nursing to justice—*The needle will pinch, but the morphine is good.* Justice or torture. They were kind enough to do their jobs. They were broad and warm, leaning over her. If told to leave with pay, they would all gladly go. But the girl didn't move.

"You're not an aide, are you? You're not from the agency?"

The girl shook her head. She was not even in the uniform of the aides, who wore white trousers and brightly colored patterned smocks. The girl wore a soft, fuzzy, gray, belted dress, and with the light behind her and her soft mass of hair, her very shape seemed to blur into the atmosphere of the room.

"Gil should have locked those damn French doors. And he didn't."

"No."

Sometimes Lila wasn't sure if she'd spoken aloud or only thought certain words. Had she shouted for Gil? In a long marriage, she and Gil had always been happiest when they'd had someone to oppose: family member, so-called friend, work associate, even on occasion Tony, their son. Someone, like this girl, whom they could trounce. It had been like that, at first, with the disease. They'd had hope at first. Lila had chosen only the best doctors, who had courted her and had seemed to love her, and a hospital whose research advances, whose very appellation, struck awe. No, the problem was not in situ. No, it was not like so-and-so's. If she could not be well, or quickly cured, then she found—to her detriment? her bewilderment?—that she needed to insist on the distinction of being grandly sick, and in fact she was.

After her first treatment, her oncologist had had the nerve to send her home with a form to donate funds toward a far distant cure. No one could help her now. Gil was already gone, or rather, he was waiting for her to go. Her disease was barbaric, and yet it lingered. She couldn't blame Gil, snoring in the next room. She must not wake him if she could help it. And Tony, their son, lived thousands of miles away. Though he had promised Lila that he would visit again before she died, he would not want to undershoot the date and have to repeat the errand. So Lila and this girl were alone.

"Where is your coat?" Lila asked.

"I have no coat." The girl's voice was calm, like a somnambulist's or a zombie's. Was she drugged? She was reasonable now, but Lila worried that a deep incomprehension existed, so that any word could set this crazy girl off. Earth, fire, air, water. Mother, father, brother, sister. Perfectly innocent words.

"Weren't you cold?" Lila said.

"It's nice in here."

The girl pointed to a bit of melted snow on the floor. A spoonful had been flung off her shoe and now the white was going icy clear, like color dissolving down the length of a graying hair. Under the covers, Lila drew back one stockinged foot, as if she'd stepped in the icy spot. But she hadn't left the chaise. She was cold, always so cold.

She wondered if she would die of the cold. On the cancer wing, she had seen a man dying in a swelter. Most doors to the other patients' rooms had been halfway closed, but his was open wide. He lay bloated and naked on his mattress, hardly covered by a small untucked sheet, like a crib sheet, blue with a nursery pattern, while the cancer sheets were white. Through the door frame, Lila had watched a hellish slapstick, scene by scene, in passing, while she made the slow circuit of a convalescent, wheeling her IV stand up and down the hall: Now the huge man pulled the sheet to his chin and uncovered his toes; now he bared one flank at the other's expense; now he rolled onto his stomach, bunching the sheet at his groin and look at that, his naked ass. Was he alone, as he appeared, or were there phantoms to whom he cried and whimpered? Couldn't the nurses do more for him than offer that little sheet, as wrinkled as if it had been wetted, wrung out by hand, and laid on his belly to cool him briefly before his body dried it out? That was one afternoon; the next day the man was gone.

"Lila?"

Had she fallen asleep? For more than a moment? Lila shivered. That pale, dour, red-haired girl was still watching her. "For God's sake, what do you want from me? Cash?" Lila nodded toward the bedroom door. "My husband leaves his wallet on the bureau. Take the money, go on."

"I'm not a thief," the girl said. "I'm nothing as bad as you. But people forgive. They let the dying die."

"Who are these goddamned 'people?' Do you mean you? What did I ever do to you?"

"I've always known who you are."

Was she a neighborhood girl? Yes, she must be, Lila thought. Back home for now. On drugs. Out of her mind. And Lila had perhaps hurt the girl's feelings when she was growing up. In childhood, she might have been a funny-looking little girl with red hair, wide-set silvery eyes, a long, slender, curved nose, and a pallor that was unearthly, no, specifically of the earth, like something growing underground. The girl had grown into a strange, unearthly beauty, but who could have predicted that, observing the funny little girl, Lila least of all? If Lila had been the girl's mother back then, she would have found a plastic surgeon to work the simplest aesthetic on the girl's flesh. Had she said as much aloud one day? Had the girl overheard? Is that why the girl seemed to hold a childish or even a psychotic grudge? She looked about Tony's age. As a boy, Tony had had his coterie, mostly other boys whose achievements had measured high, though invariably short of his. Naturally, as Tony got older, the girls would have threatened Lila more. The odd thing was, Lila couldn't remember any girls. She said, "Then you must know Tony."

The girl smiled. "Tony! Isn't Tony…perfect?"

Lila took the girl's pause as an insult, a mockery, under the guise of searching for a word. *Perfect?* Well, Tony was perfect and if he was vain, it was perfectly understandable. He had the smile of a man smiling in the mirror at himself, a smile that showed he was loved—by Lila, the figure behind his reflection in every glass. His smile also showed an intimate satisfaction, but Lila had always wanted Tony to love himself.

She said, "You know that Tony's a partner now in the premier firm—"

"Yes, Tony says that your simple boasting is never enough. You must exaggerate and fib."

"What?" Lila shook her head. "Tony's under stress. This, all this, has been so hard for Tony."

"Your cancer?" The girl's voice was flat and arch at the same time. "That's what he tells everybody."

"You're jealous then?"

"Not of you. You're his favorite pickup line."

"What? But I'm really going to die."

Did Tony think she wouldn't? Sometimes she wondered how much he would miss her, since he seldom came home anyway. In the last few years, she had often bragged of his distress on seeing aged relatives begin to fail. Her point was not that their decline seemed accelerated because he saw them so infrequently but that he was so sensitive. He had been upset to see them dying, and she blamed them subtly on his behalf. She understood why he could not be with her now. He had his own life. He was a grown man, almost thirty years old. And yet his own life, what kind of illusion was that? Why had she protected him, if not, when she needed him, to have him entirely for herself?

Had he sent this girl in his place? Was she the fiancée Lila had been waiting for? Waiting to challenge, to break and send off crying? But this one would not cry. Lila turned her head, looking at the girl's pale slender hands. "So it's you he chose. But you don't even have a ring."

"You and your rings! You set aside your most hideous jewels that no living soul would want. Tony will toss them out."

"I'll sell them myself."

"When, Lila? How?"

What did Tony see in this girl? He should have picked a happy innocent whom Lila could have told what to do, think, and say. But this crazy girl spoke to Lila as if addressing her own emotions, greeting Rage with rage and Hate with hate, and God only knew the identity and misdeeds of the original provocateur.

"We talk every week," Lila said, "but Tony didn't tell me you were coming. I didn't expect you at all. But then, he doesn't mention girls. He changes the subject when I ask."

"He doesn't know I'm here."

"Is he good to you?"

"What do you mean?"

"Well, for instance, your birthday. I'm furious when he forgets mine."

The girl frowned. "I haven't had a birthday."

"No birthdays? Smart. Then you won't get old. Or haven't you known him that long?"

"Long enough."

"Is your family still close by?"

"I raised myself."

Lila laughed. "How can that be? All by yourself?"

The girl stared hard at Lila, and Lila could see the hurt in her eyes and the smoted look of someone not quite conscious or awake, of a beauty who did not use cosmetics but had, like a mortician, fixed an expression on that face. The girl stepped closer, and Lila wondered if she'd be able to smell Tony on her, if the girl got close enough—his cologne, her perfume, beer, wine, the sea-smell of human bodies. To smell what Tony smelled. But the air around the girl was so frigid and odorless that it burned in Lila's nostrils. The girl brought the cold with her. First a stronger draft seemed to blow, and then Lila was as cold as if she'd stepped outdoors. "What do you want?"

"I'm not Tony's girl."

"Whose then? Gil's? Don't look surprised. Lying here, I've dreamed of everything." Gil would be a fool, Lila thought, with a girl this young. Though he might be happy in a simpler way—as senility is simpler—she hoped he would always be chastened from within, by a still vital, parasitical part of her. "Are you lovers already?"

"No, Lila. Your husband still loves you, almost as much, pound for pound, as he loves cash. But you're right. As you've wasted away, he's loved you less and less."

"How can you say such things?" Lila began to cry, and yet the sensation seemed imposed from without, as if her eyes were watering in the cold.

"Me? First you give me to your son, and then your husband. What kind of whoremonger are you? I'm not interested in either of those little—"

"Whoremonger?" Lila repeated. "Why are you here? Who are you? Oh, God," she said, hugging the covers more tightly, "why am I so cold?"

"I'm here because you didn't want to die alone. Remember? Nadine, Nancy, Naomi, Natalie. I found that list in a book. I chose Natalie for myself."

"No," Lila said. "I can't remember." She believed that when the healthy tried to distract the sick, their real intent was to deny the existence of pain. *Think back. Remember?* But Lila's past was so tiny and diminished. All that mattered was *now* and the intensity of cold.

"Think!"

"…can't." Lila could feel that the girl was going to harm her, as surely as if a needle were about to pierce her skin and she herself had pointed out the vein. *No, not that one.* But that's the one they always chose. The girl bent nearer. On her cheeks was the bluish tinge of hypothermia. Lila said, "Who are you?"

"Never conceived, never born, never died, never existed." The girl recited as a child might, or as a parent might somberly instruct: *This is your full name, your phone number, and your address.*

The cold was a ceaseless, rhythmless pain. Like the same old argument. Or one's own personality. In the morning, Gil would find the French doors un-latched and the little mirror and a puddle of icy water on the floor. Lila did not know where she would be. Her mouth was full of snow. The icicles she'd heard dripping along the roof all afternoon had refrozen in her outstretched arm. The girl's touch was colder still. "Hello, Lila," she said. "Lila, I'm your pal."

*Patricia Griffith*

# *Hiding Places*

PATRICIA GRIFFITH has published four novels. The latest, *Support-ing the Sky* (Putnam Publishing Group, 1996), was a Literary Guild selection. *The World Around Midnight* (Putnam Publishing Group, 1991) was named one of the notable books of 1992 by the American Library Association. Her stories have twice been included in the annual *O. Henry Prize Stories*. She is also a playwright, was president of the PEN/Faulkner Foundation from 1995 to 1999, and teaches at George Washington University.

That year a woman in Pueblo, Colorado, was hypnotized and taken back year by year to a time before her birth when she was Bridey Murphy in nineteenth century Ireland. Speaking with an Irish brogue, she sang Irish songs and told Irish stories. Her saga became a big news story and eventually a movie and my three college roommates and I, always looking for novel ideas, began discussing the probabilities of our earlier lives. I decided I'd at some point been a Russian because of my love for Chekhov and the attraction I'd had to the scenery in the one movie I'd seen set in Russia, though it turned out it was actually filmed in Canada, but I didn't know that then. Also I had always been attracted to Dostoyevsky and deep-voiced, dark-thinking Russians even though we were taught at that time and place to beware of the communist menace. But I figured I'd probably been Russian before 1917 so I'd have escaped the threat.

My roommates and I fantasized about our earlier lives and romances and one night at a pool party in Dallas, given by some airline attendants (only they were called stewardesses back then), our roommate Sandy got to talking about Bridey Murphy and a guy there said he'd majored in psychology and could hypnotize people. So one Saturday he drove down from Dallas to our apartment where we'd gathered a group of our more serious friends, believers and skeptics alike, to participate in uncovering our earlier lives.

It was our last semester of college. We'd been drummed out of the dormitory of our Baptist school for smoking. Four of us had rented a one-bedroom apartment not far off campus, taken the one double bed apart so that Charlene and I slept on the springs and Laurie and Sandy on the mattress. This arrangement took up most of the bedroom floor space, but we wanted the rest of the house free for partying and studies. This was before college students commonly lived a life of suburban luxury with DVDs and microwaves. We were poor. Since we'd left dormitory food, our diets consisted of canned tuna fish, which we bought by the case, and canned fruit cocktail we'd pour into Jell-o and declare fruit salads. The advantage was the Jell-o was cheap and we could expand it and the tuna fish salads for endless entertaining. Just add another apple to the tuna fish and another box of Jell-o to the salad. We figured that tuna fish and Jell-o salad was maybe what Jesus served when he fed the multitudes. Occasionally guys would bring steaks to grill on our greasy, blackened backyard grill. Steaks went fine with our Jell-o salads. We could afford to bake potatoes and the guys would bring a case of Lone Star and sometimes we'd spring for Mogen David wine we'd mix with 7-Up. Our drug habits were limited to cigarettes and during exam times Dexamil. The Dexamil, we believed, increased our concentration to cram for exams, and it seemed to have little other effect except for the time we watched Laurie, a philosophy major and our most dignified roommate, suddenly leap a hedge on the way home from an exam.

Laurie, Sandy, and I came from small Texas towns and fairly typical Baptist backgrounds. Charlene's family, however, lived in the country on a poor sandy land farm. Her father was a hard-shell Baptist preacher who preached so loud Charlene said he cleared the church eves of all the dirtdobbers. As a hard-shell Baptist, her father disapproved of movies, dancing, playing cards, and what was referred to as "mixed bathing," which was really co-ed swimming. He disapproved also of ironing or any other kind of labor on Sundays. To violate any of his many rules could mean, we'd learned after seeing evidence on Charlene's slim body, a whipping with a bicycle chain. Charlene, consequently, was wild as a hare and spent a lot of her time in seedy Texas nightclubs and lounges or parking in the bushes with her off-and-on-again boyfriend Robby Newkirk. She was a history major, and her senior research project focused on Sam Houston and the reasons for his short, disastrous first marriage.

That Saturday night Clark, the hypnotist, arrived, we'd gone to unusual trouble, preparing Fritos with a Velveeta cheese dip and making a Mogen David punch with lime sherbet added to the 7-Up. The four of us dressed in black pants and tops, and by the time Clark arrived the idea of such a novel event had drawn more people than we'd invited. Clark, who worked in public relations for American Airlines, arrived in a green Chevy convertible. He was a smooth-looking guy with a kind of Elvis pompadour and wearing a burgundy sports jacket and gray slacks with a splashy shirt printed with orange parrots that he'd bought in Honolulu. He had a lean, rubbery walk like a basketball player, which indeed he'd been in college until one of his knees was busted in a fight outside Luann's nightclub in Dallas.

Clark took his time before starting his hypnotism by drinking a Lone Star or two, which built up the nervous tension until finally Robby Newkirk shouted, "When are we gettin' this show on the road, Charlene?"

Clark took the big overstuffed living room chair with the beanbag ashtrays carved into either arm and we gathered around him, setting a kitchen chair in the middle where the "subject" was to be seated. We had no idea how many people Clark might hypnotize, but we figured one of us should stay compos mentis in case cops appeared or something amiss was proposed, so Sandy, a drama major who liked to "observe," volunteered to stay lucid and sober.

Clark started by turning his slightly slitty green eyes at me and offering me the kitchen chair. I admit to being a bit nervous. The atmosphere was smoky and creepy partially from the chiffon scarves we'd draped over the lamps. The filtered light made everyone in the room look a bit green either from the light or maybe the Mogen David and sherbet. But once, when I was only ten and in grade school, I'd volunteered to be cut in two by a visiting magician, so my fame for bravery was established before I even hit teendom. Also Bobby Joe Hendricks was in the room and Bobby Joe Hendricks always made me nervous ever since we'd had one date the year before and I'd fallen in love and he'd never called again but gone right back to his old girlfriend Diane whose daddy had invented a kind of oil well drill that made them rich as Croesus. Anyway, I took the chair, which was pretty straight-backed and uncomfortable and faced Clark who pulled from his pocket something that looked like a gold spinning toy on a chain. He had a silky authoritative voice like an airline pilot and told me to relax and watch the gold center spin. Just like the movies, I thought, and the room grew totally quiet as I tried to concentrate and not think about Bobby Joe Hendricks, wondering if his being there meant he'd broken up with Diane. Clark told me to count backwards from ten, which I did trying hard to focus and breathe deep like he was telling me. There were a few moments when I thought I might actually go under but when Clark told me to lift my arms I heard someone honking outside and someone giggle inside so that I realized I wasn't under at all. I had to give up and admit failure. Clark wagged his head disapprovingly and I relinquished the chair to Laurie.

Laurie was small and gentle and since she majored in philosophy I thought she might likely succumb to hypnosis, her mind being accustomed to dealing with the nether world. But Laurie, as a philosophy major, was also a skeptic, though when she stubbed out her cigarette I could see her hand shaking. Clark set his Lone Star down and removed his burgundy jacket and started again. But after a few minutes, fewer minutes than I'd tried, Laurie shook her head. "I'm sorry, ya'll, I just can't get into this and it's giving me a headache," she announced.

For the first time, I began to wonder if we were going to find out about anyone's past life. A couple more people took the chair after that, one guy who was a show off and probably hadn't concentrated on anything in his life, and another girl who'd wondered earlier if hypnotism wasn't anti-Christian. After the two of them failed, Charlene kicked off her high-heel sandals and said, "Step aside you silly people," and set herself in the kitchen chair, directed her beautiful but supercilious smile at Clark, and pulled her long black hair over to one shoulder. Clark chugalugged his beer and faced Charlene. I was beginning to worry that Bobby Joe Hendricks would leave if someone didn't hypnotize soon, then I wouldn't have a chance to find out if he'd broken up with Diane.

Clark began to talk to Charlene, and I thought he seemed to be rising to her challenge. His silky voice sounded deeper and more focused.

"Charlene…Charlene," he repeated as if savoring the word. "Just relax now, just let everything fade out of your mind, everything glide away. And you just breathe deeply." Charlene took a deep breath. "Now Charlene, lift your right hand and look at it a minute," Clark said slowly. Charlene lifted her right hand. "Now set it down and let your body relax. Concentrate on that right hand."

"Now close your eyes," Clark said leaning toward her, "and let everything go…"

We could see Charlene's deep breaths, her breasts rising and falling slowly, and she truly looked like she was in another state, somewhere we hadn't seen before.

"Now lift your arms, Charlene." And Charlene lifted her arms, a motion which gave the scene a sinister tone. The room grew very quiet and Bobby Joe Hendricks, who was standing by the door, glanced at me and smiled.

Clark told her to lower her arms and asked if she liked to go to the beach. Charlene nodded. "You like to lie on the sand…and just let the sun bake all the worry out of your body. Just sweat out all the old problems. Maybe you can hear the water lap. Smell the suntan lotion, everything is soft and easy and you're lying on a towel feeling peaceful, aren't you? Are you there, Charlene?"

Charlene said, "Yes," softly.

"And somebody's rubbing your body with warm lotion. Now with your eyes still closed tell me how you feel, Charlene."

Charlene took a deep breath and sighed. "Good," Charlene said. Outside a car passed honking, and the overhead light took that moment to burn out so the room grew darker.

"Good," Clark said. "So tell me what you see."

"I see the river and cottonwoods and sand and there's…and music."

"What music, Charlene, can you sing it for us?"

Charlene paused a minute and began to sing, "*Forever my darling…my heart will be true…I'll never part from you…*" I recognized the song since she was always playing it, an old R&B number by a Texas singer who'd died playing Russian roulette. Charlene had a good smoky-sounding R&B voice that I'd always liked to listen to.

Clark had put his spinning toy away. He told Charlene to open her eyes.

"Why don't you go in the water, Charlene, and tell us how it feels."

"I'm afraid."

"Afraid? Why're you afraid?"

"Quicksand. And I can't swim. I don't have any clothes on… I'm not supposed to be here."

"You're not supposed to be there? Why is that?"

"My Daddy…," she stopped.

"And who's with you?" Clark asked. "Tell us who's with you."

"Danny," she said quietly.

Laurie was leaning on the back of Clark's chair. She glanced at me, widening her eyes.

"And who's Danny?" Clark asked.

"My brother," Charlene said. Laurie glanced at me again. Neither of us had ever heard of Charlene having a brother.

Someone in the corner had been talking quietly, but the room grew quiet except for the slitting open of a beer can. Clark paused and looked around for a minute, and Laurie leaned over and whispered in his ear.

"Maybe we should go back to school, Charlene. Do you remember eighth grade?" And Charlene nodded. "And who's your teacher?"

"Miss Highnight," Charlene said.

"Is she pretty?"

"Yes," Charlene said, "she wears a diamond ring and she's gonna get married."

"Do you remember who's in your class then?"

Charlene began going up and down the rows, "Linda Hamilton, and Dorothy Ann Miller, and Billy Jack Cunningham…"

Charlene went desk by desk up and down the rows naming all twenty-six students in her eighth grade class and then Clark jumped back to sixth grade and Charlene again went row by row naming each student and by the time Clark got to fourth grade, Charlene was sounding like a child, her voice high and soft. I was so fascinated by then I even forgot to check to see if Bobby Joe Hendricks was still in the room.

"And what happened in the third grade, Charlene? Did you have a birthday party that year?"

Charlene stopped then, was quiet. She lifted her right hand and looked at it and then she said, "No, no…no, Danny," she said and began to cry. Clark seemed flustered for a moment.

"And where's Danny now?" Clark asked.

"He's gone," she said and Charlene lifted her hands to her ears and leaned over and wailed this loud bellowing adult wail I'd never heard before. Charlene had left the third grade.

"Charlene," Clark reached out to her, "Charlene," he said taking her hands. "Charlene, listen to me, Charlene, listen to me," he repeated trying to maintain his smooth pilot voice. "I'm going to count to seven and you're going to wake up and you won't remember, Charlene, you won't remember, you'll stop crying. You'll put your sandals back on and you'll feel fine, Charlene."

Clark began counting, "One, two, three…"

Clark counted until seven, and Charlene raised her head and wiped her eyes and looked around the room before putting her sandals on over her chartreuse-painted toenails.

"You OK?" Clark asked.

Charlene didn't answer him but stood up quickly and fled the room, and we all looked after her and then at the chair where something had happened that nobody understood.

After that we finished the Mogen David punch and the Lone Star beer and declared it a big ashtray day, which we did sometimes before Saturday morning when we'd put on a record of *Gaîté Parisienne* and vacuum the apartment. I had less than a heart-to-heart with Bobby Joe Hendricks, who told me right off the bat that Diane had gone home for the weekend. People began to melt away after that, and Clark drank a few more Lone Stars and fell asleep on the couch. When I went to bed, Charlene and Robby Newkirk were sitting on the back steps and smoking.

Laurie and Sandy and I didn't know what to do after that. Should we remind Charlene that she'd talked about a brother we'd never heard of, or let her blissfully forget whatever it was that had been so painful? We quietly debated and said nothing, and three days later we woke to find Charlene locked in the bathroom. No amount of knocking or pleading that we had to get to class made her come out or utter a word, but from the back steps we could see her standing motionless before the mirror. Finally I managed to crawl from the back porch landing over a two-story drop into the bathroom window. Even with the racket of my breaking through the screen to unlock it and knocking off shampoo bottles and jumping down from the window into the room and calling to her, Charlene didn't move. She stood in her panties before the mirror holding a knife and staring at her bloody chest. Looking in the mirror I could see where she'd carved above her breasts the word S-I-N. I unlocked the door and the three of us tried to talk to her. But even when we put our arms around her, we realized that wherever Charlene was, it wasn't in that bathroom.

Two days later, her father came to take her home. The nurse phoned us that morning asking us to pack up her clothes and deliver her suitcase to the infirmary. We'd tried to visit Charlene the day before, but they wouldn't let us see her. I asked the nurse how Charlene was doing and if we could talk to her father. The nurse said Charlene was fine and her father didn't want to talk to anybody, not even the doctor.

It was warm and windy that early spring day. Laurie and Sandy and I skipped classes and stood on the sidewalk outside the infirmary waiting to catch sight of Charlene and her father. We'd brought a sack of her books and her alarm clock she usually slept through and some toiletries like her beloved Tabu cologne and a get well card from Robby Newkirk. When Charlene and her father finally appeared, her father, a short, lean man wearing khakis and a farmer's straw hat, was obviously in a hurry. He carried her suitcase and held on to his hat, and Charlene followed carrying a pot of yellow chrysanthemums we'd sent her. We moved toward them, calling to her as her father slung her suitcase in the back end of the battered green pickup. He hurried to the driver's side where he stood until Charlene climbed inside. Their doors slammed shut one after the other with final, tinny whacks.

We were running toward them as they pulled away from the curb. Charlene turned, pushed her long hair from her face, and looked at us for a moment out the open window of the pickup. Then they were gone. We stood watching until they reached the corner and turned toward the highway.

For the next three months, I slept on the bed springs by myself. The small room had always been crowded but somehow now it felt too big. We mailed her books, the rest of her clothes, her Tabu cologne. But I don't think we ever again talked about Bridey Murphy or our former lives.

*Melissa Hardin*

# Close to Pink

MELISSA HARDIN received an MA in writing from Johns Hopkins University in 1998. Her story "Vanna on Spode" was published in *The Baltimore Review* (Summer 1998). She lives in Washington, D.C.

This was not a dream. I start by saying that because I worry you're thinking I've got nothing better to do than fantasize. The first time he called me was very late one night. I'd closed the bar down, so it must have been around two in the morning. I figured the call was Curly checking to make sure I got home all right. I know he feels bad making me shut the place up on my own. But I always tell Curly don't worry about me. I may be short but I've got some mass to me. Enough to put the drunks out at the end of the night.

So when I picked up the phone I almost started right in with "Don't worry Curly, I'm alright and yeah I locked the window in the men's pisser." But something stopped me. This kind of clickety-clackety on the line. Made me think it was long distance and I was racking my brains who it could be.

"Hello?" I said. The clicking stopped.

And this real smooth, low voice said back to me, "Hello Lenora."

And I said, "Who is this?" And he came back at me with, "Lenora, do you like s'mores?"

You know, those chocolate graham cracker marshmallow treats you make when you go camping? Well I do happen to love those. And right when he said it my mind went straight to my belly wishing it had a s'more to look forward to… That's why I let the conversation go on—didn't just hang right up on a sexy voice calling me by name in the small hours of the morning.

"Yes," I said. "As a matter of fact I do. I love s'mores."

"Did you know that it rhymes with your name? Lenora?"

I said I'd never thought about it but I supposed it did. "Maybe that contributes to my liking them so much."

"I don't think so," he said. "Because I like them too."

"Well, what's your name?"

"Pink Panther."

"OK," I said. I thought to myself, I gotta go.

"Can I call you back sometime, Lenora?"

"I guess you've got my number," I said and I hung up.

So I was a little rude that first time. I didn't give much thought to him calling himself Pink Panther. I figured he was just some lonely guy. And I know what that's all about. It's never come over me at two in the morning, but I know the feeling of wanting to call just about anyone, say anything to make them listen.

The next time he called was a Sunday morning. I was doing my cooking for the week. That's how I handle my hours situation, working late nights in the bar. I make a few big pots of food on Sunday and rotate it around during the week. I was chopping up a ham hock for my pea soup when the phone rang. I picked it up and there was that quick clickety-clackety before the line cleared and the voice came through.

"Hi Lenora."

"Who is this?"

"Pink Panther here."

"Oh hi," I said. "How are you?"

"I'm swell. Just swell. Watcha doing?"

"Choppin' ham," I said. "And you?"

"Me? I'm relaxing. Sippin' a drink."

The conversation went on like that. Humdrum, I guess you'd say, but not boring. Just comfortable. There wasn't much that voice could say that didn't feel good going into my ear. And I mean literally feeling physically good going in there. Like maybe it stroked those cilia-type hairs in my ear canal the right way or something.

It was partly this effect on my canal hairs, and the overwhelming sense of calm I got when I talked to him—like an injection of warm milk—that started me thinking maybe he actually was the Pink Panther. No human male could have this effect on me.

I asked him what he'd been doing these last twenty-odd years.

"You know," I said, "I was twenty-one when your first movie came out."

"Twenty-one," he said. "Nice age, Lenora. Like to think of you at that age."

"Frankly, I'm happier where I am now. You couldn't pay me enough to go back to then. But you? What about you? Are you sorry you're not doing more movies?"

I heard a wet slurp and the clink of ice cubes settling back into a glass. "Nope," he said. "I got my website now. TV ads. Insulation. But mostly these days I find myself on snow or sand. Vacay. I look good on white, Lenora. Solid, smooth white. Feel good."

The crunch of an ice cube made me wonder what his teeth looked like. If they were pointy and sharp like a real panther's or if they were flat, maybe from this ice-chewing, or night-time grinding under show-biz stress, or maybe they were just always flat. I enjoyed thinking about him this way—constructing and deconstructing him in my mind.

Pink Panther and I started talking regularly. Several times a week, usually late at night. Getting ready for bed. Talking with Pink Panther started replacing one of my pre-sleep activities. I would swing over, hang up the phone, lay back and drift off. Phew…like a pure shot of satisfaction.

I'd have gone on like that. Just talking I mean. The fact that it was always him calling me, me waiting and wondering, it was sort of tantalizing. But then he suggested we meet, and I couldn't get the idea out of my head. I was itching to see what he really looked like. We arranged to meet in Paul Revere Park on a Tuesday morning.

I spotted him sitting there on the park bench as soon as I rounded the corner onto Bullock Street. He was just where he said he'd be, sitting just like I thought he'd be. On the far edge of the bench with his hands—well, paws really—in his overcoat pockets, his legs crossed, one foot bobbing up and down. His wrinkled bowler hat matched the tan overcoat exactly. He wasn't as pink as I thought he'd be. It was a cloudy day so maybe that had something to do with his color being kind of muted. Don't get me wrong. It's not like you'd miss that he was Pink Panther, but he wasn't like a tacky neon sign or anything.

I drove around the square and parked right behind him. I didn't want him watching me cross the park walking towards him. I got out of my car, kind of pressed the door shut so it didn't make any noise, and snuck up behind him to the bench. Don't ask me why. It was just instinct. Like that's what you do when you're meeting your lover in person for the first time and he happens to be the Pink Panther.

I crept around the other side of the bench and sat on the far edge from him. I looked straight ahead.

"It's me," I said right out to that statue of Paul Revere.

"I know, Lenora," Pink Panther said, his leg still bobbing, looking straight ahead. "Shall we stroll?"

We both stood up at the same time, but I wasn't sure how he wanted to walk. I mean, were we supposed to look like we weren't together or something? I waited. Then I felt his arm sneak between mine and my body and we moved forward together. Not on the path. He led me straight out into the middle of the square over the grass which was frosty in places, the dew just thawing in others, turning wet. We walked a few steps and then I stopped and looked down at my sneakers. They were all damp and gray at the edges.

"Oh," Pink Panther said, following my eyes to my shoes. "Sorry. Let's take the path."

He didn't have to worry about shoes, you see. He's got paws with these quick-dry pads on them. We walked toward old Paul Revere on his horse.

Keep in mind we hadn't looked at each other straight on yet. I checked him out from the corner of my eye, sure. He was pinker up close. And I noticed how his nostrils—that spongy triangle right at the tip—it's a peachy tone, actually, and it clashes with the pink of his fur, flanked by long whiskers, fluorescent white, coming off his cheeks. That's something you wouldn't think of, I mean from the movies and stuff. They don't show those details.

We walked around to the back of the statue and stopped. Just stood there. I reached out to the horse's tail, a thin icicle hanging there. It broke off just as Pink Panther took my hand. He turned me towards him, facing, pulling close, and he looked right down at me. Into me. I came up to just about where his nipples would have been if he weren't Pink Panther. But his front's just plain smooth pink, and the fur poking out of the V of that trench coat brushed my chin.

His eyes. Whoa, his eyes. They were really something. Eyeballs deep and round, black center, fringed with green and then a thin streak of yellow, bright canary yellow, around the outside. Somewhere deep in the black there was a reflection which I was catching now and then as I looked up at him. His eyelids were covered in a finer fur. Shorter and tighter, still soft-looking though. Like the fleecy stuff all the college kids wear nowadays. Pink fleece, lashless, drooping down all lazy and sweet and sexy. I was speechless.

"Lenora, you are just how I thought you'd be."

"Really?" I asked.

"Let's go somewhere warm," he said.

All tall people look funny in my car. Even with the seat pushed all the way back their knees stick up. Pink Panther was no different, crunched up like a hairy pink accordion next to me. I took the short route home.

OK, I admit it. I guess I kind of expected him to come back to my place. So I'd cleaned up a bit. And like I said it was an overcast day so I'd left the lamp on next to the couch—the lowest setting on one of those 50-100-150 bulbs.

As we stepped in the door, Pink Panther gave a quick playful "wooh" and pressed himself up against the wall all narrow and sly, ogling my four-foot pine cone man Curly's wife gave me last Christmas. Then he flung his hat over at him, by the brim, like the bad guy in the James Bond movie. Only the hat didn't cut my cone man in half. Just fell gently over his poky head.

I hung up my coat in my closet and then turned to take Pink Panther's. I wanted to be natural about it when he took it off, not stop and stare, because of course I was wondering exactly what he looked like under there.

He was naked, like I thought. Like in the movies.

I'm thinking about my previous. He was nothing like them. I generally go for the burly type. It has to do with my own body, of course. Not wanting to look huge next to them. Guthrie, the last one, was a big boy. As many, if not more, curves than me.

Pink Panther was just all straight down. I mean except for his tail, which swung slowly like some heavy pendulum, there was nothing curvy about him. Not much width either. That coat made him look big, but it was just shoulder pads. Some vanity there. But I gave him a break…he's got Hollywood in him.

"Please sit down," I said. "Let me get you something. What do you drink? Coffee? Soda? Juice? Beer?" All right, I was nervous. Rattling off a stupid list like that. You'd have thought I was his waitress back at Curly's. But he wasn't moved by my nerves. No, not one bit.

"Whiskey, Lenora," he said. "I'll take a glass of whiskey if that's convenient for you."

I keep my whiskey in the cabinet next to the sofa down there on the bottom shelf. So that's how I came to see those pads on his feet. I was squatting down there looking for the whiskey bottle and when I got it in my hand I turned to look at him. He had his hands behind his head leaning back. Did you know that his armpits are white? His legs were crossed and he had the foot going again, bobbing right in front of my face. The pad part was black and nubbly.

"Oh excuse me," he said when he looked down and saw me staring. He uncrossed and planted his feet.

"No," I said. "Not at all. I…I was just looking at the sole of your foot there."

He pulled his foot up into his lap and held it there face up, just like you'd do if you were showing someone your plantar wart. The circle of light from the lamp fell across his foot, and the light caught all these little sparkles in the black. Winky little crystals like you see on certain sidewalks in certain lights.

"My pads," he said. "These are my pads. Keep me cool in summer, warm in winter."

"Don't they get wet though? And freeze?"

"Nope. Never. Inn-ssu-lay-tionnn," he said, spreading the word out long and smooth.

"Oh-ho," I said. "Of course."

I was right up near him then. I could feel his breath all warm on my neck as he leaned over. I tell you it amazed me how much more breath he had than…well, humans in general, not to mention the sorry fat boys I've been with. Each breath lasted a lot longer and went a lot farther. Like maybe it had longer to travel going up and down that long skinny body or something.

"Can I…would you mind?"

He didn't say anything. Just blinked all slow at me. So I put my fingers on his pad. Pads I should say. There was the usual with cats, the central larger one surrounded by four smaller at the toes. I guess it could have been sandpaper…maybe a fine 200-plus grit or so. But there was a sponginess to it. Like a little pocket of water you could push on and then it would spring right back into shape.

"I oil them," he said suddenly, low, right into my ear. "Once a week or so. Extra virgin olive or peanut if necessary. I try to avoid the peanut. Leaves a bad stain on carpets."

I instinctively looked down at mine. Not like I'm some kind of neat freak, but I do rent this place and I'm not interested in having my security deposit held for pad stains.

"Oh," I said. "Don't worry."

I stood up and poured two glasses of whiskey. He had his paws back behind his head so I set the glasses on the coffee table. I went in the kitchen and got out a box of Saltines. Put them on a wooden dish. When I came back into the living room I could see he'd taken a sip of his whiskey. In fact, there wasn't much left in his glass. I caught his long pinky gray tongue shoot out and smooth all the way around his mouth. On the way round, the tip of his tongue caught each one of those long white whiskers and they twanged for a second after his tongue was back in his mouth.

"Mmmm…aahhhh," he said to no one in particular. "Nothing like it on a chilly day." Then he looked up at me. "Sit down, Lenora. Take a load off."

"Don't mind if I do." I bent down to move a cushion off the armchair opposite him. Out of the corner of my eye I saw a narrow flash of pink over the couch he was sitting on. His tail swung out in a slow curve over the cushion next to him, the end of it twitching. It was a long tail. I'd put it at four feet. So even when he was sitting there was plenty of free movement.

I took it as a gesture, the tail. The way it waved all snaky and slow with the very tip all jittery and frisky over the open cushion next to him. I wasn't wrong. When I sat down there next to him, I got another long slow pull from those droopy eyes. I tucked my feet up under me, leaning towards him, and took a sip of my whiskey.

Reaching forward to put my glass back on the table, I felt this weight across my lap. The tail, first flickering, then settling gently across my thighs. It's heavy, you know, unexpectedly so. Like when I've tried to lift some passed-out drunkard's arm off the bar when I'm wiping up. You just don't think it's going to be such a mass, but there it is and you're struggling reaching over the bottles just to get an angle on it and drag the rag underneath.

I thought he might be pressing it down on me. But I touched it, first just with the tips of my fingers, brushing those bristly hairs that stick farther out than the rest. Then I took it in my hand, encircling it, running the length to its pointy tip. It was all floppy and relaxed. Supple. I put it up to my cheek. They were finer hairs deeper in the fur. Finer and softer. A lighter pink.

I'm not going to bore you with the details here. No. The truth is I don't remember them. It's really one pink blur from there. I remember just the right amount of wetness and dryness. The slip of my skin meeting the grain of his fur. Pinky gray on the inside of my thighs. The taste of olive oil running down the back of my tongue.

It only happened once. And you can call me crazy but I knew that's all it would happen. Maybe that was all I needed, wanted. I've never expected to hear from him again. I know that sounds weird. Like how could I let go of something that was so good? Don't I just sit here craving, dying for more? Let's leave it that there are just some connections you can only make—only take—once.

I have these dreams at night. Sometimes they're all long and soft and his tongue's smooth with just the right amount of 200 grit all over me. But there are others. There's one where I'm standing at the kitchen sink peeling a bunch of potatoes and I'm irritated. These potatoes have too many eyes and it seems like each one's got more gnarl than good. I hear this little "ptck" on the kitchen window in front of me, and I look up into the darkness outside and there he is. Staring in at me. My Pink Panther all frosty and glowing from the fluorescent light over my sink. And in that first instant I feel this wave of relief, almost crushing me so that I drop the gnarly potato and the knife and grab the edge of the sink. Then I notice his eyes…all the sexiness has run out of them. That droopy fleece eyelid is stuck back up all dry in the socket and the eyeballs are these flat desperate black circles. I'm drying my hand on the kitchen towel now. My mouth is open to say…what? Maybe just an abbreviated exclamation…an "aye," maybe the start of "I knew you'd come back" or "I can't." I'm not sure. It's something that sticks in my throat though. So much so that when I wake up my throat's sore. Bruised. I have that dream enough though so I wake myself up before I rush outside in the dream. I know when I get out there I'll find this Halloween costume hanging there off my dead dogwood tree. Flapping in the wind and the neighbors' kids giggling, scuttering off into the bushes.

*Judith Harris*

# *Damnation*

JUDITH HARRIS is the author of *Atonement: Poems* (Louisiana State University Press, 2000) and *Signifying Pain: Constructing and Healing the Self through Writing* (SUNY Press, 2003). Her new book of poems, *The Bad Secret*, is forthcoming in early 2006. Her recent work has been published by *Tikkun*, *The Southern Review*, *The American Scholar*, *Antioch Review*, *Prairie Schooner*, *The Writer's Chronicle*, and *Ontario Review*.

It was one of those sweltering August days, abuzz with humidity and crickets, when the people across the street, new to the neighborhood, came out on their front stoop fanning themselves with folded notebook paper or magnolia leaves, knotting their T-shirts above midriff blubber, using watering cans to cool down. They dragged everything from inside out: chairs, magazines, portable radios, and an inflated wading pool. They made quite a commotion. The children set themselves down on the front lawn as if their parents were holding a bone fide yard sale. They had even relocated their yarn and button-eyed dolls and assorted sand buckets; some of them were trying to sell watered-down lemonade for five cents a cup.

My family was fortunate to have bought air conditioning units from Montgomery Ward's on my father's overtime bonus. It was Sunday afternoon, and my mother held a blue ice pack to her forehead as if she had a headache from someone giving her too much grief. She was just feeling hot. Rousing herself, she parted the curtains at the kitchen window, and complained about the eyesore of the house tumbled inside out across the street, like the tissue wrap half-pulled out of an open shoebox. She said people like this, who couldn't keep their private matters private, would take down the property value of the whole neighborhood. My father said that she just needed some time to get acquainted with them. Then she let the venetian blinds go back down with a nervous rattle.

"Look, they've got that kid out there without any clothes on! Do you see that, Sam?" My father was relaxing on the comfortable chair, reading the newspaper.

He had on his shorts and a pair of flip-flops. He got up and came over to the window, and squinted to where my mother was pointing.

"Miriam, she's not naked. She's got her underpants on."

Just then, the little girl squeezed her fountain yellow ducky toy on the parched, bleached-out grass. Her mother, in a housedress and sponge curlers, was frugally cutting out coupons from the back of the Food section of the newspaper. Suddenly, the woman waved at us, and my mother backed up, panting a little from a bad conscience.

We were all hoping for relief from this record-breaking heat. We were tired of sleeping on the floor of the living room where we could feel the air conditioning pumping its cool rescuing air. We had popsicles for breakfast, and Helen and I didn't even try to dodge the sprinklers when we walked to the mailbox in order to mail our subscriptions to *Beat* magazine. My mother didn't feel like folding laundry or cooking, so, after taking in the scene of the neighbors, she sank in a wicker chair, crunching ice from a recycled grape jelly glass and opened her Belva Plain paperback.

In Sligo Woods, nothing eye-popping happened anyway, except maybe a screaming match at the Kolbs, five houses down, or the sign on the golden arches of McDonald's adding up two million hamburgers sold. And then there was always the excitement over Donny Gillian's getting lost again, and getting home so late he'd probably get a licking.

Donny's disappearing somewhere in the woods happened at least once a week. The Gillians lived three houses away and were the only ones in the neighborhood to have planted zoisia grass. For the first few years, their front yard was a mud slab, and only gradually did it grow its own superior, chemically concocted green breed of grass. My mother said Donny had a neurological problem, but they hadn't been able to take an X-ray that would show what it was. His father, an Episcopalian, was an ex-marine and kept to a strict code; he took, he said, "no flack from inferiors." And he considered all children inferiors because they were younger and inexperienced. So when he couldn't see Donny in the backyard or around the gooseberry hedges, he would take out a duck whistle and blow three times, then twice just for the purposes of warning. We all knew that if Donny didn't show up in five minutes after the third screech, Donny was in for it.

Donny was a mystery to me. I was a good friend of his sister Brenda's, who was a year older than me and a grade higher in school, but we were in the same Girl Scout troop. Mr. Gillian's whistle went off again like a bird's muted scream, and then we saw him adjust the lenses of a pair of binoculars he'd lifted to his eyes. Sweat was sticking to his crew cut making it twinkle like a crown. He was calmly preparing for the reasoning behind this policy of punishment after three warning signs.

My father, on the other hand, never seemed to plan his punishments; he was stylistically less sadistic and more improvisational. We only got walloped when one of us, including my father, had a temper tantrum. I would have preferred a silent treatment, or grounding, or extra chores. But my father was impatient. He would charge messily around the house, on all fours, looking for me behind chairs or under the table, in a weird parody of playing horsey with his bare hands ready to grab hair, or ankle, just so that he could get a few good slugs in.

With another hour to kill before Helen and I could go to the swimming pool, since they were cleaning it up after a meet, I found a place in the shade under the dogwood and kept my eye out for Donny. Now Donny had made it back up the hill, tramping barefoot, swinging his grass stained sneakers by their tied-up shoe-laces in one hand, his khaki trousers still wet from all that dipping and stone-hopping in Sligo's viscous, scabby water. Donny was red-faced, and head-bowed, and crying the alligator tears that seem less from fear than from rage; spitting on liver spots of the sidewalk. Mr. Gillian stood on the front porch. We imagined soon he would be wailing into the summery air, adding to the bird's cries and crickets' chirping, as if a being hit on the buttocks with an open hand, or a belt, or even a paddle, was all perfectly natural. His mother tried to intercede, with her raised, and righteous, prideful voice, a voice used to singing the high notes of Sunday hymns in the ladies' Sunday choir.

Brenda was probably on her father's side about Donny. She knew that his infractions would only shine a better light on her good behavior. I watched her come out, just as her father pushed Donny back in, slamming both the screen door and the hard door; so I knew it was serious, a double-seal, like when parents locked up at night to keep thieves out. Brenda cut across the Binder's front yard, her just showered hair fastened with hair pins that stuck out like needles in a ball of brown yarn. She came up to the sidewalk and to the path leading up to the stoop. I smiled mildly, inviting her to sit down. She gingerly agreed, her legs skidding to a stop at her tan line, which was lower than her short-shorts.

"Hi, Lou."

"Hi," I said, evenly.

"Got a new cat?" Brenda was inspecting the side of my house where I kept a cut-out-cardboard carton with a saucer of milk beside it.

"Uh, huh. Butterscotch. She must be somewhere around."

"Donny's going to get the strap," Brenda announced, circumambulating around herself as if she were motorized.

"I know," I said, wondering if he'd been burning fireflies under a magnifying glass at the creek, something I'd seen him do. He and Terrence Brown were notorious for shooting their cap guns or starting fires and stomping them out. Donny was always smuggling matches from his mother's handbag.

Brenda had a fresh Ivory soap scent about her and a few freckles dotted her nose and her forehead. Her teeth were preternaturally, but whimsically, straight.

"Did you hear about the Boston Strangler?" Brenda was always more apprised of newspaper headlines than the rest of us. Her mother pointed out evil; and spent hours delivering sermons on the dangers of going to hell. The strangler was up north, a good distance away, and I knew about the nurses; it had been permanently etched into my mind that one had been choked with her own nylon stocking until she turned blue. Then he stabbed her just to make sure she was dead.

"What did Donny do?"

"Don't know."

"Does your father know, or does he just get him because he's late?" It seemed to me to be a question of crime and punishment; the two should be in balance.

"Look Lou, bad things in this world are happening. And God is going to put an end to it. There's going to be a new dawn, and God's going to come down in all His glory and bring all of us up who believe in Him. We're going to the next and better place; at least us good Christians."

"You mean Christ, or God?" I was never sure of how the Christians saw the difference between those two. Christ always seemed to be sandwiched between God and the Holy Ghost. Being Jewish was easier. God was God, and Christ was a man—a good man, my mother told me—but a man just the same.

Just then, I could hear Donny yelling and crying through the screened in porch of the Gillian's house. His father's shadow was stretched on the wall. Brenda didn't look that way towards her house. She kept her eyes fixed on me. A lightning bug flashed in front of us.

"Our Savior, Jesus Christ," Brenda said, and crunched her knees. She said it with a conviction that reminded me of the time she led our class in the Pledge of Allegiance. Then, as if suddenly energized by my interest in what she was saying, she continued, wide-eyed. I rarely listened to Brenda closely; but this did seem, in the large scope of things, if not urgent, at least consequential.

"Brenda, what happens to Donny in there? Does your father hit him with a belt or the Ping-Pong ball paddle?"

Brenda moved closer to me. I was having one of those moments in which I realized how much I loved her. She was a born beautician and knew how to make her hair shiny with a gloss of peanut oil.

"Doomsday is coming in the year 1971 and then Christ is going to float down with all the angels in heaven and He's going to pick us from the others. And we're all going to be in white robes under the trees, holding hands, with harps like angels, and we're going to rise up, naturally levitated, and live forever in the most beautiful air castle where everything is good. But you have to believe in order to be saved."

Brenda declared this as if she were daring me to do something dangerous, like jumping off a carport roof. She just stared at me knowing that I didn't, couldn't, believe in Christ, because I was Jewish. I would be a traitor to my family, and all my family's family.

"What about the Jews?" I asked, still casually, not wishing to give myself away, the way in which Donny hadn't wanted to reveal his fear to his father who was already there to punish him, having nothing else on his mind, not work or gardening or unpaid bills, but to punish him.

Brenda drew in her breath, exhilarated with the power of delivering bad news, in fact, catastrophic news:

"The Jews are all going to burn in one big fire in the pit of Hell. They'll be cremated in a huge pot of boiling oil."

I was quiet, thinking of Ali Baba and the Forty Thieves. Why would God want to damn Jews all over again? How many times can a single body be punished?

The sun was strong I had to blink back at her, and then we both turned, in silence, to the strange picnic across the street. It was hot as Hell in the Christian religion, I thought. Beads of sweat appeared on her forehead just below her widow's peak. I took a microscopic look at her pores; she had complexion as clear as Snow White's. Meanwhile, the inside out family was sitting down to a cookout. The mother was putting out paper plates and mustard and ketchup dispensers like the kind you see at restaurants. The child had on her underpants but was still topless. Suddenly, I envied them; it was like they were on a vacation. I could hear starlings, a car backfiring, the arc of sprinkler fans relieving the dry grass with shower.

I felt uncannily bare, as if Brenda was seeing right through me and my skin, and I was on fire. Someone had told me that our blood is blue until it hits the air, and then the oxygen turns it bright red through a chemical reaction. I felt like my Jewish blood was boiling. Something was happening to my words, too, they were beginning to sound like somebody else's, as if I were on the verge of betraying a loved one.

"But see, Lou, Christ is all good, so he doesn't blame children for any of this. If you can take Christ into your heart, if you can really believe in Him, and pray to Him, even if you don't open your mouth, He'll save you before you get to be thirteen. But your parents are too old. They're irr-evoc-ably damned. Do you know about Satan?"

"Save me?" I asked, nearly stunned.

"You have just a couple more years, now. Jewish children didn't know better when the Jews murdered Him. Did you know the Jews killed God?"

I couldn't answer her. I imagined myself turning away from my mother, father, and Helen in order to save myself. I imagined myself crossing the line. Being an orphan. Having to change my name. Going to another city. Taking on a new identity. Brenda rose to her feet, so that she'd have to be concentrating on the top of my head when she finished talking.

"I guess the fight's over by now." She paused, and then waxed more philosophically. "Donny's going to have to mop the floor for a week."

I rubbed my legs in the baking sun and stood up. My whole body felt hot, and my hair was beginning to get wet at the back of my neck. "I'm going to the pool," I said.

Brenda didn't belong to the same swimming pool. I was a good swimmer. I didn't think Brenda could put her head under water. She wasn't finished talking about salvation.

"There's nothing they can do to you on earth that'll match what happens to your soul, because damnation is eternal. Remember that."

"OK. I'll think it over."

"OK. I'll give you a toothpaste facial when you get back from the pool. Maybe I can do your hair, too. It's looking kind of dry."

Just then Mr. Gillian came out with Donny in tow; his ears were bright red, and Mr. Gillian had him by the shirt collar. Donny glared at Brenda and me, and Mr. Gillian shouted across the lawns, "Better come home, Brenda."

"Got to go, Lou."

I watched her walk away, and then glared back to my house behind me. Helen was probably talking on the phone. My father was reading the newspaper. They were not hurting. I thought about how good Jews say the Shema morning and night, and just before they die. I'd even heard that my grandfather who couldn't speak for three years after they operated on his esophagus had been able to sing the Shema. Then I wondered if Donny had cried or denied his humiliation at getting the strap. Then I did what I thought was probably the safest thing to do, which was to ask for forgiveness for us all, especially the smallest, cruelest things that we don't know we do.

*Donna Hemans*

# Access to the Gods

Jamaican-born DONNA HEMANS is the author of *River Woman*, which was nominated for the Hurston-Wright Legacy Award in 2003 and was a co-winner of the 2004 Towson University Prize for Literature. Her short fiction is forthcoming or has been published in *Thema, Crab Orchard Review,* and *Caribbean Writer.* She has taught at Georgetown University and is an instructor at the Writer's Center in Bethesda, Maryland.

Maureen had read somewhere that ancient Egyptians wrote letters to the dead, letters that sometimes held a simple hello, an explanation, a plea for a healthy life. They wrote for easy access, a direct line to the gods. She was thinking though of doing no such thing, sending no pleas for immortality, or a long life at least, no pleas for a godlike son. Besides, to whom would she have written? She wasn't particularly close to anyone who'd died. Charmaine, a friend from primary school days had died escaping a fire, choking on inhaled smoke. A cousin, who shared her birthday, had died in childbirth. Charmaine and her cousin both deserved some peace now, at least.

There was her mother's mother of whom she had vague memories, no memories strong enough to suggest the old lady, even in death, would do anything more than kiss her teeth. Of course, there was her father, whom she'd met in her late teens. Having lived for twenty years in a London suburb, he was by then a proper Englishman and she could only imagine him saying "Righto then," and "Blimey," words she'd picked up from British TV imports. Each time he returned to Jamaica, his accent was more pronounced, his clothes more flamboyant than the last. He'd always said "I'll ring you," never following through on his promise. He'd been buried in one of those flamboyant suits, and he looked in death like a pimp. He'd failed to follow up on his promises in life; there was no reason she should believe he would not do the same in death. And even though those dead folks, now so close to the gods, could have read a letter and taken her plea directly, she still didn't want to disturb the dead.

But Maureen wanted a change and she composed as she drove, laid out thoughts that could form the body of a letter. The composition, spoken out loud and drowning out the newscaster on the all-news radio, seemed to be the most natural thing. She'd long stopped praying for hers weren't the prayers that were answered. She thought of praying as a lottery, the gods shaking a bag to see which prayers would be answered and which would remain unheard. It was no wonder, she thought, that her ancestors used obeah to reach the gods. Obeah, though, was not an option an educated woman from the city should consider.

Maureen was turning thirty-five, a number she considered the mid-life point; seventy, she thought, was a sufficient number of years to live. The years stretched behind her like a road at midnight with lights flickering occasionally as cars maneuver bends in the road, dip into valleys, jerk suddenly at a gully looming close. Maureen preferred to think of the years as a trek up a hillside road that had been worn out over the years by rivulets of water cascading rather than as a leisurely drive from one coastal town to another; she preferred to think she had made significant efforts, at least. The years and the description of the journey mattered now, more than ever, because she had looked in the mirror and pictured herself the way others saw her. An accomplished woman, yes. But despite what she achieved there was always someone asking about a family and a husband, reminding her that without either she was still incomplete. A grand-aunt had told her once, "Don't be like me. When you get to my age, that's when you really miss it."

She'd spent her life being careful, the daughter every mother wanted. She'd played the angels in school Christmas plays. Once she even played the Virgin Mary, rocking a footless doll wrapped in an adult's shirt. In high school, a boarding school for girls that prided itself on turning out ladies and not women, a high school that adhered to antiquated British colonial traditions, she was always the student pulled out as an example for the other girls to follow. Her black shoes always shone, her white uniform sparkled in the sun. Her socks never drooped, but lay flat against her ankles. She was known for her deportment and diction, and each year she got prizes at the annual prize-giving ceremony for both.

Now, though, she was contemplating, voicing out loud actions that were not at all characteristic of her. She'd looked around at the other cars on the road, and placed a headset over her ears to give the impression she was having a conversation on her mobile phone.

The ad had said "Healthy Females, 18–35." There was no consideration of race or height or weight or inherited diseases as yet undetected. She was healthy. She was the right age, trying then to capitalize on what she thought could be her last chance to carry a baby. The baby wouldn't be hers she knew, but she hoped there would be several fertile eggs, twins or triplets. At the very least, there should be one child for the couple and another for herself. Fifteen years earlier, she'd seen similar ads in newspapers on campus but it had never occurred to her that she would one day give the ads more than a passing glance.

Looking left and right, she ticked off all she'd done to establish her life for what she thought was inevitable—a husband and children of her own. She counted her undergraduate degree from Howard University, graduate studies at Columbia, her patriotic return home to a coveted job with one of Jamaica's two television stations, a house with two seldom-used extra bedrooms, the committees she chaired, and the endless dinners, dances, and cultural events for which she volunteered. She'd even modeled for fashion shows. Though she placed herself in the midst of all the action, it seemed she'd been moving too swiftly, a bee flitting far too quickly to capture the pollen it was expected to deliver to another flower to keep nature in balance. Her life was unbalanced.

Maureen was on her way then to the couple's Red Hills home, what she imagined to be one of the mansions overlooking Kingston. She'd worn a dress she'd found in an outlet mall outside Washington, D.C., shaved her legs, and opted for sandals. She wasn't dressed for business, and business it was, but she preferred the loose dress, its flirty neckline and hem, to a more formal suit. She'd pulled her hair back away from her face, hoping as she dressed in white that there was innocence in her actions, in the way she looked.

જ

A Doberman pinscher sat by the gate, its head resting on a bandaged paw, its ears perking and eyes blinking rapidly. She honked once, and a gardener emerged. He opened both sides of the gate, prodding the wounded dog and shouting at two others that were running toward the car. Maureen drove the car in slowly, glancing through the rear view mirror at the dogs rushing around the car, teeth bared, eyes hungry. There was no obvious movement within the house; no curtains fluttered; no windowpanes were lowered to hide the body of the person behind. The gardener approached the car, shooing the dogs, and telling her through the cracked window to go on through the door.

A maid met her. "You looking for Miss Grant?"

"Yes. I'm Maureen. She's expecting me."

The helper wore a plaid dress, with buttons down the front, pleats from the waist; the style was the same as Maureen's primary school uniform. She shook her head; the way the household was run was not her concern.

"Come through. She's right here."

Maureen had expected a sterile house, white tiles, white walls, museum-quality sculptures and art, an American or European woman dressed for afternoon tea. Yes, there were the sculptures and the art, but they were inviting rather than distancing. The woman, about her age, sat on the floor amidst pieces of a puzzle, helping two young children who were twisting and turning the pieces for a perfect fit.

"Maureen, come on down, nuh."

The woman spoke with an accent Maureen couldn't identify, an accent that tried to sound Jamaican. But there was a lilt, a hint of another language, another culture buried beneath her tone. She looked too at the woman's light brown skin, a single braid down her back, and thought Indian or Spanish.

Maureen stepped down into the sunken living room, and eased herself into a chair.

"I'm Maya." The woman unfolded her lanky body and patted the children's heads. "Let's sit outside." She patted Maureen's arm as she would a long-time friend and called for Eileen, the housekeeper, to bring them a drink outside.

The heat had begun to lift. Maureen had forgotten that the hills were cooler than the valley she'd just left. She walked to the edge of the verandah and looked down at the garden, vibrant and beautiful, the plants she saw daily and whose names she'd never bothered to learn, and then out at the city below. She could feel the woman's eyes on her body and regretted immediately that she'd worn the dress.

"You're not what I expected. Most of the other girls, I mean women…well… they weren't so polished. Haven't I seen you on TV?"

"Yes. I'm a newscaster."

"Then, why?"

Maureen expected silence, an immediate dismissal, not the inquisitive and concerned look, not the woman's body bending forward as if she were getting ready to share a confidence with an intimate friend. She'd thought her answers out, how she would allay her mother's fears; handle those who'd say self-righteously that the American way of life was infiltrating every aspect of Jamaican culture, down to a woman's womb and causing an accomplished woman to sell her eggs to another woman. Between her mother, her aunt Rose, and herself, they'd laughed a thousand laughs about the urgent need of Americans to talk through every problem on daytime talk shows as if talk alone could solve the deepest of issues. They'd laughed at the women who wanted to motivate listless husbands, the middle-class unfulfilled who wanted to find their inner selves, the middle-aged women who were desperately seeking husbands and families. Maureen wasn't laughing then because she had become one of those women willing to buy fulfillment.

"Most of the other women were doing it for the money." Maya, sensing Maureen's hesitancy spoke, and moved quickly to sit next to Maureen on the chair. The chair, a sofa-length swing, glided. "Some because they wanted the chance to go abroad. You know we'd be sending you to America for the procedure, for the duration of the pregnancy. It's not just business to me." She laughed. "After all, you might be giving me your eggs, carrying a child and giving it over to me. You're going to be part of me. As close as a sister."

Maureen looked out at the sun going down, the orange glow that was like a cracked egg, a sliding egg yolk.

"Yes, I know. I probably have what the other women don't have, a life everyone envies. I probably shouldn't say this, but I think this may be my last chance to carry a child. I'm thirty-five." She stopped, thinking she'd said too much and feeling like a child rather than the woman who commanded attention when she read the morning or evening news. Maureen had wanted to be businesslike, to outline her demand that she be allowed to keep one of the eggs or one of the children if there were multiple fetuses.

"Yes, it's the emptiness."

Maureen looked up quickly. She knew Maya wasn't referring to the emptiness of a silent house, but the emptiness of a womb that could bear no children. "The children, they're not yours?"

"No. My husband's from a previous marriage. He wants a boy." Maya flicked away a tear. "Men never feel complete unless they have a boy."

"He doesn't want to adopt?"

Maya laughed, a bitter sound that was more a bark than a sound of joy. "It must be his offspring. I prefer this, this arrangement, to his finding a mistress. Nobody will ever know the baby wasn't adopted. And if I go away for a year, nobody here will know I didn't carry the baby myself." Maya moved then and by the movement it seemed she reasserted herself, regained the poise that Maureen expected. "Let's talk business."

Maureen wished then for the suit she was accustomed to wearing, the bright studio lights that intimidated the guests she often interviewed, the microphone that represented a censor monitoring what she said, the prompter that ensured she rarely stumbled over her words and her questions always appeared well thought out and witty. Without those she felt vulnerable, naked.

"Your husband, is he going to be a part of the decision?"

"No, no. It's all mine. He met two women and gave up. I can understand why. Their greed was almost tangible." Maya looked steadily at Maureen as if she realized something then. "You're not here because of the money."

"No. I'm not here for the money." Maureen stood too, gliding across the tiled verandah to lean also against the railing.

From a distance the two women, standing side by side, their backs to the city winding down and lighting up, would look like close friends conversing at a party, sharing a secret. It was a house built for parties. Maureen imagined a bar set up at one end of the long verandah, dinner at another, guests wandering the gardens, losing themselves in the spacious house.

"If I am to carry a child fathered by your husband, and if I am to give over the child to you, I want a guarantee that I will be able to raise at least one of the children. I won't deny you your child or your children. But I want a guarantee that I will be able to later implant another of the fertilized eggs and raise that child myself."

Maya turned her head away from Maureen, shielding her emotion. "The emptiness," was all she said, not referring then to the emptiness of her womb, but the emptiness that could prompt Maureen to make such a bold request. "There are sperm banks you know. Anonymous donors."

"I don't want to buy sperm." Maureen thought she again sounded like a child rather than the woman who'd laid out a business proposal. It was all business, she reminded herself, but her request had opened a chasm. She felt Maya sliding, the rapport they'd developed slipping. She hadn't thought fully of a reaction to her demand. As a journalist, she asked questions and expected answers. She was not expected to be concerned whether the answers were delivered defensively or honestly.

With no current boyfriend, and no possibilities in the near term, she'd considered old friends, new friends she thought would consent to lending their sperm. That wasn't something she wanted to discuss though.

"Your demand is not so innocent," Maureen said instead. "You're buying the essence of a woman, the ability to carry a child. You're buying a child. We both want the same thing." She hesitated before adding, "It seems to me to be an equitable exchange."

"Yes. But it will be the same as my husband having a mistress, a bastard child, the children having a sibling they'll never ever meet." She stressed ever, bowing and shaking her head. "A bastard child. That's what you call such children here, no?"

"And what name do you call the child I'll carry and hand over to you?"

It's all business, Maureen told herself again. She took out a business card. "Here's how to reach me if you want."

⨍

They agreed not to taint the process with the exchange of money. Maya would pay for the procedures, of course, but Maureen would handle the cost of any procedures beyond the first successful pregnancy. They'd met in a blues café in New Kingston with an atmosphere reminiscent of New York City's East Village cafés and spoken word events. A poet raised her voice in defense of her body. Maureen thought of the poem as an extended scream, the poet as a petulant child.

"She makes poetry seem painful." Maureen turned away from the stage.

The poet's voice rose and fell. The hum of the café enveloped the two, imbued their exchange with a layer of innocence.

"Pray with me," Maya said.

"I don't pray."

"I'd feel better if God blessed this."

"Really, I don't pray."

"OK, just hold my hands."

They joined hands across the table, Maya bending her head in prayer, Maureen looking at Maya's bent head, her hair pulled back, the length of the plait disappearing into a bun. Maureen forgot the semi-dark room, the voices of the poets that seemed to only get louder as the night wore on, the variations on the poets' anger. An African student poet talked of guns and blood and incessant wars. Maureen blocked the poet and concentrated instead on Maya's bent head. Maya's prayer, she hoped, would serve the same purpose as letters to the dead, extending to her direct access to the gods.

⨍

Maya and Maureen flew together, but Maya's husband would travel separately, coming days later to fulfill his end of the pact. They'd sublet a furnished Brooklyn Heights apartment through a friend of Maureen's. Together they walked through the house, strangers peering at another stranger's things.

"We'll be together for a year so we must at least be friends." Maya stood across the living room, looking out on the portion of the river allotted to that window, a portion as small as the image from a child's view finder. She didn't look at Maureen as she spoke. "Think of me as a sister-in-law you have no choice but to welcome."

"Yes, we must at least be friends."

Maureen had wanted the exchange to remain as it had been before their departure, a contract overseen by corporate lawyers. They hadn't met in the months since they sealed their pact with a prayer at the blues café, Maureen preferring to contemplate her fate alone rather than succumb to Maya's pleas that they forge a friendship from their shared desire. In those months Maureen had not met Maya's husband, and she preferred not to think of the child she would create with an unknown father. She preferred not to think at all whether he'd sanctioned the peddling of his sperm. Perhaps he didn't know. Perhaps he didn't care. Still, she preferred this arrangement to buying sperm from a bank. Together, so far from home, she felt that yes, they should at least try to be friends. They began awkwardly, as ungraceful as new lovers on a date doling out the basics.

"How'd you and your husband meet?"

"He was on a diplomatic mission. Not a diplomat, but chief of staff. Like everyone else, he thought I was Indian. But I'm South African. White mother, black father. A mixed child coming of age in a country coming to terms with years of keeping races separate. I wanted to be somewhere else. To be in a country that had had years of dealing with mixed children. And I found him. Not very romantic, is it?"

Maureen preferred not to respond. She wanted not to be judgmental, not to say anything trite.

"How is it you haven't married?"

"The question should be, 'How is it I haven't met a man I'd marry?'" Maureen laughed, joining Maya at the window. The two women looked out on the view allotted them, a small piece of the world. "I've met men. The hard part is eliminating my expectations. My mother's expectations."

"You learn."

"I don't want to learn."

"It's not a fairy tale."

"No, it's not. There are never happy endings."

"My father would ask, 'What is happiness?' And he'd say 'It's a state of mind.' Attitudes can be adjusted. Look at South Africa now."

"We're beginning to sound like philosophy students."

That first night, lying beneath an open window, Maureen wished she could pray a prayer she truly believed but she didn't believe in a single God and she'd long accepted the futility of praying for what she believed she needed. She had considered the financial aspects of her plan, detailed the cost of raising a child. She'd even scripted conversations explaining or not explaining her choice. Over and over, she heard her mother's voice, "Is not here you learn that behavior." But she had yet to assess the emotional impact. She didn't think of herself as a surrogate, but rather as a woman bearing a child she'd later give up for adoption. She'd grown up with a distant father in a culture and a class that valued matrimony, and a mother who belittled herself for never achieving the ideals established by the ruling class. Though Maureen had achieved what her mother hadn't, she was contemplating bearing a child without having even seen the man who'd be its father. That was a prayer she had to bring directly because she couldn't think of any ancestor, hers or the ancestors of friends, who'd take such a prayer to the gods.

꒔

Maureen and Maya's was a friendship sealed by the rhythm of a woman's biology. Maureen knew and Maya understood Maureen's menstrual cycle and period of ovulation. There were no secrets there. Though Maya would have preferred in vitro fertilization and the implantation of her own eggs fertilized by her husband's sperm, they chose traditional surrogacy—Maureen's eggs, Maya's husband's sperm—for the quality of Maureen's eggs, the simplicity of the procedure. Maya, mother-like, nurse-like, recorded Maureen's body temperature, and learned to use fertility monitors to determine when Maureen would likely ovulate. Maya monitored Maureen's diet, her intake of vitamins and herbs and the mild fertility drug prescribed to better time ovulation. But the friendship didn't go beyond the basic understanding of Maureen's biology because Maureen wouldn't allow it.

Through ultrasounds and fetal monitors, Maya experienced the development of a life. Later Maya would also come to expect, but never fully understand, midnight cravings and mood swings. Maya wanted Maureen to keep a journal, to log how she felt at specific moments, so she could fully immerse herself in the experience of gestation and birth. Once, Maya said she felt like a man, a voyeur, instead of a woman preparing to bring a new baby home. And indeed that's the way they lived, Maya fetching and carrying, trying to anticipate her partner's needs; Maureen expanding and demanding care and attention.

Maureen, feeling guilty, thinking that she shouldn't be enjoying her body spreading, the flutter of the baby's first kick and seemingly responsive movement when she sang or whispered, began a journal, recording for Maya her thoughts upon waking, the joy from a single fetal movement. The baby she was carrying was, after all, Maya's, and it would be Maya who would one day respond to a child's questions about her early days. Maureen didn't share her diary though, preferring to wait until they'd both returned to their separate lives. Five months into the pregnancy she wrote:

Dear Maya,

I'm thinking Baby M, as I have begun calling it because of
both our first names, must be a boy. Or at least a very
spirited girl. Today, the minute I sat on the train, Baby M
kicked. He kicked so hard, my hand jerked, squeezing
water from my water bottle on the passengers all around.
The woman next to me asked if I was OK. I laughed.
Perhaps she didn't know I was pregnant. And I wanted to
tell her, "My baby's just alive, that's all." It's the little
things that matter, you know.

Maureen

The call came at three one afternoon. Maureen, seven months and fourteen
days along, was watching, though not participating, in aerobics for the mom-to-
be. She had enrolled in classes to try to speed the year along, and she'd returned
too exhausted to even reach for the remote that controlled the VCR. Instead, she
watched the aerobic video, thinking that the women exaggerated their energy.
The video couldn't be continuous, she thought. But the call came and she reached
for the phone, expecting to hear Maya asking, as she did every day, if everything
was still all right.

She heard instead an unfamiliar voice, a nurse from Downstate Medical, asking if she could come to the hospital because Maya had been injured in an accident. She moved, she thought, with the energy of the women on the video,
fitting one swollen foot and then the other into shoes that were already feeling
too tight. She hailed a cab rather than take the bus. Though she'd spent two years
of graduate school living in Brooklyn, the roads seemed unfamiliar still, and the
route the cabdriver choose seemed like a roundabout way. Only then did she miss
having her own car, the ease of getting around Kingston, a city she'd known since
her birth.

Amid the bustle of the emergency room, watching the visitors coming and
going, the emergency technicians wheeling patients in, the nurses and doctors
moving without grace, waiting for a doctor to come speak with her, Maureen
began to compose a letter for her journal: Dear Maya, Baby M, I'm sure, cried
today...

Patti Kim

# Bashy and Me

PATTI KIM is the author of the novel *A Cab Called Reliable* (St. Martin's Press, 1997) and is working on her second book. She lives in University Park with her husband and daughter. They're expecting their second child in December.

I got hit by a truck. I was trying to catch the ice cream man who was starting to drive off and away already ringing his bells for the kids up at the swimming pool. The only thing I could feel after my head bounced off the license plate was the quarter in my fist. Hard and round and hot. I didn't get run over. I just got hit. I told the man who drove the truck I was all right. When his friend with the pencil behind his ear asked me where I lived, I told him it was none of his business. The kids at the basketball court started gathering around me like I was a dead dog, so I got up, brushed the gravel off my knees, and pushed my way through. First to the swimming pool for my Orange Push-Up. Then home to the bathroom to clean the blood off my knees.

My mother and father found out I got hit by a truck because the *ah-jim-mah* downstairs called right when they got home from the dry cleaners. I could hear her through the floor. She said that they really ought to keep a closer watch on their one and only daughter. She said we didn't immigrate all the way to America from Korea to have our children hit by cars. She herself keeps her eyes glued on her daughters, Mina and Jina, because you just don't know what can happen in this strange country. Dad hung up, told me to take my clothes off, and had a good look at my body. My mother told him to beat me so I wouldn't do it again. She said she was too tired, too tired. She said she couldn't live anymore, couldn't live anymore. She said that all the time. I wondered how she kept on living and living. Dad lifted my arms, turned me around, touched my knees and asked if that hurt. It hurt, but I said it didn't. He called me a liar, told me I was too skinny and to be careful, patted my butt, told me to get ready for dinner, and threw my shirt over my head. Hiding under my shirt, I ran into the bathroom.

I had two ways of crying. When they hit me for not getting straight As on my report card or forgetting to press the ON button on the rice maker after school or for doing something stupid like losing my purse that had eight whole dollar bills in it or for playing with Bashy, I'd wail for a long time, hiccup myself to sleep with swollen eyes and a sore throat and dream about turning into something like an octopus with a big head to house a big brain and many many arms to whip away the stones that came my way. When they didn't hit me. When my mother just said something mean under her breath. When my father said something funny to make me laugh. When they let me go, I cried silently. The tears gathered, and I tried to hold them in, hoping they would uncross my eyes. But I blinked, and the tears slid down my mask of a face with its one eye still eyeing the other.

When I asked my mother how my eyes got crossed, she said it wasn't her fault since I wasn't born this way. When I was born, my eyes were perfect just like hers, the two brown pools dead center. She could always tell what I was looking at. She said the eyes of children who thought bad thoughts about their mothers crossed themselves, a punishment from God. If they didn't change their ways, God sooner or later blinded them. Anyone who hates her mother doesn't deserve to see.

Hee-ah, do you hate your mother?

No, I don't hate my mother.

Then why have your eyes crossed?

I don't know.

Isn't it true you sometimes want me to go away?

No, it's not true.

Isn't it true you sometimes even want me to die?

No, it's not true.

Isn't it true you love your father more than your mother?

I love you the same. It's all the same.

I wanted to ask her what happened to mothers who were mean to their children? Did they also turn into monsters? But I didn't. Instead, I tried my best to uncross my eyes by imagining me in the pictures I had seen of my mother when she lived in Korea. Instead of alone on the beach, she sat with me, both of us hiding our hands in the sand. I rode on the handle bars of her bicycle. I held the flower she bent down to sniff. I sat on a branch of the tree she stood beneath for shade. That night, I went to bed with the hope that I would wake up the next morning with the eyes my mother had made for me. But it didn't happen. I woke up still looking like the monster God must have known me to be.

"Where is this girl?" my mother said from the kitchen. I wiped the tears with my shirt, got dressed, and hurried out of the bathroom and to the kitchen sink where it was my job to rinse and wring out the sponge three times before wiping down the table. It was also my job to rinse the cups, chopsticks, spoons, and bowls. Everything had to be rinsed because of the roaches my mother blamed

Bashy for. Bashy was my secret best friend who lived in the apartment next to ours, his door faced mine. My mother swore she had seen roaches crawling out from under their door and in through ours. I had seen them crawling back and forth. She didn't like Bashy and his family because as she said they were the color of dirt. And I got slapped for saying I liked that color. It was better than the color of pee.

My mother and I prepared dinner, while my father sat at his desk counting the money they had made today. His calculator tap, tap, tapped out numbers onto a long strip of paper. I liked listening to the sound because the more tapping I heard, the more money they made. As I poured water into our cups, my mother said the rice looked perfect tonight. I had cooked it with just the right amount of water. The pot of dehn jahng casserole simmering on the stove. The smell pulling at my tongue. Steam rising from our three bowls of rice. The bucket of fried chicken wings, fish cakes, kimchi, bean sprouts, and pickled cubes of radish waiting to be eaten. And my mother telling me I had cooked perfect rice made all of those bad feelings go away. Happy and hungry, I skipped to their bedroom and leaned into my father's arm to tell him dinner was ready. He spit into his fingers, counting a handful of five-dollar bills.

"We're rich, aren't we?" I asked.

He finished counting the pile and said, "You just study hard. All this is none of your concern."

"When I grow up, I'm going to make lots of money," I said.

"And how are you going to do that?"

"I'm going to study hard and become a doctor."

"And what are you going to do with all your money?"

"I'm going to buy you and mom a big house and a nice car and lots of food so that you don't have to work anymore and you don't have to live in an apartment and you don't have to drive your junky car that breaks all the time."

"Keep on dreaming," he said, looking down at me with the corners of his eyes.

"Watch me. I'm going to make it happen."

"You're not keeping any of the money for yourself?"

"I'm going to keep just enough."

"Just enough for what?"

"I'm going to get surgery done on my eyes so that I can see straight."

"What are you talking about? You have magical eyes. You can see what ordinary eyes cannot. Why do you want to change that?"

"Because I look like a monster."

"I'd rather be a seeing monster than a blind human."

"I don't care what I can and can't see. I just want to look normal. I'm going to be rich and I'm going to get my eyes fixed."

"Are these people coming to eat or not?" my mother called from the kitchen.

My father pressed his hand on my head, using it like a cane to push himself up from his chair. I liked feeling the pressure and straightened up to brace his weight. I took his hand and pulled him to dinner.

We ate, my father crunching the bones of a chicken wing, me blowing on a spoonful of rice, and my mother scraping her teeth against the steel chopsticks because she didn't want to mess up her lipstick. My mother always wore lipstick. I think it had something to do with people back in Korea once telling her she looked as pretty as Sandra Dee. I had never seen Sandra Dee, but I figured she was very pretty and worth the trouble my mother went through to keep looking like her. I didn't know how my father with his foldless eyes ended up marrying a Korean Sandra Dee, having me, bringing her to America to live in an apartment with roaches, and having her clean other people's dirty clothes for a living. I looked nothing like my mother. I had my father's Chinese-Japanese-dirty-knees-look-at-these eyes on a big square head with a nose the shape of a plump heart turned upside down. Maybe if I looked like my mother, things would have been different. Maybe if I looked more like her, she would have loved the reflection of herself in me.

Bashy looked just like his mother. Puffy brown cotton candy hair on a perfect egg-shaped head. Dark brown skin, really dark brown. It was night-time dark, almost black, so dark that when he smiled, his teeth glowed white, even though they were yellow. A soft shiny pink tongue that looked liked chewed-up bubble gum. And a plum of a mouth I planned on kissing someday.

Bashy's mother worked at Zayre as a cashier. I had seen her there once while shopping with my mother. She was wearing pencil-pointy high heels with straps that tied around her ankles. Her African dress sparkled with bronze and gold, and her head was crowned with that cotton candy hair. When it came time for us to check out, I told my mother to go to her line because she was my friend Bashy's mother, because she would be nice to us, because she was our neighbor, but she shushed and pulled me into a longer line, hiding behind a rack of batteries and candy, pretending not to have seen her.

Bashy's father was a taxi driver who carried a briefcase to and from work. My mother teased, saying even taxi drivers must have felt the need to appear important. I figured it must have been full of the cash he had earned that day.

My mother dropped a chicken wing in my rice bowl and told me to eat it, bones and all, because I needed the calcium to grow tall like the American girls.

I hated the wing's tip because it sometimes had a nail that wobbled like a loose tooth and feathers that had been left unplucked. The wing's tip always reminded me I was eating a bird that couldn't fly.

"What are you going to do the next time you cross a street?" my father asked, spooning out the last piece of meat in the casserole.

"Look left, right, and left again," I said, washing a cube of kimchi radish in a bowl of water. The red spices floated to the surface. I pulled out the cleaned radish that now looked like a cube of flesh and bit into it.

"You have to be very careful," he said.

"Yes, sir," I said.

"Anything can happen, just like that," he said.

"Yes, sir," I said.

My mother reached for a toothpick and said, "Don't you remember how Joon-oh bbah got hit by a car and had to go to the hospital because all the bones in his legs were broken? His family didn't have any money to pay for the hospital. That was so much trouble for his family. I think they're still paying the hospital bills. It's not like Korea where everyone has insurance. In America, you have to give up your child's name to get insurance. And the police didn't even catch that driver because he got away, but even if he did catch him, he probably would have let him go because the police around here don't like us. Aigo, we don't have anyone on our side." I wanted to tell her that a police officer had visited our school once, and he was very nice to all of us, but instead I put another spoonful of rice in my mouth and chewed, wondering how I would talk them into letting me stay home this summer. All my summers had been spent in stores. First, the liquor store in Baltimore where my father stocked the shelves and my mother received money through a hole in the bullet-proof plastic wall in exchange for bottles of liquor. Then, the gas station in D.C. where my father tried to be a mechanic and my mother received money through a sliding drawer in exchange for gasoline. Then, Mr. Chae's dry cleaners where my father cleaned and pressed clothes and my mother stapled numbered tags on them. Then, my parents' very own store, Betty Brite Cleaners in Silver Spring, where my father had built a loft in the back for me to sit in while memorizing vocabulary words, U.S. presidents, state capitals, planets, and parts of the human brain in front of an oscillating fan.

"I'm getting straight As again," I said.

"You got straight As the last time. We didn't expect any less from you this time," my mother said, pulling a chicken wing apart.

"That calls for a reward," my father said.

"You should do well for the sake of doing well. Excellence is a reward in and of itself," my mother said.

"Hee-yah, what do you want?" my father asked

"It better not be another bicycle. You don't even ride the one you already have," my mother muttered, scraping meat off a chicken bone with her teeth.

"What about encyclopedias?" my father asked. "What about a globe? Or an atlas? You could learn a lot from an atlas."

"The girl doesn't want a boring atlas. It's just a waste of money. She should earn straight As because she wants to do well not because she wants a stupid atlas," my mother said.

"Hee-yah, what do you want?" my father asked.

"Anything?" I asked.

"First tell us what it is," my father said.

I cleared my throat and said, "I would like to stay home this summer." My mother stopped chewing her food and looked at me. Before she could say how I would get the family into big trouble by getting hit by a car, in my best Korean I said, "Please don't give me an answer right now. Please think about it. If I stay home, I could study better. Father, I appreciate the loft you built for me, but it gets very hot up there in the summer and I have a hard time thinking in the heat. It feels like my brain is melting up there. If I stayed at home, I can study with a clearer mind as well as take care of the apartment by doing extra chores. Mother, I know how much you dislike vacuuming because of your allergies, so I can vacuum in the morning right after you leave for work. By the time you return home, the dust would have settled and you won't have those sneezing attacks. You know how sneezing messes up your lipstick. And it won't be just rice I'd be cooking for dinner; I can cook casseroles and fry omelets and steam cabbage leaves to wrap our rice in. Mother, you spend your Sundays doing the laundry. I can take care of that during the week so that you can rest on your day off. But most importantly, I'll be able to study in a comfortable environment, get straight As year after year, go to a good college, become successful, and take care of you. And I promise that I will not get into any trouble. If you're going to say no to the entire summer, please say yes to just the first week of it. You can see how I do. If you're not pleased with me, I'll return to the store. Please think about it."

"How old are you?" my father asked.

"I'm ten years old." I answered, knowing he knew my age.

"I don't know. That seems too young. But it does get hot at the store," my father said.

"Hee-yah, it's not that we want you to stay home and be a maid all summer. What's most important to us is that you study hard and get into a good college. If we let you stay home this summer, that is our reason, not that you'll be getting extra chores done around the house. Do you understand?" my mother said.

"Yes, ma'am," I said.

"I don't think it's a bad idea," my mother said.

"I don't know," my father said.

"This is the best studying environment for her," my mother said.

"It is," my father said.

I wasn't sure if my mother was more concerned about my studying environment or her days off. I didn't know how many more chores were going to be stacked on me, but I appreciated having her on my side.

"What's the word of the day?" my father asked. Last year my parents had bought me a dictionary for Christmas. Since then, they made me learn the spelling and meaning of a new word each day. I was still in the As. The change of subject meant he would think about my request.

"Today's word is accuse. A-C-C-U-S-E," I said.

"What does it mean?" he asked.

I had forgotten the definition, but I told my parents accuse meant to make better. When I thought I saw suspicion in my father's eyes, I used it in a sentence and said, "I accused my vocabulary by learning a new word every day."

My father smiled, pushed his chair back, and said, "What would I do without my Hee-yah?"

As soon as he stood up, I placed my bowl, spoon, and chopsticks in the sink, ran hot water over them, and hurried to my room to look up "accuse" in the dictionary. It meant to charge with a fault, to blame. I shut the book, held it to my chest, and hoped they never used it at the store with their customers. I clean your shirt. I accuse it. See? I press your pants. I accuse it. See? I take spot out of jacket. I accuse it. See? The customers' lips would curl up, their brows would press together, their eyes would look at my parents as if they were strange little creatures daring to talk like them. Then out of their mouths would come, What are you talking about?

I make better. I accuse.

Accuse?

Yes. A-C-C-U-S-E.

That's not what the word means.

Then, my parents would return home, kick me, and blame me for the humiliation I made them feel. Tapping my forehead on my desk, I prayed they would forget that word as they forgot all the others I ever tried to teach them.

~

That evening, my father cracked open my bedroom door and asked how my knees were doing. Swinging them under my desk, I told him they were doing just fine. Strong, in fact. I could probably climb a mountain if I had to. I wanted to ask him if he had made up his mind about this summer, but I didn't want to press my luck. He knew the day after tomorrow was my last day of school. Just be as good as can be.

"May I go on the balcony and catch fireflies?"

He opened the door wide. I thanked him, as I walked through, ducking a little to keep from brushing the top of my head against his extended arm.

"Not too long. It's dark out there," he said.

"That's the best time to catch them," I said and tried not to look like I was hurrying outside.

I parted the curtain, slid open the heavy glass door, slipped on my flip-flops, and slid shut the door. It was dark and warm outside. I smelled fabric softener in the air. The dryer in the laundromat downstairs was running. I heard the tumbling. I heard a zipper hit against the metal one, two, three times before the sound got drowned out by nervous crickets. The moon was out. The stars were out. The fireflies blinked on and off. Leaning against the rail, I waited for the sound of Bashy's patio door to slide open then shut. When he came outside, he stepped up onto two bricks and leaned over his railing to get closer to my side. I stepped up onto the hibachi grill to get closer to his side. I saw the whites of his eyes and smelled dinner on his breath. It was quiet between us until I fingered him over, pulled his ear to my mouth, and in a whisper, told him how I had almost died today.

Karen J. Kovacs

# The Scottish Vampire

KAREN J. KOVACS (The Artist Formerly Known as McCaney) is a mum, writer, poet, artist, editor, and sometime vampire stylist living 3.5 miles from Captain Tasty in Silver Spring, Maryland, which is 3.5 hours from Cabins, West Virginia, 3.5 hours from Cape May, New Jersey, and 3,644 miles from London, U.K., which is 3.5 hours from the lair of the real Scottish vampire. Kovacs has had fiction and poetry published in the United States and United Kingdom. "The Scottish Vampire" is excerpted from a novel-in-progress.

*I*t's been five weeks since Todd's accident. An entire change of season. Spring, and he stares out the window at new leaves, marveling at how tiny they are, and how pale. Against a simmering, pre-storm sky, they shudder gently; Todd wonders when he last noticed the beauty of a frail leaf, the grouping of storm clouds. He remembers lying on his back beneath a pine tree twenty-eight years ago, eating tiny strawberries plucked from the field behind his house, noticing a bit of tarry sap on a branch just overhead, loving the smell of needles both fresh and fallen, wondering if his girlfriend was still angry at him for pressuring her the night before. The rising crescent moon had disappeared into an almost white sky that late afternoon.

The memory is clearer than more recent ones he could summon. Todd's been reading a lot since the accident, including an article suggesting that there are specific cells whose function it is to carry genetic memories of one's forebears. If that theory were true, Todd muses, as he follows from his living room window the flight of a passing great blue heron, it would go far toward explaining a few things in his life. Scotland, for example, sang to him like a siren. And why not, if those memory cells were chock-a-block with the history of wild men who warred and roared through the hills of Scotland, maybe even some who painted compli-cated patterns all over their bodies. What were they called? Picts? After forty-five years, his regular, non-genetic memory isn't what it used to be, save the occasional lucid flashback. But yes, the more he thinks about it, the more he's convinced that certain cells are crowding his unconscious mind with images of rough-hewn men who waved spears, built castles, blew music through pipes loud enough to wake the ghosts of their own slain ancestors slumbering in the heather underfoot. Todd's cells definitely remember golf as it was when first invented in Scotland, and that nothing is better than treading through tall wet grass under a pearl sky, with no one to trouble your peace but a quiet companion. Nothing can top that, except the "knowing" of a woman. More than one woman, if possible. Do nothing by halves, the old cells sing to other cells, the ones in charge of making new memories. Or so it seems to Todd. Nothing by halves, nothing by halves.

"So, Jonathan," Todd says aloud to the heron, who's landed, as he does daily, on the bank of a pond at the bottom of Todd's property, "what am I supposed to do, living in Pennsylvania and carrying around all those ferocious auld Scottish memories in my cells? Me without so much as a kilt, let alone a scrap of land to call my own."

He roars at his wife, but that isn't enough. He listens to music many decibels louder than most civilized people can stand, but it's never music of his own making and boasts no bagpipes. His house is on a grassy hill, but it isn't a castle and there's no scent of heather blowing though the open windows on a stormy night. It isn't even *his* house. He rents it from his aunt. He's possessed more women than he cares to count, has married three of them. He's a damn good golfer, and didn't the game originate in Scotland? Still. Nothing's ever felt right, nothing fits into place.

Maybe he needs to return to Kirriemuir, a dot on the coast where Scotland borders northeastern England, and the last place Todd's maternal ancestors had lived before emigrating to America. A shadowy group of Bavarian memory cells from his father's side of the family occasionally make a bid to be recognized, but Todd's affinity lies with the Scots.

*Kirriemuir.* As soon as he ponders going, he can feel his ancestors or memory cells or whatever leaping in anticipation. He starts rolling the idea over and over in his head until after a few days it tumbles coolly across his thoughts like a brook-polished stone.

He'll have to go without his wife, that much is certain. Wife number three. Robinn has stayed with him the longest. Going on two years, three if you count the year they lived together before tying the knot. She's out late this evening, to some awards dinner at the college. She didn't want him going to this one, which is a sure sign she'll be cozying up to the newly appointed girls' volleyball coach. She always tries to recruit the new staff into her camp, in case she needs their loyalty to rally around her over some faculty issue or another down the road. Todd imagines telling her his plan before they turn in for the night.

"I want to go to Scotland," he'll say.

"During semester break? That could work. Let me check the dates," she'll say.

"No, I want to go alone," he'll say.

"Why?" she'll wonder, looking hurt. That's where he gets stuck every time. Why alone, is a question for which he has no answer. She'll think he's off in search of a new woman, a Scottish one. He isn't, but he knows her—she'll think history might repeat itself. After all, it was she who bulldozed his artist girlfriend out of the way. The artist was another like himself, did nothing by halves, probably had a lot of yammering genetic cells like he did and no clue how to stifle them. Todd's heart tightens at the thought of her, his enemy because his mirror. She broke more easily, and he couldn't wouldn't didn't want to deal with that. But she would've understood the whole Kirriemuir thing. And he probably would have taken her.

Robinn is neither twin nor foe, though once she threw a dish at him when he said he wasn't ready to give up being friends with the artist. But it didn't matter anyway, since the artist fell to pieces and moved to New York to recover. Soon thereafter, Todd and the dish-thrower had settled into life among the misty hills of Pennsylvania. They married, in spite of a lot of hand-wringing from his parents ("the dust hasn't even settled from your second divorce, Todd") and his sister ("she still has a *girlfriend*, Todd"). Robinn, already on faculty at the local university, started flying high when they let her teach a class she dreamed up called Classical Theories of Aesthetics in Athletics. Todd, restless and jobless, took to spending his days driving and brooding along the nearby Delaware River. One day just after dusk, his tires skidded on a patch of ice and hit a snowdrift; seconds later, an approaching pickup truck rammed into the driver's side of his MG. The doctors told him he was lucky to have escaped with only six broken ribs, a few bruises and such a juicy out-of-court settlement from the other driver.

Todd doesn't feel lucky, and the painkillers have started to become addictive, so he's dumped them out and switched to Extra-Strength Tylenol. Useless.

He gets to thinking about how it's written that God pulled a rib out of Adam's side, from which He fashioned Eve. Clearly, Todd muses, he himself is not a man for whom one ribmate would ever suffice. And even if he found his Eve, would he realize it? He's been told by dozens of women that he doesn't know his own happiness when it stares him in the face. But what if he met his Eve and did recognize her as his missing rib and plunged right into the fiery heart of love with her, only to be driven mad by her in the end. Because that's what would happen, he was sure, if he met up with his rib. Madness.

All the thinking about ribs make Todd's own broken ones start to rumble and mutter amongst themselves. Todd's ribs can out-talk almost any part of his body. "What's he talking about, a missing rib? I swear the man is never satisfied." "We've done a perfectly good job for forty-five years. You can't blame us for getting broken. If he'd bother to drive a car bigger than a popsicle, he wouldn't get himself smashed up by the big boys." "Anyway we're all still here, none of us are missing." "It can't be as bad as he's whining, I mean, if he's in so much pain, how come he can still have sex?" "He isn't." "He is so, his penis said he is." "You can't believe anything his penis says. Anyway that isn't having sex. That's just something to tide him over." And so on.

Todd phones his doctor's office and asks the receptionist to have his pain prescription refilled. "I flushed them so I wouldn't get addicted to them, but my ribs are screaming at me." The receptionist agrees to have the doctor call in a refill. In the meantime, Todd swallows a few ibuprofen tablets with a shot of whiskey. As a rule, he prefers wine or beer, but the memory cells are pushing up an image of warm, drunken camaraderie amongst a clan of Scots, and he wants to join the fun. Maybe this is what makes people believe in reincarnation, he speculates drowsily. They think they're remembering a previous life, when in fact it's one of their ancestor's lives.

Once the ribs are sure Todd is breathing deeply and regularly, they start nudging one another. "He's out cold, finish the story," two or three implore the largest of the unbroken ribs. "Yes, finish it, finish it," several chime in.

"Very well, very well," says the big rib. "Someone remind me where we left off."

"The part when he leaves his fellows and heads for the wilds of the Black Forest?"

"No, we were considerably further along than that," a medium unbroken rib insists. "Remember? He leaves the company of his fellows and heads for the heart of the Black Forest, where he hopes to find solace in the ageless beauty...there where the leaves are so thick and deep the sun never penetrates beyond the highest branches, where time seems suspended in perennial twilight. But his tranquility among the majestic trees and the curious but quiet creatures of the forest is disturbed by a tiresome band of gypsies."

"Oh yes, the majestic perennial twilight thing and the tiresome band of gypsies. That's where you left off," two more ribs agree.

"All right, all right," says the big rib. "The tiresome band of gypsies set up camp in a clearing near a brook a mere two hundred yards from where the Scottish vampire had fashioned a rough hut for himself. Their music kept him awake night after night, and their tales filled his head with strange and troubling dreams.

The curse of Anya worried him most of all. He'd heard it on the third night, when the gypsies had just eaten a couple of roasted rabbits and were drinking a cheap-smelling wine and smoking pipes around their meager fire. Sophia, oldest of the gypsy women, had stared into the flames and spoken."

"'Bela, remember the curse of Anya?'

"Bela spit into the fire. 'Anya couldn't curse a horse to be plagued with horse-flies. Nobody believed that curse would take.'

"'Bold words, old man. But I see you've never removed that garlic from your neck.'

"'It keeps the mosquitoes off,' Bela grumbled.

"'What mosquitoes?' The other gypsies laughed.

"'Why did Anya curse you, Bela?' the youngest of the women asked.

"Bela silently fingered the rope of garlic round his neck. The young gypsy stared at him, waiting, but he turned away.

"'He compromised her reputation,' Sophia cackled.

"'Her reputation, that's a good one,' one of the men snorted.

"'It's true," Sophia said. 'True enough anyway. She hadn't known a man before that night. Not in the proper sense. But Bela lusted after her and—'

"'You're daft and drunk. You don't know what you're talking about.' Bela glowered a warning.

"'She fought him off tooth and nail. Especially tooth,' Sophia continued with a sneer. 'He still has a scar on his neck. Go ahead and show her, Bela. Take off that filthy scarf and show her the marks, why don't you.' Sophia reached over to snatch the scarf, and Bela pushed her hard, toppling her off balance. She fell on her side in a torrent of profanities.

"'I'll kill you for that, Bela,' she shrieked. 'Better yet I'll curse you. And you know mine will stick.'

"'Keep your claws and curses to yourself, old hag. And while you're at it, keep your lies to yourself.' Bela stormed off toward the caravan.

"'What became of Anya?'" the young one asked, helping Sophia to her feet.

"'She was never seen again, but there were rumors among some of the Romneys that she bore a fairy child with teeth every bit as sharp as her own.'

"'When did all that happen, Sophia?'

"'Ach, it has to be nigh on thirty years ago.'

"The Scottish vampire felt a chill pass over him, and soundlessly retreated to his hut.

"After that night, the curse of Anya haunted him. Nevertheless, he continued to stand in the shadows, watching the gypsy faces in the firelight, but always remaining hidden from view, not only because he was unwilling to give up his solitude, but because he feared he'd be tempted."

"Tempted to bite one of them?" a small rib interrupts eagerly.

"Sssh," the others hiss.

"Yes, tempted to sink his teeth into the neck of the young one. She wasn't a true beauty, and always looked in need of a good washing, but she was pretty enough, and possessed beguiling eyes and a fey charm, and the Scottish vampire found his eyes returning to her face, her form, and most of all her neck, again and again."

"Why doesn't he just go ahead and bite her? I would," another small rib says.

"Because he's a *reluctant* Scottish vampire, remember?" the unbroken medium rib says impatiently, in the way of all medium ribs. "He doesn't want to make anyone suffer the way he has. Why do you think he drinks the blood of animals, hmmm?"

"Quite right," says the big rib. "He isn't, as you recall, a vampire by choice."

"That's why he parts the company of his fellows," medium rib reminds the small rib.

"Not very nice for the animals, though," a small rib points out.

"Indeed." The big rib continues. "As I was saying, the Scottish vampire is drawn to the young gypsy woman, but cloaks himself in trees and shadows, listening to their bickering and scheming by day, their intoxicated ramblings and soothsaying by night, eventually returning to his hut for a few hours of fitful sleep. Finally, on the eve of their departure, when the moon is full, he follows the girl to his bathing brook and watches her slip out of her clothes and wash her lissome body in the cool, murmuring waters."

Several ribs whisper uh oh, and others sshh them.

"The moonlight plays upon her body in rivulets and petals, and the Scottish vampire stands mesmerized, forgetting himself, forgetting his vow to hide himself from all women forever. He steps closer and closer, the woman's lighthearted splashes muffling any sound his careless footsteps might make."

The big rib pauses abruptly, and the others sigh as Todd turns on his side, then back again, then lifts himself out of bed.

"He has the world's worst timing," one of the little ribs whines.

"Never mind, I'll finish telling the story tomorrow night," assures the big rib.

"Can't you tonight?"

"No, the story's gone into his sleeping head and he's already getting aroused and that always spoils everything. We should get some rest while the painkiller is still working its magic."

A few ribs grumble in protest, but they soon settle down for the night. The largest of the broken ribs whispers, "If I weren't a rib, I'd be a gypsy."

ॐ

In the morning, as soon as Robinn has left the house, Todd paces around awhile, stares out at a gray sky full of low, racing clouds, and finally phones directory information. The artist's number in Greenwich is unlisted. He phones her mother, who still lives in his town, and she reluctantly provides her daughter's address, but only after Todd takes the trouble to make his voice crack a bit. He spends the entire afternoon writing and rewriting the perfect letter imploring the artist to accompany him to the wilds of Kirriemuir. He's still sitting at his desk when Robinn returns from campus.

"Hi, honey. Sorry I got in so late last night. Whatcha writing?" Her glance darts everywhere but Todd's face, eyes flitting like minnows, avoiding his own.

"I'm going to Scotland."

Robinn's eyes come in for a landing, meeting his defiant look dead on.

"And I'm going alone."

*Robin Alva Marcus*

# *Birdie*

ROBIN ALVA MARCUS is a native Washingtonian who received her MFA in creative writing from the University of Maryland. She is a winner of the Katherine Anne Porter Prize for Fiction, recipient of the Mary Boyle McCrory Award for Excellence in Writing, two-time D.C. awardee of a Commission for the Arts and Humanities Fellowship Grant for Literature, founding member of The Theatre Collective and former columnist for *Sister 2 Sister* magazine. She has led writing workshops at the National Museum for Women in the Arts and for the Zora Neale Hurston/Richard Wright Foundation. She teaches at Howard University and the Duke Ellington School for the Arts and is the proud mother of three sons.

In a few weeks Dominique's grandmother will turn her head to face the window of her bedroom and will not be able to turn again. Her fingers will freeze into a permanent curl, like the hands of a beggar. When she discovers this, Dominique will smooth the fingers down, press them flat, and watch them slowly close into themselves again. She will also notice that her grandmother's hands are still soft, that the skin still moves easily over her knuckles when the visiting nurse rubs lotion into them.

A week later, she will notice that the skin on her hands has changed: it feels like canvas stretched taut over a plywood frame. Her grandmother's feet reached this stage earlier; they are dark, hard, and lifeless as if death entered through creases in her soles and then crawled through her body inch by inch. When the nurse trimmed her thickened toenails and accidentally clipped off a crescent of skin, the wound did not bleed.

Dominique's grandfather Carlton sleeps in a recliner. A neighbor's sons carried it up from the TV room on the first floor and into his bedroom. They put it in the airless space between the bed and the wall. It's hell on his back but Carlton refuses to sleep away from his wife until he has to, until she's gone.

He's driven a cab for thirty years. Before she lost the strength to talk, his wife made him promise that he wouldn't quit working and just sit around the house all day waiting for her to die. It would make her feel, she said, as if she had to hurry up. On Tuesdays, the days she used to go to the hospital, he would take the cab back to the lot and leave for an extended lunch. When he came up the walk whistling, she would be sitting in the living room with her purse resting on her lap and enough morphine swimming through her veins to make her unsure about the distance between her feet and the carpeted floor. At the sound of his whistle, she would smile and begin taking in deep breaths.

Their walk to the car took fifteen minutes although the car was so close, just at the end of their short walkway or double-parked just beyond. Their heads nearly touched as they walked; they held onto each other like old friends sharing a secret.

Once they reached the car, Carlton would put his hands on the sides of her waist to steady her as she gripped the door frame, then lowered her body, small as a child's, into the passenger seat. In the beginning, after the visits to the doctor's office, they would ride out near National Airport and watch the planes take off like they did when they were teenagers. She could still nibble on the bag of gourmet jellybeans or Bridge mix he would buy for her then. Eventually the trips to the doctor's office left her exhausted; she could sleep into the middle of Wednesday after her Tuesday trip. Now of course, she doesn't go at all.

Her grandmother is a presence, a constant, like her own heartbeat. Like the questions that shadow every mundane enterprise whatever it is, carrying a load of clothes to the basement, pulling off socks and rolling them into a ball, squeezing toothpaste onto the toothbrush. *Is she dying right now, this exact second? When I go back in there will she be gone?* Nine years ago, when Dominique was born, her grandmother nicknamed her Birdie. At not quite five pounds, the baby seemed light enough to fly away if the window was left open. Dominique's lullaby, the song her grandmother sang to her until she fell asleep in her grandmother's arms, was a song she and Dominique's grandfather danced to when they were dating, *"Got a black magic woman, got a black magic woman, I got a black magic woman got me so blind I can't see…"*

It's a song that slips into Dominique's head when she's swinging on the swings at Garrison playground or sitting anywhere by herself with nothing to do. Sometimes when she visits and the clack and whir of the respirator almost sound like music, Dominique pretends that she can hear her grandmother singing to her from *inside her brain.* She listens as she sits on the floor at the foot of the bed drawing pictures to tape on the wall next to the window that her grandmother faces but of course, can't see.

It's hard for Dominique to imagine her grandmother any other way now. She studies the framed photographs that are everywhere in the room, on the dresser, the nightstand, and on the walls, but they're images from another time. In one her grandmother is dressed for Mardi Gras wearing a crown of jewels and feathers with multiple ropes of colored beads looped around her neck. In another she is sitting in the living room posing in the fur coat Carlton bought her when his number came out in 1987 and he won $5,000.

On good days, her grandmother will say, "Is that you, Birdie?" when Dominique comes into the room and touches her shoulder. She'll listen with eyes closed as Dominique complains about Jelly, her younger brother, whose sole purpose in life is to get her in trouble. One complaint will bleed into another, and then another about something that might have happened last week or last year. When Dominique says, "You listening, Grandma?" her grandmother will raise her eyebrows to assure Dominique that she is.

Before the respirator came she occasionally stopped breathing for seconds at a time and even with it standing vigil beside the bed she sometimes seems so still that Dominique leans in close to make sure her chest is rising and falling. She doesn't always wake her grandmother; sometimes her visits are silent. She'll walk over to the bed and wonder how the same illness that is stealing her grandmother also makes her seem radiant. A persistent low-grade fever leaves a film of perspiration glistening on her skin if the light is touching it in a certain way. Her burnished cheeks, heated from fever, shine deep and red like the apples that she used to peel in one uninterrupted motion and pass dangling from the paring knife to her enchanted granddaughter.

When her hair grew back after the first round of chemotherapy and radiation, it was thinner than before. It falls over her shoulders like strands of mixed gray and silver yarn. Dominique's favorite thing to do when she visits her grandmother is to loosen her braids, scratch her scalp gently with a rubber-tipped comb, and then brush her hair with a soft-bristled brush that belonged to Dominique when she was a baby. Her second favorite thing to do is to lie down next to her grandmother and feel the heat from her grandmother's body reach into hers through the blankets.

While Dominique bathed upstairs this morning, her mother Cheri set a dining room chair against the kitchen sink backwards and stacked three telephone books in the seat. After she dries off, rubs Vaseline into her elbows, knees, and heels, and peeks in on her grandmother hoping (as always) that her grandmother is sitting up and magically healthy, Dominique counts to ten twice at the top of the stair-case. She wills herself down the stairs, stepping on each step with both feet. Midway down she bends low to look at the name of a boy she wrote on the baseboard in letters so small only she could see it. Out of habit she hops from the last step onto the floor, walks through the living room and dining room, and finally enters the kitchen with her eyes cast down and the resolve of a martyr approaching the guillotine. Her mother, thick from neck to thigh, stands at the sink with her fists jammed on her hips and a folded towel thrown around her neck saying, "Nikki you know I got other things to do," as Dominique kneels on the stack of books and places her neck on the sink's edge.

Her mother's fingernails leave behind trails of raw skin on her tender-headed scalp. Her mother believes that only hot water will rinse shampoo well and Dominique's head feels as if it's on fire. Shampoo burns her eyes. Squirming is punishable by a pinch in the ribs or a yank, but Dominique tries to adjust. She turns her head hoping to redirect the path of the shampoo, but her mother's hand pushes her head so that she's face down again and the suds collect exactly where they'll do the most damage, in the pockets of her eyes.

There isn't enough time this morning to shampoo twice; one good scrubbing will have to do. Afterwards Dominique's neck is sore and her eyes are red, but at least they won't sting too much. She wipes shampoo suds from her ears and dabs at her watering eyes with the corners of the towel draped over her wet hair.

Her brother Jelly stands at the kitchen door. "See there?" he teases, "That's why you a crybaby."

"I ain't no crybaby, Jelly," Dominique tells him. "Keep messin with me, *you* gonna be the one cryin."

"Stop fussin, ya'll," Cheri warns. She drops the telephone books on top of the refrigerator and drags the chair back to the dining room.

"Like you gon do somethin," Jelly continues, ignoring his mother. "Like you *want* some a this. This is a *soldier* over here. For real." He tugs his T-shirt sleeve up to show his sister the small mound that barely rises when he flexes his muscle.

Dominique sucks her teeth. "Yeah, right. A *gay-lo* soldier if anything."

"Quit, Dominique and go head on, Jelly," Cheri says, drawing the comb down the center of her daughter's hair. "Go help your grandfather."

Their mother seems to have chosen sides: hers. "See there? That's what you get for doin stupid stuff," Dominique teases. She sucks her teeth again as Cheri brings the wooden part of the brush down on the crown of Dominique's head.

"Ouch, Mommy, dang!"

"You two play too much," Cheri says. "And I told you to keep still Nikki."

A blow dryer with a comb attachment tames Dominique's knotted mass of tangles. In another hour, Cheri's quick fingers would have organized her hair into twenty perfectly spaced cornrows. Rubber bands would have been secured on the ends of each braid. But Cheri has decided to take a break here and get back to her work in the kitchen. Her shoulders have begun to ache from the pull and struggle with her daughter's hair. As she pushes up from the sofa, she grabs Dominique by the forearms and points her toward the stairs saying, "Go change your clothes so you'll be ready when company gets here and you can help out." But Nelly is on *106 and Park*, and Dominique leans over the balustrade to watch.

Pale pink chicken wings, rinsed and patted dry, are waiting in a heap on the counter to be dropped in a bag of seasoned flour and then fried in a heavy black skillet. Three family-sized cans of pork and beans have been emptied into a pot. Chopped onions, a chunk of fat back, mustard, and brown sugar have been added but not stirred in, although heat from a slow flame is beginning to make its way up from the bottom of the pot. Ribs simmer on the back burner. Cheri wets her fingers under the faucet and flings drops of water into the grease to make sure it is hot enough for frying.

Carlton rakes patterns of wavy lines in the dirt around the picnic table like his mother did in her front yard in River's End, Georgia. A jug of his barbecue sauce, a concoction that he mixes up in a crab pot at the beginning of summer and stores in gallon-sized milk containers at the back of the refrigerator, sits on the picnic table surrounded by industrial-sized bottles of mustard, ketchup, relish, and hot sauce. When his raking is done, he lifts the top of the grill, a converted oil drum sawed in half and reattached with hinges. A plume of smoke envelopes his face and leaves a scent on his shirt that will last all day. He's done something new this time, added hickory and mesquite chips to the charcoal pile, according to directions, when the flames had died down and the centers of the briquettes were glowing like ingots in a furnace. He looks up to the second-story bedroom where he'd left the windows open so that if his wife wanted to, she could at least *hear* her relatives and friends out in the yard, she could smell the party.

His brother Squirrel, a bus driver who lives in Richmond, has pulled up in a maroon Crown Vic weighted down with female relatives who are large and not ashamed about it. Squirrel and his wife have triplets. The clan has welcomed twins before but never three at a time. "Squirrel n' them here!" her grandfather calls from the yard and, in spite of her mother's instructions, Dominique runs outside to see this miracle of babies. She is barefoot and wearing only the thin cotton jumper she put on after her bath and occasionally sleeps in at her grandmother's house. She leaves the front door wide open behind her, like people raised in a barn. Her hair is slicked flat against the sides of her head with Dax grease and sticks straight out from the back stock-still, as if it's frozen, not at all ready for the scrutiny of other black women. Cheri yells from the kitchen doorway, "Nikki! Who told you you could go outside? Get your little *narrow* behind back in this house!"

The triplets are worthless, Dominique soon realizes. Three little brown teddy bears with bald spots on the sides of their heads where the soft baby hair has rubbed off and the wool has not yet grown in. All they do is sit in their car seats and occasionally loose a shoe or stick a finger in their mouths releasing a rivulet of drool that eases down their chins and soaks into their bibs. Their names have been written on the cuffs of their jeans with a bleach pen: Kelvin, Kendel, and Kayvonne.

After a while the blur of activity that their arrival unleashes, hugs and backslaps, picnic baskets, a chest of iced beer, and stacks of Tupperware containers hauled in from the trunk of the car, subsides. They were parked on the sofa and left there as if Dominique wanted to sit and watch them while everybody else got to whoop and holler, as her grandmother used to say, out in the kitchen and in the backyard where a card table has been set up under the cigarette tree for a game of spades that will not end until midnight.

They take up all the space on the sofa; their diaper bags and a bag of Pampers have been deposited on the armchairs. Dominique has to sit on the floor. *And why?* She wonders. Her ankles are crossed and her heels bounce against the rug, and she looks over at the triplets from the side of her eyes. She squinches up her nose; the babies *stink* too. Now Dominique folds her arms, a situation has developed. Is *she* supposed to change their diapers, she wonders? For three babies? For free?

"Didn't nobody ask me," she says beneath her breath. "Didn't nobody say, 'Nikki, could you watch the kids?'" The laces on Kendall's left Nike have come untied. Dominique ties it in a double bow, turns the channel to the BET, and goes upstairs, taking the steps two at a time.

Her clothes are laid across her grandfather's chair. As she dresses she describes the scene downstairs, telling her grandmother about the babies, about how Auntie Roberta looks like she's got some more babies up under her big dress. "Grandma, they all poop at the same time. Smells like all poo poo down there."

Babies begin crying all at once. Dominique runs for the stairs, taking two steps at a time. The triplets have somehow knocked themselves off the sofa and tumbled to the floor, upsetting the glass top of the coffee table with its uneven leg. An ashtray, the crystal potpourri bowl, and one of her Uncle Vaughn's football trophies that had been carefully positioned on the table to give it balance are strewn across the carpet. The babies are lying on either their sides or face down, still buckled into the car seats, arms and legs flailing.

Two of the triplets look like human turtles; she can't help it: the sight makes Dominique laugh before she can think to get to her knees to help them. Uncle Squirrel and Auntie Roberta come running. Dominique's grandfather, Auntie Lorie, big-headed Jelly, and Miss Francine from around the corner who's been friends with Dominique's grandmother for forty-five years cram into the room. Her mother pushes through the crowd of relatives and snatches Dominique up by the arm strikes her wherever her hand falls and screams, "What did I tell you? *What did I tell you?*"

Dominique twists free protesting, "You ain't tell me nothin!"

Bodies shuffle between them. Dominique moves out of striking distance, grateful for the interference. "Go on upstairs," Cheri says, "you *know* you getting whupped. And you *bet* not wake up Mama."

The coffee table glass is replaced on its crippled frame. Someone has pulled the vacuum cleaner out of the closet and begins cleaning the ashes from the carpet. The potpourri is scooped back into its bowl. Three sets of arms reach for Kendell, Kelvin, and Kayvonne to soothe the unhurt babies as their mother unfolds a changing pad on the floor and lines up the baby wipes, Pampers, and a tube of Desitin to clean their nasty bottoms. Within moments they will be gnawing on ears of roasted corn while perched on alternating laps in the backyard.

Barbecue smoke and Lysol tangle in the air of her grandmother's room as Dominique settles in on the floor. She props her back against the wall. Few things are harder to wait for than a whipping. Her grandfather's sack of candy lies in the V made by her legs and her feet disappear under the bed. She picks through the assortment, searching for candy corn. This isn't her first raid on her grandfather's stash and there aren't many left, but she drops the few that she finds into her open palm. As always, she bites the white tips off first then eats the orange middle and yellow bottoms together; they taste the same anyway.

Maybe Cheri will forget, forget to peel a switch off the cigar tree and come looking for her. "You think she'll forget, Grandma?" she whispers, softly, like a prayer. The carpet scratches the backs of her knees. She shakes the candy corn in her fist like dice and listens to the song that drifts from her grandmother's pillow, *"Got a black magic woman…"*

## C. M. Mayo

# Manta Ray

C. M. MAYO is the author of *Sky over El Nido* (University of Georgia Press, 1999), which won the Flannery O'Connor Award for Short Fiction, and *Miraculous Air: Journey of a Thousand Miles through Baja California, the Other Mexico* (University of Utah Press, 2002). Her most recent short fiction has appeared in *Chelsea*, *The Kenyon Review*, *Natural Bridge*, and *Turnrow*. Her other awards include fellowships to the Bread Loaf, Sewanee, and Wesleyan Writers' Conferences; residencies at the MacDowell Colony, Ragdale Foundation, Virginia Center for the Creative Arts, and Yaddo; and, for her travel writing, two Lowell Thomas Awards. A native of El Paso, Texas, Mayo currently divides her time between Mexico City and Washington, D.C. She is writing a novel titled "The Last Prince of the Mexican Empire." Her website is www.cmmayo.com.

Now that she was trying to write a novel, Consuelo Kennedy had become exquisitely sensitive to noise. But today, on this summer morning of her seventh month in Washington, it was the stink of burning fruit that woke her. "Something's burning," Nick said, sitting bolt upright in their bed. "Something is definitely burning." He sniffed loudly, moving his nose around like a dog. Consuelo had been dreaming a delicious dream, something about Tom Cruise and a sofa-sized and pillowy (if strangely tasteless) marshmallow, but already it had faded—*poof,* like a wisp up a chimney.

"It's pie," Consuelo said crossly. She touched the ring in her eyebrow, which was a little bit sore from the way she'd been sleeping on it.

"It's burning."

"No kidding." Consuelo stretched her arms long and lazy like a cat, and yawned. She was half-Mexican but with the pale and moonlike face of a model in a photograph by Horst. Little in her life of twenty-nine years seemed to have perturbed her; had she been a pond, she would have been hidden deep in a thicket, her surface mirror-like over the pile of rocks that lay scattered along the bottom, slowly accumulating silt.

"I don't like it," Nick said.

Consuelo wrinkled her nose. "It's just spillover onto the oven pan." She yawned again. This was the Watergate; all kinds of smells seeped in with the air conditioning—cooking curry, burnt toast. Just last Tuesday the neighbor had forgotten a teriyaki squab in the oven when she went to have her hair permed. ("Oh, diddly!" Mrs. Tuttle had said when Consuelo found her, the service door to her kitchen flung open, flagging her apron to clear the air into the hallway.)

Nick was up and wriggling out of his undershorts. "Well," he said, still sniffing suspiciously. The whole bedroom stank.

"Don't crack your coconut," Consuelo muttered, but Nick couldn't hear her; he was already in the bathroom.

Nick was quick in the mornings, *splash boom bah*, as she liked to make fun of him. All of a sudden, there he'd be, leaning over her for his good-bye kiss, holding his Hermès tie to his chest, his face razored smooth and bay leaf fresh. "*Ciao*," he'd say. "Save the world," she'd say, because Nick worked in Project Evaluation at the World Bank—today a sewage treatment for San Salvador, tomorrow a hydroelectric plant for Nicaragua. For two years straight, Nick had crunched the numbers for the new superhighway out of Mexico City, which was where they'd met in a bar—and though that sounded sleazy to say, it was La Sirena, a cutting-edge cool kind of bar (faux ostrich leather banquettes, Louis Armstrong rasping on the sound system, geometric little cucumber and ginger-seared ahi tapas) where Consuelo's photographs of the Revillagigedo Islands were displayed, each one framed and halogen spot-lit on lipstick-red lacquered walls.

"That's a place to check out," Nick had said, gazing at the one over the bar.

She had been entranced by the way this gringo looked, slim in his suit, the sharp famished-Tartar planes of his face. His jaw flexed as he crunched a mouthful of ice.

"That's the Revillagigedos," Consuelo had offered, and because she'd sucked down a couple of glasses of *jérez*, she rather too voluptuously rolled the "r"— *Rrrrrr-vee-ah-hee-hay-dos.*

"Scuba?" "Yes." "Golf?" "No." "Just kidding." It had started like that.

And then—*zup*—here she was, living with him for seven months already in Washington.

"*Ciao*," Nick said.

"Save the world," Consuelo said.

"I don't like that smell," he said. He had his briefcase in his hand.

"Well," she said, her cheek heavy as a stone on the pillow, "I wouldn't bottle and sell it."

So warmly cocooned in the down-filled duvet, for Conseulo, there was nothing more tempting than to sleep just a little bit longer. Every morning after Nick left, the urge came upon her like a spell. The room remained dark (Nick left the curtains closed); blue quiet enfolded the building like a thick felt blanket. When she'd first moved into Nick's apartment, she'd been startled by this quiet. After all, the Watergate was walking distance to K Street and Georgetown, and right on the expressway along the Potomac. As for the celebrities who lived here (somehow, she'd associated them with sparklers, party crackers, whoopee cushions), other than Senator McDudley, and the bottle-blonde woman named Springer whose picture she'd happened to recognize in *Architectural Digest*, she'd no idea who they were. Older people lived in the Watergate mostly, slow-moving dowagers with helmet hairdos, their husbands (if they still had them) shuffling downstairs in cardigan sweaters on errands to the pharmacy. As for any noise, across the hall, there was a pug that would let out an indignant yip when he wanted his walk; and next door, the Tuttles might leave their tea kettle to whistle for a few (excruciatingly long) minutes at a time. Now and then, an airplane or a helicopter would roar over the river on the way to National Airport or Andrews Air Force Base. Otherwise there was only a muffled *zizz* of traffic along the river, and the air conditioner's faint, soothing *thrummmmmmmm*.

She pulled the pillow over her head.

She'd grown so weary with photography—the clamorous weddings, the bar mitzvahs, not to mention the likes of a lingerie catalogue that featured black-laced red satin teddies ("*muévete el brazo*," move your arm, she kept having to tell the model, to hide the tracks). The highlight of her career in Mexico—though the word "career" struck her as unnecessarily sharp, like trying to portion out flan with a knife—had been the shoot in the Revillagigedo Islands. Rigoberto Castro, the shopping mall magnate, had sent her out there along with a tuna fish spotter's helicopter. (A squirrely man who fancied ascots, Castro reminded her of Fred Astaire but on three pots of cold coffee. He'd *oohed* and *aahed* over her prints, then for six months—she'd called and called, leaving messages with his increasingly testy secretary—he wouldn't cut a check.) They *were* gorgeous photographs, damn it, so gorgeous they didn't look real. Two hundred and fifty miles off the end of the Baja California peninsula, the Revillagigedos appeared suddenly up out of the carpet of the sea, spires and soaring arches of sun-shocked volcanic rock. Her own memories were even more strange and wonderful than her photographs. On the shore of one of the islands—a mountain of ash like a slab of cake—thousands of bits of pumice tumbled against each other in the surf, making a noise like children humming. Her cameras around her neck, Consuelo had waded into that sea, which was warm as bathwater, the little rocks, light like sponges, dancing and tickling around her ankles. She'd made friends with a visiting marine biologist named Sofia von Holtman and together they camped on a beach of crushed moon-white shells, they climbed a mountain of raw rock the color of blood, and one afternoon, with scuba gear, Consuelo and Sofia rode on the backs of giant manta rays. Fast the manta rays swam, their hides soft like gloves, their wings working through the water with long, elegant curls.

Nothing after the Revillagigedos could compare. And the shoot had been a fluke, this rich man's whim. Back in Mexico City, though she'd lent prints to La Sirena, the only business she could muster was the same stale stuff: weddings, bar mitzvahs, more weddings. A men's tie catalogue (every one of them polyester).

Oh, the lace curl of a shell-strewn shore, swirls of chocolate lava, the rush and spume of surf against sun-dazzled rock: to see the Revillagigedos there, spot-lit on the lipstick-red lacquered walls of that dark and noise-addled bar: they taunted her, glassed-over portals. Above the swinging door to the ladies' toilet: a magnificent frigate bird aloft in blue. Had she, Consuelo Kennedy, really taken that, or had it been a dream? She'd felt so trapped then, as if she'd been closed into a room that was filling with smoke. But she'd had to keep working and working because the thing was, she'd sunk every peso of her savings into her studio and state-of-the-art equipment—until, one night while she was knocking back a beer in La Sirena with Nick, someone jimmied the lock on the door by the fire escape and carried off the cameras, zoom lens, the lamps and booms and tripods, even the umbrella diffuser with the kink in the latch so she could never get it to close, even the pans, even the paper. Her space was cleared of everything but shadows. And there, on the floor, the faint rime of dust outlining where her equipment had been. And a wadded-up yellow candy wrapper. She kicked it.

"Sunk costs are sunk," Nick said with a shoulder-padded shrug. That was Project Evaluation lingo, something he'd said to her the first night they'd met in La Sirena. It meant that you could sink a couple of hundred million bucks into an electric plant, and if it turned out you'd built it on the wrong hill, you walked away.

"Like that?" she'd clicked her fingers.

"Yep," he'd said.

And so, flush with insurance money, she decided—why not?—to move to Washington with Nick and write a novel.

"Funds are fungible," Nick had said, fast, as if it were an incantation: *funzrfingble*. That was another bit o' lingo she hadn't yet fathomed the point of. It seemed like saying, for example, flammable stuff can catch fire.

As for that funky smell, well, she thought as she thrashed off the duvet and scrunched her toes into the rug, that's the kind of bother one puts up with living in an apartment building. At least there was no one here who would blare their stereo, as in Mexico City, bloody hell, the neighbor's bass used to drive her mad, *dum-dum-dum*.

In the bathroom, she slipped into Nick's terrycloth robe. Taken from a businessman's hotel, the once spongy and swan-white terrycloth was now splotched with coffee and frayed at the sleeves. She flipped her hair behind her shoulders, stooped down and splashed water on her face. All the towels were in the hamper; she used the robe's sleeve as, from the mirror, her eyes gazed back at her eyes. ("Witch," Nick had whispered in the dim of La Sirena that night she'd decided to come and live with him. He'd hooked a strand of her hair with his finger and wound it around her wrist in a cuff.) How she hated wearing white; this robe made her skin look moon-pale, and her crow-black hair, falling down now over the collar in dark hanks, lackluster.

She should jog, she thought, eat more vegetables. Maybe haul Nick's bike out for a ride along the river.

(But in that heat?)

Forty-five minutes later, she was still in his bathrobe, sipping a second cup of coffee. She did not particularly care for *The Washington Post*; it printed too many comics, all crammed together, so that she had to hold it up to her face and squint to make out the words. No matter, she always read "Zippy the Pinhead." Now she was on "Dear Abby" (and she had yet to read "Hints from Heloise" or the horoscopes or the movie schedule). Her novel—or rather, The Novel, as it loomed dimly in the corner of her mind—piled the dining room table, Chapter 1 in a Tower of Pisa-like stack of drafts, Chapter 2, Chapter 3, Chapter 9, and 11 all dusted like Nick's flea-market oak tabletop itself, as though by some flying gremlin, with shreds of eraser. Post-its peeped from the layers of the scattered stacks, once-optimistic flags of lemon-yellow long faded from the sun that poured in every morning from the balcony. In the middle of this mess, its black cord drooping over the end of the table and tangling across the floor, sat the toad-like interruption of a telephone.

*Lovers Lost* was The Novel's original title, which Consuelo now judged too dramatic, lacking art. For two days in April, she'd called it *Far Journeys*. Nick had snickered—*Far Journeys* was the name of a book about out-of-body experiences; he'd thumbed through it in the Georgetown Barnes & Noble. Then—it came to her in a beautiful dream (she was a bird soaring over a glassy sea)—*Lost Horizon*, until Nick told her that was the title of a classic Hollywood movie. Photography had seemed so simple—you point your camera and click (she used to exaggerate)—but coming up with a title for The Novel was torture, like the writing itself, slow, so lead-footed slow, as if for each word she had to wade through an ocean of muck.

It was—so far—about an American actor named Ned and a half-Mexican investment banker named Carmen O'Reilly, who met in a bar in Mexico City, which sounded sleazy to say, but it was El Tritón, a cutting-edge cool kind of bar (faux crocodile banquettes, Billie Holiday sweetly moaning on the sound system, geometric little chèvre and raspberry-smoked shrimp sushis). Plus they both knew the owner, the heir to a beerbottling fortune named Roberto Chávez.

So, what? *What?* Would Carmen O'Reilly give up her investment banking career (so chic she looked in her alligator heels and shark-gray Armani suits) and move to LA but not be able to work because she couldn't get *Tío* Sam to slap out the Green Card? (Even if, mangoes to the U.S. Immigration and Naturalization Service, her granddaddy was a railroad engineer from Pittsburgh?) Unemployed, alone in the apartment all day, surrounded by pots of dehydrated ferns, Carmen O'Reilly would laze on Ned's pigskin sofa watching TV, licking up spoonful after spoonful of Chunky Monkey ice cream. She would grow fatter and fatter, her face puffing around her eyes, her chin swelling as if it were filled with sand. Her thighs, striped with stretch marks like welts, would rub together (in the most annoying way) when she walked. Until one day—and it would be a hot and gritty afternoon with the pounding of cars on the freeway and a sooty, Raymond Chandler kind of Santa Ana soughing through the palm trees—Carmen would waddle over to her closet and find that she had nothing left to wear but… (she would sink to her knees and sob into her fleshy hands)… a black muumuu. And so that chapter ended: *She knew her life was rotten like an orange left on the tree after the harvest. Finally it fell*, plunk, *on the dirt*.

That draft lay deep, near the bottom of the pile.

Or, more optimistically, would Ned decide to stay in Mexico City ( *"Dig the energy," he liked to say in a voice as smoothly nutty as Chunky Monkey ice cream*), and land a role as a DEA agent in a TV Azteca soap opera?

Nah. She had crumpled that and aimed it at the window: *tik*.

Next: Consuelo tried flying Carmen and Ned in Roberto Chávez's Lear jet to the Revillagigedos. There they came upon an uninhabited crescent-shaped beach fringed with coconut trees. Such beautiful coconut trees, snake-slim and lushly feathered, silvered by the sun and the reflections from the water. They began to build a hut, setting the moon-white shells—so playfully, like children—into the sandy adobe of the walls. Which was, she realized as soon as she lifted the pen from the paper, like: Hello Zippy!

Maybe, Consuelo wondered—and she raised her frayed sleeve over the pile of it—a tsunami should wash the whole thing away.

*"Sunk costs are sunk,"* as Carmen O'Reilly would say, her voice smoky, her eyes batting at Ned over the rim of her Chunky Monkey ice cream carton (—or tin camp mug?).

When she looked at Ned, who was wearing his DEA agent sunglasses, what Carmen O'Reilly saw was her own reflection, huge, bloated, distorted. Like the face of something that slithered through the deep.

And then what did Ned say? *What?* (*Water makes things wet?*)

Nick hadn't read a word of it. ("Art doesn't light my fire," he'd said once. He'd raked his hands into her hair and breathed into the hollow of her throat: "You do.") What Nick read, deep in his four-thousand-dollar Roche-Bobois to-bacco-leather sofa, his bare feet up on his battered college footlocker of a coffee table, was *The Wall Street Journal*, which he loudly rustled, his arms spread wide, the paper a screen across his face.

Could that stink be burning apples?

Maybe cherries. Whatever it was, in her mind, Consuelo could see it blackly bubbling, the filling of a pie on the bottom of—Mrs. Tuttle's?—oven. Whatever it was, it was giving her a headache, a dull pinch like two thumbs cratering into the backs of eyes.

Of course, had there been an actual fire, someone would have rung the fire department. Still, she considered, it was odd that a smoke alarm hadn't sounded. When she'd first moved in, an only slightly over-browned piece of toast (not even a puff of smoke!) had set Nick's off wailing like a banshee. How it had made her mitt her hands over her ears and cringe! The instant it stopped, she'd climbed up on the stepstool and popped the batteries.

"That's illegal, you know," Nick said. She'd smirked as she chucked the batteries in the trash.

It occurred to her now to slide open the glass doors to the balcony—framed by Nick's burlap-brown curtains, the sky looked deep and invitingly clear. But she didn't want to suck in more of that stink. On an afternoon just last week she'd opened the doors and the stink of charred meat had whuffed in so strong, the whole scene developed in her mind like a Polaroid: Mrs. Tuttle in a fetal stroke-victim curl, and smoking furiously on her stovetop, the lump of hamburger. Consuelo flew to phone the front desk. "Oh," said the clerk, his voice acid green with condescension. "That's just a barbecue, oh, *waaaaay-way* up on the 11th floor. It's been taken care of." Later, she happened to see Mrs. Tuttle in the elevator and she explained, "It's the negative pressure, honey. You open your balcony door, your apartment just sucks the smell right in, *whish!*" Mrs. Tuttle had waved her hands at herself like flippers. "You don't know where in diddly it's coming from."

Consuelo had graduated from the American School in Mexico City; still, she'd had to phone Nick at the World Bank to ask him, "What does Mrs. Tuttle mean, 'where in diddly'?" He'd laughed—and in her mind she could see him, his Greek God nose high, laughing from deep behind his sternum, the whole of him—even his feet, Italian tasseled loafers up on his desk—so smooth and suave like Tom Cruise. Yes, Tom Cruise deciding the hydraulic fate of the Nicaraguan People. "Hell," Nick said when he'd finally caught his breath. "She means, where in hell."

The smell from hell. But the air conditioning was so cool, so comfortable. Now, still on the sofa, she held the corner of *The Post* with one hand and tipped up the mug for another swallow of coffee, which was cold. She'd finished "Hints from Heloise" (three nifty new uses for aluminum foil), and was about to peruse her horoscope (Pisces) when, with a toad-like croak, the telephone rang. It rang again, *rrrbit*.

The receiver felt at once light and heavy in her hand the way her zoom lens had felt. (Who was shooting with it now? What scenes?)

"*Tenía un presentimiento.*" It was her friend the marine biologist Sofia von Holtman, calling from Mexico City. She'd had a premonition. "Are you all right?"

"*Sí,*" Consuelo made her voice soothing as a hand laid on a furrowed brow. "*De veras..*" Really. The cord of the telephone snaked behind her as she padded into the kitchen to reheat her coffee. The linoleum felt warm on her feet. She placed her mug in the microwave. "How's tricks?" She punched the button for HOT BEVERAGE.

She'd made another field trip to the Revillagigedos, Sofia said, and just flown back from a conference at UC San Diego. A professor at the Universidad Nacional, Sofia had published a long list of articles and three books, no less, the most recent—it would be out in the fall with University of Arizona Press, she was saying—on the mating rituals of the blue-footed boobie.

Consuelo listened, the phone jammed between her ear and her shoulder, to the soft patter of Sofia's voice. She planted her elbow on the counter as she watched her mug in the microwave hum-whirr around and around and around. She could see Sofia seated at her desk, her pale dishpan blonde hair tucked behind her ears. She would be wearing a pastel linen jacket and a tasteful strand of tiny perfect pearly shells. Behind her there would be the neat rows of books, the filing cabinet and the poster—PROTEGE A LAS BALLENAS—of the breaching whale with its sun-sparkled muzzle and its tiny swollen-looking eye. Consuelo liked Sofia, she really did; they'd had a grand time together in the Revillagigedos those months ago. But honestly, how could anyone get so hepped about those beady-eyed birds? Blue-footed boobies. They made such a nasty racket, and on that one island, their guano—gag, there were carpets of it.

Oh, she had a hammer of a headache. Careful to avoid the ring in her eyebrow, she touched her fingertips to her eyelid.

"And your novel?" Sofia asked. Finally.

Consuelo sighed: to even think about The Novel made her stone-heavy with fatigue. And anyway, could La Profesora Sofia von Holtman really give a diddly about a cooked-up character named Carmen O'Reilly? And her American actor boyfriend Ned (who just might—Consuelo hadn't yet pinned it down—take that gig playing a DEA agent in a TV Azteca soap)? "I'm not sure yet where I'm aiming," Consuelo tried to explain it, and as she did, she carried the telephone over to the sofa and she plopped her body down, *whumph*, on the cushions.

And how was it living in the Watergate? Sofia wanted to know. "Do you ever see Senator McDudley?"

"On CNN, like the rest of the planet." (Consuelo wasn't going to mention that she'd gotten into the elevator with Senator McDudley twice, and both times he'd farted.) "Actually, the Watergate is very—" She was going to say, quiet, but a *thud* sounded in the apartment below, *thud, thud,* and another *THUD*. She could feel the vibrations through the cushions.

"*¿Bueno?*" Sofia said. "Are you there?"

"*Caramba.*" Consuelo sat up. Remodeling, she explained with another, extravagant sigh. Everyone in the Watergate, it seemed, was doing it: the granite countertops, the herringbone white-oak floors, the Sub-Zero refrigerators. *The Post* was spattered with the advertisements. She rolled her eyes. "It'll go on for *an eternity.*"

"You can use a library, can't you?"

*Thud.*

"Yeaaaaah." Consuelo slouched lower into the sofa. It simply fried her, the idea of hauling around all her papers, the little Post-it notes and drafts and sketches and ideas, the pencils, the eraser (like a broken lens cap, the eraser would swim in the depths of her bag with mint wrappers and Metro tickets and wads of tissues.)

But—*thud! thud!*—there were other things to talk about: La Sirena was a Tuscan restaurant now, the Pesto Presto, had Consuelo heard? They'd collaged the walls with shellacked basil leaves. (Yes, her photographs were still there, though that big one with the leaping manta ray, they'd moved it to over the back door to the parking lot.) Rigoberto Castro's divorce was all over *Reforma*, his wife wanted five hundred million dollars and a penthouse in New York.

"May she boil his balls," Consuelo said.

"He was such a *cabrón*, wasn't he?" Sofia had written the text to go with Consuelo's photographs which Rigoberto Castro published in a book—after he'd edited it to shreds of tourist-grubbing fluff.

"*Cabronsísimo*," Consuelo agreed.

Another *THUD* and the *krashshsh* of shattering glass.

But Sofia had to run—she had a classroom full of students waiting. "*Cuídate.*" Take care of yourself, she said.

"*Besote.*" Big kiss. Consuelo made a pretty little smacking sound and with her lips still pinched together, hung up the phone, *clack*. She had an urge to kick it. Instead, she rubbed her foot.

She touched the coffee to her lips: cold. Out the window to the balcony the sky was ablaze with an empty summer light. Already it was near noon. Time was flying fast. She felt it passing over her like the shadow of a bird. But sunk deep into the sofa, her body dead-fish-limp, she'd melded with the cushions. How could she possibly write? And she detested libraries, they were so dreary, so full of nose-pickers.

The phone croaked again. "Finally!" Nick sounded agitated.

"What do you mean, *finally?*"

"Well, what happened?"

"What do you mean, *what happened?*"

"That burning smell—"

Consuelo sniffed. The air stank of burnt sugar, though she now realized, as she'd been talking with Sofia it had turned acrid with melting plastic. She clinked her mug down on the coffee table; the liquid made a little *slop* over the side.

"Check it out," Nick said. It was the very same tone of voice, Consuelo thought, that Ned the TV Azteca DEA agent would use: *That black Cadillac down there in the parking lot? Check it out.*

She lowered her voice, to make fun of him: "I'll check it out."

"Call me back."

"OK. I'll call you back." She pouted the way she did when he could see it. "*Ciao.*"

She didn't bother to say, save the world.

She ambled over to the sliding door to the balcony for some fresh air, and it was as she touched the handle that she spotted the crowd of people, bright dots of color on the grass of the inner garden, six stories below. She pulled open the door and *whush*, in came a blast of summer, billowing in the curtains and sending the open newspaper on the table *zig* and *zag* to the floor. Several pages of The Novel flew off the table behind it, skittering and flapping like birds with broken wings. Deep in the apartment, a door slammed shut.

She recognized some of the people—there was the front desk clerk in his navy-blue jacket, and that bottle-blonde Springer woman in her white track suit and a turban; and three of the elderly ladies she always grudged a hello to in the elevator but whose names she couldn't remember. That pug darted around their feet, frantic with excitement, *bark! Bark!* The faces were looking up right at her, so many moons of worry. Consuelo waved—too serenely, she realized, because no one waved back. She cinched the bathrobe belt tighter, and she called down over the railing, her voice Adult Concerned: "What's going on?"

"Oh my God," a woman's voice floated up, thin as a thread.

"Go up to the roof!" Mr. Danforth, the building manager, made a bullhorn with his hands. "Go now, and use the stairs!

In a flash, she was in the hallway. Smoke hovered near the ceiling in a lacy agitated cloud. She covered her mouth with her sleeve, sprinted down the hall past the elevators to the stairs, and dashed up, holding high the hem of the bathrobe, two steps at a time—seventh floor, eighth floor, ninth floor. On the tenth, the air still stank of burning plastic, but she could drop the sleeve and breathe; she climbed more slowly, though still fast, to the eleventh, the twelfth, the thirteenth. At the roof, she threw her weight against the bar on the door and it swung open.

"Mrs. Tuttle!" Consuelo, her chest heaving, squinted into the glare.

"Oh honey!" Mrs. Tuttle gasped and took a step back. "Are you all right?"

Consuelo nodded.

Behind her stood Mr. Tuttle, his face, ponderous with jowls, beaded with perspiration. He wore a sweat-soaked Hawaiian shirt stamped with little pineapples.

"I thought you'd gone downstairs!" Mrs. Tuttle said. "We would have knocked on your door."

"Where was the fire?" Consuelo addressed Mr. Tuttle, who regarded her warily from under his scraggly eyebrows. He shielded his eyes, as if making a salute.

"He's not got his hearing aid in," Mrs. Tuttle said. "We ran out in such a hurry when the fire trucks came! Mr. Danforth called the fire department, oh, and a very long time after he should have. I'm not sure where the fire is, but I'll wager it's Thelma Chávez's apartment."

"Where is that?" Consuelo hadn't begun to sort out the names and locations of all Nick's neighbors. She dabbed at her forehead with the sleeve of the robe.

"Why, it's the apartment directly below yours."

The thudding, the breaking glass—that must have been the firemen! And *the warm kitchen floor!* A stone of fear plashed through the surface of her and slowly settled down heavy and cold in the pit of her stomach.

"Nick's?"

Mrs. Tuttle was saying, "But it's so hard to tell where anything's coming from in this building. I figure something was probably smoldering in there for hours. I'll bet the maid left something in the toaster oven. Thelma's in Florida, you know."

Consuelo didn't know. She didn't even know who Thelma Chávez was. She said, "How long have you been up here?"

"Oh my!" said Mrs. Tuttle, fanning herself with her hand. Her wedding band flashed. "With this sun, we're going to end up broiled like a pair of lobsters! I'd say *at least* twenty minutes."

Mr. Tuttle boomed: "We have been waiting here for twenty minutes!"

"Yes, dear." Mrs. Tuttle and made a downward motion with the flat of her hand that meant, *Drop the volume.*

Consuelo said, "I didn't hear any sirens."

"That's because you're on the back side of the building," Mrs. Tuttle said. "Plus you've got those extra-thick glass doors, and the noise of your air conditioning at full throttle, I'm sure."

Consuelo brushed a pebble off the sole of her foot. She put her foot on the hot gravel again; there was nowhere else to put it. She glared at Mrs. Tuttle's espadrilles. They were the exact same Pepto-Bismol pink of her skirt. Her hair, the color fake as shoe polish, looked as if it had been screwed down onto her head. And those little pearl clip earrings! The badges of the damned.

Mrs. Tuttle was pursing her lips—at the ring in Consuelo's eyebrow, no doubt, and her coffee-stained man's bathrobe, and her bare feet, and her hair, which was mashed on the side she'd slept on it. Mrs. Tuttle's right eyebrow lifted up, a little inverted V: "You weren't still asleep, were you?"

Consuelo coolly focused her gaze. "Yes," she lied.

She hadn't brushed her teeth, either. She ran her tongue over the front of them. Gritty, they tasted bitter, of coffee. *¿Y qué?* So what? She turned her back and began walking, gingerly over the gravel, towards the railing at the rim of the roof. She was curious to see the firemen, what would happen—and if the fire burned into Nick's apartment? *¡Andale!* Ugly curtains, a lot of lousy junk. As for *Lovers Lost, Far Journeys, Lost Horizon,* (whatever The Novel was), not a soul on this planet would miss it—certainly not Nick. He would fret for a moment over his Roche-Bobois tobacco-colored sofa, because it had cost him four thousand dollars, and his suits and his Italian shoes and his battery-operated rack crammed with who knows how many dozen Hermès ties (enough anyway that he could have used the cash to feed a few thousand starving *campesinos*). He'd punch his fist into his palm, like a baseball into a mitt, *punch, punch,* but then softened up a bit, he would throw his head back, crazy number-cruncher boy, and huff out a laugh.

"Sunk costs are sunk!" And Nick was right, she knew this in the marrow of her bones.

"Excuse me?" Mrs. Tuttle called to her.

How Consuelo wished she had her camera up here! An airplane had left a stripe in the sky, like a scrape on the inside of a blue glazed bowl. There was so little noise; even the cars down on the expressway were muffled in the distance. Everything seemed to be happening silently, the flock of starlings wheeling below in a burst of confetti, the trees shimmering in the oven-hot air. Just over her head—she ducked—a gull dove and then swooped down, towards the great sparkling belt of the Potomac. In the middle of the river, a white boat cruised towards Memorial Bridge, its wake trailing behind like the train of a dress.

Yes, she knew how to swallow the world into a lens: the light dancing on the curve of the river, the gull (yellow legs tucked against its breast) as it swooped down, those clouds in the distance, the ones laying low over the trees like shreds of lace, or wisps of smoke. She had been brilliant in the Revillagigedos, monstrous with that power. And if, suddenly, she had been drawn down deep into the sea, to ride for a brief and miraculous moment a manta ray, here she was in the sky, flung like a fish out of water: to see.

She stood now with her hands curled on the sun-warmed railing. It was a curious sensation: the air on her face felt so silky and somehow viscous. Her feet rested lightly on the gravel, as though she had suddenly lost a great deal of weight. From here she could see the crowd of her neighbors, far below in the garden. The Springer woman's turban was a dot like a Q-tip. And there was the pug, tiny as a flea, its barks pinpricks of sound. From a hydrant in the bushes, a hose like an albino python slithered out and up a ladder. A fireman shouted—tiny, tinny voice— "Get back, get back!"

The soles of their shoes crunching loudly, the Tuttles had come up behind her, but they could not reach her, they could not touch her—the hem of her robe, the heel of her soft gravel-dimpled foot—she was floating up, up and over the railing, higher, up higher.

Higher.

Soon the monuments of the city rose up, the obelisk, the dome, the great hulking masses of white. Washington was a very green city—she could see that now; it was a sea of green, so very lush, such a richness that obscured the sidewalks, the people. Cars moved, wee toys, disappearing into maws of green. A gull flapped past, so close that her fingers could have brushed its feathers. Beneath her, a jay: quick flit of blue. It was so easy to relax into this air that held her like a womb. Spreading her arms, she soared. Her hair unfurled behind her, flowing like water. Soon the belt of the bathrobe came loose. She was moving towards the center of the Mall now, her shadow flitting over the runway of grass. After a while—she was nearing the Library of Congress—the bathrobe fell open; she rocked her shoulders, gently, and let it slip from her body. It landed, as in the arms of a gentle goddess, in the branches of a cherry tree.

Which startled a tourist who happened to have been posing for his wife.

"Why d'ya move?" his wife said. Her camera hung from her swan-like neck on a rainbow strap. She wore a diamond stud in her nostril, designer sunglasses, spike-heeled alligator sandals, and a parrot-red T-shirt that clung to her body like a dancer's leotard. Her name was Carmen O'Reilly. His name was Ned. They'd flown in from LAX.

"Did you see that?" Ned pointed to what looked like a towel swagged over the topmost branches of the cherry tree.

"OK then," Carmen said, pointing to a different tree, "move over there."

"But didn't you see it drop?" Ned was so beautiful, the way his face registered every nuance of an emotion. He was up for an Emmy for his role as the rookie cop in a made-for-TV movie, *DEA: Dead or Alive*. But here, in his three-day beard, a baseball cap, and shorts, only a few people had recognized him. At the Air & Space Museum, a grandmother from Iowa had asked him to autograph her plane ticket.

"What?" Already the blister on Carmen's bunion was bleeding. And right now—Ned *knew* it—Carmen could've scarfed down an elephant! (Wasn't this just like Ned? Diddling around.) She wanted to get going, get the photo and find Bullfeathers. Senator McDudley—they'd sat next to him on the plane—had said that place served gonzo hamburgers and onion rings.

"Come on," she said. "Bust a nut."

"But didn't you?" Ned had heard it drop, he was sure of it. He craned his neck. He did not see a soul on the roof.

*Julia Meek*

# Be Careful of Desire

JULIA MEEK, the author of *Lollapalooza* (Nimrod House, 1996), which means "a wild tale," grew up in Washington, D.C., where she worked as a photographer, storyteller, inspirational speaker for parents of ADHD children, and as a manager in a psychiatrist's office. She has had humorous stories and articles published in diverse journals and magazines, including *Medical Economics*, where she explored what goes on at home when Mom and Dad are at a sexually transmitted disease convention. A single mom who has finally seen the last of her eight children off to college or better after thirty-six years, she is currently starting her second life.

Pulling up in front of the house with my boyfriend Taylor, I saw Harrison's black Saab parked at the curb. Harrison was my daughter's boyfriend.

"That kid's here so often you'll need to get him his own parking sticker," Taylor said. He'd had his sticker for three years now.

He turned into the neighbor's drive then, slamming his big Suburban in reverse, accelerated into my driveway. Sometimes I held my breath when he drove, not because he frightened me but because I wished I had that kind of confidence. He used his side mirrors instead of turning around, assuming that the right road would always be there waiting for him. And it was.

"My house is awash in hormones," I complained.

"With the way Melody looks, it's only been a matter of time," Taylor said. The bucket seat rocked slightly under his weight. I thought of it as a giant leather hand cupping his haunches.

"Whenever I go into a room, I find them in some corner kissing." I reached over and grabbed the inside of his thigh briefly. I liked the way his muscles tensed under the skin. Shorts were good for this.

Taylor stomped on the emergency brake with such force that I wondered if he intended the car to take root. "You better watch out," he said. "Next he'll be boinking her."

"Come on." I made a face like I was annoyed but it was only a token face. He liked it if I acted upset when he talked this way. When we were alone we said all manner of things about boinking. "I've had the sex talk with Melody," I said. "But I don't think she listens to half the stuff we tell her."

"At our age we don't have anything she wants," he said.

"I told her to wait until she's in college."

Halfway out the door, he paused. "Oh sure," he laughed. "Did you?"

"Yes, but not because I wanted to." Unlike Taylor, I had to use the running board to reach the ground.

"I suspect your mother was a lot more on top of things than you are." Taylor slammed the door and clicked the keyless entry to lock the car.

"Believe me, my mother had nothing to do with my not getting laid," I said.

My front door was never locked. Taylor pushed it open and stood back while I walked ahead of him into the empty living room. Three puffy gray cats lounged on the sofa watching a television program about orcas giving birth. Taylor took off his windbreaker and hung it on the back of a chair. Settling down at the end of the couch nearest the lamp, he picked up the newspaper with the crossword puzzle in it. He'd left the carefully folded section on the coffee table before we'd gone to the movies. A pen clicked thoughtfully against his front teeth. For a big man, he had a small mouth.

"Where are the young lovers?" he asked. "You may already be too late."

"You're not helping." These conversations made me defensive. Sometimes I felt as if I was at war with Melody and sometimes I felt as if I was at war with myself. At other, more confusing moments, I felt as if I was still fighting my mother, which was silly because she'd been dead for ten years.

I walked around the room trying to detect movement above me. I heard the distant rise and fall of commercials on a television upstairs. "I have a rule that Melody can't have boys up to her room," I said.

"You have a lot of rules you don't follow through on," Taylor said without looking up. "Why are you so excited about this one?"

"Because she's so blatant. Why can't she just have sex when I'm in another state?" I said.

His round blue eyes regarded me over the rims of his glasses.

I went to the bottom of the stairs and yelled up. "Melody!"

I heard footsteps in the upstairs hall. A door closed with a whispered click.

"Melody, you are not allowed to have boys in your room!" I shouted. I started to take the steps two at a time but had to pause and catch my breath.

Melody materialized at the top of the stairs. "Honestly, Mom. Chill out! What is with you?"

She stood with her hands on her hips and her lips pushed out. I could practically smell the mating juices wafting down the stairwell. "What do you *think* we're doing?" she asked.

"It doesn't matter what you're doing or not doing." I moved up a step, wondering where Harrison was. "It's the rule."

Melody turned to glance quickly back at her room. I imagined she was checking to see if she'd pulled the leopard comforter up to cover the rumple of disheveled sheets. "It's a stupid rule," she said.

"It just doesn't look good," I said, knowing as soon as the words were out of my mouth that I sounded like my mother.

"We were just watching television," Melody said. In the dim light of the stairwell, her features looked smeared. "You and Taylor do it all the time. He makes funny noises."

"He falls asleep and snores," I said, knowing that snoring wasn't the only sound she heard.

Sometimes Taylor had a board meeting in the evening and turned up wearing his corporate suit instead of his carpenter clothes. The pants, still creased from the dry cleaners, made me want to melt him. My hands became busy creatures under the flaps of his suit jacket. He'd groan with pleasure and frustration. When we heard the distinctive plup-plup of Melody's slippers on the uncarpeted stairs as she came down to do her laundry we'd stop fooling around and adjust ourselves.

"And you guys are right in the living room where anyone could see you!" Melody continued, her voice rising. "What would my friends think?"

Time to switch channels, I decided. "Driving comes with a lot of responsibilities," I began.

"Yeah?" Her eyes focused on me. "And your point is?"

"Your learner's permit expires in three weeks," I said. Frenetic barking came from below. The nature program must have shifted to wild dogs.

"I'm doing real well in Driver's Ed." Melody sat down on the top step. Our eyes were almost even.

"Whether or not I let you get your driver's license depends on what kind of judgment you display."

All three cats bounded up the stairs, trying to get away from the television dogs. Their footfalls were heavy. They sounded like small children running through the house.

"If you can't follow the rules I set down at home, then how can I be sure you'll obey the rules of the road?"

"This is blackmail," Melody said. I noticed that she didn't grab one of the cats and bury her face in its deep neck fur the way she usually did when she was stressed. Harrison was allergic to cats. His eyes swelled shut.

I climbed a step.

"OK. I got it." She threw up her hands. "No guys in my room."

"By the way, where is Harrison?" I asked.

She flicked her head back toward the bathroom door. "He locked himself in." A toilet flushed. "He's scared you're going to yell at him."

"Tell him it's safe to come out now."

↣

I stopped talking to my mother the summer of 1963 after I began to drive and make out on a regular basis. When my parents realized that teaching me to drive wasn't healthy for their relationship, they hired an instructor. Mother thought it was important for me to take some of the lessons at night in the city so that I would be comfortable driving in downtown Washington, D.C., and not just out in the suburbs where we lived. The instructor had me drive him to Hains Point where we would make out.

For my lessons Mother insisted I wear flats and a shirtwaist dress.

"People don't get dressed up to drive," I protested.

"Driving is a passage and you need to dress like the young lady you are becoming," she said.

"Mother, this isn't like a date." I wondered if we'd do more French kissing. The texture of tongues was something I'd never thought about before.

"Of course it isn't." She reached out to pat down my round collar. I jerked away. "You're missing the point."

A horn sounded in front of our Spring Valley home.

"There he is," she said. "Now drive carefully and remember not to change lanes without signaling first."

The instructor went to a local college and had shiny copper hair that glinted in the streetlight. In spite of the fire in his hair I had no fire in my belly for him, but it was pleasant and I thought of these lessons as a two-fer. After I got my license I never saw the instructor again but I did take my boyfriend, Vince, back to Hains Point.

Vince was the gatekeeper at a small swimming pool on the grounds of Beauvoir, a private elementary school. My parents had bought a family membership and Mother dropped me off to swim every afternoon when she picked up my brother from camp. I knew Vince from Saint Albans, which was the brother school to National Cathedral from which I had just graduated.

That winter I had even signed up for Religion Club so I could stand next to him once a week. I loved the way his thick wrestler's neck grew out of his white shirt collar. Every now and then I was close enough to breathe in the Old Spice aftershave. Once he turned suddenly and asked me if I had a cold because I kept sniffing. I coughed and told him I was taking time-release Coricidin. After that, I breathed him in more carefully.

"You're working here?" I asked on my first afternoon at the pool. I couldn't believe my luck.

"This is great," he said. "You're the first person over six and under forty who's come through." He sat on a folding chair with yellow nylon strapping. The seat stretched low under his weight.

"You want to see my membership card?" I began ransacking my white wicker purse, which opened on brass hinges like a book. Combs. Brushes. Chap Stick. Tissues. But where was the card?

"Not necessary." He shook his head. A film of perspiration glistened on his forehead. "What're you doing here?"

"My whole family went to Beauvoir so we get a discount." I ticked my head toward the school up the hill and imagined placing my hands flat against his chest. I hadn't seen chest hairs up close in the sunlight. "I like swimming," I added.

"You could do this whole pool in three strokes," he said.

"If I stay home, my mother makes me baby-sit." I sat down on the lounge chair next to the chain link fence to get my purse under control. A packet of exploded Kleenex fell into my lap. I couldn't remember if I'd used the tissues to wipe my brother's nose. I jammed them back in my purse. "I can't use the car in the afternoons," I said. Suddenly I worried that I might be making the lounge chair hang down too far. I stood up. "This way I get out of the house. Besides, I like to practice diving."

He leaned back in his chair. It squealed. Heavy thighs emerged from his brown and green madras trunks. "What's your best dive?" he asked.

"The jackknife." I tried to suck my stomach in.

"You look like a diver."

I tipped my head, watching the way his dark hair fell over his sweaty forehead.

"Long and—" His chair lurched forward.

"It's also called an inward, because I do it toward the board." Was it good to look like a diver? I wondered.

"If nobody else shows, I'll come watch. It's pretty slow. Everyone's out of town." He glanced down at the open notebook. There were only a few names. Some were written in childish block letters. The number two pencil was placed carefully inside the wire spiral so it wouldn't roll away.

"I can show you how to do the dive." I hugged the folded towel against my breast. I could smell the Ivory Snow detergent my mother used.

"Not me. It's too dangerous."

The word dangerous made my feet itch. I slid out of my flip-flops. The cement was firecracker hot. I jiggled from foot to foot.

"You could break your neck and there goes your whole life." He reached over and twisted the handle above a wall spigot. Water gushed out of the dark metal throat.

I worked my bare feet up and down in the puddle. The deck steamed.

"I'm going to Yale in the fall," he said.

"Great." I knew all about him being a Merit Scholar too, but that wasn't what I wanted from him.

"How about wrestling?" I asked. "Isn't that dangerous?"

He'd wrestled heavyweight on the varsity for two years. Last winter I'd finally worked up the nerve to go to one of the matches and watched from the back row. He'd been sitting on the bench waiting to go on when he turned to look over the crowd and saw me. I fled.

"If you get caught in a full nelson, but that's illegal." He picked up a pale blue towel with bleach spots and wiped his chest. I imagined my hair trailing across his skin, the ends capturing drops of moisture and pulling them along. He balled the towel up in his lap. "Didn't I see you at one of the matches?"

I nodded. My face flushed hotter than the summer day.

"I looked for you afterwards," he said.

"You did?" I said, noticing how much he smiled. Maybe his teeth just looked whiter because he was tan. "I had to catch the bus."

The entire area was flooded. Water ran under the chain link fence and down the rocky path to the parking lot. Muddy rivulets spread out like veins.

"Pretty soon I'll be able to swim right here," I said.

"Put your suit on and come back and talk to me," he said.

"OK."

"You never talked very much in Religion Club."

I ducked into the dressing room to change. I couldn't tell him that I had difficulty standing next to him and breathing, much less talking.

I had two bathing suits, a green-and-white-checkered two-piece and a turquoise tank with howitzer-shell-shaped cups. Both had come from Garfinkel's. I was afraid I looked fat in the two-piece so I put on the turquoise tank with the pointy breast cones.

"This is the worst book." Vince threw down the paperback he was reading as I came out of the dressing room. The denseness of the July heat muffled the cries from the pool on the other side of the changing area. "Nice suit," he said.

I spread my towel out on the lounge chair and sat facing him. "What're you reading?"

"*Equus.*"

"About the boy who stabbed out the horses' eyes?"

"Yes," he said. "It's crazy."

I decided not to tell him how much I'd liked it. He'd think I was sick. "I'm reading Eugene O'Neill."

"Summer reading is such a drag."

I didn't mention that I was reading it by choice. I was halfway through the complete works.

"You really look good," he said.

"Thanks. I have to wear a one-piece if I'm going to dive," I said, embarrassed by the attention. "Why are you reading a book you don't like?"

"It was the shortest one on the list of recommended titles for freshmen." He took off his heavy tortoise-shell glasses and put them on top of the splayed paperback. "It's too hot to read." He rubbed his forehead.

"How blind are you?" I asked, touching the smooth plastic of the glasses.

"Pretty bad."

"Let me see," I said.

He got up and sat on the end of my lounge chair. Without glasses, his brown eyes looked soft and unfocused. They were deeper than I expected. Bending forward from the waist he rubbed his forehead against the Lycra covering my stomach. The weight of the summer heat tamped down the sound of the cicadas. I held my breath. "I can't believe how hot it is," he said into my stomach. I could feel his mouth moving right through my body to my spine.

I put my hands over his ears. They stuck out slightly but thick auburn hair covered them. I brought his face up to mine. His lips were little pillows of flesh that flattened against my mouth but then got more muscular as they chased into me.

From time to time he pulled away to check the path for swimmers. A string of saliva lagged behind when we separated. His hand moved up to the stiff cups on my bathing suit. The straps on the lounge chair stretched and whimpered as our weight shifted.

"Are those real?" he said.

"Let's see." I peeled the top half of my suit down.

"My God!" He jerked back and glanced frantically around. "What're you doing?"

"Looking." The air felt good on my bare skin.

"Anyone might come." His fingers dug into my shoulders.

"I thought you wanted—"

"I didn't expect you to actually do it." He kept glancing over his shoulder and then back at my breasts.

"Why not?" I said.

Perspiration ran down his cheeks. "I've never—"

"OK."

"No. Wait." He swallowed and closed his eyes. Pulling me against him he rubbed his bare chest back and forth across my nipples. "Oh, Jesus," he whispered again and again. "Oh Jesus."

It felt so good I couldn't speak.

࿒

The monologue on *The Johnny Carson Show* was just ending when I sat down on the edge of Mother's bed. She muted the volume and set her empty dish on the bedside table. Every night at eleven-thirty she allowed herself one scoop of pistachio ice cream. At midnight Dad came up from his office in the basement and they went to bed.

I began to rub her legs. She suffered from varicose veins and enjoyed having her legs messaged. The skin was freckled and smooth. It amazed me that she never had to shave. She didn't sweat either; she just got very red when she was hot. Now she sat propped up on a rose satin pillow. A blue hair net covered the silver pin curls nesting in her dark hair.

"You were out with Vince?" she asked.

"We saw *The Great Escape* at the Uptown," I said, not including the side trip to Hains Point. "It was very exciting."

"You see him a lot." She rearranged the layers of her creamy nylon nightgown.

"I like him a lot," I said self-consciously. I'd gotten out of the habit of talking to her but the rhythmic motion of my hands up and down her glassy shins and the distant impersonal chatter of the television relaxed me.

"What's he interested in?" she said.

I was disappointed. I wanted to discuss how I felt about him. "He wants to be an archeologist—dig up ancient people—and study them."

"Where?"

"Egypt, the Southwest. Dry places where remains are preserved." I imagined lying in a tent with the desert wind beating at the canvas walls and his weight on top of me. The dry heat would make our sweat evaporate. We'd have to get a double cot.

"I meant where is he going to college," Mother said.

"Yale."

"He must be very smart."

"Yes." I was going to a small women's college outside of Boston, not a Yale. I was going to get away from home.

"What does Vince think about what you intend to do?" Mother crossed her legs so I'd work on the other one.

"Being a war correspondent?" I shrugged. "He thinks it's too dangerous."

In fact, we didn't spend much time talking about what we wanted to do. Less than an hour ago we'd been lying on a blanket in the grass by the Potomac. Weeping willows lined the sidewalk that ran along the riverbank. In places the feathery branches trailed to the ground, creating a private cave. Random breezes played across the water, stirring the leaves and tracing whispers of pleasure across our bare skin. His white Jockey briefs made him easy to find in the gloom. I loved the way the thick stock of his penis nestled against my palm and grew to fit so handily inside my curved fingers.

"Going to war is not very ladylike." Mother folded her hands on her stomach and looked at me. "Journalist sounds much better."

"I'm not *going* to war; I want to write about it," I said.

"Slow down, you're going to take off a layer of skin."

"Sorry."

'Boys don't like girls who are too forward," she said.

"What's that got to do with it?" I asked, flexing my wrist.

"War is an aggressive act." She reached up and adjusted a clip under her hair net. "Men don't like women who are aggressive. You have to be careful," Mother said.

"Of what?" I said. "Getting shot?"

"Of not acting like an animal in heat and ruining your reputation." Her hazel eyes turned in the direction of the television. Doc Severinson was being introduced.

Vince kissed with a voracious mouth; sometimes our teeth ground together. When his hunger was greatest he licked my entire face with his tongue. I felt devoured. I wanted more and more, craving the meat and heft of him. He was always the one to put on the brakes and pull away. I was out of control. Now my skin burned with a shame like sunburn. I felt blistered where he'd touched me.

I stood up. "I'm going to bed."

"Good night, dear." She reached up and pulled my face down for a kiss. Her Oil-of-Olay cheek was smooth and cool. "Could you please take my dirty dish out on your way?"

Leaving it on the drain board in the darkened kitchen, I marveled that she could be satisfied with just one scoop of ice cream night after night. I'd want to eat the whole fucking thing.

ふ

As Melody cruised along 495 on our way to the Department of Motor Vehicles, her driving reminded me of a very aggressive soccer player weaving and dodging down the field at top speed.

"Do you have the certificate from the driving school?" I asked her.

"Why do you think I can't take care of stuff?"

"The speed limit here is fifty-five," I said.

"Susan and her boyfriend are having sex," Melody said.

"What!"

"You need to get a hearing aid. I said Susan and—"

"I heard that." I said. "I was just surprised." What now, I thought, or rather what was I supposed to say?

"She can't tell her mother, though. She'd spaz." Melody cut in and out of traffic. "How many people are in carpool?" she asked.

"What?"

"Why can't you admit you're going deaf?"

"What have carpools got to do with Susan having sex?"

"Nothing. Can I drive in the HOV lane?"

"Yes."

"Cool beans." Melody slid across three lanes of traffic. A tractor-trailer blew his air horn. The blast made me jump. Melody waved and gave the trucker a big cheesy grin. He sounded his horn again but was rapidly falling behind us.

"Jesus Christ, Melody! Slow down. Getting killed on the way to the test is not good. At least wait until you have your license."

"Chill out, Mom." She examined a chipped purple fingernail.

"And signal when you change lanes." I said.

"If I'm going to have sex, I promise I'll tell you."

Before I had a chance to react, Melody turned on the radio.

"The Red Hot Chili Peppers OK with you?" she asked. "I'm so nervous, the music helps."

I nodded vaguely and tried to think. I didn't want to say the wrong thing and shut down communication. I pretended to admire the buildings along the I-270 techno-corridor, which were flying past.

"Mel, how do you feel about Susan having sex?" I asked as we turned off on the Clopper Road exit.

"Fine. They've been going together for two months." She leaned sideways into the turn. We were definitely not taking the ramp at the suggested thirty miles per hour. "He said he loved her. That's the key."

I remembered how it was with Vince, how the touch of his hand on my summer shoulder would saturate my body with longing.

"The problem with having sex too soon," I told her, "is that girls attach a great deal of emotional significance to the act and think it's love because it generates such powerful feelings."

I worried that my sentence was too long. "At sixteen you don't have the emotional perspective," I tried again.

"Then you think she should've waited?" Melody accelerated to pass a refrigeration truck.

"Yes."

"I went to the clinic with Susan because she was scared," Melody continued. "She got birth control pills."

"That was responsible." I took a deep breath. Why did I feel like I was going to be sick? "Melody, when you get to that point, tell me and I'll take you to a regular gyn."

"Should I follow the blue signs?" she asked.

I hoped she'd heard me. It was so important I didn't dare repeat it.

"Watch for the green and white ones. The blue ones are for the train."

"Gotcha." She slowed down, searching.

"There." I pointed. "Make a right into the parking lot. The test is around back."

We turned into the DMV and got into a line of cars. An officer put a large number on our windshield.

"Stay with your vehicle until the examiner arrives," he told us. "Then you can wait inside the building."

Melody wrapped and unwrapped her fingers around the steering wheel. I could feel the tension gripping her.

"You're going to be fine." I ran my hand under her hair and rubbed her neck. "You're a good driver." At this moment confidence was more important to her than the truth.

She leaned her head against my arm. "Any last word of advice?"

*Be careful of desire,* I wanted to whisper. *I can't help you.* What I said was, "Be sure to signal when you change lanes."

"I know, Mom." Melody straightened up. Her mouth dropped open as a huge bull of a man opened the passenger door.

"Out you go," the officer said to me. "I'll take it from here."

↜

Down by the river at Hains Point in the early sixties the planes shook the ground as they thundered in and out of Bolling Air Force Base. Vibrations surged through us each time the sound wave hit. We wrestled and strained, struggling to crawl into each other's skin. Then one night we finally got to the moment where there was only one place left to go. Vince abruptly got up from the ground and walked away, parting the leafy curtain. I trembled on the itchy wool blanket. Jet engines clubbed the air overhead. Vince came back with his shirt tucked into his khaki pants. He squatted down in front of me, just out of reach.

"I can't," he said.

I swallowed and sat up. Waltz music from a passing cruise ship slid across the water. I waited. The river lapped at the bulkhead with soft liquid slaps.

"It would ruin three lives," he said.

"What?" Who was he talking about?

"Yours, mine, and the baby's," he said.

"Vince, we can use—"

"No." He shook his head. "Just, no."

I tried to see his face in the dark. Slowly I understood that he wouldn't make love to me because I had been too forward. My mother was right. I had become the fevered animal she'd warned me about. The music was gone now, following the boat downstream. I shivered and pulled my dress up.

Driving home the silence in the car was suffocating. When we stopped at the light on Constitution Avenue, the weight of it became intolerable. I got out of the car, took off my dress and threw it in the back seat. In my white cotton panties and bra, I walked across the street. Under my bare feet the pavement was still warm from the heat of the day.

## Margaret Meyers

# Eau de Paradis

MARGARET MEYERS was born in Belgium and raised in the Congo. She moved to the United States after graduating from the Ubangi Academy in the Equateur Province. She holds an MA in philosophy from DePaul University and an MFA in creative writing from the University of Virginia. Author of the short story collection *Swimming in the Congo*, Meyers also teaches writing and literature at the Johns Hopkins University Advanced Academic Programs.

Cream-colored boots, wispy blonde tendrils, and—oh dear—a Burberry plaid miniskirt she probably wears because she had a similar one in high school in 1968. She'll want—really, this is so easy it's boring—a girlish perfume. Yves Saint Laurent's Baby Doll, probably, though it's beyond me why anyone pays good money to smell like weak grapefruit juice. Then again, a girlish dress sense sometimes goes hand in hand with a taste for aggressively sexy fragrances. My money's on Chanel's amber-and-spice-rich Coco—or, if her vamp instincts are a bit on the vulgar side, Giorgio. But no, she's passed Chanel, she's heading my way, Baby Doll or Giorgio it is. Why don't people wear good old-fashioned spikenard ointment anymore? Wonderful stuff, spikenard, but does anyone come into Saks and ask for it? Not in my lifetime… ("I'm sorry, madam, but we don't carry Giorgio. But I know you can find it at Lord & Taylor.")

Black silk sweater, sleek black chignon, cranberry-red lips from Nars or maybe Trish McEvoy. And oh, what delectable little Jimmy Choo heels! She's a bit more of a challenge, but the category is clear: classic and pricey. *Very* pricey. Patou's 1000, if she's read that Jackie O. wore it and knows the bottles are individually numbered. Or Joy, if she knows about the limited edition Baccarat bottle for the not-so-bargain price of $800. ("Thank you madam, and may I congratulate you on your good choice? The Baccarat is already a collector's item.")

Oh Lordy, look at *this* one—thin-lipped, thin-bodied, tweedily genteel in a vintage Jaeger suit of periwinkle blue. All she needs is the famous flamingo brooch, and the Duchess of Windsor is back from the grave. Unquestionable Youth Dew time. How did she miss the Estée Lauder counter anyway? Ah, Emile's with her. She must be Somebody. Or Somebody's Wife.

"Magda, darling, would you assist mademoiselle with a Caron perfume? Narcisse Noir, I believe."

Oops. Miscalculated this time. And how attentive Emile is, smiling fiercely and flattering her with "mademoiselle," his hand hovering at her withered elbow. He can't stand her. He'll imitate her. Mercilessly.

"Delighted to be of assistance," I murmur, and Emile heads back to Lancôme with the insolent swagger of a model. His trousers drape fluidly from his narrow hips, and his buttocks have elegant but well-defined curves. He must be working out again. I only hope his little Marty is as appreciative as I am. I tell the Duchess of Windsor that Narcisse Noir is one of my personal favorites even though this is absolutely not true. The sweet, festered-lily stink of Persian black narcissus makes my nasal passages shut down. Besides, I dislike any perfume made with civet. But the bottle design is from 1912, and ravishingly gorgeous. Late Art Nouveau.

"Well," the Duchess says with a slight flare of her thoroughbred nostrils. "I don't like it at all, frankly. I just buy it out of loyalty to Ernest Daltroff. He was devoted to my grandmother and created the perfume with her in mind."

"Ah." I feel rebuffed for my polite lie. I also refuse to be impressed.

"I don't care for scent in general," she says. "I never have."

"Ah." I now decide the Duchess of Windsor is One Unholy Bitch. Really. Because the fact is, good scent has genuine spiritual meaning. Where do people think the high-church love of incense comes from anyway? The great Christian tradition. The "odor of sanctity." The sweet smell that distinguished the personal presence of saints. The delicious floral perfume of St. Veronica Giuliani's stigmata that permeated her entire cloister. The trademark scent of violets that clung to the tomb of St. Catherine de Ricci for years after her death even though her body was encased in a lead coffin. Everyone knows that warlocks, wizards, and the exceptionally evil emit a horrible smell. Noisome Philistines! Poor St. Catherine of Siena almost died of suffocation in the malodorous presence of a notorious sinner. OK, I know the Duchess doesn't actually smell *bad*, but her lack of appreciation isn't much to her credit. At least her disgust of scent in general means she doesn't like—or worse yet, *wear*—the appalling Giorgio. I tend to think one whiff of Giorgio and poor tender-nosed St. Catherine would've given somebody a nice bloody slap.

"Are there any fragrances you like at all?" I ask the Duchess as I wait for her American Express card to ring through. "Even just a little?"

"Only one," she says, and an impish, albeit thin-lipped, grin cracks the lacquered perfection of her makeup. "The sweet smell of success."

Disarmed, I burst out laughing. How wonderful it is, this excuse for laughter. And how equally wonderful this sensation behind my breastbone: a great sparkling flood released from some deep river-vein of joy. I know I often talk like work is Hell, but I will freely confess that I'm just conforming, just trying to keep my little euphoric surges under control. And, more importantly, unnoticed. I don't want other people to realize that for me the Saks perfume department represents mountains of myrrh, hills of frankincense, orchards of fruit, and beds of spices. I don't want to realize it myself, most of the time. Because I do have mixed feelings about who I am and what I do. Given the choice, I'd rather be a person of more serious, substantive talents—a history professor, maybe, or a medical doctor in a third world country. A Brain or a Heart has infinitely more gravitas than a mere Nose.

"It wasn't *that* funny." The Duchess's voice is dry, but her grin widens delightedly as her eyes meet mine. I can tell she is not in the habit of making people laugh, and is pleased with herself. For a frivolous moment I think maybe Saks is actually so far from Hell that it's Heaven—and I feel again that occasional, eerie rending of some important veil. Though peculiar (and it is always, inevitably, that!), my rent-veil sensation is not so rare that I'm thrown off balance by it. But today there is more. Today I hear something as well. A voice, a distant voice, speaks words that seem directed at me—or maybe someone very close by: "This day you shall be with me in Paradise." I glance up at the high white ceiling, half expecting to see deep fractures zigzag down the plastered arches and bright bulbs explode from the tactful recessed lighting. Half expecting to hear a gusty drumroll of thunder and the glorious blare of a dozen trumpets. None of this happens, and I feel a little ridiculous that my legs have gone weak at the knees. I hand the glossy little shopping bag to the Duchess, take a deep breath, and say, "When you invent a perfume called The Sweet Smell of Success, count on me to buy a bottle."

"That'll be in my next life, when I'm reincarnated as a perfumer," she replies. "You know how some people are tone deaf? Well, I'm scent deaf. I was born that way."

As I watch her head for the escalator, I lean my elbows against the counter. We're not supposed to do this for fear of smudging the glass or endangering expensive merchandise—and God forbid the manager sees me!—but my legs are still wobbly. Besides, I get nervous when people make jokes about reincarnation. I realize they don't mean anything by it, that it's just part of casual modern discourse. But I still don't like it. Last year one of the bigwigs from Guerlain was here to lecture on "The Perfumer's Art," and he asked several us to determine the composition of one of the more obscure Guerlain scents, Vol de Nuit. My ability to do this ("Top notes are definitely bergamot, orange blossom, mandarin, lemon…then jonquil, galbanum, aldehydes of some kind, oak moss…um, a little orris, very high-quality Italian orris—") had excited him into offering me a job on the spot. You are a Nose, mademoiselle!" he had cried. "The first real Nose I've encountered in twenty years. We need you in Paris!" I was flattered, even briefly tempted, until he said, "You must have been a perfumer in a former life. A French perfumer, *naturellement.* Maybe even our great founder, Pierre-Francois-Pascal Guerlain himself." He seemed so perfectly serious, even fanatical, about this possibility that a coldness shivered down my spine. I rejected his offer so emphatically that he was offended and gave me a lecture on the irresponsibility—the immorality, *enfin!*—of squandering a remarkable gift.

"Magda, my love, my sweetest one, my dove."

I start, whisk my elbows off the glass, and glare suspiciously at Emile. He doesn't usually waste his fulsome endearments on his colleagues. He's too tired out from catering to the expectations of a certain kind of shopper by fulfilling a certain stereotype of gay behavior even though he isn't gay. ("How they adore feeling titillated and daring and tolerant all at once!" he says. "And how I adore the way my sales go up, even though the act gets tedious.") I wonder what he wants. Lancôme must be really slow today—and why not, since the whole store is—but I think he's up to something.

"Planet Magda must be a really interesting place," he observes. "Did that old Narcisse Noir bat get to you or something? Her suit was as ancient as she was, I swear. And talk about Eau de Mothballs!"

"Don't be ridiculous," I snap, suddenly much offended by the mindless arrogance of the young, the unlined, and the gorgeously fit. "That was just good old-fashioned Pears soap. I know the difference, I promise you."

"Of course you do," he flares back. "Mademoiselle Magda of the Magnificent Nose!"

Poor Emile. There's nothing he'd like better than a glamorous job in Paris with Guerlain, and he hasn't forgiven me for casually rejecting an opportunity he will never have. Emile is wonderful with color, appreciates the infinite subtleties of different beige-toned foundations the way an Eskimo is said to distinguish variations in snow, but he's hopeless with scent. Once I actually heard him tell a client that Lancôme's floral semi-oriental Tresor had "A sort of fresh green smell, like a newly mown lawn." I like him, though. And I like his little Marty too. They were high school sweethearts and ten years later they're still going strong, which is pleasant to see in our world of short-lived loyalties. But that doesn't mean I'm in the mood to hear him trash old ladies just because they're old. I'm not as young as I used to be either.

"Spikenard," I say meditatively. "For some reason I woke up today thinking about spikenard."

Emile's beautifully arched brows lift, and he says, "What's spikenard?"

"An aromatic plant substance from way back when," I tell him. "They used to put it in expensive ointments or perfumes. Just imagine: once upon a time you went to your friendly neighborhood apothecary and said, 'Listen, mix me up a bit of spikenard cream, would you, Gaius Octavuis Augustus?' And no snotty, critical people like us intimidated you with unbelievably high prices or bewildered you with hundreds of choices or openly jeered at your fashion sense." Emile looks hurt, opens his mouth—and I rush on. "Now don't take it personally, Emile. I was just thinking how it used to be, that's all."

"Like you really know, Mrs. Methuselah!" Emile snorts. Then he pats my arm and says, "Never mind, Magda darling, my dove, my sweet, I'm going bonkers too. It's the lack of customers. First dry sunny day in weeks and nobody wants to be inside. Including me." A significant pause. "Especially me."

"So that's it," I say gleefully. "You want to take a long lunch, and you want me to cover for you."

Emile looks both pained at my bluntness and embarrassed by his own transparency. He explains that, well, as a matter of fact, darling Marty has the day off. Darling Marty has just called from Whole Foods where she has picked up brie, paté, and French bread. They've both been absolutely perishing for a picnic, he tells me soulfully. And he'll make it up to me, of course—doesn't he always?—so what do I think?

I think he and Marty are lucky, adorable, and straight out of the Hebrew poets. *Rise up, my love, my fair one, and come away. For, lo, the winter is past—*

"Come on, Magda. Please? Pretty please?"

I surface. I say, "Yes, alright, if you really are perishing." And I hope to God I haven't been mumbling from the *Song of Solomon* out loud.

Emile rushes off to phone Marty. I sell a curvaceous bottle of Diva to an elderly man in a conservative suit and cannot help speculating about his private life. Then there is a long lull, broken only by one irritable woman who just can't *believe* we don't sell Revlon's Charlie and goes off in a huff when I suggest CVS or Sears. Emile leaves with a grateful wave, and I divide my time between Fragrances and the Lancôme counter. Even so, there isn't enough going on to keep me busy, so I amuse myself by spraying Jil Sander No. 4 on my wrist and taking judicious sniffs. Geranium, peach, plum, with just a hint of rose, I think. And then heliotrope, violet, carnation—mercy, can that possibly be tarragon?—and, ah yes, myrrh. I do so love myrrh. It isn't used in scent that much anymore. Though there is Oscar de la Renta, I guess, and Laura Biagiotti's Roma. Caron's Parfum Sacré too, of course. I wander back to Lancôme, catch a glimpse of myself in a makeup mirror, and decide my face could do with some color. I try a tiny dab of the new highlighting cream Emile is so enthusiastic about on my browbone, then apply a little orchid-colored shadow on my lids. I admire the results in the hand mirror. It's gratifying to realize I could still turn heads if I felt like making the effort. I don't feel like it though, not as a rule, which annoys all the Saks makeup gurus who palpably itch to get their hands on my makeup-free face. Emile says I'm not living up to my advertising potential and one of these days the management will probably apply a little pressure. As I study my face from another angle, guiltily pleased that my cheekbones are still to-die-for (not that anybody ever did, of course, but certainly some very extravagant things were said), I tilt the mirror just a little to the right. And feel all the blood, all the warmth and color, leave my face. *Oh Duchess, no. Please no.*

For there she is, my Duchess, standing close against the wall with the built-in shelving that holds all the marvelous Annick Goutal fragrances. There she is, ostensibly examining one of the larger trademark cream-and-gold eau de toilette boxes in her right hand while her left hand slips a smaller box into the inside lining of her unbuttoned Jaeger suitjacket. There she is, about to be caught—although she doesn't know it. For I can have security here in ten seconds. If, that is, they aren't already on their way. The Duchess can have no idea about that huge bank of video screens in the Security Room downstairs. Nor can the Duchess realize that the new Head of Security, for all the disaffection suggested by his greasy ponytail and tight black jeans, is a tremendously earnest thief-catcher who likes nothing better than watching those screens right through his lunch hour. ("He doesn't trust us," his two assistants tell anyone who will listen, which is why we all know so much about the new Head. "He's so afraid we'll miss something that he doesn't drink fluids all day so he won't have to break for a leak.") The Duchess is about to be arrested for stealing perfume, and the Duchess is—or so she claims—scent deaf.

Instead of discreetly pressing the alarm, I leave the Lancôme counter at an unhurried pace. I cross the shining floor toward her, and even from a distance I see the galloping of the pulse in the chic scrawniness of her neck. My hands are trembling so much that I clench them behind my back like a guilty child, and I have no idea what I will do or sat until I stop in front of her and ask very quietly, "Which one, Duchess."

"Folavril," she replies.

"Why?"

"It smells like pomegranates."

"No it doesn't." I say, taken aback. "It's jasmine. And mango."

"Maybe. But it's pomegranate too. All at once I could smell it." The Duchess is suddenly and strangely radiant. "I could feel it in my nose, taste it on my tongue—like champagne. And it's fabulous."

She's right. I can smell it myself now, and it is fabulous, and it is definitely pomegranate. Invisible waves of pomegranate swirl around us so that I am dizzied. *How much better than wine is the smell of thine ointments... isn't* that how it goes? I think so, yes... *The pomegranates have budded, the orchard is pleasant with fruit, with camphire, with saffron, with spikenard—*

Striving for the prosaic, I say, "How much did you spray on yourself, anyway?"

"None," the Duchess replies simply. "I just sniffed it from the bottle."

Never in my life have I been at such a loss. Never have I been so uncertain about the rightness or wrongness of things. Why should the Duchess experience this—this miracle? And why should she celebrate it by stealing? Since our vigilant Security has not arrived after all, judgment is up to me—and I am no fit person to do it. I have never been the judging kind, which may be the main reason why I haven't aspired to one of those substantive Brain and Heart professions. No, I ought to qualify that; I am the judging kind, really, but I don't judge *out loud* and I don't judge with a view to punishment. The very thought sickens and disorients me. I know how it feels to be judged out loud. I even know what it is to grow *comfortable* with a role of The Judgee, to feel that I have actually found my proper niche in the world. Honestly, you should have heard those men on the subject of my spikenard ointment wickedness alone. A flamboyant display, they said. A prideful gesture with no true repentance behind it. A sinful waste, they said, when with good management forty orphans might have lived for forty days on that money. And they picked up the lustrous shards of the alabaster jar and waved them accusingly in my face...

"You're not going to faint on me, are you?" There is wonderment in the Duchess's old blue eyes as she grips my arm.

The veil is well and truly rent at last. And I am furious.

"No, I most certainly am not," I tell her firmly. "I'm going to aid and abet. I'm going to be an accessory—or whatever it's called."

"Why?"

"Because I think He's got an absolutely rotten sense of humor. I was *right there* when He told the thief on His left that he'd be with Him in Paradise. And me? What happens to me?" I stab my breastbone with my forefinger. "Well, I'll tell you. *Saks* happens to me, for God's sake! A *Nose* happens to me! Century after century of Saks—or its equivalent—and here's what I'd like to know: Is the Saks Fragrance Department any kind of substitute for Paradise?"

The Duchess's lips twitch as she says, "I shouldn't think so, dear."

And I can't tell if her twitch is from amusement or nervous alarm, and I don't much care. I sweep on, tumbling my feelings into words: "He was always saying I took myself and my sins far too seriously—but even so! To play a joke like this on me, century after century—why, it's mean. It's perverse. Under His circumstances, I'd even say it's thoroughly deviant behavior, don't you agree?"

"I don't really understand perverse or deviant," the Duchess says calmly. "This is the most deviant few minutes I've ever spent in my life, and I suspect it doesn't even count since it was sort of an—an hysterical reaction. Because I honestly never did smell anything before, and this pomegranate—"

Her voice is almost reverent, and I stare at her for a moment. Stare at her hard, and pityingly. However privileged, however well connected and respected, the Duchess has missed out. She has never used her favorite mortar and pestle of Egyptian marble to make the best spikenard ointment in Israel. Never scampered across the steep green hillsides of Capri gleefully collecting the spicy wild carnations exclusive to the island. Never picked French jasmine by night, sightlessly following the blissful scent from bloom to bloom. Never made her own attar of Bulgarian rose in her own Balkan castle stillroom, her fingers redolent and her spirits high for days afterwards. Never been apprenticed to the monks at the Farmacia di Santa Maria Novella, perfumers to the Medici family and entrusted with the secret recipes and priceless essences. Never been the artist behind the Empress Josephine's favorite musk cologne. Never helped the great Balzac create his own customized scent. Or Sarah Bernhardt. Such a terribly demanding and finicky woman, the Divine Sarah, but once I steered her in the direction of Moroccan *rose de mai,* she was as sweet as... *Good God, I HAVE been a Nose at Guerlain.*

I give the Duchess's thin arm a gentle pat. I tell her to enjoy her purchase. I tell her that if she should ask for me next time she comes in, I'll give her a free 2.5-ounce tube of Annick Goutal's Eau d'Hadrien lotion, which smells like a Sicilian lemon grove with a few cypress and grapefruit trees thrown in.

As she heads for the exit, I say aloud, to the ceiling, "Alright, very funny. And maybe You were right. If You are penitent—truly and really—I might, just *might,* forgive You!"

*Mary Overton*

# *Fire Bones*

MARY OVERTON is the author of a story collection, *The Wine of Astonishment*, published by La Questa Press (1997). Her short fiction appears in both commercial and literary magazines. She was born and raised in Missouri, moved to Arlington during her high school years, and has lived most of her adult life in Northern Virginia.

People began wild, and the milk of she-people was wild milk. Infants drinking that milk belonged to the people.

A child born wrong was given no milk that it might die.

Burning woman began as a child born wrong. Her small body emerged, white-hot and shining. The flames killed her mother and scorched the hands of she-people.

Such a baby that burned was meant to die.

She-people gave her no milk. They abandoned her beside endless water.

The baby cried, and hot wind came from her burning mouth. Birds knew that voice. It spoke the first language, from which all other languages came.

Bird mothers flew down to her, built a nest about her, gave to her food meant for their own young. Birds sheltered the baby with their wings. Her flames scorched their feathers.

The child grew to be a woman who burned, white-hot and shining. She came back to people, as birds were not her own kind. She lived with people but not of them. She was to the people as one with no kin.

༜

Burning woman marked the beginning of time.

Prior to her birth, there was no time. People lived without fire. They lived naked, barefoot, and mute on land by endless water. They gathered meat from the ocean and fruit from the trees. Sun ruled over sky, making it a warm land.

Burning woman became the first teacher to people. She mimicked her bird mothers. She painted her body with fruit pulp to color it like the bodies of birds, and people were amazed. She invented song by answering bird calls and dance by miming bird courtship. In all these things, people did the same and followed her.

Burning woman tried to fly and discovered longing. People learned this longing. How they yearned to fly! If only they might see as a bird sees when it flies away. Desire brought upon people the first discontent.

People could not bear the suffering of discontent. They were compelled to act. They seized birds and cut out birds' eyes. People then plucked out their own eyes. They placed in the empty sockets the eyes of birds.

When it was done, people looked through these new eyes. But they saw nothing of flight. They saw nothing a bird might see as it flies away. People looked at each other and saw instead their own trickery, which could not be undone.

Only burning woman contained her discontent and kept her first sight.

To this day, a bird will peck at your eyes, wanting to reclaim that which was stolen from its ancestors.

~

At the beginning of time, birds were many and people were few. A day came when birds gathered for the purpose of revenge.

Angry and pitiless birds swarmed upon the people. Those who fell were eaten by birds. Confusion and torment ruled. People fled, and birds hunted them.

Day and night, without rest, birds chased people far away from their land. Babies fell, old ones, sick and weak ones, all fell and were eaten. Strongest of people suffered near death.

Burning woman might have been spared. She might have cried out with hot wind in that voice of the first language. But she remained innocent of trickery. Burning woman fled with the others.

In this way people realized their longing. They came to see through bird eyes places that were far away. Their flight, however, was wingless.

~

Flight took people to where sky ruled over sun with a cold, dark hand. In this place, birds let go their pursuit. Birds gave people over to a merciless land.

People sought an ocean from which to gather meat, familiar trees from which to gather fruit. They found, instead, snow and his bitter sister, ice.

Burning woman alone greeted snow and ice and the dark hand of sky without concern. Where she walked, snow retreated. Where she reached out her hand, ice turned away. Her flaming body, white-hot and shining, was visible through darkness as lightning is visible through storm.

In this way she came to lead the people, who hated her because she did not suffer.

ॐ

Beasts in the merciless land were innocent of trickery.

A she-bear, pregnant with twins and the foreknowledge of her death, came to burning woman. In the hot wind of the first language, she-bear said, "Your kind are not suited to this place." She offered her coat to the naked people. "Only save my cubs," she implored, "that they may remember me."

She-bear died in the effort of birth, and burning woman saved her cubs. Burning woman removed she-bear's coat and made coverings for all people but herself, who remained without.

People warmed inside their new clothes. Even so, they were bitter with hunger. People ate the meat of she-bear. When it was done, they killed her twins and ate that meat as well.

To this day, when a bear cub is grown she cannot remember her mother. She hides during winter to keep safe her coat.

If a creature is clever, one trick is enough. But innocence is a hard thing to lose.

A doe, pregnant with twins and the foreknowledge of her death, came to burning woman. Doe said, "Your kind are not suited to this place." She gave up the stiff soles of her hooves to the barefoot people. "Only save my fawns," she implored, "that they may remember me."

Burning woman saved the fawns and made shoes for all people but herself, who remained without. People warmed inside their new shoes. Even so, they were bitter with hunger. People ate the meat of doe. When it was done, they killed her twins and ate that meat as well.

To this day, when a fawn is grown she cannot remember her mother. She startles and flees at the least noise, to keep safe her hooves.

Wolves were the most clever and advanced of beasts. The better to hunt, they borrowed from the first language to invent their own words. Still, innocence is a hard thing to lose.

A she-wolf, pregnant with twins and the foreknowledge of her death, came to burning woman. She-wolf said, "Your kind are not suited to this place. Take my words and use them to hunt. Only save my pups," she implored, "that they may remember me."

Burning woman saved the pups. She removed she-wolf's words and made language for all people but herself, who remained mute.

Once people shared a language, they spoke bitterly of hunger. People ate the meat of she-wolf. When it was done, they killed her twins and ate that meat as well.

To this day, when a wolf pup is grown she cannot remember her mother. She howls at having given up her words. She howls to warn beasts against the trickery of people.

✦

Burning woman led people to the face of an iron mountain. Within its caves they found shelter and an end to flight.

Now began a time of settlement. She-people took men as mates and became pregnant.

People learned to hunt. They used trickery and language. From the skins of beasts people made new and finer clothing that they might better greet snow and his bitter sister, ice. From the hard parts of beasts—bone, tooth, claw, hoof—people made decorations that they might better sing and dance on long, dark nights. This is how magic was invented.

People lived without fire. They had instead the shining, white-hot body of burning woman. She gave heat and light to the people, who hated her for keeping to old ways. Her eyes looked unknowingly. She continued to be naked, barefoot, and mute. Burning woman lived with people but not of them, as one with no kin.

✦

Where people settled, beasts were many and people were few. A day came that beasts gathered for the purpose of revenge.

On that day she-people did not hunt. They were heavy with unborn children. Men went out to hunt but never came back. Angry and pitiless beasts killed men and ate the meat.

Beasts advanced upon iron mountain that they might kill and eat the meat of she-people and their unborn children. Burning woman alone greeted beasts without concern. She stood at the face of iron mountain. Her flaming body, white-hot and shining, burned between she-people and beasts.

Day and night, beasts challenged her fire. From one new moon to the next, burning woman stood before the beasts who cried for blood. This was a battle between fire and blood.

In the first language, beasts shouted their grievances.

"We regret our sacrifice for you," said bear and deer and wolf. "Give back what is ours, that the young may remember us."

"I have nothing to give you," said hot wind from the woman's burning mouth, and it was true. She was indeed naked, barefoot, and mute.

Burning woman stood fast, and over the turning of one moon her fire disabled the will of beasts. Animals fled from iron mountain, defeated.

To this day, a beast is unable to pass by fire.

To this day, a woman knows with her blood the turning of the moon.

Now began a hard time when people had no men. She-people gave birth and raised children, but cherished sons above daughters.

With hard times came a change of memory. She-people retold the exodus from birds and the siege of beasts. She-people retold their lost men as heroes. Their lost men grew into the stuff of legend, into champions, into small gods.

To this day, a man strives to be a hero and a woman secretly regrets his constant failure.

Fatherless children came of age in a new time when sons ruled over mothers. Sons took daughters as mates and ruled over wives. She-people grew old and died, content that they might rest from years without men.

Only burning woman did not grow old. She did not die. She would not be ruled. White-hot and shining, naked, mute, unseeing, she kept to forgotten ways. By night her flaming body stood outside iron mountain. By day she stood within. People hated her that she should not be understood.

Wives said, "Make burning woman bear children as we do."

Husbands said, "We will rule her children and own their burning."

Youths said, "We will divide her burning children among us and make new nations."

People began a contest to establish a hero, to discover the man who might rule burning woman. A winner was sought. He must kill the fiercest beasts, fight the bravest hunters, and keep the strongest wives. This is how the first king came to be. He ruled for the turning of one sun.

For the turning of one sun there are thirteen turnings of the moon, each measured by a woman's blood.

At year's end, the king put his hands upon burning woman. He took her as his mate. It was like taking a beast. She received him like a beast, in rage and terror. Burning woman consumed the king with fire so he died.

People hated burning woman that she made them mourn the first king.

Burning woman knew only her own grief. She abandoned people. She descended through unknown passages into the mountain's iron belly. Her anguish melted its iron core. Burning woman stood in a bath of liquid rock and wept so tears boiled upon her face.

Twin babies grew in her own belly. The twins smoked and sweated, each with an inner fire.

᎒

People awoke from lamentation to find constant midnight closed about them. It sucked warmth from their breath and light from their eyes. Without burning woman, the iron walls where they dwelled turned black and frozen.

At the face of iron mountain gathered birds and beasts, hungry for meat.

People cried out bitterly. Then they began to die.

Wives rebuked the men who ruled them, saying, "Heroes took what was needed from birds and beasts. Did all heroes die with the king?"

Men said, "We will pursue this woman and take her burning."

People covered themselves over with skins of beasts until they no longer appeared human. They descended into the belly of iron mountain. Through black and frozen passages people descended. They came to a place unlikely made, a place inside stone yet blazing with its own sun.

Burning woman, white-hot and shining, stood before them in a bath of liquid rock.

"We forgive you!" people cried. "We forgive you for leaving us!"

Burning woman heard words taken from a she-wolf but did not understand them.

"Come back to us!" people cried. "Come back that we may care for you!"

Burning woman saw before her the shapes and skins of beasts but did not recognize trickery.

"You are kin to us!" people cried. "You belong to us!"

Burning woman walked out of her fiery bath. She had no fear because beasts are unable to pass by fire. But people are different.

People put their covered hands on burning woman. Fire consumed the skins they wore. Fire killed and maimed the first, bold ones, the heroes.

Heroes dismembered burning woman. They broke open her body.

Inside, they found her bones, white-hot and shining.

Heroes broke open her bones. Inside, they found fire.

This was the first fire held by people.

ॐ

Once people owned fire, they had no use for burning children.

People tore from the belly of burning woman her twin babies, each no bigger than a thumb and hot with an inner spark. People threw the babies down the face of iron mountain, that they might die and be eaten by beasts.

But once people owned fire, beasts retreated.

A she-mouse found the crying infants. She suckled them on wild milk.

The twins, a boy and a girl, thrived on her milk. They grew to be strong and wild and no larger than their mouse mother.

Stories about the brother and sister are legion: how they came to fly on the backs of birds and learned to see trickery, how they bathed in stump water and learned to make magic, how they mixed trickery and magic to steal wings for themselves.

The twins spoke all languages, wild and tame, but for one, the hot wind of the first language. That one is lost.

After a time, brother and sister lay together. There were no others of their kind. From the union came fairies, the small, wild people of the forest and meadow and river.

To this day, fairies keep fire in their bones.

# Frances Park

# Walks Home in the Dark with Abby

FRANCES PARK wrote her first book on an ancient Underwood type-writer at the age of ten and has never quite returned to the real world. Her three novels are *When My Sister Was Cleopatra Moon* (Miramax, 2001), *To Swim across the World* (co-authored with Ginger Park; Miramax, 2002), and *Hotline Heaven* (Permanent Press, 1998). She has also published many short stories and children's books (co-authored). Her books have been translated into German and Korean. While she's had the fortune to be inter-viewed on CNN, *Good Morning America*, NPR, and the *Diane Rehm Show*, she's most comfortable at home and writing. Pres-ently, she's putting the finishing touches on a new novel. She can be reached through her website at www.parksisters.com.

## CHAPTER 1

My mother and Mrs. Brown are at the kitchen table clipping reci-pes from magazines with Christmas cookies on the covers. Some-thing about Thanksgiving for the needy, rosemary bread, and sweet potato pie. Still saving the world, or at least their remote corner in Cabin Creek. I'm serving tea for three. Behind us a big bay window frames the backyard where piles of leaves smoke like teepees and stacked logs wait for winter. A scene from a Hallmark calendar. *November nostalgia*... Whenever Cookie the cat swings through the porch door, the smell of something from the attic of my memories, something like sunshine and birds' nests, squashed acorns and pumpkins, makes me long for something I can't quite touch—like a long-awaited kiss at a bonfire against muffled voices and a stereophonic sky, or those long walks home in the dark with Abby. The calendar flips backwards and forwards until I remember.

I am home again.

I come back with my family to Cabin Creek every Thanksgiving to see my mother. My brother and his family come for Christmas. For years, this revolving door arrangement has worked in a silence-is-golden way. When we leave, we know they're coming. When they come, they know we've been here. There's probably some hint of us lingering around like faint echoes, like ghosts. But this Thanksgiving I'm alone. No sign of my husband Mark or my son Owen will be left behind. Only my footprints, down the path of my thoughts with Abby.

Some nights are immortal, some glow. 1976: A bonfire behind the school, a bottle of beer in my pocket. Both blazing in my eyes. I wanted more bonfire, I wanted more beer. More kisses, too. Afterwards, the boy offered to walk me home, but Abby took my hand—*good-bye, Clyde!*—and dragged me past trees, past a clearing, the stone church on the right. This was our path home, which ran parallel to Appleseed, the main road. The forest lit up by the light of a passing car and for a split second I caught Abby's seventeen-year-old face, all bluesy as she crooned "She's Gone." I could still feel Clyde's warm tongue in my mouth, wanting more, something deeper, and this made me feel naked, like I wanted his hands all over my breasts right here in the woods. Abby would howl at the moon at such a confession. When it came to sex, we were in different leagues. That night she reminded me, spitting beer like bullets: *"Whenever I do it with Donnie or Chip or Kurt—especially with Kurt!—I'm kicking myself. I can't stand him, Maggie, he's so dumb. Do you know he's never heard of Ayn Rand? Never HEARD of her! Three years of Spanish and all he can do is burp up burritos! That's enough to make love go pffft!"*

There was something worldly in her talk that made me believe no matter how crummy I'd been feeling that day, we could jump through the trees tonight, all giddy and beautiful, and never have to come back down.

We never talked about it, but I was different.

Abby loved me anyway.

Orientals, if they belonged anywhere outside Asia in those days, belonged either on islands or in cities. Not in Cabin Creek. Not a small town in the heart of Virginia. My father had been the town doctor and his wise Korean face put calm in the hearts of concerned mothers with coughing kids. No one would ever guess Dr. Moon would run off with one of these mothers, a Mrs. Hardwick. A middle-of-the-night elopement to a new life one heat-peaking summer. I was entering my last year of high school. My mother, as a young woman in Hawaii, had refused to marry any of the island boys after her, claiming they were all *good-for-nothing Don Hos*. She had picked my father like he was a prize orchid. Nineteen years later, on the morning of discovered abandon, she shut her bedroom door behind her. When she emerged that evening, she was wearing a moth-smelling muumuu and had aged a bitter year for every hour she was in there.

"*Mom—*"

"*Shhhh!*"

That *Shhhh!* meant my brother and I were not allowed to talk about what my father did. He was gone, and that was that.


Abby stuck by me during that period of shock. I told her what had happened, but not another word after that. She knew I was hurting; she lived next door and could see that my light stayed on all night. And because she knew me. She *knew* me. She also knew the first days back at school were hard for me to face. Everyone had heard what Dr. Moon did.

Day two, we ditched Home Ec for a smoke in the woods. She slipped her arm in mine while we walked to nowhere and back.

"*Maggie Moon, don't bunch it up inside of you. You gotta lay it all out like a blanket under the stars.*"

"*Please, Abby—*"

"*Come ON!*"

"*I can't talk about it.*"

To nowhere and back we walked and smoked. All that existed was silence. Abby broke it by stepping on a branch. Snap!

"*Well, damn you, then!*"

My face was one twitch from breaking down. "*What do you mean?*"

"*Why did we skip Home Ec? We could've learned how to make the perfect meringue and watch its stiff white peaks brown to perfection*"—only Abby could whip up erotica out of imaginary meringue—"*But noooo… and now that Betty Crocker bitch is gonna wanna flunk our butts!*"

My cigarette spat out with crude accompaniment and I started to laugh. At first it felt good, only I couldn't stop, I… just… couldn't… stop. And then the path and the trees and the sky morphed into a blurry merry-go-round from some nightmare forgotten in the light of day. I dropped to my knees and quietly shriveled into an unsightly ball. Soon Abby's arms were around me, saving me from dying right there in the dirt. And then:

*"You'll be OK, Maggie Moon, I know you'll be OK. My dad's long gone, and I'm OK."*

## CHAPTER 2

Abby was different, too. Deceptively so. She was tall and the boys at school called her *Your blonde highness* to which she responded with a Janis Joplin sneer. And while her green eyes caught more attention than emeralds, her foul-mouthed bark often drove it away. She loved that. *Loved* that. Only I got close enough to her eyes to see what was in them, a sparkle for the taboos in life: Secrets, mysteries, even porn.

*"I met someone,"* she whispered into the phone. Even in that whisper, I heard titillation. It shot up and down my spine and left me shivering. With Abby, the promise of meeting up with hungry-lipped, long-haired boys was always right around the corner.

*"Who is he, Abby?"*

*"It's a she."*

*"She?"*

*"Her name is Tess."*

*"Oh."*

*"She's a new secretary at school."*

*"Our school?"*

*"Yeah. I was in the office arguing with that boozer Mr. Cooper—God, he was drunk as a skunk and here he is a GUIDANCE counselor—over transferring out of Miss O'Toole's class. He told me to give it another couple of weeks; that Miss O'Toole just takes some time warming up to. I told him the old biddy farts in my face—wasn't that warm enough? That's when I met her—Tess, I mean. She heard us arguing and elbowed her way into the conversation."*

*"What did she say?"*

*"'Joe, let the girl transfer. The old biddy farts in her face.'"*

*"No! Really? What did Cooper do?"*

*"He let me transfer."*

After school, Abby had waited around for Tess, just to thank her, she said. They ended up at McDonald's, drinking coffee and smoking. And making plans.

*"She invited me over to her apartment this Sunday. She lives in Berrysville; just moved here from Charleston, West Virginia. You're coming, too, Maggie. You'll love her. She's a far-out lady. A strong lady. Liberated by divorce! She knows how to put a man in his place."*

A far-out *lady*? A strong *lady*? In Abby's world, females were chicks unless—

*"Is she old or something?"* I wondered.

*"Yeah, pretty old. Over FORTY old. But beautiful."*

*"How can anyone over forty be beautiful?"*

*"I don't know, Maggie Moon. But she is. She reminds me of Mae West with a munchkin voice."*

Abby's instant adoration of Tess filled me with dread. Tess. An older lady who could boss Mr. Cooper around. Tess. Who could smoke in broad daylight, theatrically flicking her ashes while she trashed politicians. Tess. Who probably had a juicy past that left Abby thirsting for more. Tess. Divorced. Tess. Even her name was threatening.

I didn't want Abby loving anyone more than me.


My worries were soon over—only because of Tess's all-embracing halo-like charms. Her big loop earrings and peasant skirt set me at ease, as did the musk oil from her skin and her just-out-of-bed blonde hair. I smelled eucalyptus.

*"Incense,"* Abby said.

*"You must be Maggie! I've seen you in the hallways! Aren't you a cutie!"* this Tess lady cried in pure munchkin fashion, now stepping back and taking in the both of us. Even when she was still she was moving, and the hurricane in her spirit made her hair fluff out like mad. *"There's just too much gorgeousness in here. I guess they can't evict me for that. Did the bus work out OK for you girls? I wasn't sure about the Sunday schedule."*

*"It was cool,"* Abby replied.

Tess clapped. *"Cool is good!"*

She lived in a building, once a mansion, now divided into apartments with a view of cows set against mountains. This was Berrysville. Peaceful, but I couldn't for the life of me figure out how anyone who wasn't born here would end up here. What would be the attraction? Especially to a woman with exotic spices bubbling in her blood—like Tess. It was early October but she breezed from the kitchen to the dining room in flat gold lamé sandals from India that showed off her glittery copper-polished toes.

*"Tess, will you sit down?"* Abby yelled in a loving manner.

*"I just want us to have a proper tea, young lady. Just because I have a tattoo doesn't mean I'm some wild, uncivilized beast—although a night of that behavior would be fun!"*

I grinned and gasped at once. *"You have a tattoo?"*

*"You bet your sweet doily I do!"* Tess's laughter was voluptuous, as she was, now unlacing her white peasant blouse. Out popped more pink bosom than I'd ever

seen in real life. Mine had grown *all they're gonna*, as Abby had woefully re-marked, peaking at 34B—kids' stuff next to this. And then the most magnificent shock: A heart tattoo on her right breast. In my eyes, throbbing.

*"Wow!"* I shouted.

*"Isn't it great?"* Abby squealed—obviously not for the first time.

*"Not bad for a fifty-year-old broad,"* Tess said, lacing up.

*"FIFTY!"*

We almost fell over.

## CHAPTER 3

Tess's love of teas and tattoos was, I would note that fragrant afternoon, like the white-laced shawl dangling from her chair. She was proper in some ways and bohemian in others.

Her china looked very Victorian and over a century old, as did her silver tea set. Everything seemed too miniature and too exquisite for my hands—the tea-cups, the spoons, the plates, the fancy food. I was so afraid of dropping some-thing and making a mess. But tea was old hat for Tess who ate with delightful abandon, never spilling a drop or a crumb.

*"My biggest joy in life was being a mother to my four kids. I loved every minute of it. The sleepless nights, the diaper-changing, the broken curfews. We fought like alley cats. See these crow's feet? Lines of love. One day you girls will have them, too."*

Abby coughed up a blueberry. *"Kids are a pain. I don't want any."*

*"I do,"* I said. *"A little boy and maybe a little girl. But a little boy for sure."*

Tess was pleased with my reply—but not with Abby's. *"You might change your mind."*

*"Some things I'm not sure of. Like, do I dislike or despise KC and The Sunshine Band? Do I or don't I believe in God? But I do know one thing for sure: I'm never having any brats,"* Abby restated.

Tiny sandwiches, assorted berries, and bite-sized pastries still crowded the table. It was almost too beautiful to eat. In the months following my father's disappearing act, my brother and I fixed our own food—chili dogs and fried eggs—and ate off paper plates.

*"Tess,"* I held my breath, *"do YOU believe in God?"*

Winking: *"I try to cover all my bases, Maggie."*

I learned that Tess's husband of twenty-odd years, a functional alcoholic with some important jet-setting job, had an affair with another woman. Not a woman he loved, he kept insisting, as if that made any difference. His goal: To stay mar-ried.

*"But I mooned him."*

Tess vowed to make it on her own. But first she stopped eating and ended up in the hospital for three months. Those days were long over; her heart-wrenching past only wrenched a little, now.

*"It's a funny thing, girls, when a part of you dies you either wither to nothing or build character. I did both, in that order. After my divorce, I worked for a judge in West Virginia. I was hired to be his secretary, but he had me getting his lunch, picking up his dry cleaning and babysitting his son. After a while, I had to put my foot down. Then the bastard fired me. Somehow the Women Libbers got a hold of the story, and urged me to sue him. So I did. And I won! Not just the judgment, but something more: Emotional independence. The experience made me realize my one big regret—even though I was happily married for twenty-two years, I should have made a life for myself that was mine and mine only. Sculptured something unique in the shape of Tess. Every woman should do that—are you girls listening? Anyway, I was a heroine across the country, but I didn't really feel welcome in Charleston anymore. There were still a lot of very traditional types around who thought I shouldn't have opened my big fat mouth and gotten the 'good judge' in trouble. And that's how I ended up here. I've got two sons nearby. Their wives are sticks-in-the-mud, but their kids are darling little beasts. God, I love them."*

*"Tess was in all the newspapers,"* Abby bragged. *"She was a—what were you, again?"*

*"A* cause-célèbre. *And don't you forget it!"*

Abby applauded her. *"You had the guts to stand up for yourself. Thank God!"*

*"Oh,"* Tess winked at us both, *"I do thank Her."*

## CHAPTER 4

I want to ask Mrs. Brown how Abby is doing these days up in the foothills of Canada doing whatever she's doing—forestry, I think—but that would rattle our teacups with a gust of harsh, ancient wind. Unlike her sons who still live in the area, George in Clarksburg and Fred in Walnut Way, her once-lovely daughter has faded from the family portraits, replaced with grandchildren in ceramic frames the shapes of hearts. When Mrs. Brown mentions her, it's with a flinching pain as though Abby died twenty years ago. Maybe she blames me, just a little. Maybe, she thinks, I misguided Abby; put stars in her eyes and talked her into moving to New York with me that fateful winter. Yes, if only Abby had stayed in Cabin Creek, she would have married Kurt and her crazy notions would've never got started. Surely it was the late hours and the punk rockers in the East Village that pointed her the wrong way, made her go left when she should have gone right.

When I come home, she remembers Abby; conjures up her ghost next to me. The reminder is too much for her. The spoken truth, too, I suspect. If Abby had died I think Mrs. Brown would have had an easier time accepting her daughter's direction instead of torturing herself with *whys* and *hows* and *will she ever come back home?* When will she realize Abby doesn't even remember the way?

"I like the look of that stuffing," Mrs. Brown says.

My mother nods. "Pecan raisin. We could do that in a pinch."

My mother and Mrs. Brown are best friends, next-door neighbors for as long as I can remember. The children are grown and gone. One husband died, the other disappeared. Both so long ago they don't seem like real people anymore. Is that what happens when someone's gone? Slowly they fade… first from your heart and then the family portraits? What if you loved them the way I loved my son? More than God.

My mother and Mrs. Brown are quiet women, donating most of their time to The Virginia Volunteers. They're good at knit-a-thons and small talk, but nothing that cuts skin deep. No bangs, no applause, just hushed emotions. They've always been that way. When Abby and I were in the tenth grade we won a county-sponsored Virginian Award for Best Picture Book—I was the author and she was the illustrator of "Dreams, Streams and Reams of Possibilities"—but our mothers, in the silhouette of my memories, merely ho-hummed and got on with supper. Whenever I call my mother, the long distance separates us further and I ask myself, *What's a little Hawaiian lady doing there?* Then I think, *Those two should just live together.* But that would crowd one woman's life and abandon the other's. My mother and Mrs. Brown are best friends, but not close friends. Not like Abby and I were.

*"Maggie Moon, promise me something,"* Abby said, splashing vodka into Dixie cups. We'd just left Keg Night at a local hangout called Love, Pizza. The jukebox played "Shake Your Booty" six times; we counted.

*"OK,"* I said, thirsty for this high. Then we'll fly through the forest like neon kites and dream of the night that just passed.

*"Promise me we'll always be best friends. No matter what else happens."*

*"Of course we will!"* I said.

She chugged her vodka and poured another. Her tall blondeness swayed over me. Her speech slurred, her face bulldogged. *"It's not so simple! People change! Times change! What's real and meaningful right now could be crap in your lap tomorrow. Someday you might look back and not even know me from the hag next to you on the bus."*

I stopped in my tracks. *"What are you talking about?"* I wanted to party and dance home, not be hit with this like the stark kitchen light whenever I walked in the door. *"I promise we'll be best friends forever. God's honor."*

*"Yeah, well what about your DAD'S God's honor? Didn't he vow to stay married to your mom?"*

*"What's your point?"*

*"Quit being such a dope, Maggie! Tell me how you're feeling! Your old man splits and you don't even act like anything's wrong!"*

I started to run; the Dixie cup fell out of my hand; I wanted to get away from her, her bullying shadow at my feet. Then she grabbed me and spun me around. *"Maggie, look—"*

*"My dad is gone,"* I spat, the vodka and emotion messing me up. *"Don't rub it in my face."*

Abby took my arm and led me out of the forest. We fell into a spell. Finally she said, *"Don't be mad at me, Maggie. You're the only person in the whole world I love."*

With my face in my tea I'm trying to decode Mrs. Brown's silences and pauses like the dots and dashes of Morse code. I need to hear a secret message from Abby.

"Mrs. Brown?"

She looks up. "Hmm?"

My mother, who swears there was something different about Abby from the word *mama*, darts me a don't-you-dare look before getting up to answer the telephone.

So I say: "I hear Fred's having a hard time."

Mrs. Brown nods. "Janet left him."

"Oh," I cringe as Cookie jumps onto my lap. I was referring to his recent layoff from the furniture company. "That's terrible."

"Apparently there was someone else," she sighs.

This comes as no surprise. Janet was cheating on him in junior high. "What about the kids?"

"Oh, she left them, too."

"Poor Fred," I say.

She murmurs.

Moments like these I can't help but wonder: When my father walked out on us, did Mrs. Brown just sigh and murmur at the kitchen table while my mother made more coffee, wondering whether she'd live through another pot? And what about when Mr. Brown passed away the summer Abby turned twelve? Did my mother console Mrs. Brown or merely make her an extra big batch of brownies? Death and desertion never seemed to enter into their conversations. If they touched it at all, it was with the dread of touching a corpse.

"Maggie," Mrs. Brown speaks softly so my telephone-talking mother can't hear her, "how are you?"

I freeze. How am I?

"I'm OK. Thank you for asking."

Her eyes tear, her voice squeaks—"I can't even begin to imagine how you feel. I'm so sorry."

*No! Don't say anything more. I won't survive this day, this minute, if you say another word. You can't comfort me.*

"Thank you," I say.

Abby, on death: *"I hope dying isn't like sleeping—when you don't know what's happening to you. You may as well be dreaming when you go. I hope it's not some slip-into-oblivion event; I hope it's more conscious. You know what I hope most of all, Maggie Moon? My dad could be a dope sometimes—like when he got lost going over to Petersburg and drove two hours out of his way, and remember the time he went to pick up his car at five in the morning when the mechanic meant five in the after-noon?—but wherever he is, I hope he knows what's going on. I hope he's not lost like he was in life."*

## CHAPTER 5

Tess became *Abby's* blonde highness. As for me, I found mystique in Tess, not just from the stories she told but more the ones I suspected she didn't; the tears that sprang from something as subtle as the breeze; and, yes, most of all, the naughty décor under her blouse. Knowing it was there, a vivid red heart kissed by cleavage. For such a flourish—what an impression! Tucked away but not a secret, she'd whip it out for us any time, in a flamboyant show of flesh and art. In the early days of our friendship I thought about it whenever we were together, chatting; and I thought about it whenever I was alone, falling asleep. When the novelty of her tattoo finally wore off, her mystique didn't. I...loved her.

But Abby's love was different than mine. More savage. Her need to be near Tess—as though her close-by breathing could fix fate—was unquenchable. One night after a football game, Abby yanked me out from under the bleachers and we headed home. Our trusty path awaited us. We'd been drinking Cold Duck, the world had a boozy rhythm, my lips were swollen from French-kissing Clyde and some ponytailed guy named Jeremy where it was too dark to tell who was who. To anyone who was listening, I hollered:

*"What a blast!"*

*"You're a slut,"* Abby said darkly.

I swayed under white moon, black sky. *"What?"*

*"The way you let yourself be manhandled by those losers!"* Her disgust blew owls off their branches.

*"What about you? You're the one who's done it with more guys than I can count!"*

*"Yeah, but they don't mean anything to me! Meanwhile, Maggie Moon will go home and croon about all the boys who tell her how pretty her long black hair is. God, it makes me want to vomit!"*

*"Big deal, what's a little kissing? And besides, I was drunk, OK?"*

*"There was a lot more than kissing going on!"*

I blinked myself back to sobriety. Under the bleachers. Passed back and forth. Clyde, Jeremy, Clyde, Jeremy. Suddenly, my memory flew at me like a bat and I crumpled under the horror of it: My breasts, exposed. I reached in my bra where it was wet and raw. My nipples were sore.

*"I think I'm bleeding,"* I cried.

She snorted. *"You're not bleeding. Well, maybe metaphorically."*

*"Huh?"*

*"Look, just don't love them, Maggie. Do whatever you want with them, but don't love them. Otherwise you'll get hurt. Didn't you learn that lesson from Tess?"* She inhaled the whole night, every star in the sky, lost her balance, then fell down like some drunken hobo. *"We'll go see her tomorrow! She'll set you straight and the sky will be bright blue again! Hallelujah!"*

*"Why? Tess isn't my mother!"* I whined.

*"Exactly!"*

We were too hungover to go see Tess the next day, but in time we did. Actually, Abby saw a lot more of her than she let on—half the school day she was hanging around the office on the pretense of learning secretarial skills.

One Saturday the three of us went to a little art exhibit in Berrysville. Tess had painted in her youth, gave it up for a family, and was now getting back into the groove.

*"Opening my eyes again,"* she said with loving inspection, then whispered dreamily, half to herself: *"Girls, go wherever your heart goes and don't ever look back."*

The gallery was wall-to-wall paintings of female nudes. The artist had frizzy red hair and a million moles. Her unfortunate features betrayed her angelic poise.

*"Hello, hello, hello,"* she walked around, greeting everyone one by one. *"I'm Donna."*

Nudes everywhere. It was almost assaulting. Nudes reading, nudes sleeping, nudes swimming. Nudes, nudes, nudes, all dimpled and fat.

*"These are far out,"* Abby said. *"Wish I could paint like this."*

*"Maggie showed me the book you girls made. You've got talent. Both of you do,"* Tess said.

*"Yeah?"* Abby reacted. I knew what she was wondering: When did I show it to Tess, why did I show it to Tess, did I see Tess behind her back? The truth was, I just brought it to school one day as a gesture. Tess was my friend, too.

Before we left, Tess purchased a little sketch of a nude rising from a bear claw tub for ten dollars.

*"Just to show my support,"* she shrugged while Abby and I peeked at a picnic lunch she had packed up for us. *"I wish I had some money to throw around but my ex-jackass made sure I'd have to scrimp and save till the day I dropped. Girls, when love ends on a sour note, you can't imagine ever singing its praises again."*

Tess had the perfect spot picked out for us, on a stone bridge the sun had warmed up nicely. She was an interesting eater: Tarragon chicken salad, sunflower muffins, dried fruit, and rainbow-colored bottles of juice. She wiggled her way into a cross-legged position and proposed:

*"Let's do what nudes do best."*

I gulped down muffin. *"What?"*

Tess smiled at her goddess, the sun, and said, *"Lounge."*

*"That Donna chick knows how to hold a paintbrush,"* Abby said, drinking juice.

*"This is gross. I thought it was mango but it's carrot."*

*"They were OK,"* I said, *"but can't she do anything besides nudes? I'd rather look at paintings of sunsets or mountains or a basket of flowers."*

Abby shoved a finger down her throat. *"How pedestrian."*

*"OK,"* Tess posed, *"how about some food for thought, girls? How would you feel if the artist were male? Maggie?"*

*"What difference would it make?"*

*"Abby?"*

*"I'd tell him where to go."*

*"Why?"*

*"He has no beeswax painting nude chicks, that's why."*

*"Abby, Abby, Abby—haven't you ever heard of an artist's freedom of expression?"*

*"Yeah, but I've heard of dog poop, too."*

*"What if I decided I wanted to paint male nudes?"*

Abby, mortified: *"Why would you WANT to?"*

Tess and I lost it and soon our laughter lured Abby in. First, with a little hiccup of a giggle that progressed to full-fledged howling.

Glorious sisterhood!

Later, tearing at a dried apricot like beef jerky, Abby said, too casually:

*"Maggie lets boys take advantage of her."*

*"Oh, I can't believe that,"* Tess said. I doubted her surprise was genuine. *"You seem like you have a good head on your shoulders, Maggie."*

I snapped back at Abby, *"Maybe I take advantage of THEM!"*

*"That's no good, either,"* Tess said.

*"Look, they both said I was cute,"* I said.

*"Jesus Christ,"* Abby muttered.

*"Maggie,"* Tess said, *"listen to me very carefully. At night all cats look black. Do you know what I'm trying to say?"*

*"I'm not sure…"*

*"You're a gorgeous girl. You're both gorgeous girls!"* Tess declared. *"God help the men on this planet when you're both full-grown women. But right now, don't believe what any boy tells you after dark when he's got ants in his pants."*

*"This all happened after Maggie's dad left,"* Abby volunteered.

*"Abby, don't,"* I warned her.

*"Well, it's true,"* was her chewy retort.

Naked, I was stark naked. But this wasn't art. My dad was gone.

*"I just don't want to see you hurt, Maggie,"* Abby said with rare sweetness, so sweet I began to cramp. *"Your old man takes off with the town bimbo and you act fine with that. Meanwhile, you let any gross-out with a pierced ear and a ponytail suck the life out of you. Don't you know all they wanna do is wiggle it in every girl's face?"* She bore so deeply into my eyes I swear she's still there, somewhere. *"Your dad split. Deal with it. Please. PLEASE?"*

Tess knew the whole secret rotten story—I could tell. Her face was a beautiful old wreck and at that moment her true goodness, the Mother Earth in her, beckoned me. I crawled into her arms, into her bosom, home of her heart and tattoo and a flowery smell that made me feel safe. I would stay here, in this dark fragrant cave, because out there it was too bright, blindingly bright, people died in such light. At some point Abby joined in the huddle and prayed for my soul and never in my life did I feel so protected from all the evil out there. When I finally cried—and I cried like my guts were being torn out of me—every buried emotion bubbled up and gurgled and puked out.

*"Korean men don't do this, up and leave their families! It's unheard of! He must have hated us so much. Can you imagine how much he hated us? He didn't even*

*leave us a note. I don't even remember the last thing he said to me. Why didn't he love my mother? Why didn't he love us? How could he abandon us in this hick town where there's nothing for us? Where we stick out like sore thumbs! Here he'd get mad if we used forks when we ate mashed potatoes—does eating mashed potatoes with chopsticks make any sense, any sense at all? If he were so traditional, why'd he leave? What a creep. What a devil. Yes, he's the devil. He deserves to burn in hell. I hate him. I hate him!"*

And then, I was told, I slept.

## CHAPTER 6

Tess, our priestess, our life force, fell in love just a few weeks later. Ironically it was with the new town doctor, the man who replaced my father. Dr. Kowolski was a widower with white hair and a white moustache and the kindest smile I'd ever seen. He was good to Tess, and treated her like a princess. And she was happy. And she painted.

And she sang!

Abby and I went to colleges on opposite sides of the Blue Ridge, but we kept in touch like two mountain climbers listening for each other's echoes. She always addressed her letters to *Maggie-Moon-with-the-moody-blues* or *Maggie-Moon-with-the-zit-on-her-tit*; and she always drew cartoons of me dancing inside a full moon or hanging off a crescent moon blowing kisses. Meanwhile I shot back some radical poetry; mostly, I think, because that's what she wanted to hear—fragmented moans over the mountains. *If I'm fighting a war with myself, there's no way I'll ever win/ If I'm fighting a war with God, I'll be condemned for the sin/ If I'm fighting a war with the world, then life should never have been.*

But behind the cartoons and the poems, our messages traveled to an imaginary path where we met halfway, a place unchanged by the light of passing cars. Like the actual path that paralleled Appleseed, here it was always safe and secretive, uplifting and eternal, no matter how bad the war was going or how late our periods were. Merely a projected reflection of where we used to go, it was more real than the traffic at night around us.

That January after graduation, Abby and I moved to New York. The year was 1982. I would become the famous poetess, and Abby, the famous artiste. We were naïve—despite our portfolios, we remained in the shadows and ended up taking jobs as phone solicitors from six o'clock to midnight. The only place we could afford to live was a railroad apartment on East Sixth Street with dirt floors, a tub in the living room and cockroaches falling from the ceiling as we slept. But that was OK with Abby. It was enough for her to just *be* here; suddenly she walked with the freedom of a prisoner stretching in the sun. I watched her undergo some liberation of soul in the East Village and it was as disturbing as watching a mannequin in a punk shop come to life. In my animated memories she grew a neon glint in her eye and searched for weirdos in dark café corners writing suicide notes. She spent her free time picking up men with poor teeth and corroded fingernails, then driving them away with her manic talk of schizos and scuzballs, her mockery of the human race.

*"We philosophize until we're blue in the face. The meaning of life is this. The meaning of life is that. But the problem is that we're too dumb to know the meaning of anything. How can we have philosophy when we're so fucking dumb?"*

When Abby tired of men she started befriending women. The one I remember the most was a woman she met in a museum who had witchy white hair and worked in the theater. No expression, no eye contact—she gave me the willies. In the afternoons Abby would disappear to meet her and be back at our apartment at five o'clock to walk with me to our jobs near Washington Square. These walks were nothing like our walks back home. The East Village in winter had the air of post-war gloom and sometimes we walked all the way in silence, hiding our faces with scarves like Ukrainian peasants. No matter how drunk Abby and I got—and we got drunk most nights on a jug of Gallo as the heat rose up on the loft bed where we spoke with underground urgency—we never came out and talked about this woman. Why? Because it touched on something we were too afraid to touch, something we inherited from our mothers. Their relationship ended abruptly one day and Abby went back to men for crude jokes and quickies.

One night in a Village bar I caught something in the arch of Abby's brow and the parting of her lips after she drank from a glass she had just tilted a stranger's way—yes, a woman. A transformation so gradual it almost seemed natural, even inevitable, here, amid the screaming of ambulances outside our windows and the howling of drug addicts in the stairwell. If I were older I would have confronted this situation with some level of maturity; I would have been able to simply ask: *Abby, are you gay?*

Instead, three months after we arrived, I left Abby in New York.

## CHAPTER 7

I could say we lost touch over the years, but the truth is that Abby left me behind. Not in Cabin Creek or New York but on a path where we had met in our minds long after the true treading of that path when we walked home from football games and parties and, more often than not, from nowhere. Even now as I spinsterishly sip tea I can conjure up the forests around us ink-blotting the sky; and how I shivered from the bottle of beer I held in my hands, my neck tingling because I had almost been made love to. Abby and I talked about everything, so sure of our clear-sightedness; and if we concentrated hard enough we could move mountains and constellations with our minds. We would grow up to be great women and as vulgar as men. We would cuss in urban fashion like drunks on Broadway. Our path: Immortalized in my memories as a place holy to ourselves, our once-walked youth. *Dried leaves in my hair, I lay on the hard, lumpy ground. Above us, an infant blue night sleeping, cradled by God, rocked by the moon. I'm in child wonder of all that stretches ahead of me like a great big magical sky.*

The next time I saw Abby was six years later in 1988 when I was in New York for a seminar. By then I'd graduated from law school, married and settled down in the suburbs of Philadelphia, three hundred and twenty-four miles northeast of Cabin Creek. It wasn't the first time I'd been back to New York, but it was the first time I called her. She agreed to meet me at the bar of my hotel on Central Park. It was winter and everything was lit up like a skating rink. Even then I was feeling skittish about my marriage, like I'd rushed onto the ice without my skates. Abby was late and hurried; her face was powder pale.

"It's Maggie Moon." She bit her lip, and then I knew why she had stopped answering my letters: I was a reminder of a life she was on the verge of forgetting. *"And she's pregnant."*

"Well," I said awkwardly, *"I wanted a little boy and I'm having a little boy. Do you remember me saying that, that afternoon with Tess?"*

Abby barely nodded, refusing to let her memory budge.

I said: *"Tess died last April. She had a heart attack in her sleep. Did you know?"*

Abby's eyes, emeralds still, met mine and flickered for one sentimental second. *Tess died? No, no, no...* She was shaking but fought it, conquered it—that is, coming back to me, what we shared.

*"No,"* she replied.

When I say Abby left me behind, I mean that when she declared her sexuality, she didn't want to leave a trail that led back to me.

Mrs. Brown waddles off to the bathroom. Too much tea and she didn't touch the Lorna Doones.

My mother remarks: "Whoever believes 'absence makes the heart grow fonder' doesn't know her behind from her brain."

"It was Mark's idea to spend Thanksgiving apart," I inform her.

"Oh?" She looks surprised.

My mother only knows the soft-spoken son-in-law who takes walks in the wilderness whenever we visit, not the broken middle-aged man he's become. And who could blame him? Not me.

"You and Mark have been through a lot, Maggie. God knows some marriages wouldn't survive this."

My lack of reply visibly upsets her.

"You two need to spend more time together," she says. "I know you're what they call a power lawyer but don't get caught up in your exciting job. You'll regret it later."

"I hardly call talking to disgruntled partners and horse-faced wives who don't understand why their husbands leave them exciting. No *cause-célèbres* in my appointment book, believe me." Wrong thing to say. My mother was no horse-faced wife. My father was just a creep who left us to feel our way alone in the dark. And in that darkness my mother chose to reach out to save others instead of herself. A Socks and Mittens drive. The Sweet Charity Ball. Annual Thanks-a-thons. But what does that leave me?

"I think about Owen every day," she whispers, she trembles. "Every minute of every day."

The sound of my son's name murders me in cold blood. Every night for the past ten months I've lain in bed, more stone than human. And then it hits me... Owen is gone.

My beautiful brown-haired boy is not coming back. If I believed in God, and I try to believe in God (but what kind of God would allow a child to die?), then I would fall asleep and enter a picture book world of dreams, streams and reams of possibilities. But instead I pass out and into some netherworld where the only sounds are echoes from a voice I'll never hear again. Owen is gone. And now I know what death feels like.

"Me, too."

Now that I am back in Cabin Creek and settled in for the week, I can't imagine packing up and leaving. When I ask myself *Where I will go from here?* it's not a geographical question but a philosophical one. One that Abby would answer from the lips of Tess: *Go wherever your heart goes and don't ever look back.* But that's where my heart goes—back, before I lost Owen. If Abby had any idea how often I wish I could go back to that night of the bonfire, she'd call me a dope and say, *This is what happens to people who abandon their art; they dwell on dumb things.* She'd say, *Wake up, Maggie Moon-with-the-moody-blues, you're dreaming of an old universe.*

An old universe. It all looks and feels the same, but nothing's the same. My mother and Mrs. Brown are organizing their Thanksgiving menu while I'm clearing tea for three. Behind us a big bay window frames the backyard where the ashes of leaves pile like autumn potpourri. A scene from a Hallmark calendar. *November nesting...* If only I could pull some magic and a handful of stars out of the air and flip the calendar back to 1976 when my whole life stood still against muffled voices and a stereophonic sky. Now we're running home, Abby and I— *good-bye, Clyde!*—laughing like we're about to pee in our pants. *"I'm gonna do it with Kurt tomorrow after school, Maggie, and then I'm gonna tell him what a lousy lover he is. Isn't that a howl?"*

The calendar flips forward and I run to meet Abby halfway on the path, past trees, past a clearing, the stone church on the right, run to hear her tell me one last time—

*"You'll be OK, Maggie Moon. I know you'll be OK."*

# Carolyn Parkhurst

# Becoming a Dog

CAROLYN PARKHURST is a writer living in Washington, D.C. Her first novel, *The Dogs of Babel*, was published by Little, Brown & Co. in 2003.

When I was a small girl, and not a dog at all, I used to think that "Old Mother Hubbard" was the saddest thing I had ever heard: When she got there, the cupboard was bare, and so her poor dog had none. When I thought of that dog standing there hungry and not knowing why, I could feel myself standing in his place. I could see myself looking up and pleading, not able to say a word.

It was Allison who told me that there was more to that story. She had an old book of nursery rhymes which contained more than a dozen verses I had never heard, and they told the story of how Old Mother Hubbard finally made it up to her dog. Finally, I saw, she learned how to take care of him. "She went to the fruiterer's to buy him some fruit; when she came back, he was playing the flute… She went to the barber's to buy him a wig; when she came back, he was dancing a jig." But my favorite verse was the last one: "The dame made a curtsy, the dog made a bow; the dame said 'Your servant,' the dog said 'Bow-wow.'" The dog, it seemed, was finally happy, and Old Mother Hubbard had learned to love him back.

All this is by way of explanation. To try to show why, when the moment came and I stood there as speechless as a dog, I made the choices I did.

Allison has been my friend for a long time, but it's only recently that I looked at her and saw the way her eyes looked when she laughed. The way that sometimes she spoke with such passion her cheeks flushed. It's only recently that I looked at her and saw the way I had been in love with her for years.

I wanted to tell her—really, I did—but there were so many times I couldn't. There was a day when we were talking, and she was lying sprawled across my bed, and I knew I couldn't ruin it all by opening my mouth. She yawned and stretched her arms out, not even aware of the tension I could feel spreading through the room. She asked me some question about my day, and my tongue was like clay in my mouth, and I couldn't answer. I sat there and watched her, and all I could think of was the way she looked and the stupid way the words stayed stuck to my tongue.

One night, we went out together to a club, and we danced to the swaying music. I saw the way her hair fell around her face, and I thought that maybe the music was loud enough for me to tell her. But then a man came up and stood right in the middle of us and started dancing with her. And even though he wasn't the one I cared about, I felt the old teenage sadness that he didn't want to dance with me. After a while, I went back to the table and drank different colored drinks and watched the way he urged her with his body, the way he moved on every side of her until she couldn't help but dance with him. I had had a moment when I might have changed everything, but I let it pass, too concerned with looking at her hair, and now the moment belonged to him. He put his hand out and touched her for the first time, on the back of her neck, underneath her hair. And I have known her as long as I can remember, and I have never tried to touch her there. I sat alone, and my feet were stones, and my tongue was clay, and my sweet drinks tasted like what I had lost.

His name was Gareth. He had wild red hair that fell to his shoulders, and he worked for an organization that helped the homeless. He was perfect for her. She fell in love all at once.

Lucky for me, Gareth had a friend he thought I might like. His name was Alex. And I did like him. He was sweet and considerate, and he could always make me laugh. When he touched me, it felt like he was petting me softly, nothing more.

The four of us would go out together, and when Allison and I retreated to the ladies' room, she would put her hand on my shoulder and lean close to talk softly in my ear. When Gareth gave her a new pair of earrings, she let me take her ear in my hand to get a better look. We seemed closer than ever. This went on for six months.

We decided to go away for the weekend, both couples together, to look at the fall foliage and shop in the outlet malls. We were staying in a cottage Allison's parents owned. While the guys chopped wood for a fire, Allison and I went for a walk in the woods.

"You look so pretty today," she said. I nearly stopped walking. I couldn't take a breath. "Alex can't stop looking at you."

I looked down and made myself laugh.

She bent and picked up a leaf from the ground. It was beautiful, big and vibrant and orange. "I'm going to take it back and give it to Gareth," she said. "I love to give him little things."

"That's a nice idea," I said. My throat was as dry as dirt. "Gareth is lucky to have you."

That night before bed, Allison came into our room to bring us towels. "I hope the bed's OK," she said. "It's where my parents usually sleep. I would've felt weird staying here with Gareth."

Alex was leaning back against the pillows. "It feels great," he said.

"Okay. Good night, you two," she said and closed the door. When she left, it seemed like she took all of the air in the room with her.

I went to turn off the light. "No," Alex said. "Leave it on."

The light was my ruin. If the room had been dark, then I might have been able to be honest with him. I might have been able to hide my face in his shoulder and whisper how I felt. But when he took my hand and said, "I love you" and I looked at his unbearable, hopeful face, I panicked. "I love you, too," I said.

He was so happy. I couldn't stand how happy he was. I wanted to cry for what I had done to us. He touched me as if he were touching something holy. He made love to me slowly in the light, and I had to look at his glad face the whole time.

Once Alex was asleep, I got up and went to look out the window. There was a stone outside, alone in the chill, and I thought that if I went out to sit there underneath the moon, I might be able to make myself feel anything at all. I left the room quietly and let myself out of the house. But when I got to the stone, it wasn't what I wanted it to be. It grew warm beneath me as I sat, but it was always just as still and as hard as a stone sitting in the moonlight. It was nothing to me. I had begun to shiver, and I knew that the night would only get colder, and it wouldn't matter where I sat.

The next day, I was quieter than a dog. I didn't want to talk at all. I said I wasn't feeling well, and we decided to drive home early. Alex sat with me in the back seat and made me rest with my head in his lap. He stroked my hair and checked my face for fever.

When they dropped me off, Allison got out of the car and walked me to the door. "Guess what?" she whispered. "Gareth got a new job, and he's moving to California, and he wants me to go with him!" She hugged me tight. Over her shoulder, I could see Gareth smiling at us through the window of the car.

"Wow," I said.

"I know," she said. "I'm going to start looking for a job there tomorrow."

I couldn't smile. I couldn't speak. "Well, listen, go get some sleep," Allison said. And she was gone.

I was awake all night, thinking about it, and when the dawn came, I had decided what to do. Alex called in the morning to see how I was feeling. "Listen," he said. "I want to cook you dinner next weekend."

I didn't think about the way his face must look on the other end. "I'm sorry," I said. "I can't do this. I love somebody else." And I hung up.

I got to Allison's house as quickly as I could. I love you, I was going to say. And, you're beautiful. And, I think about you all the time. But when I got there, she was already on the phone with Alex.

She covered the receiver with her hand when I came in. "What's going on?" she asked. She looked angry. She held the phone out to me. "Talk to him. He's really upset. You've got to talk to him."

I looked at the phone, and I looked into the bare cupboard of her eyes, and all I wanted was to lie with my head in her lap and to feel her stroking my hair. I wanted to kiss her hand and to taste the sweet salt of her skin. But I couldn't say the words.

I closed my eyes and thought of Mother Hubbard, and I could feel myself shrinking down. I felt the fur growing out everywhere to hide my shaming flesh. I bristled the hair on my back as I looked at her hand holding out the receiver, and I let out a low growl.

Now, when I bark, it means everything all at once. I don't have to say a thing. When Allison comes home at the end of the day, I leap and turn in my little dog jig, and she speaks to me softly and fills my bowl with everything I could want. I bring her rubber balls and the carcasses of birds, and she places tidbits of meat in my mouth with her slender fingers.

When Gareth comes over, I jump up on the couch between them and she scratches me behind the ears. When he stays overnight and she closes me out of the bedroom, I crouch under the coffee table and pee into the thick carpet. I sink my sharp teeth into the leather of his shoes when he leaves them on the living room floor. When she scolds me, all I have to do is lie on my back and offer her my belly to rub, and she smiles at me like I've been her best friend all along. She takes care of me, and this is the way it will always be. My love, she will curtsy, and the dog, I will bow, and she'll say "Your servant," and I'll say bow wow.

*Sally Pfoutz*

# *Sea Anemone*

SALLY PFOUTZ is the author of two published novels, *Missing Person* (Penguin, 1993) and *Red-tail* (Publishamerica, 2002). Her poems have appeared in *Phoebe* and *Fugue,* and she's had several articles in national publications. Her short story "If You Were a Tiger" won the 2001 Alice Abel National Literary Award. She's currently working on a preschool curriculum workbook, also called "If You Were a Tiger." She is in the planning stages of a sourcebook for young adults called "Goodbye, I Love You, Take Care." Besides continuing to write novels, she's researching the life and works of Anna Hyatt Huntington, with the idea of writing a biography.

One clear, bright, April morning, Seth Feinstein's wife, Ailene, gave birth to a miniature porcelain beauty. April, they called her, and she was as perfect as a spring day can be. She had a fine crest of silky hair, huge eyes the color of midnight, a chip of a nose. Her features were exquisite; it was clear to all who saw her in those first few moments that April Feinstein would have grown up into a true beauty. If only she had not been missing the back of her brain.

Seth held her against him while doctors and nurses clustered around Ailene, who was unconscious. One look at her daughter and she had fainted dead away after fourteen hours of frightening, exhausting, unwanted labor. Seth wouldn't sleep, he'd never sleep again, that's what he thought as he ran his eyes up over April's pale swoop of a skull. The soft spot pulsed in response. Her ears were so delicate, did she know what they were saying about her, could she hear their tones, earnest, sorrowful, excited?

Seth had seen it, once for a few seconds and the image was burned on his memory. One quick look had planted the vision in his sight forever, the tip of her spine was exposed like a tender sea anemone. It opened pearly pink, the nerve endings swimming gently, then it closed; opened, closed, with every breath of air, like a normal baby's tiny fist. In a moment that could have been eternity, April, the only child Seth would ever have, died in his arms.

Seth imagined the gift list. Her dazzling blue eyes would give corneas to Lucian Mays, a pharmacist in Cincinnati, Ohio. Her kidneys would go to Donna Lynn Padgette of Ocracoke, North Carolina, and John Lorenzo of Vineland, New Jersey. Her heart would be implanted in Baby Reba Smith of McKenzie, Tennessee, and her liver would be lost in a failed transplant attempt in Pittsburgh, Pennsylvania, recipient unnamed.

His baby would be used for parts, transplants, and research, Seth knew, because he had given permission with his harried, haphazard signature. "Here…here…here…here…," the nurse's finger pointed and he scrawled. If anyone knew what he had done, no one was saying.

Then Seth Feinstein, professor of mathematics, kissed his wife of fourteen years on her chin, noticing how it puckered and trembled even as she slept, and he left the hospital forever. Outside, like a relentless storm, a raging fire, or a deadening drought, Seth knew he'd have to face the founder and leader of the Rights of the Fetus Society. A childless, wifeless man who wore the Bible as an armor and claimed divinity as his defense. A man who declared himself far and wide the Great Protector of Human Life. Caleb Brown, who bulldozed over the lives of living breathing human beings in order to guarantee the births of terminally sick babies. He was ever spread-eagled in Seth's path, blocking his passage, snarling and spitting.

Seth shoved Caleb hard, and then walked right into the face of a camera. So many were pointed at him like eyes in a peacock fan, a giant colorful array of hands and eyes and open mouths. One long-nosed lens branded Seth's forehead. "Hey," someone shouted, "what about your baby?"

Seth got into his Saab and drove far out into the country to a neglected sunflower field. Uncut from the year before, its brown stalks gawked at him like a host of blinded scarecrows. The forgotten flowers were wasted, shriveled, their blackened faces identical. His fancy Saab rattled across the rutted field, flattening every sunflower scarecrow before him, two and three, sometimes five went down against the hood of his car, or reared over backwards to be taken by his wheels.

In his mind, April's spine winked open and closed like a tissue paper fist. He knew it would always be there, in his sleep it would grab him, hold his dreams, squeeze the life out of him. When he awoke it would be adhered to his Adam's apple, begging and sucking, stealing his breath, his thoughts. Seth took out the scalpel he had lifted from the hospital, the one he had taken for April. If his hand over her mouth and nose hadn't worked swiftly enough, he would have felt for the soft place between her twiggy ribs where her heart beat like a fingertip on a tom-tom, and he would have plunged in the scalpel, swiftly. He wouldn't have been sorry. His thoughts were pure, there was a deed, the time was certain, his hand on the knife would have acted quickly, efficiently. When April ceased to breathe, he thanked her in his mind, just as his wife wailed in grief. The doctors and nurses attended Ailene like priests at a christening.

Now he was outside, under the sky, sheltered from the road by hoards of leftover sunflowers. Seth poked the scalpel into the spot on the side of his neck where his own pulse wagered its hold on life. The pain surprised him, made him cry for the first time that day. He wept for his loss, groaned in agony, and gasped as the sting of the knife pierced his flesh. There was a deepening ache as he pushed its point into his artery, the flash of terror as he ripped it across his throat. Then his forehead thudded on the steering wheel. The last thing he saw was a fountain of blood. It drenched the windshield like a sheet of rain; cool, dark, April showers.

Leslie Pietrzyk

# Showered with Gifts

LESLIE PIETRZYK is the author of two novels: *A Year and a Day*
(William Morrow, 2004) and *Pears on a Willow Tree* (Avon, 1998).
She lives in Alexandria, Virginia.

Our hostess loves her role. This is the fourth shower (two bridal, two baby) she has given in three years. She has a routine: pulling down from the closet shelf the cut-glass punch bowl that belonged to her grandmother, the stack of wicker trays from Pier 1 Imports that permit people to easily balance plates of food on their laps, several oversize ceramic platters. Ironing, organizing, polishing. Stationery shop, grocery store, florist. The hostess owns all the right implements: Saucers to match every coffee cup. Four extra serving spoons in her silver pattern. Trays. Bowls. Baskets. A nifty plate for pickles and olives. Even a tough-but-gentle spot remover stick that has never failed to get rid of any stain on the lace tablecloths or linen napkins, even the dropped blackberries, even dribbles of coffee, even lipstick. The hostess is well aware that details always mean the difference between a shower that is memorable and one that, sadly, isn't.

The idea, in case anyone has forgotten or doesn't know, is to "shower" the happy bride (or expectant mother) with the gifts she will need in her new role.

A good setting is important; everyone knows that. The hostess's house—almost paid off, thanks to a top-notch divorce attorney and a guilt-ridden ex-husband—boasts a kitchen large enough to accommodate insistent "helpers" (women accomplishing little more than being in the way, though the hostess cheerfully accepts all offers of assistance because that's how it's done at showers). The house also features a formal living room that seats forty in a pinch, a separate dining room, and a recently redecorated sunroom that opens out onto a large deck. There is ample street parking, and the house is situated close to the Little River Turnpike exit off the Beltway in Virginia, making directions a snap; even the people from Maryland and the District can find the house without a hitch.

The largest shower she hosted was for thirty-seven women—too many, really; opening the gifts took nearly three hours, and with all those presents, duplicates were inevitable. Two All-Clad butter warmers, two different pepper grinders, a host of picture frames—why do people insist they know better than the bride and forgo the registry? She, our hostess, always gives something nice off the registry.

The smallest shower was a mere six women, making for a cozy afternoon. One guest was the lawyer in charge of an important murder case that had been all over the front page of the newspaper, so it was a thrill to have a local celebrity present. She'd bought off the registry—a lovely set of rosewood-handled steak knives.

Our hostess knows all the best shower games—asking people to guess what's inside baby food jars with the labels torn off; wearing the ugly hat if you're caught exclaiming, "Cute!" while opening the baby clothes; choosing nouns and verbs that end up in a funny story about how the bride and groom met. And all the traditions—making the paper plate bouquet with the gift bows; designating some-one to keep a list of gifts and givers; asking the guests to copy out favorite recipes to compile into a scrapbook for the bride. But of all these traditions and games and details, this, what we're doing now, is the single thing the hostess likes best about each shower, baby or wedding: when she hands out slips of paper and perfectly sharpened pencils and asks us to write one piece of advice for the bride- or mother-to-be. These "words of wisdom" are collected and placed in a basket with a satiny pink bow tied around the handle. Some are read out loud to the group, breaking up the monotonous block of gift-opening. The rest go home with the honored guest so she can ponder at her leisure the accumulated wisdom based on the years of our experience.

Today we are being asked to offer advice to a bride.

The hostess watches with pleasure as several women, all regular shower-goers, quickly scribble words on the slips of paper. Other women seem to be thinking hard, chewing the eraser ends of their pencils. (The hostess always throws away the pencils afterwards because she knows people can't keep things out of their mouths.) There are always several women who glance at their watches, impatient with these beloved traditions. But soon the papers are folded and dropped into the basket, which is set at the bride's feet.

Perhaps this advice will make a difference. Perhaps the hostess's marriage would not have failed if she had been told these things before the wedding. We all long to believe this, so we dutifully write down our secrets to a successful, happy marriage.

The bride—just turned thirty last week; met her fiancé on an airplane out of O'Hare—has dark circles under her eyes. Some people say that's hereditary. She's a beautiful girl: tall, slender, elegant, quite like the young Jackie Kennedy. She's very polite, mindful of introducing her friends to her mother's friends, good about repeating our names when she talks to us, like that's a trick she's learned, and maybe it is. In her business—something political—a memory for names is essential. She's sitting in the big wingback, the guest of honor chair, as the hostess has directed. Everyone today has told her she will be a beautiful bride, and she will—she glows with intense happiness, that singular joy brides feel because they're convinced their love is better, stronger, deeper, realer, more honest than anyone else's love for another person ever, anywhere. Without that illusion of certainty, could any of us walk down the aisle?

The bride reaches into the basket, rustles the folded papers, finally selects one. She unfolds it and reads out loud: *Tell him that you love him at least one time every single day. No exceptions! Not even if he's being a pain in the!*

That was probably written by Jeanne. She won't write or say vulgar words—though she wants to use them. "That f-ing son-in-law," she might mutter to a friend while she's on break from working the register. "He's a real p in the a. Not half as smart as he thinks."

Jeanne's real objection is that he has moved her only daughter (pregnant with twins) down to Atlanta. When the grandchildren come, they'll barely know Jeanne. She'll be a voice on the phone, the woman linked to presents and airports. Not to mention that cornball accent they'll pick up.

Jeanne knows you rely on daughters to take care of you when you're old, not sons (not even sons as wonderful as hers). If you're counting on sons, what you're really counting on are daughters-in-law, so good luck. And now her only daughter is settling into faraway Atlanta—buying a house in a good school district, registering at the parish, enrolling in the frequent shopper clubs. Jeanne can't put it out of her head, though why does growing old worry her so?; after all, she considers herself healthy—soy milk on her bran flakes, yoga classes, a calcium supplement and vitamin daily. Actually, unfortunately, there's a tiny lump growing in Jeanne's right breast. In less than a month, she'll come across it with her index finger, and she'll stand naked in front of the mirror, whispering, "F, f, f, f," then finally, "Fuck," but it will be several more months before she tells anyone else, even her doctor, and later there will be people, including her daughter in Atlanta, who will wonder if earlier detection would have made a difference. But everyone knows there aren't answers to questions like that.

A number of gifts have been opened—happily, most are from the registry so far!—and now the bride unfolds another piece of paper she's pulled from the basket. She clears her throat—she's been coughing quite a bit this afternoon; is it a cold or has she started smoking again? She reads: *Kiss and make up after every fight. Never go to bed angry.*

A murmur of agreement arises. This bit of advice is offered frequently and could've been written by Audrey or that younger woman, Kim, who is balanced on the edge of the sofa. Probably Kim. She was only four when her mother died, and she's self-conscious about having grown up motherless. Other women know things she doesn't, secrets and tricks about being a woman that their mothers passed along to them; there is a knowledge of the ways of the world that Kim thinks she lacks. For example, until recently she didn't actually know what she was doing when she pressed one hand to the forehead of someone who said he was sick. Or why and how to use fabric softener. And she still can't tie a silk scarf stylishly. The only wisdom Kim could claim to have learned from her mother was "look both ways when crossing a busy street so you don't get run over by a car and leave your only daughter motherless." Hardly advice to write on a piece of paper at a bridal shower, so Kim goes with the tried and true.

Not that she feels qualified to comment on matters of the heart: her last three relationships with men ended badly. One man was married, which Kim knew and ignored—so that was destined for failure. Another man suddenly moved to New York one day, swiping all of Kim's Prozac and leaving a terse note magneted to the fridge. The most recent of the three has repeatedly told Kim he will not get rid of his three cats though they make her sneeze and give her an itchy rash which he calls "a psychosomatic reaction." He doesn't like most of her friends and scorned the shower as "an old-fashioned hen party."

Kim knows that if she had grown up with a mother the way everyone else did, she would not keep dating men her therapist has determined are "inappropriate."

Though Kim and the bride work for the same company and usually eat their brown bag lunches together, today Kim barely pays attention to her friend. Instead she focuses on her friend's mother, seated on a stiff chair next to her daughter. She takes each gift after it's been opened, neatly tucking it away, watching to make sure the card doesn't get misplaced. Clearly, she likes helping.

The bride looks very much like her mother; that has been the source of early conversation at the shower. Kim noticed the resemblance immediately, though she felt too shy and sad to mention it to the mother, even though she was standing beside her in the foyer with only that single observation in her head. So the mother excused herself and walked off to talk to someone more interesting, more chatty, less awkward. Kim should have known what to say to make her friend's mother laugh and respond with something amusing. Everyone else managed to chat with the bride's mother.

Kim squirms in her seat, wishes (again) that she were the one getting married so she could have a daughter and do all the right, motherly things. If the man with the cats proposed, she would say yes. Someone at the shower told her about Zyrtec. Apparently it is very effective on all kinds of allergies.

Of course it is clear the man with the cats will not propose. No man will ever propose to Kim, though she'll live to be ninety-three.

The hostess holds out the basket again. She has been careful to keep track: unwrap four presents then read advice. Makes for a good rhythm that keeps the pace from lagging. No one will get bored.

The bride giggles as she grabs a piece of paper that has been folded over many, many times, until it is the size of a wad of gum. Everyone laughs to think how someone would compress a piece of paper in that way; who would do such a thing?

Desiree.

The bride reads Desiree's words: *Love means never having to say you're sorry.* Someone murmurs, "That was a sad movie"; heads nod; "Ryan O'Neal," sighs one of the older women.

Desiree draws her long dark braid over the front of her shoulder, strokes the fringed tips of her hair. It was just something to write. Who knows what it really means? It seems to her that love means constantly having to say you're sorry. Her partner wants more than anything to have a baby, and Desiree has to keep saying, "Sorry, I don't want one, I don't know why, but, sorry, I just don't, I never have—why do you want one? And, sorry, but it's not like the kid would be genetically related to me anyway," and so many more words to that effect. Sorry. Imagine that the world's most painful conversation is also the world's most boring. That is what Desiree has been dealing with all year. Simply put, she would not have come to this shower if her friend were having a baby; she's sick of babies and of thinking about them.

Yet she can't imagine leaving her partner, who is wonderful and perfect in every way except this new and ridiculous need for a baby. The two of them have been together since college; they had a commitment ceremony six years ago on a Greek island. Desiree is waiting for her partner to change her mind. A matter of time, she believes.

In fact, seven months from now, Desiree's partner will be raped and murdered late one night on her way home from the Metro—she probably shouldn't have taken that shortcut through the empty school grounds, but she was eager to get home and surprise Desiree with the news of her upgraded job title. A horrible tragedy—more does not need to be said. Except this: In the months and years that follow, Desiree will desperately regret that there is no baby and never will be.

All the gifts have been opened and noted on the master list; the bow bouquet is complete and has been properly admired. Now we have come to the last chance for one final piece of advice, one more thought on the secret to a good marriage. The bride reads this: *Buy a new item of lingerie once a month.* Everyone titters; there are some whistles; one or two of the older women blush in a sweet, ladylike way. Probably good advice, though the hostess is a bit surprised. She's never heard that one at any of the countless showers she's attended.

The woman who came up with this titillating suggestion is the woman whose name no one (except the bride) can remember—she's sitting in the far corner. She didn't take any cake, didn't want coffee, picked at the salad on her plate, dropped her buttered roll face-down on the carpet and left it there.

This woman has an entire dresser drawer jammed with lingerie, all of it ordered privately, very, very late at night from the Victoria's Secret toll-free number which she has memorized. At the way bottom of this drawer, hidden underneath the silky teddies and merry widows and seamed stockings that her husband can't seem to get enough of, is a handgun.

Which she will successfully use on herself before summer's end. Her husband will tear apart the house—searching all the closets, all the drawers—looking for a note but won't find one.

Enough. The bride can take home the remaining slips of paper to read (or not) at her leisure. In fact, her mother is sliding them into a small envelope, specifically set out for this purpose.

The hostess circulates through the room, pouring coffee into cups. She is adept at maneuvering through outstretched feet, bodies on the floor, finding the cups that need refilling, avoiding those that don't. She fields a few requests for hot tea. If she didn't enjoy giving showers so much, she might feel like a stewardess at this point. But thankfully, things are winding down; good-byes and thank yous waft from the foyer, women are free with their hugs and promises to call soon.

There is a point—and we are almost there—when the hostess simply wants everyone to be gone and the mess and disruption to disappear, when she wonders why she invited all these noisy, sloppy, clumsy, sticky people into her nice, clean house, her pristine sanctuary. She worries that she is becoming too accustomed to silence and aloneness. Her house is too big for her, of course, there are too many empty rooms now. She should move into something smaller, but she is reluctant, though several of her real estate agent friends have made discreet inquiries. Would the kids take that as their opening to start spending Christmas at their father's fancy mountain home instead of her sensible condo? It seems as if

Christmas is the only time she sees them anymore. And she couldn't possibly host showers in a condo. She would miss that terribly, providing these happy send-offs for brides and new mothers.

She glances at her watch. Everyone will be gone soon. She will insist that she needs no help cleaning up, she will nudge all these lovely women out the door so sweetly they won't realize what she's doing. Then she'll turn the deadbolt behind the last one, stack the dirty dishes in the sink as quickly as she can, and take down her blessed bottle of Maker's Mark bourbon from the back of the cupboard. She'll drop five ice cubes in a Waterford glass and pour bourbon until it reaches the top of the fleur de lis, give the glass a quick shake. Our hostess will carry the glass to the couch, where she'll sit and stare at nothing, listening to nothing as she slowly drains that first glass dry and then a second one, a third. This is what she does every night, what she looks forward to. Our hostess believes there is a certain comfort gained from the knowledge that all of the days—all of them—seem to end this way.

*Barbara Ann Porte*

# *Honeycomb*

(FOR ALEXANDRA MARIE THOMAS)

BARBARA ANN PORTE is the author of nearly thirty books for children and for adults, most recently *Beauty and the Serpent, 13 Tales* (Simon & Schuster, 2001). Awards include American Library Association Notable Book and Best of the Year list citations. Her poems and stories frequently appear in literary magazines, and her essays have been published in *The Washington Post Book World*, *The New York Times*, *Newsday*, and elsewhere. She is currently completing a novel. She is also a librarian, and lives in Arlington, Virginia.

*O*nce, and not that long ago, either, there lived a man and a woman, happily married for many years. Alas, one day the wife took ill, and died soon after. How sad! Surprising, too, as it was the husband who'd always been ailing: heart problems, diabetes, prostate trouble, and so on. His several sisters-in-law could hardly do enough for him; a man who'd never had to do himself. Poor soul!

Then, within the year he remarried, his bride a sweet young thing, not half his age, with nothing at all to call her own, except what was his, and that considerable. How shocking! The sisters-in-law were horrified.

"Gold-digger," they called her. "Jezebel!" All three predicted the worst.

"He'd better pray that one day they don't find him dead at the foot of the stairs, pushed," said the eldest.

"Or in insulin shock," said the next.

"Or overdone by too much hootchy-kootchy," the youngest one added.

"Serve him right, too," they told one another.

It didn't help, either, that none of them, or any other of their relatives, had been invited to the wedding. Nevertheless, the upshot was, within a month of it, the three sisters descended en masse on the house to gather up their dead sister's stuff: jewelry, clothing, wigs, and so on. "Over our dead bodies will Miss Teeny-tiny wear these," they said.

The pink china, though, was another matter; comprising service for twelve, of fine English bone, acquired ages ago, from goodness knows where. Not counting one missing cup and its matching saucer, the set was in pristine condition.

"It's staying," said the husband.

"Uh-uh," said his in-laws. "It's a family heirloom from our mother's estate. It was only on loan to our sister."

"Not hardly! We bought it in Barbados on our honeymoon." Naturally, the husband meant his first one. "It's mine!"

Possession being nine-tenths of the law, that's how things stood at the time. What time? The time when Juliet, a college freshman at the University of North Carolina, Chapel Hill, received a box in the mail from her paternal grandmother, youngest sister of her deceased great-aunt.

"Care package from Mumsie?" one roommate asked.

"Is it your birthday?" said the other.

Both roommates are white. Why should it matter? Juliet isn't a prejudiced person.

Still, from long experience dealing with Caucasians, not to mention dealing with relatives, Juliet has learned to practice discretion. Therefore, she makes up her mind to wait until both roommates are gone before she opens her present. A wise decision as it turns out.

First, she shakes the box. Not a sound. That probably eliminates home-baked cookies. What then? Removing the tape, she lifts the lid, peers inside. What is it? It looks like some sort of animal, dark brown, with long flowing fur. A mink or a marten? A pika, perhaps? She tells herself, Don't be silly. No one sends live animals through the mail. Not mammals anyway. Chickens, maybe, day old and cheeping, yellow and fluffy. Juliet and her brother once raised some. A dead animal, then? A fur piece? A fox collar? She certainly hopes not. Gingerly, she reaches inside, lifts out what's there. Oh, my. It's hair. Falls of it: long and short, black and brown, coarse and fine, curled and straight. A note is enclosed. Juliet reads it: From great-auntie's estate to the only coiffeuse in the family. Love, Grandma. Juliet blinks, and reads it again. To say she's surprised is a vast understatement. Not that she doesn't love hair.

"It's my passion," she's told her relatives on more than one occasion. She dreams of life in Hollywood, herself a famous stylist to the stars. Hair designs by

Juliet, will read her on-screen credit line. Naturally, her relatives are horrified. Professionals all, with advanced degrees, they continue to hope she'll change her mind. They're determined to help her; and also, so they say, willing to meet her halfway.

They tell her: "What you want to do first is finish college. Get a business degree. Open up a string of beauty parlors. Then you can do anything you like." They supply her with informational books, including the latest on Madam Walker, legendary African American entrepreneur, philanthropist, and inventor; daughter of slaves who revolutionized hair care for black women with products she'd invented and opened a chain of beauty schools, becoming a very wealthy women in the process. "It wouldn't hurt to take some chemistry, besides," they advise her.

Of course, what her relatives really hope is once on campus, Juliet will get some sense, alter her plans, become a doctor or a lawyer. It hasn't happened yet.

Now this! Juliet doesn't know what to make of her present. She's had no experience—none whatsoever—in dealing with dead people's stuff, plus hair seems so singularly intimate. She does have some questions, for instance: When did her aunt wear it last? Was she already ill? Has it been shampooed since? Dry cleaned? (Disinfected is what she really means.) Also, exactly what was the cause of her great-aunt's death? Liver problems is all Juliet's ever been told. That could mean almost anything. But was it contagious? And what of the hair's original owners? Were they all in good health when they sold it?

So many questions have made Juliet queasy. Gingerly, she picks up the hair and drops it back into the box. Is she supposed to send a thank you note? If so, when? Dealing with her great-aunt's bequests is about to take up all her spare time. Right now, for example, she has to decide what to do with the hair.

Hastily, she retapes the box and slides it under her bed. Out of sight, out of mind, she tells herself. But it isn't. Then she remembers her pesky brother. "Just don't think of a purple elephant," he used to tell her before she went to bed, after which she'd lie awake for hours, visions of a purple elephant running through her head. Now, recalling this, she retrieves the box, carries it down the hallway to storage, finds her suitcase, and unlocks it. Other stuff's already in it, including a pink china cup and a matching saucer she'd almost forgotten were there. Where had they come from?

"You keep those." Had her great-auntie told her that—say when she was three or four or five—after a tea party, held, perhaps, to take her mind off the weather. As a child, she'd been terrified of electric storms. Or had Juliet, instead, when no one was looking, tucked them into her duffle bag during one of her overnight visits, then walked off with them in the morning? Who remembers anymore?

Lifting them out, she places the box of hair in their stead, and carries the cup and saucer back to her room. She sets them on a shelf above the sink alongside several mugs already there. Then she washes her hands.

Well, that's that, she tells herself. But it isn't, by a long shot.

Exactly one week later, here comes a second package in the mail, this one an oversize, padded, brown manila envelope, carefully sealed.

"Another birthday?" asks one roommate.

"Another teacup?" says the second.

"Umm," says Juliet. Circumspect as ever, she waits until they're gone to open her present. She removes the contents cautiously. First the note: *Accessories from Auntie. We're still going through her things. Love, Grandma.* Then, piece by piece, the rest: a voluminous purple silk scarf, diaphanous—unfortunately with several, not quite invisible, runs; a pair of white cotton gloves, slightly soiled at the fingertips; a black beaded evening purse; and a pair of rose-colored dancing slippers; the likes of all of which Juliet has only ever seen in old movies, rerun on late night television.

Thinking the purse might have possibilities, Juliet unsnaps it. Inside is a wrinkled yellow hanky, with ivory tatting. (She's surprised to find she even knows that word.) Dismayed, she snaps shut the purse, stuffs it and everything else back into the envelope; then, carrying the envelope down the hall, she deposits it too in her suitcase, on top of the hair. Sighing, she wonders, what next? She won't have long to wait.

In exactly seven days, a third package arrives, large and square. Neither of her roommates being there, Juliet opens it at once, though not without some trepidation. Removing the brown outer paper, she uncovers a hatbox, white cardboard with cloth ties. Unfastening them, she takes off the lid. *Quelle surprise!* It's a hat. There's also a note: *Don't worry if it doesn't fit. It's meant as a memento. Love, Grandma.*

Juliet lifts out the hat and examines it. It's white, straw-like, with ivory tulle around its wide brim. The tulle is bountifully decorated with dots that look like tiny pussy willows. Turning the hat around in her hands, Juliet reflects. By now she's had time to get used to the idea of proximity regarding her dead auntie's stuff. Also, she's interrogated her mother.

"Exactly what kind of liver problems did Great-Auntie die of?"

"Cirrhosis," her mother finally told her. Then added, "You needn't think there's only one way to get it, either."

Having since looked it up, however, Juliet's pretty sure it isn't catching. Besides which, the hat appears never to have been worn. It still has its sales tag attached, the price marked down several times. Why not? Juliet thinks. Then, facing the mirror, she tries it on.

Of course she looks beautiful. Like a Watusi princess, as her father would say; or a picture: pretty girl in chapeau. Unfortunately, though, the hat doesn't fit. It's way too small. But with such an extravagant brim, will it fit into her suitcase? Juliet wonders. It is awfully pretty. It would seem a shame just to lock it away. So she doesn't.

Instead, she sets the hat on her bed and traipses, yet again, down the hallway to storage. Once there, she retrieves from her suitcase all her auntie's other stuff. Carrying it back to her room, she goes to work.

Using the only item she can find for a base, a toilet plunger, she pads it with towel-stuffed pillowcases to fashion a head and a body, which she dresses in a sweatshirt and pants, then places in a sitting position in the rocking chair near the window. At the ends of her figure's appropriate limbs, she pins the gloves and the slippers. Around its shoulders, she drapes the scarf, and lays the purse in its lap. She covers its head with falls of hair, then at the very top goes the hat.

She steps back to admire her efforts. One more thing, she thinks. Fetching the pink cup and the saucer from over the sink, she hands them to her aunt. (Well, in a manner of speaking.) "Have some tea," she offers.

At just that moment, Juliet's roommates come in.

"Carnival time?" asks one.

"A voodoo ball?" says the other

Juliet regards them coolly. "It's from my great-aunt. It's my legacy," she tells them. She gives the chair a push, starting it to rock. It goes on rocking—for a very long time. Then, just like that, it stops. "Uh-oh! Black magic, perhaps?" Juliet smiles. "My aunt was very spiritual."

"Creepy," says one roommate, moving away.

"Crazy," says the other.

That night, Juliet's awakened by a crashing noise, like thunder. Sitting straight up in bed, she's just in time to see a fearful flash of lightning go streaking past the window. She listens for the rain; hears huge drops splashing on trees, on leaves just coming out, pounding the pavement. In the midst of all this, comes a familiar, wholly unexpected, sound—the creaking of a rocking chair. How eerie! But then she thinks, of course! The chair is by the window. A draft must be coming in through the sash. She thinks she sees the white chiffon curtains blowing. She considers getting up to make sure the window is closed, except, the truth is, even now that she's grown, lighting storms still make Juliet a teensy bit nervous. Therefore, instead, she pulls her pillow around her head, and slides deeper under her covers. Eventually, she falls asleep to the unsyncopated rhythms of her roommates' snores. How can they sleep through such a wild storm?

Come morning, Juliet says, "That was some storm last night, huh!"

"Storm?"

"What storm?"

Both roommates look baffled.

It must be white people can sleep through anything, Juliet tells herself. In an effort to show them, she goes to the window, and, pulling back the drapes, opens it. She pokes out her head. Everything's dry. Bone dry, as they say. How can that be? Well, it's true there's been a drought going on, but what of last night? Did she dream it?

Just then the telephone rings. Juliet turns to pick it up. "Hello," she says, noticing at the same time that her dead auntie's hat has come askew. She reaches to straighten it. Wet! It's very wet—as though it's been out in a storm. Oh, my! The hair is wet, too. Before Juliet can explore any farther, her mother's voice comes over the line.

"How are you doing?"

"Fine, how are you doing?"

"I'm fine, too." Then, for all the world as if she'd been there, Juliet's mother says, "The weirdest thing happened last night." Wow, Juliet thinks. How would my mother know?

"Weird how?" she asks her. This is what her mother tells her:

"To begin with, we had a terrible storm. Such thunder you'd think the angels were bowling. Lightning lit the sky, and rain came down in buckets. The large tree in front of our house was blown down in the wind. Still, we were lucky. We didn't even lose power.

"First thing this morning, I turned on the television to see how other folks had fared. Imagine my surprise seeing your late great-auntie's house on the screen; struck by lightning, according to the news. Only your uncle and his new wife were home at the time. They're both fine."

"New wife?" Juliet interrupts to ask. It's the first she's heard of it, which goes to show she isn't the only circumspect member of her family.

"Ummmhmmm, don't ask!" says her mother. "Daddy and I weren't even invited to the wedding. All I know of her is what I saw on television. Looking not much older than you, there she was being interviewed. But here comes the weird part. Listen.

"She said, 'My husband is not a well man. He was already in bed. I was getting ready to join him when the storm hit. Then this happened: A streak of white light whished down through the chimney. Like a demon from hell, it flew room to room, lighted up each as it went. It stopped for only a split second when it got to the china cabinet. Then came such a flashing, and a sizzling, and a sputtering, that all I could think to do was to close my eyes and pray. That's when the rattling started, followed by sounds of crashing, noise so loud I covered my ears. Over it all, though, God must have heard me. The rumpus ended. Opening my eyes, I was just in time to see a blue-white ball of light bolt into the kitchen and disappear down the kitchen sink pipe. It left behind a strange and a powerful smell, something like bleach, something like sulfur. When I went to check on my china, a pink powder was all that remained.'

"Humph, *her* china, indeed!" says Juliet's mother. "Still, I guess it puts an end to the family fight."

"Family fight?" Juliet echoes.

"Just be glad you're not involved," her mother tells her.

"Oh, I am," Juliet answers. But which does she mean—glad or involved? In either case, events have left her nearly speechless. Not that she'd have much to say, anyway, with her roommates both still in the room, listening.

"Well?" they say, when she hangs up the phone.

"Well what?" Increasingly, Juliet thinks white people must have a whole different standard of manners. She means from the rest of the world. Ignoring them, she takes a towel from the bathroom, wipes off her legacy, and begins to dismantle it. She speaks to it as she goes: "Don't think I won't miss you," she says. "But at your stage, so much sitting up *can't* be good for you."

Her roommates look on, dumfounded. Then, "Stage?" one of them says, having recovered her composure.

"I think she said 'age,'" says the other. Openly curious, they watch as Juliet retrieves from under her bed: a hatbox, a carton, and a large mailing envelope and starts to pack them. Into the first goes the hat; into the carton, the hair; and all the rest she stuffs into the envelope: the beaded bag, the slippers, the gloves, the large purple scarf ruined by runs.

Ready now to tape everything up, she reaches to move her pink cup and saucer out of harm's way. That's when she notices that both are cracked; a pair of hairline fractures bifurcate each. She's positive they both were fine when she put them there, alongside what wasn't quite her aunt. Then in a flash, it comes to her—that ancient formula contained in old-time tales. Exactly how did it go? For sure it was something to do with a rag, and a bone, and a hank of hair, ever an incendiary combination. Not that she believes this, but who knows? She should have listened to her relatives and taken chemistry. Or better still, not bothered that bone china to begin with. Why wouldn't her aunt want it back?

Thinking this, Juliet wraps the cup and the saucer in a new towel, and tucks them in with the hat. Nothing to cause trouble there, she tells herself, sealing all three packages. Whatever's left—the pants and the shirt, the pillowcases and the stuffing—goes into the laundry. She replaces the toilet plunger under the sink. A flying machine, she thinks. Finally, dressed herself, she puts her trio of bundles into her backpack, then adds a large serving spoon and a stainless steel knife—digging utensils.

"I'm off to see the Wiz!" she tells her roommate audience.

As the door closes behind her, they discuss the situation.

"A leaking radiator, perhaps," says one.

"Spilt tea?" suggests the other.

Outside now, Juliet pauses briefly to consider, then sets off for a forsaken, overgrown graveyard she knows of just beyond the west edge of campus. She chatters as she goes: "sugar, petkins, baby cakes"—sweet-nothings to appease the dead, keep anyone from coming back to haunt her. Not that Juliet believes such things, but a bit of precaution never hurts.

Arriving at the cemetery, she digs a hole deep enough that she can stack her three packages in it, which she does, then covers them over with dirt. "There," she says, standing back up. "I guess you've got what you wanted. No more need to go traveling." Then, whispering, she adds for good measure, "Rest in peace; you're sweeter than a honeycomb."

Only later does it come to her to think how soft, how easy to dig, was that dirt; like well-drained soil after a rain that follows a drought. By then, however, Juliet has no time to dwell on it. She's head over heels in schoolwork.

"I've switched my major from business to science," she tells her grandmother on the telephone. "Paleontology to be exact. It's much more demanding, but worth it." Naturally, her grandmother is pleased to hear it.

Then, perhaps not wanting to sound ungrateful for her grandmother's gift, Juliet adds, "Well, I'm still in love with hair, but there's a lot to be learned from old bones."

Coming in at the tail end of the conversation, Juliet's roommates query her the moment she hangs up.

"Hair?" says one.

"Bones?" says the other.

"Hairybones," Juliet tells them pleasantly. "Just dug up in China. They're thought to be a missing link between the hairy caterpillar and the wooly mammoth."

"Wow!" one roommate says

"Cool!" says the other.

Used to them by now, Juliet smiles indulgently. Some white people, she thinks, will believe anything. Some *people*, she thinks. *Almost* anything. "Amazing, isn't it?" she says aloud.

*Nani Power*

# I Am Kurt Cobain's Twin Brother. Really.

NANI POWER's first novel, *Crawling at Night* (Grove/Atlantic Monthly, 2001), was a *New York Times* Notable Book of the Year and a finalist for the Los Angeles Times Book Award as well as the British Orange Award. It has been translated into six languages and optioned for film. *The Good Remains* (Grove/Atlantic Monthly, 2002) was also a *New York Times* Notable Book of the Year and a finalist for the Virginia Library Award. Her third novel, *The Sea of Tears*, is due from Counterpoint Press in 2005.

*"I need to be slightly numb in order to regain the enthusiasm I once had as a child."*
—Kurt Cobain, from his suicide note, April 1994

There are only two routes. The red or the black. There is even a book with that title, though I never read it. Maybe Stendhal has the same idea.

The red and the black. Kurt took the black.

And I took the red.

## THE RED

It is a still afternoon in August. Cats sleep. A train's whistle is heard. The air is hazy because of the heat. Claire is told to stay put, in bed, as long as the twins lay curled inside her. Her stomach is stretched out, taut and shiny and her bellybutton protrudes like a plum. I am on the top side, vertex breech, they would say, lying head towards her heart and nestled next to Kurt's tiny crunched form, his eyes puffed, closed slats, his fists nut-like and transparent.

About an hour later, after she drank some iced tea, waddling to the bathroom with our weight in front like an awkward wheelbarrow, we were born in a whoosh of fluid on her petal-pale chenille bedspread, writhing in a pool of transparent blanket-like tissue.

As soon as I was born, I shrieked for food, air, touch. The air was hard and blue and filled my chest like cold, wet knives. My mouth was a vacuum and I grasped for anything to fill its void.

Kurt was still and gray. His stomach was concave and she reached for him and held him to her soft, downy chest. He made soft little cat mews.

It was always this way.

He almost died then, they would later say. I sucked all the nutrients from the umbilicus and Kurt got peanuts. He was shriveled and way underweight.

Then, he took over. He was a tiny little blonde thing, with relentless transparent blue eyes, surrounded by prickly black lashes. His hair stuck out in shocks of cornsilk.

I was big, with coarse red hair. I was the boring one, who glued models of the Starship Enterprise in my room, while Kurt played the electric guitar downstairs.

At picnics, he stood on the bench and sang "Yesterday." Aunt Landis clapped and laughed so hard food came out of her nose. She held a glazed-nail hand over her mouth, her body shaking. Then, finally, she took a deep breath.

"Oh, Lor-dee. Jesus. That just beats all."

I sat, next to her, eating my third warped paper plate of oniony potato salad.

Next, I zeroed in on a few freshly fried chicken thighs, still warm inside.

I weighed two hundred thirty pounds when I was thirteen.

At thirteen, Kurt wore tight Wranglers and got laid.

In the car, on road trips he would press his bony knuckle in my arm.

"Say uncle, fatty" he'd whisper. We'd pass road signs, clumps of trees, shiny diners. The pain would throb, ache.

"Wuss." His breath was hot and candy-like in my face.

"Mom!" I'd finally bleat. He'd pull back, his face turned to the front.

"*Jeremy.* Stop picking on Kurt. He's smaller. It's unkind."

He'd roll in a ball, snickering.

He once opened the jar of honey Mom bought at an Amish road stand, and it slid across the woolly seat like an unctuous wave of gold. Dirt became embedded in our clothes, hands, and hair from the honey glue. There was no air conditioning.

"Jeremy Lloyd Cobain," she said, her mascara spreading beneath her eyes from the hot oil on her face. She heaved a painful pocket of air from her mouth as she wiped down the seats with tiny lemony Wet 'n Dries.

I always liked the sharp, cool folds of those things.

روح

I'm twenty-seven now. But he's gone.

Sometimes, in the dark, if I get in bed just right with my eyes closed and crunch up in an almond shape, like a fetus, I get a strange echoey feeling of suspension in space, of buoyancy, of flesh and visceral surrounding. Memories of the womb.

In total darkness, eyes closed, the sounds of warm waves, drips, and rushes. The feeling of Kurt. There, next to me.

Quiet. Warm. Quiet. Warm. With each breath, I feel his thoughts.

Quiet, he says.

Warm, I answer.

He's gone.

So how do I know I still exist?

## THE BLACK

A Directory of Commonly Misused Pharmaceuticals

By Kurt Donald Cobain

Age: 16

Mrs. Gertman, English

*Acid slang* Lysergic Acid Diethylamide.

Let's see. *Well.* First you eat this tiny square of the world's most expensive paper. You wait. Maybe an hour. Has lots of slang names: *Dragonslayer, Windowpane. White lightning. Microdot.*

You start to notice streaks from lights every time you move. Laughter is increasingly a byproduct. The inner machinations of all that confused becomes glaringly obvious. Piss looks weird, like a crystalline tube.

Inside the car with Terry, Chris, and that idiot, Turtlehead. Terry is pretty.

Terry is a beaming X-ray. With acid, women lose their cold, glossy exteriors. Their guts glow with kindness. You want to kiss their kidneys, spleen. Your tongue can be a sonogram paddle. You can search and destroy the tumors inside with your magic .

Drinking with acid is like swilling water after a marathon. It's tasteless and lacks strength. Everything lacks strength after this. You could fuck on the Moon and it would feel normal, but when you see your Mom's tired-ass face in a nylon, pilly bathrobe coming down the stairs,

She makes your head explode with fear.

If I wasn't laughing so much, I'd like to fill my whole mouth with Terry's tit. I'd like to save her mouth in my wallet, and call it "my first child."

*Your mouth* will taste like it's coated in copper. The next day, you'll feel the phantom of a different self around your edges.

*Bernice* AKA Coke. Addictive central nervous system stimulant derived from Coca plants.

Bernice, you are a cold piece.

She'll be sour and bitter in the back of your throat. Burns going up your nose. Then you rub the last trace left on the mirror on your gums. Don't ask me why.

Bernice is a cruel and heartless friend. Anger is a side effect.

*Crack* is just the sleazy stepbrother of Bernice that sleeps in the basement surrounded by beer cans, and raids your wallet. You can just check out the pipe losers out by The Frawley trailer park for more on the definition of "Crack."

*H* comes from Poppies. "Addictive narcotic opium derivative produced by treating morphine with acetic acid."

Junk, Horse, Smack, Scag, Boy.

When I think of Heroin, I think of Maria and Thanksgiving:

Mom hires a maid. She comes from El Salvador. I like her. She cooks pretty well (ask my fat brother). She is plump, about forty, had a few kids, really black hair pulled in a braid. Cross around her neck. It's Thanksgiving, when I'm sixteen. Family's over, and actually I like Thanksgiving. I like Turkey. Football. Crisp air. Pumpkin pie. The whole *she-bang*.

According to *Mother,* Turkey needs to get greased down with butter, to make it crisp and golden, so Maria gets a vat of butter and proceeds to slap it on, I'm chomping on some Doritos, just watching, and she's frigging rubbing it up and down the Turkey leg. Up and down really fast. Like she's *jerking off* the Turkey leg. First, my head gets light—no, well, first, I get this out-rageous woody—and then my head spins and, then something just *clicks*.

I'm putting lots of loose ends together in that speedy, synapse way it happens in your brain. You know. Part of you is saying—ununh, don't do it, but the other part is listing, calculating, adding—*Maria*—/hair/glossy eyes/red lips, pouty/ cavity between breasts brown, silky/hands agile, stroking Turkey way too well, way too sexual/DING DING DING. There you have it. A full-blown obsession, created by the triggering of one simple action that must have been building subconsciously or something. Like Dominoes.

I wanted Maria after that. I *had* to have her. After the Turkey, everything started to look good, even the plumpness which is not my thing. "Dog don't want no bone without some meat on it," I'd say. The age, well, she *knows*, she's been around. The cross. Well, that would be amazing to see shaking back and forth between her…

I was choking the chicken five times a day with various Maria fantasies, even singing this ripped version of "Maria" from *West Side Story*, when it just hit me. Kurt, make a *move*. I mean, guys in South America get it on with maids like constantly, right?

I convinced myself. First, I put on my best shirt, my Sex Pistols red one, which is only because my arms look one iota bigger in it. She was scrubbing the floor in the kitchen. I decided my strategy. No suaveness, just direct hit.

She got up from the floor to rinse the mop.

"Hi, Curse. Whatcha doin'?" Can you believe that? She called me "Curse." I adored her for that.

"Hey, Maria."

"You hungry, mister?" I was damn hungry. Shit. I'm starving to death here, Maria.

"You have no idea." I grabbed her hand and kissed it. I tripped on the dull, metal bucket. What the fuck! I'd totally lost it. Was that like the corniest Ricardo Montalban thing you've ever heard of? Worse. I couldn't let go. I kissed, I fucking licked. Her hand smelled like Ajax. I almost came right there. She was, well, not amused or aroused. A wet circle of gray suds covered the linoleum.

"Curse. You baby. Get out of here." She pushed me away and even slapped me on the butt as she pushed me out the kitchen.

She was laughing, though.

"I don't have time for you crazies," she said, and slapped the stringy mop on the spill.

I ached. I went out with girls with black hair, or her nose, or even just the way gold looked against their skin. They chattered on the phone as I watched Maria wring out the mop, cool gray water sliding through her fingers. In their warm bodies, I felt empty, cold, scoured.

Maria acted like it never happened. She gave me a Jehovah's Witness pamphlet that said "Is Hell Funny?" I slept with it.

Then she left because her son was in trouble in San Salvador and Mom replaced her with Glovinia who was cruel and burned food.

I never got over Maria. It hit me *way* deep inside. I started riding in Jimmy Cactus's crew, taking rides. I got messed up. I left my body and all its hungry needs and put it away. I forgot about food, sex, and even my chest felt hollow and cool with wind blowing through it like a drafty tunnel. Days lost meaning and Monday became Saturday, and Tuesday was gone, and Maria became a small red drop somewhere on a lost piece of paper, one I lost and couldn't find, but I kind of remembered.

Sometimes I'd been floating on a dream, in bed with Maria holding me, rubbing me with oil, talking in Spanish and I'd kiss her and she smelled like Ajax, and the sun would burst through and warmth would explode around us, with colors, and horns playing, like those Mariachis or something, and the best fucking feeling you can imagine, Pure Heaven, and she was my good, warm Maria, and then in a second I look down and I see a big syringe hanging in my arm and it seems like Jimmy's yelling something about MUSIC OFF or HIS TURN but fuck him, fuck him, I don't have time for that now, it's my turn, my turn, my turn to take a ride on the big, soft gray, gray, gray pillow named Maria.

*Methadone* "synthetic opiate used to replace heroin in treatment of addicts."
See Maria/Thanksgiving.

*Ritalin* Misused Pharmaceutical for treatment of Healthy, Active Creative Geniuses.

Mom gives me Ritalin every day since I'm five. Because I'm disruptive. I fidget. I'm compulsive. It calms me down. I stop eating. I stop growing. I'm the shortest guy in class. Thanks, Mom. Oh, and by the way, Kurt. Drugs are *bad*. They are evil, evil things. This is your brain on drugs. Sizzle. This is your brain with Bacon and Toast.

*Opiate*
See Maria/Thanksgiving.

Kurt—

Interesting take on the assignment. although not exactly what I expected for "What I did on my summer vacation." I'm hoping it's all a fictive frolic, and not a serious journal of drug addiction. That would be a shame. Because you are a special kid, Mr. Kurt. Despite your lackadaisical jokes in class, there is a lean intelligence that shines through. In fact, after these disgusting years of study hall, smelly lockers, screwing girls in backseats, Black Flag blaring, there will shine a new Kurt Cobain, one you never imagined. You will pick up that guitar and sing and people will pay good money to hear you wail.

What's with Mr. Gertman, Kurt? Does he feel? Better yet, does he have a soul? What is a soul? Mr. Gertman talks of bills, payments, timelines, schedules. Mr. Gertman says his shirt has a stain. He says did you go to the bank, the post office, the drugstore? Do you believe in love at first sight, I ask? Mr. Gertman says, we need more Raisin Bran. This one is empty. Yes, Mr. Gertman is a very smart man. Very responsible, a good family man.

Why should he radiate this sparkling, haughty sense of sexuality you have? Mr. Gertman has no time for magic. There are things to do.

In fact, when you gain popularity and women flock around your blonde, scraggy, grungy self, especially the queen of evil, Courtney Love, please don't forget Mrs. Gertman, the one who will make her furtive move in study hall, on a Tuesday afternoon, and you will sleepily look past her, out the window, standing there, looking at the soccer field, the players, the ball spinning and bounding up and down, a beautiful black and red ball, black and red, black and red, blood and death, pain and shame, horror and nothingness, two twin brothers, nothing to lose, hating the same, spilling the honey, dual universes, oil and water, power and blame, staring at the ball, no tears, no smiles, no good-byes, no suitcases, not even aware of Mrs. Gertman's hand stroking his cheek, his neck, his chest, his stomach, his crotch, to no avail, all over now, so sorry, it's useless, that part gone, faded, leaving just the whisper, the faint pop, the crack, the smoke, the echo, of a gun, somewhere in the far distance.

*Mary Quattlebaum*

# Suzuki

MARY QUATTLEBAUM's fiction and poetry have appeared in *The Gettysburg Review*, *Poet Lore*, *The Washington Review*, and several anthologies. Her twelve children's books include *Jackson Jones and the Puddle of Thorns* (Random House, 1994), *Underground Train* (Random House, 1997), and *Family Reunion* (Eerdmans, 2004), and have garnered awards such as the Marguerite de Angeli Prize, *Parenting* Reading Magic Award, and the Sugarman Award. Of "Suzuki," she says, "Modes of transportation seem to figure prominently in my writing. As a kid, I wrote a whole series of teeny books about a girl and her pet donkey. The plots revolved around getting the donkey to move." Quattlebaum teaches creative writing in Washington, D.C., where she lives with her family.

I watch from the top as Anita and Mama heave old Nick up the stairs. His body dangles between them like a sagging hammock between two trees. One side of the old man's face is drawn up, the other side hangs loosely. His wrinkles look deep as ditches. The flap over one eye droops, and the other eye, black and bright and moist, shifts as he glances around.

"Rose!" Anita, hoisting her pregnant belly before her, bleats instructions at me. "Support his head. Help Mama, he's too heavy for her. She'll drop him! Uhh!"

Mama grunts with each step. The loose skin on her arms flaps back and forth, and her large buttocks tremble with the great effort. Her fat hands clutch the old man beneath his arms; Anita has his feet.

"Rose, Rose!"

"Anita, be careful!"

"Jesus," I mutter. I cross my arms across my tits, nice-sized for a thirteen-year-old (that's what Frankie says) and growing every day.

For days Mama has moaned about her ex-husband's father coming to stay ("that no-good son of a bitch, your father, who run off and left me when I was p.g. and now *I* have to take care of *his* flesh and blood?"), but the old man was

225

sick and someone or other was going to pay her to take care of him. Which didn't lessen her moaning any, but did set her to work making preparations, namely having me clean out the old catch-all room, scrubbing 'til my fingers reeked of Pine-Sol.

The old man is bumped up slowly, the drool sliding from the corner of his mouth and making little wet spots on the stairs. Anita almost drops him at the top. "Bitch," he says.

Frankie has a motorcycle, a high-powered Suzuki, black. I ride behind him, my legs perched high on two pegs at the sides. I hang tight to his waist, dig my face into his denim jacket. (On the back are studs in the shape of a star and they scrape my nose.) We curve around corners; our bodies hang for a moment, then straighten. Bugs smack against my helmet and bounce off, their small bodies flattened, broken, dented, their antennae bent, their eyes askew.

"So how long's the old man supposed to be with you?"

"'Til he gets well, I guess, or dies. It's not too bad. Mama pays me five dollars a week to take care of him."

"Jesus, but he could last forever! Can't we go out at night anymore?"

"Frankie, why are you being such a baby? We can go out after I feed him and put him to bed. And I'll have some money of my own, all right?"

"Put him to bed! Jesus, sounds like he's the baby! Why don't your mama take care of him?"

"'Cause she's too fat to keep going up and down stairs. And she needs to take naps to keep her blood pressure down. Rose doesn't want him. She's Miss Hoity-toity now she's moved in with her boyfriend and says old men smell terrible. Nick's not too bad. Actually, he's kind of funny. He thinks he's a cowboy."

"Rose, you are a good girl, a good girl. Turn on the TV. To take care of your poor old grandfather. When you want to be with your boyfriend. Does he get jealous, maybe? Hmm?"

I help Nick do exercises, holding his old legs at the ankles and pumping them up and down. His legs are stiff as two sticks in a popsicle. He likes soup with alphabet letters and wheat crackers. He sucks on the crackers until the drool runs brown out of the corner of his mouth. I wipe his face, empty his pot. He watches cowboy movies on TV and holds his fingers like pistols.

Sometimes I sneak out of school and buy hamburgers at Howard's Pizza and Grill. The buns are best there, soft and soggy from the hamburger grease. They also have a great pinball machine, Beach Women. I can make one quarter last for at least three games and, once, I won twelve free games. A record for Howard's, I think. Outside, children play step-on-a-crack-break-your-mother's-back and young men lounge by the street lamps with their caps pulled low and their 'fros hanging over their ears. They yell among themselves and at women passing by. The women pretend not to hear; the men yell louder and jab each other with their elbows.

I slam my body against the pinball machine. Bright lights bang on and off and the numbers whirr, change to higher and higher totals. The boobs on the women light up. Their faces never change expression, the shapes of their bodies never change, neither does the style of their bathing suits.

Frankie takes me wherever I want to go on his Suzuki. My body now is upright, relaxed. I know I won't fall, won't lose the little control I have over the bike's balance. My hands are at my sides, no longer clutching Frankie's waist. I know how to move, when to shift as well as he. I squint my eyes to black out the back of his head and pretend I am alone.

I buy a hat with a red feather and show it to Nick.

"Tee-hee," he laughs. "Won't you look fine. Like a whore all trumped up in her nightly best."

"Nick!" I mock-scold him. "I thought cowboys were clean-living men. Didn't like women, only horses."

'Tee-hee, girl, you are wrong. We loved the women…those saloon girls, the stiff black petticoats…the garters just begging to be plucked…their hair piled high and stuck with feathers. The times we would have on a Saturday night, full of beer and filling women. But forget 'em we always did, always. When the open range called and our good pintos stomped their feet, we were off, raring to go."

I twirl the hat on one finger, tweak the feather to make it stand up bright and sassy. I stick the hat on Nick's head. It tips over his bad eye at a jaunty angle.

"Oh, ho!" he crows. "Ride 'em, cowboy!"

Nick used to wash dishes, Mama told me, standing on a mug rack to reach the rinse hose. He moved those dishes through, smooth and slick and stacked them, billowing with steam. Did it for years and years, his finger pads growing soft and white and bloated with water. Once he was a counter attendant for two weeks but got fired for yelling at a man who left a lousy tip.

Young Jeans is selling chances for a motorcycle, a white Harley-Davidson. It stands in the display window with a straw hat on the handlebars, a lavender T-shirt draped over the seat.

I buy six tickets. At a dollar apiece.

On Friday, Anita stays with Nick so Frankie and I can go to the movies. She is so pregnant the buttons on her shirt stretch at their holes. Some pop open.

"I should have brought my belt for you to wear. It's a gold belt. Mike bought it for me, right before I got pregnant."

"Don't need it. The skirt doesn't have loops for a belt."

"But it would have looked so nice. I should have brought it just in case... What would you say if I told you I was getting married?"

"Wouldn't believe it."

"Well, maybe in a little bit."

"Oh, ho! So you have to talk Mike into it, huh? Waste of time. What you want to marry him for? Why don't ya just move back home?"

"And be stuck here with Mama and that dying old man? With Mama sleeping and him stinking? I'd go bananas!"

I shrug and spray La Nuit at my cleavage. Take stock: my skirt fits well, tight over the rear; my rump is high and, I think, very lovely; tits in proportion to hips. Beside me in the mirror, Anita looks like a little kid dressed up for Halloween and stuffed with pillows. A big lump juts beneath her red-striped shirt. Her mouth is puckered and pink with gloss.

Frankie buys me a box of jellied fruits from the candy counter. He touches me, my hair, my blouse, and kisses me during the boring parts of the movie. His breath smells like limes; his tongue is smooth and firm as a long, jellied banana.

"Um," he says, "I'd like to bump off that old man and have you all to myself again."

We go to Howard's after the movie. The men outside all look at me, at my skirt, at my moving legs. They don't say anything, not a word. No "Hi, babe" or "Hey, white sugar." (Frankie looks pretty solid in that studded jacket and those boots with the thick heels.) Howard's wife is the waitress. Legs bulging with veins, wedgies scuffing, voice booming "So, what do you kids want?," she takes our order—two hamburgers, two Cokes—tears the top sheet off her waitress pad and hands it to Howard. Almost all the sheets have been torn from the pad, leaving a growth of ragged paper edges at the top. Almost all the other couples around us have ordered hamburgers and Cokes. All those sheets sent back to Howard with "two hamburgers" scrawled on the first line, and "two Cokes" scrawled on the second... Jesus!

In the booth across from us, the boy has one hand up his girl's skirt. She feeds him bits of hamburger, and he kisses the tips of her fingers, her long, red-painted nails. The grease shines on their faces. The bass on the jukebox is too loud and I feel it echo in my belly. Three guys are playing the pinball machine. They drop quarter after quarter in the slot (just dying for those boobs to light up) and they never win a game. I won twelve.

"Heard you were out with a boy."

"Yeah."

"All night?"

"Maybe."

"Anita told me. She never comes to see me. All I see is you. Sometimes I get tired of seeing your ugly face."

"So close your eyes."

"Anita and I talked. All night. And she gave me two bowls of soup."

I straighten the bedside table.

"Actually, we watched TV, and didn't talk any...except when I had to go to the bathroom."

I straighten the lamp.

"I know you want to be doing things with your boyfriend. All kinds of things. You will forget about me. You will be mean to me."

"Shut up!" I shake old Nick, but not hard, and his good eye moistens and tears. He farts dismally.

Nick sucks mentholated cough drops. He has a bad cold and wheezes every few minutes.

"Rose, I am tired of being an old man. They have no fun. I remember the days when I used to ride the range on Thunder...wide-open spaces. Go, Thunder! Ride 'em, cowboy! Round up cattle, with my spurs a-janglin'. Whoopee-ti-yi-yo!"

He slaps his skinny old flanks. The cough drop dribbles out of the corner of his mouth.

"Show me how to work your motorcycle."

"Why?"

"'Cause it might be worth your while, why not?"

I hang onto Frankie's arm while he points out the tachometer, the speedometer. He pulls out the choke, turns the key in the ignition, and presses the starter button. It is an easy process, this starting of the bike. Fluid, almost effortless. I make up a little song to remember the motions. Pull the choke-turn the key-press the starter. Pull-turn-start. Pull-turn-start.

I buy six more tickets for the motorcycle at Young Jeans.

I clip coupons from magazines. All kinds—7¢, 10¢, 15¢, 50¢, for dog food, rug cleaner, disinfectants, frosted Pop-Tarts. I had started reading an article in the *Reader's Digest* at the public library. It was about a woman who bought all her groceries with coupons and always got extra money to boot.

Anita calls me on the phone. The baby is jumping in her now, making her nervous about every little thing.

"Don't you ride that motorcycle anymore, you hear? It will bring bad things. Bad things will happen to you."

The public library sells old magazines for ten cents each. I buy *Western Horseman*, *Ladies Home Journal*, and *McCalls*. I cut out pictures of cowboys and horses for Nick and tape them to the walls of his room. The ladies' magazines are full of coupons.

One day I bought a *National Geographic* and looked at the pictures—the animals running, their hard horns bent in shapes; the wing flips of birds captured against the sky. Old ladies smiled with no teeth, and long, black people danced, looking as if they were about to eat someone up. There were green stretches of grass, a dog herding sheep. A sweep of beach littered with people. A smooth, flat desert plain.

They had the drawing for the motorcycle at Young Jeans. It was held over the radio. Meg Cornell wins the lavender blouse. Kinsey Kennedy wins the straw hat. Jeneatte Eloise Jordan wins the Harley-Davidson.

Nick lies flat on his back in bed. He wheezes, and his bony old chest rises and falls. We can take him to the doctor in a week or so, when Mama gets her check. I don't even try to help Nick do his exercises anymore. The horses on the wall careen around barrels, and cowboys with tanned faces and tight jeans twirl ropes. One man rides a bronco, his arm lifted high. Nick's legs are like pencils and his knees like two knobby erasers. He wheezes and speaks to the pictures on the wall.

I think I saw the Harley-Davidson today. The rider had long hair that slapped her back and a helmet, white to match the bike. Her rump in tight jeans was squeezed against the seat, her arms at an easy angle from her body.

I ride Frankie's bike whenever he lets me. I like to ride at night, after sponging Nick's body and getting him ready for bed. I ride past the men standing tight against buildings. Past the whores on the corner of Fifth and Broad, with their high boots and low-hanging earrings. I don't zip in and out of traffic. Too hot-doggy, too childish. Speed smoothly right along. My hair is swept up and under the helmet, my jacket shapeless. No one can tell who I am, where I am going. At the all-night grocery, I buy a pack of cigarettes. Light one in the parking lot. Stamp it out. I practice the pull-turn-start movements, reliving, each time, the moment when the engine roars to life and the whole bike starts to tremble. *I* control the thrust into city traffic. *I* guide the way through the casual flow of night-cruising Fords, Lincolns, and Mercurys. My bike headlight bites a path that runs parallel to the street and glows like the jackpot light on Howard's pinball machine.

"Hey!" A man in a Chevette rolls down his window. "Can you tell me where I can find Washington Street?"

I point the way with a flick of my wrist. I know this city too well.

Anita was married in what Mama called a civil ceremony.

My pile of coupons is growing. I stuff them in a plastic sack with a zip-lock opening.

Nick coughs and hawks into a piece of paper towel. The TV blares and small cowboy figures flicker across the screen. Nick holds his fingers, like pistols, to his own chest. "Bang-bang," he says. One cowboy clutches his throat, falls, kicks dust. I say the rosary for the old man but he doesn't listen. "Bang-bang." I say the prayers very fast, running the "Hail Mary's" together, getting only six to a deck.

There's a new girl at school. Long, blonde hair. Good ass, small tits. I see Frankie looking at her sometimes in the halls. He doesn't care whether I see him or not and I caught him polishing his studs with this special cleaner that made them twinkle. The girl is no catch—quite common but for the hair—and she better not come near me; I'll give her something to mince about. My fingers itch to grab that girl's cheeks and pull them wide. Dig in 'til her mouth opens in a bright, red smile, wide, wide, very wide. The corners crack and bleed. I want to twist her hair around my hand and yank until out it comes, roots and all, and I hold it like a prize. I'll tie it to the handlebars of the Suzuki, my bike, where it will stream in the wind like a horse's high-flying tail.

Frankie has stopped calling me as often. "Sure, sure," he says when I talk to him about anything.

"Will you pick me up from school?"

"Sure, sure."

"Do you want half my sandwich?"

"Sure, sure."

"How're you doing?"

"Sure, sure."

I saw him talking to Miss Small Tits the other day. His hands at his side curved like an animal waiting to glide onto that round mountain of an ass. I swear his fingers twitched.

"Sure, sure," Frankie says when I ask to borrow the Suzuki.

"Thunder, Thunder! Here, boy," Nick calls out in the night. Sometimes he mumbles "Yippee-yi-yay."

"Shh," I say, moving to the bed. Nick thinks I am Thunder and tries to stroke my nose. He tangles his hand in my hair and tugs as if it were a horse's mane.

"Yippee-yi-yay. Yi-yay," he mutters.

My hair hangs over his body. Over that heap of bones that show through his skin, sharp and distinct as points on a sheriff's star.

I park Frankie's bike in front of my house. Children stand around it and run their hands over the handlebars, the wheels, the headlight. "Get away," I shout from the kitchen window, but they don't move. I pack a lunch of cheese Nabs and Animal Crackers and place them in the bag with my coupons. I put all my money and some of Mama's into an Animal Cracker box. The coupon bag bulges. I tie the bag to my side with a belt.

"Thunder," Nick cries. I mash twenty-nine aspirins and dissolve them in a glass of warm water. The water is white, swirling like clouds, and I help Nick drink it down.

"Water."

I hold his hand tightly for a long time as his breath becomes regular, then stills. His hand is like an old, brown knot in a shoelace, each finger thin as twine. The knuckles are lumps. I smooth his hand, smooth the blanket over his chest. His eyelashes are sparse and no longer tremble.

My black boots have good-sized heels, a rounded toe. They strike the ground with a surety, an intensity, that makes the cracked sidewalks ring. The children around the Suzuki scatter.

Pull-turn-start.

"Hey, miss, give me a cigarette. Give me a cigarette."

The words are deadened by the helmet and the noise of the engine as I whirl off. The street lines flash beneath the bike wheels; the lights glower, green, red; the pocked city sidewalks zip by. Behind me, I can almost feel Old Nick clinging, one hand clutching my jacket, one arm raised high.

"Yippee-yi-yay," I shout into the wind I have created. The machine beneath me is hot and powerful. My arms are steady, an easy grip on the handlebars. Around me, the world rises. Stretches out. Falls away.

## Lisa Schamess

# What the Body Is Saying

LISA SCHAMESS lives in Washington, D.C. She is the author of the novel *Borrowed Light* (Southern Methodist University Press, 2002), which won the Texas Institute of Letters Steven Turner Award for Best First Fiction in 2002 and was a finalist for the institute's Jesse Jones Award for Best Fiction, 2002; and the Paterson Fiction Prize, 2002–2003. Her short stories have appeared in *Glimmer Train*, *Antietam Review*, and elsewhere.

The summer after you die I take our daughter and go stay with your parents. It rains and rains. The rivers swell and blur their banks. The streets and driveways are studded with twigs and scattered rocks and fallen branches. The asphalt seems to be melting. By some miracle, the earth does not shed its surface.

Each day in your parents' house is enough like the one before to make me trust the next day. Living here now, I begin to understand why your slim, perfectly lovely childhood was precious to you. You told and retold your memories to me, bringing them together in the night and at the breakfast table, among friends and with family, kissing the four corners of your life prayerfully: past, present, present, past, *and then, and then, and then, and then*. Like the time your brother told you the sidewalk mica was really atoms, sparkling forth from the concrete, threatening to burst its surface any moment. You looked and looked, closer and closer, trying to really see.

Memories from last year rise in my throat each night when the baby sleeps, chopped phrases of a forced language I can't unlearn. Like: We sat each week in the prayer circle at the hospital, learning different methods of facing absence. During a meditation I saw myself as a snake in the grass, low to the ground, safe. You, sitting next to me, saw bones.

The counselor called these images the body's words.

During one session, your body's words were three stones in your heart, smooth from a river's rapids. You felt you were protecting them. Then you were on the river in a small boat. The river twinned—one stream green, the other red. You tried to steer into the green branch, but your boat was sucked into the other. Then the branches spiraled each other in a helix.

One Wednesday near the end, a visiting Qi Gong master taught us the five-phases exercise. You were so weak I had to do it for you. I wanted you to be strong again, like the tree. You said that was your favorite exercise. It made you feel more solid.

After you died, it was a snail I wanted to be. Soft and vulnerable, but with a shell made from some intrinsic substance of its own.

*Just see what the snake sees.* I imagined myself close to the ground, just seeing enough to find the next opening in the underbrush, then the next, then the next.

I have lived that way for months.

Our daughter is speaking her first words, learning basic concepts for living: up, more, please, no. She holds out to me the things she finds on the floor, not to ask or even show me, but because she has just learned the gesture. She repeats and repeats this offering.

Are memories the body's store of gestures?

When you were a toddler, your mother took you and your older brother to Central Park every day to play under the wide-splayed old trees. The mothers designated a Pee Pee Tree so they wouldn't have to take the kids back up past their doormen and into the elevators and up to their apartments every time na-ture urged. The trunk of this venerable being, perhaps planted by the hands of Olmsted's original crew, was redolent of all the piddlings it had borne since the last rain. You were old enough maybe to inhale deeply and feel some pride under its generous branches, squatting in the dirt and later aiming against the rough bark as you perfected one of man's oldest skills.

*And how are you feeling today? And what is your body telling you now?*

And where are your memories now, your gestures? Where is your voice, the actual sounds, the words you said?

In the morning the baby hands me toys and I hold them, waiting for more.

Your hands were strong and large, set on slim wrists. There was not an ounce of extra fat on you. You were wiry and stubborn. You insisted on carrying heavy things by yourself, up and down stairs. When I was pregnant, you never once warned me to be careful, to refrain from lifting this or carrying that.

Those hands molded clay, wanted to work wood.

A massage therapist came to our house three weeks before you died. All we wanted was a measure of comfort, a refreshing day's sleep. She saw you upstairs in the middle room of our house, between our bedroom and our daughter's.

After she was done, she had a cup of tea before departing. She wouldn't take the money from my hand.

"I am so sorry, but I just can't come back," she said. "It would depress me so."

I looked around at our cozy house, the baby's bright toys, thought of you upstairs in our clean, sunny middle room, still so beautiful, skimming just a hundred pounds, still the strongest man I'd even known, still with those amazing hands on their slender wrists. I honestly didn't see what could depress a person about this house.

At night, I lie on the floor by the baby's crib to let her breathing soothe me. I like being down here, looking up through the rails at how the light curves around her thigh and diapered bottom as they push up from under the blankets. *Don't stop moving, but try not to hurry.* I am still living that way.

As a little boy you developed a hip problem that could only be cured by time. Off your feet for three weeks, an eternity that could have been agony. And then you made a crucial connection: doorbell rings, visitors for you, presents on the table. You bumped down the steps one at a time on your bottom as you'd been told you could do. For a long time afterward, the sound of a ringing doorbell made you look up with great expectation.

I tried to see the good of those three stones in your heart. I tried to believe your body was saying, *the self is like a gemstone, entire of its own, hard to change.* Except through well-placed blows, some sharp, others blunt. And once changed, changed always.

I tried to see love in that red river inside you. I wanted your body to speak of the heat and demands of love, the way it had spoken when we met. The hard work of living for love. Love the fire underground, that lights the self's way.

Warm clothes, right out of the dryer. On a cold wet day. Your mother buttoning you snug.

Look up from where you are. Even when you are low, can you see some light through the tree's dense canopy, light between the leaves, offering?

Love burns, and the burning leaves behind ash. And something else: the burned lip of the place fire touched, the beginning of what remains. Where we have been burned most deeply, there the most astonishing new life grows. Where trees fall, rain comes, and some of the seeds of the old trees awaken and turn, roots finding earth, tendrils finding light.

Who knows—the plants can't tell us—but that every part of it hurts, the dying and the growing and the staying put to root. If fire sweeps toward them again, the new are as powerless to stand elsewhere as the old were. Tender, living, vulnerable, we are all fire's nourishment.

And once I saw the body as a translucent blue pane, a rectangle of pale light, dimensional like the water, full of space and sparkling.

The last time we were at your parents' house together, it was winter. You went out for firewood one bitter cold day. You banged the door when you came back, stamping the snow off your boots and cursing. I came down to the bottom of the stairs and kissed you quickly, an everyday kiss, nothing to speak of. But you decided to make it last. You grabbed my waist with your icy fingers. You opened my mouth and made prayers of us right there at the doorway, your lips deliciously cold from the outside, your warm tongue a miracle within.

*Myra Sklarew*

# The Guardians of the First Estate

MYRA SKLAREW served as president of the artists' community Yaddo and has been a faculty member at American University since 1970. Her books include three poetry chapbooks; six full-length collections of poetry, most recently *Lithuania: New & Selected Poems* (Azul Editions, 1985); a collection of short fictions, *Like a Field Riddled by Ants* (Lost Roads Publishers, 1987); a work on Lithuania, *The Witness Trees* (Cornwall Books, 2000); and a collection of essays, *Over the Rooftops of Time* (SUNY Press, 2002). Earlier work in neuroscience has resulted in a current research project, "Holocaust and the Construction of Memory."

*D*aughtergirl was set up for it. After years of sitting in the darkened examining room of an eye doctor's office. Her mother off in the distance. Her with her nearsighted eyes. Him with his penis set right out on the chair between them. He breathed hard. His hand searched for hers. The two hands hovered in the vicinity of his organ. And came down together gently on top of it.

The eye examinations were interminable. The small light of his ophthalmoscope shone for long periods onto the back of her retina, causing her rods and cones to discharge erratically. Her mother never guessed what was happening so near to her. And Daughtergirl at age six had never come this close to the private parts of a grown man. Why Dr. Kapoyr was willing to risk all for this brief probe was not something Daughtergirl knew enough to ask. But there in his elegant downtown, wood-paneled office it is very likely that half the girl-children of that city had direct contact with Dr. Kapoyr's organ.

The mysterious bit of life which lay beneath her small hand was soft beyond anything she had ever felt. And years later she could imagine its warmth and quickening, the tender surface as her hand rode up and down it, guided patiently by his own hand. She did not look down. Likely she would not have seen anything had she dared to. Between the darkness and her dim eyesight. But it was a time in her life, though she was curious enough, when she would have been too polite to look at what was occurring.

Her mother was given the chair of honor. Against the far wall. Her voice came crisply across the room from time to time as though from a distant yet fashionable part of London. "How are the child's eyes today, Dr. Kapoyr?" she would inquire. "Has there been any significant change since we were last here."

And Dr. Kapoyr, fully into the business of enlarging his organ, as well as seeing to the dilation of the pupil of the eye, the better to have at the interior parts, would call back to her in a thin, abstracted voice, "Mrs. Mother-daughter, we will have our conference as soon as the examination is finished." This seemed to satisfy her. Doctors in those days were not to be trifled with.

Daughtergirl could feel the hairs curling out from his nostrils. The odor of tobacco and aftershave lotion. His breath on her face. Her eyelashes reflected back to her in the bare light his instrument gave off. And years later she remembered how the inside of his thigh felt through the white coat he wore. Through the finely tailored trousers. Though at the time she hardly knew which continent she was swirling through space on. She hardly knew the names of the various apparati she was so calmly manipulating.

She had been tripping, stumbling over things. Falling down. She had no idea that others saw more than she did. She couldn't see the blackboard at school and didn't realize for some time that she was supposed to be able to. Above all, Dr. Kapoyr restored the world to her by bringing it into proper focus.

❧

She was sitting in the front seat of her teacher's dark green Packard. This was years later, in a parking lot during a thunderstorm. Luc Choirloft (they had trimmed Lucretuis down to a manageable size but tried unsuccessfully during all of ninth grade to find out what his mother called him) and her father were inside the high school attending a meeting on recent vandalism and delinquency. Her father had no idea at all that she was out there. Choirloft had set it up with her. That she would wait for him in his car.

Luc Choirloft was an interesting case. He was fond of American history. You could say it was one of his specialties. And pubescent girls. Medieval art. That was something he was big on. And pubescent girls. He brought his two main interests together on occasion in that perfect intersection so rare in life. He took the pubescent girls to the Cloisters where among the medieval statues and gothic ceilings he fondled first the statues and then the girls. Sometimes he did both at once, bringing into his employ both left and right arm.

There among the beatific faces of the young girls raised in prayer and offering to the heavenly Father, Lucretuis Choirloft managed to feel up any number of girls in close range of the guards without ever incurring suspicion. Never once did an irate father or surprised guard catch him at his exploits. Often one or another of his subjects would think better of the enterprise and break away, hiding behind a cloistered figure for a brief moment. Choirloft knew the museum exquisitely well after all his years in it. He would come upon the poor girl crouched behind a madonna and lure her out again, starting up the whole hotly entertaining game once more. It was, in fact, this juxtaposition of becalmed madonna with pubescent girl that so set him off.

Daughtergirl and Choirloft played it closer and closer to the edge, always increasing the odds of discovery. They never knew if it was some perversity that was behind this or if the greater danger provided more excitement. Daughtergirl didn't know at the time just how much of the proceedings were her doing. Some, she decided in retrospect.

Choirloft would occasionally take her home to visit his wife and kids. Daughtergirl felt that she knew something about them all that they separately had no way of knowing. As she watched his wife diaper the baby. Or as she tiptoed into a child's room one night, with Choirloft holding her hand, to witness the peace of a small son sleeping.

Was it in the nature of men, she reasoned with her newfound logic, as with turtles and fish, to disseminate sufficient seed to guarantee the continuation of the species? Perhaps, she ventured, our own quite recent code of morality was simply an overlay that had nothing at all to do with survival. Suddenly the urge of men to inseminate with great frequency wherever it seemed feasible struck her as a profound virtue. Daughtergirl felt like standing up in the middle of the high school gymnasium and cheering for mankind and his abundant seed. She too longed to be the recipient of such life-giving force as her teacher had to offer. Which is why she was spread across the front seat of his Packard when he appeared, suddenly illuminated by a flash of lightning.

Choirloft had managed to slip out of the meeting just before it ended. In moments, Daughtergirl's father would appear in the same parking lot, climb into the family's blue Plymouth shaped like a box turtle and drive off, never suspecting that his Gibson girl, his own sweet daughter was waiting, hot-blooded, in the front seat of Luc Choirloft's car, only a few feet away from where he was parked.

The question was: To which theory of teaching did our fated couple ascribe? Was it the "stuff an apple in the teacher's mouth and serve him up to the hungry student" variety? Or was it the "dump truck" method where the teacher loads up his blue dump truck, backs it up to the door of the classroom, unloads, and drives off? Or a third: "infusion and exchange," where the student is responsible for at least part of what happens? And where the student, with the teacher's help, must undergo some basic change? Daughtergirl felt that she was about to make some essential contact with the third method.

Choirloft started up the Packard. The broken muffler let out a sputtering roar, dropping engine juice like a series of dashes across the asphalt surface. Daughtergirl pondered the condition of Choirloft's front seat. She wondered how many other girls had been there before her. She wondered what he said to them and how many more would take their turns long after she was gone from this place.

They drove out of the school parking lot and onto Main Street. It appeared to anyone who might think to look that Lucretius Choirloft was entirely alone that night. But when they pulled off the road and headed down the narrow stretch leading to the bay, Lucretius Choirloft's other half, his pubescence, leaned mightily against him, all the while his hand traveled as though on its own. It wound around her shoulder and down her arm, touching the fingers of her right hand. Slowly, slowly, it made its way along her plaid wool skirt until it came to the edge of the hem where it began its ascent. Those fingers moved deftly up under her slip, finding places even she hadn't known she had. "You're wet there," he told her admiringly. She couldn't tell if he was pleased with his prowess in causing that to happen or if he was imagining how pleasant it would be to place his organ inside that wetness. These were matters she hadn't read about or even discussed. He continued to work those fingers of his right hand until she was feverish.

Years later she thought of him. Of that moment in the old Packard with him. Of her own sexuality proclaimed and admired. And she thought of Dr. Kapoyr staring with sublime concentration through the dilated opening of her pupil into the great velvety darkness which lay just beyond his reach, while far below he fumbled for a small hand in order to begin a ritual he had generously participated in many times before.

# Mary Ann Suehle

# A Scream of Her Own

MARYANN SUEHLE passed away in June 2004. Her fiction has recently appeared in *Antietam Review*, *Café Irreal*, *Del Sol Review*, *Gargoyle*, and the *New Orleans Review*. She is the recipient of a Maryland Individual Artist Award and has been nominated for the Pushcart Prize. Her novel-in-progress is "By the Sword."

Christmas morning, we tear into the usual boxes of gloves and overlong sweaters, the necessary socks, the board games, craft kits and gadgets. Our holiday lies in ribbons and balled paper at our feet. The only thing missing is a good scream. "Go ahead, Evie, try one on for us. For Christmas's sake," Mom says.

I sit on the floor, wedged between the plaid couch and a coffee table that displays Mom's cotton ball snow scenes. I take a breath of the dried glue and when I open my mouth, out comes a strange bark. "Ahk." It's a seal's bark. "Ahk, ahk, ahk."

In reply, Mom stands from the couch, and leaning slightly forward, she shreds the air with a scream. It's the very best kind, shrill if a bit tart for the Christmas season. A cry of delight follows it, a hiccup of satisfaction about the same volume as my bark.

Every daughter develops her scream with the help and use of her mother. But I'm nineteen by now and haven't yet plucked out a decent protest. I try again, hugging my knees to my chest. My voice struggles up my throat... "Ah ha!"

"That's no effort at all," says Mom. "Just look at you, Evie. Just look." She sits down hard on the couch, her back straight. She's a teacher at Century Middle School and somehow believes thirty-five pairs of eyes are always watching her.

"Let me try one," says Dan-Dan. He kicks through the Christmas debris to straddle the arm of the couch next to her. His mouth is sugared with red and green cookie sprinkles.

Mom cups her hand over his mouth. "Quiet now, you know boys don't scream. Men aren't built for it, the poor darlings. You could hurt yourself." She brushes the sugar sprinkles away.

"What about me?" I say from the floor. "Aren't you worried I'll hurt myself?"

"Maybe that's your problem," she says. "You need to feel pain in order to scream. Have your father and I failed you so completely?"

"Excuse me," says Dad, "this screaming business isn't going to scorch the dinner?" He leans forward in the recliner. He is just waking up from his new coffee table book, *Lost Screams of the Anaconda*. His new socks and ties ornament him like a nest of benign snakes, brown and blue and colorfully striped.

"Your sister was a late screamer, wasn't she, Gerald?"

"Don't recall it," he says. The footrest thumps into place. He steps along the edge of the Christmas mess. "More eggnog," he says, heading for the kitchen. The eggnog is mostly nog, a tonic to dull the edges of holiday screams.

Dan-Dan follows him out, steering with his electronic game around toppled piles of presents. He stops to wiggle his pajamaed butt at the explosions scored by his pixel-drawn hero. He's eight, my mother's change-of-life baby.

"I'll bet he can scream like any girl," I say.

Dan-Dan belches before shimmying from the room.

Mom doesn't have to say anything. Her disappointment is sharp as icicles on the tree. I can hear the glass Christmas balls crumbling under the pressure of her expectations.

"Just what are you going to do with yourself? What are you going to do?"

"Ugh!" I say. Not technically a scream. Too unhysterical. I offer it in recognition of the facts rather than in declaration or protest. A truly feminine wail could rip open this day as if it was unwrapping something unnamable and irregularly shaped.

I seize on a rubber-stamping kit, hold it aloft, and announce: "I am going to stamp. Stamp, stamp, stamp." My slippered foot stomps the carpet. The laminated box displays stamped greeting cards, flowerpots, candles, a pair of tennis shoes with ladybugs at the toes. I have a vague idea I will stamp my way to a good scream and punctuate my resolve with, "Hey!"

"That's no better," says Mom.

We shoulder the scream inequity between us into the kitchen, where I slice cranberry sauce from the can, and she stirs lumps from the gravy. I whip the potatoes; she butters and salts them. This is how holiday meals have been prepared for generations, when she was the daughter, when her mother was the daughter. That's how it will always be. It's the same in every house, down every street. Every woman screams. Why can't I?

∽

Despite Mom's best efforts, the dining room she converted from the spare bed-room is a do-it-yourself disaster. She uses it as a workspace to plan home econom-ics projects for her middle school students. I feel as if I walk uphill in that room, both coming and going. Perhaps the pink-striped wallpaper hangs crooked. Or the root-bound houseplants are to blame, weedy at the front windows and dig-ging unevenly into the flaming pink shag.

When I was thirteen, I had plenty to say about it. "Pink-striped wallpaper isn't bad enough? Now this rug?" All the makings of a screamer were lodged in my complaint.

At the time, Mom settled the matter with a cry that melted the chandelier's globes.

Dad agreed the rug was certainly a colorful addition but suggested the chandelier's globes be replaced. Afterward, he ventured into the dining room for holiday meals only, about twice a year.

The dining room has since become a testing ground for soda-bottle Easter bunnies; salt ceramic napkin rings that dissolve in the dish water; even sculptured guest soaps, swans—or ducks—and some kind of petaled or scaled object. Later, these are reproduced on the desks of every Century Middle student. The thought sickens and soothes me. It strikes me as something I can scream about.

After the holidays, Mom brings down boxes from the attic as fast as she puts the Christmas decorations away. She stacks index card boxes, envelope boxes, file folder cartons, even cookie and candy boxes from long-ago valentines onto the table's plastic-covered lace. The dusty lids flip off to reveal a stash of family memora-bilia, photographs layered in with ticket stubs, school programs, certificates, report cards. Mom announces she will introduce scrapbooking to her third-quarter classes.

"Third quarter," I say from my place at the table. "Isn't that usually themed recipe books?" I drip blue food coloring into a plastic vial of yellow and shake it. I'm going for green, crocodile green.

"This time, it's scrapbooks." Mom stands across from me where Dan-Dan usually sits. She considers me a moment before saying, "What if I make this scrapbook for you?" A teacher's smile rides her lips.

"What do you mean, a scrapbook for me? Do I get to put what I want in it?"

"All we have is what's already here." She waits as if we are both listening in the distance for the same thing. "It's true, you haven't screamed yet. I'll leave some blank pages."

I pick through my stamping kit, now organized in a plastic toolbox Dad brought me. Its graduated trays and shallow compartments keep the stamps, paints, inks and brushes separate and organized. I love its new-molded plastic smell, its tight hinges.

"Remember that oratory contest?" says Mom, turning a photo upright. "You were afraid of the mike. Thought it would bite you." She shows a picture of me tapping the head of a microphone.

"Not bite, just shock. It had static in it." I remember the ticking sound it made, like something about to strike.

I test-stamp crocodiles along the narrow margins of the daily gazette, and we drop into a bottomless silence until Dan-Dan drives into the room with another electronic game. He zooms around the table, mimicking an engine shifting gears at full throttle. "Vroom, vroo, vrahhh."

In a fit of mute inspiration, I stamp him. The imprint on his forehead reads, "Happy Birthday!" faint and crooked.

Dan-Dan speeds past me to Mom's place at the table, where he imagines the game's finish line. I stand behind him to ink a rabbit on the back of his hand. I stamp a rooster on his cheek, a pig on his chin. He brushes aside the gummy stamper bites until the video game sings a victory song, its digital flags flying. He waves a stamped hand. He is a winner. "Hooray, hooray," he says.

"Just what do you think you're doing?" Mom says.

"Look, a snake has eaten a rabbit for dinner," I say, pointing out overlapping stamps. "No, the rabbit hopped down the snake's mouth. Which is it? Which?"

Dan-Dan swings at me. "Quit it. Quit."

Mom's scream puts a metallic shine to the pink-striped walls. The shag pills beneath our feet. Even the potted fig sheds its leaves, yellow and green indifferently. Still deaf with sound, I toss off another attempt, "So there!"

"Not even close," says Mom, upsetting a box lid with discarded photos.

"Now I have skin *poisoning*," says Dan-Dan, availing himself of every vowel and consonant.

"Pretend they're tattoos," I say.

"If you think this is the stuff of screaming, young lady, you're mistaken."

Dan-Dan feels his face for his stamped skin. "I can feel them. I've been stamped!"

"See what comes of your silence? See? You're acting like a caged animal." Mom wants to belt out another one, I can tell, but screams are precious, too, and not to be over-used once a point is made. Besides, Dan-Dan is on the verge of a scream himself, so she drives him into the bathroom to scrub off the stamping ink.

Meanwhile, I rifle through the photos Mom has set aside, hoping to remove the ones that mark me for silence. How embarrassing to be put before the kids at the middle school. To be made an example of. A bad one.

❧

The slant walls of my attic bedroom suggest a life of stooping. At a shorter age, I would stand on the mattress near the footboard and unscrew the light fixture's shade, blowing out the insect carcasses and talking into the bowl-shaped glass. It magnified and deepened my voice. I'd put the shade up to my ear, listening for evidence of my future scream. But there was nothing, only the rush of blood in my ear.

I still use the student desk Mom bought at the school's surplus sale. It sits beneath the window peeling yellowed varnish. Pen marks score the desktop with the usual arrow-struck hearts, names and initials: Jeri and Leo, LN and LB, MS and JSS. In red pen, someone carved the whole opening jingle of an old TV program. Mom has said it was hard to find a desk without obscenities cut into it, but I can see the ghost of them in scrubbed patches near the pencil holder. By now, the desktop markings are so familiar to me, sometimes I mistake them for my own.

In high school, I sat here doing homework despite the handicap of my screamless academic career. I am still folding myself down into this desk, the seat sized to a ten-year-old, my knees pushing against the underside of the desktop. In the window, I see myself bending over the desk as the sun sets behind the shingled rooftops. The only sound is the scratch of my pen as I draw zebra stripes on an animal greeting card. It's another in what is fast becoming an entire line that I dub, "Evie's Ark."

Before long, I hear someone on the stairs. Dan-Dan won't dare come up, not after the stamping incident, and Dad rarely stirs from the recliner. It must be Mom. I don't turn around when I feel her observing me from the doorway with silent disapproval.

"So how's the greeting card girl?" she says.

The ink pen has left a fresh stain on my thumb and index finger. I examine it more carefully than it deserves.

"You know, Evie, I suppose you could spend your life up here coloring. But there's a whole world out there."

"I'm not 'coloring.' I don't call it that when you do it."

"When I do it, there are a hundred and twenty middle school children who learn to copy it." She walks into the room, her chapped hand folded on her hip. Her fingers are always reddened whether from putting them in bleach or working with glue and paints. She must wash them all day, during every class. She picks up my card with those hands, to examine it.

I colored my greeting card zebra in black and red stripes. He is an embarrassed zebra, carrying another card of himself in his mouth and whinnying from inside the card: "Happy Birthday, *Late*."

Mom looks at me as if I have somehow given her the wrong card for the occasion.

She takes a breath—not a screaming breath, a talking one. "You should know by now, we have to scream for what we want," she says. "Our educations, our jobs, our promotions. We scream at our future husbands to see if they will walk. If they stay, we scream out their children. If you can't do that, Evie, I'm afraid the rest doesn't matter."

I lean back, balancing on the legs of the chair. "I can't scream. I'm not a screamer." It's a quiet confession.

"Yes you are. You are a screamer, but this isn't it," she says, shaking the zebra card at me. "Do you hear me? This isn't your screaming." To prove it, she tosses the card into the trashcan.

That's when I feel a scream filling up the room. It stirs against the walls, tuning itself up for an audible blast. I look for its tone and amplitude jutting through the paint like plastered joints along the wallboard.

"If you think you can scream right now, you'd better do it," she says. She grips her hands, holding herself back from filling up the empty space. Her mouth is open, but there's no sound. She slaps her hands at her sides to stop herself from screaming, then turns silently toward the door. As she goes, she switches off the light. It's a habit of hers to conserve electricity. She cannot break it.

The whole room cools down as my eyes adjust to the light. Something brushes against my ribcage before it turns itself around, curls up, and dozes. "Help!" I call, then strain to hear a rattle at the window, a ping on the ceiling light. Long after Mom's footsteps are gone, I listen to her shoes crushing the rug all down through the years.

In the weird light from the street, I open my toolbox, pick out a stamp and press it into the wall. *Hello?* I say. *Is anybody there?* A faint blotch clings to the paint. It's a blue monkey. I open an inkpad and stamp a sibling, darker, bolder, facing the opposite direction. *Hello, hello?* A second pair, a third. The animals gain momentum, forming ill-fated pairs: a lamb then a lion; sheep, goat; roadrunner, coyote. By then, I have stamped clear to the door. *Can anybody hear me?*

The animals circle the entire room, and still nobody hears me. I stamp over the windows, fill the walls to the ceiling. *Hello?*

I fall onto the bed and wait for the animals to move in the constant light. I wonder if I will find their dried carcasses some day inside the light fixture's glass shade. Blue hippos, red rhinos. A yellow elephant. Snakes and flamingoes. *Hello? Anybody at all?*

၁

To take the edge off a screamless summer, Mom and I visit the local scrapbooking and stamping paradise known as the Cut-N-Paste. The store is all things paper, ink, glitter, and glue. The store owner, Darla Pitts, has stocked the pegboard aisles with every available talent-enhancing widget: stencil rulers, templates, and pattern-edged scissors. A feather-tipped fuchsia pen instantly transforms my ordinary stick printing into a designer font.

Darla fills her shop with paper dreams by holding contests for gift certificates and displaying the winning entries inside the store. My line of animal greeting cards won second place last month and now hangs from red ribbons in the pad and paint aisle. Mom and I stand beneath the cards, watching them twirl and jostle like a mobile over our heads as the air conditioner fans the tepid air. She pulls down my crocodile and flamingo card, examining it in hopes of discovering its secret worth.

On a weedy background, I stamped the crocodile snapping the heels of the flamingo in diagonal lines going down the card. The two chase left to right, front to back. The croc gains on the bird, closer, salivating, poised to strike. Turns out, I couldn't let the crocodile eat the pretty champagne flamingo, so I stamped her balancing atop the croc's toothy snout. She's a marvel, that flamingo.

Mom says she doesn't get it.

"It's a funny turn of events," I tell her.

"Too bad 'funny' doesn't get you anywhere."

"I won in this contest."

"Second place," she says. Besides, what's there to joke about when you can't even scream? She doesn't say this, not in so many words. I hear it in the way she taps my card against her thumbnail.

Darla interrupts, slipping a flyer in each of our hands. It's an ad for the national contest sponsored by Craft Planet, manufacturers of practically the whole craft industry.

"It's perfect for you and your girl," she says. Today she wears an animal print scarf, flattening the tail of it along her shoulder. Darla knows I can't scream, though she herself can put a shine to the scissor blades, but she doesn't seem to mind.

"The winning entry will be installed in the lobby at Craft Planet's headquarters in Cleveland!" She points to this statement on Mom's flyer. Darla is enthusiastic about almost everything. I like her for it.

"I know just what I'll send," Mom says. She hefts the croc card in her hand, folding it flat.

I retreat to the paper aisle, entertaining the notion that Mom finally sees what Darla sees and will enter my cards in the contest herself. I pretend I don't notice her taking my cards down as I finger the blooming, ribbon-bordered stock. The paper aisle is my favorite part of the store: hand-made, cotton-made, bark-made papers stacked in ream-sized cubby holes. I smooth a cockatiel rag, closing my eyes to hear the color sing. Instead, I hear the die-cut machine lurch through a pass. Roll-flack-roll. There's a second pass, then another.

The die-cutter. It punches card stock into sailboats and laced gloves and fashion dresses on hangers. When I join her at the back of the store, Mom holds up a tiny paper purse. She has folded its tabs and sides and swings it by its crescent-cut strap. It's a party favor. I've seen the shape before. And the purse's croc and flamingo pattern, I've seen that before, too. It's the same weedy background, the same green and champagne stamping inks as my award-winning card. It is my card.

Mom leans on the stencil display, the die-cut machine spotted with scraps. She wears the same expression as when she finds a remnant of my childhood decaying and moth-eaten in the attic crawl space. Then as now the item has a sad, untouchable familiarity.

I plunge my hands into a bin of pencil sharpeners and gum erasers, picking them up by fistfuls and dropping the items into the bin. The force of what comes over me prods the plastic-encased scissors and knives. "How could you do this? How?" My voice curls to the highest octave although I strangle its volume to a whisper.

Perhaps Mom is giving my scream a running start, the way her voice keys the scale of hysteria. "See that? See what can happen? Go ahead, you know what to do."

Die-cut holes are shot through all of my award-winning cards. She has reduced the entire grouping to paper skeletons. I hear machine-guns and rapid-fire BBs.

"Let's hear it," she says. "It's pain, just sing it out."

I see my scream funneling through the stencil shapes behind Mom's head, blooming into bands of shrillness the way light fans out in water. If I open my mouth, my teeth bared, the scream will bolt right through me and into the shop. It will resound throughout my life and in every life that touches mine. Even Darla nods from across the cutting table. She is waiting for me to blow the torn bits of my cards right through the store.

Mom is serene, anticipating this long-awaited event.

So I pick up a ruined card, put my lips to the die-cut bones, and whistle.

*Elly Williams*

# The Yellow Bathrobe

ELLY WILLIAMS is the author of the novel *This Never Happened (Random House, 1998)*, an adjunct instructor at Johns Hopkins, a faculty member for the Sewanee Young Writers' Conference, and a PhD student in English at Ohio University. She is at work on a new novel, "The Divine and Miss Johanna." She has been a fellow at Sewanee, the Virginia Center for the Arts, the Hambidge Center, and the Georgia State College and University. Most recently, she was a Jackobson Scholar at Wesleyan University.

Frances sat up in bed, clutching the sheets. *There's something wrong with Grace.* Her son-in-law Jonathan's late-night words hummed in her ears. She struggled to look at the clock. Six-thirty. Leon must have set off running on the trail around the lake. It was too early in the morning to grab the phone and call Grace. Please don't let there be anything wrong with my silly baby girl. Not another *episode*. She couldn't bear it. And hidden beneath this prayer was another one: *Forgive me for thinking there's not a damn thing wrong with Grace but selfishness.*

Frances got up and shrugged off her nightgown, hanging it on its hook inside the closet. She left on her underpants, practical white cotton underwear she bought in packages of six at Wal-Mart. She special-ordered her white padded bras, insisting they be delivered in plain brown wrapping paper, but they still cost under twenty dollars, shipping included. A good thing, too. Someone in the family had to watch their pennies. The Lord only knew if they would have one cent in their IRAs if she didn't. Bankruptcy had not stopped Leon from spending money. As for Grace, she went through Jonathan's money faster than he earned it. New house, new van, new this, new that. No doubt in her mind that Grace had pushed Jonathan to build the new warehouse for his tire business.

Frances hurried into the hallway, snapped on the overhead light, and took a long look in the full-length mirror. She sighed. Her breasts, small as they had been before, had shrunk after menopause. No wonder Leon had a roving eye.

She shook her head. She refused to remember the *incidents*. That was all in that past. Still, she tried to recall the last time Leon had seen her body. Or touched it. Would he have noticed the small lump in her right breast? Frances was sure Jonathan got an eyeful of Grace once, maybe twice, a week. She shut her eyes, tried to blank out the image of a naked Grace radiating lush heat and damp invitation.

Frances shut off the lights and returned to the bedroom. Maybe another baby was on the way. Maybe that's what was making Grace upset Jonathan. Hormones. She hated that part of her felt pleased at the thought. But there it was, a sliver of pleasure at the idea of Grace not being able to hang onto that voluptuous figure of hers forever. Not if she's popping out babies. And about time, too, with Theo close to seven years old. What on earth had she been waiting for? Grace was no career woman like she had been. All she had were silly dreams of designing her own clothing line some day.

Frances pulled on her worn pink quilted bathrobe and as she did, she remembered an afternoon she had walked in on Jonathan wrapped in this same robe. Yes, Jonathan. Frances sat down on the bed. It had been the damnedest thing. She had come home early from the office one afternoon Grace's senior year in high school to find Jonathan's truck parked in the driveway. She pulled her old Valiant around it and drove into the port cochere. She entered the house quietly. She headed down the hallway, past Baby Nathan's locked door to Grace's bedroom. The door was shut, and she heard a scuffle, followed by a giggle.

"It's not the right size," Grace said. "You've got to let me fit it."

Another scuffle, followed by a crash.

Frances flung open the door. Jonathan stood on Grace's hope chest wearing Frances's pink bathrobe. The sewing table chair lay on its side. Grace sat on the bed, a red cape slung over a much too small black bodysuit. The legs hit her midcalf. Her bosom strained the top. She leaned toward Jonathan, tape measure in her hand.

"What are you two doing home from school?" With his dark coloring, Jonathan looked adorable in pink. And, oh, my, he was so hairy. Frances grew faint. Her heart fluttered, a little whisper of butterfly wings. She collapsed on the bed beside her daughter, nothing but warm melted butter.

Jonathan leaped down from the chest, and Frances caught a glimpse of boxer shorts covered in pink-and-red hearts. She knew he knew she saw them. "Grace," he said. "Grace made them for me for Valentine's Day."

"What is that you're wearing?" she said to Grace.

"It's a costume. Minette's. For *Cats.*"

"And Jonathan?" Frances turned to Grace's boyfriend. "What's he doing in my bathrobe?" She gave him a sidelong look. A flush crept up her neck. "Not for a musical, is it?" she said, her voice low, lingering a bit on the words *my bathrobe*.

Jonathan ran out of the room. Frances started to follow him, but Grace put up her hand. "His clothes are in your room," she said. "Stay here. You'll embarrass him." She tilted her head to the side in that way that she had, as if listening to what wasn't being said.

Frances was certain Grace thought she'd been flirting with Jonathan, and her flush turned dark. "What are his clothes doing in my bedroom? What's he doing in my robe?" She pressed cold fingers against her hot cheek.

"He loves that bathrobe," Grace said. "I was measuring him so I could make him one his size." She paused. "There's nothing odd about it. Bathrobes are unisex," she said. "He didn't want pink. He told me to make it yellow."

Frances had looked at Grace and at almost the same moment, they started to laugh. Poor Jonathan had fled the house without saying good-bye to either one of them.

Now, these six, seven years later, Frances sat in the same spot on the same bed. Why did she feel at least twenty years older than she had that afternoon giggling with Grace? *Please, God, help her feel less what? Old? Like her life was over?* She walked over to the dresser and picked up her framed picture of Jesus and touched her lips to His. No lighting a bunch of candles, gulping wine, and dropping to her knees in some melodramatic swoon for her. No hysterical claims that Jesus had visited her in the flesh like Grace. No trips to the Psyche Institute for her. No, Francis pulled out the prayer cushion tucked beneath her bed and knelt down. "Thank You, Lord," she prayed, "for Jonathan's phone call. Please help Grace see the light." She put a hand inside her robe and bra and lightly pressed the lump.

ॐ

Silver Lake stretched two miles in either direction, the Catskills all around. Frances pressed her nose to the cottage kitchen's window screen. A hazy day, hot for May, no breeze, not even one blowing up from the lake. A damp, cottagey odor, a melancholy scent, lingered in the air. The Thayers' raft bobbed in the water, its worn buoys faded orange. She reached for the Saltines and began to nibble.

Off in the distance a canoe moved. Now who could that be at this early hour? Dan Connelly? Phil Berkheimer? She pulled the binoculars from the drawer beside the window. Dan Connelly with a blonde-haired woman. Where there's smoke there's fire, she thought. Not that she would ever say anything.

She returned the binoculars to the drawer. Twenty-five after seven. She knew her daughter's schedule as well as she knew her own. Jonathan would be at the tire store, Grace waking up, Theo on her bed, playing with his super figures. Keeping an eye out the window for Leon's return, Frances snatched up the telephone and hit speed dial.

"Mom," Grace said. "I'm glad you called." Her voice sounded tired. "Can I come out to the lake today?"

Frances sighed in relief. No need to mention Jonathan's urgent call. She pictured Grace chewing on a nail. There was nothing wrong with her silly girl, there just wasn't. She wondered again about a baby. Well, she had plenty of advice for Grace if indeed she were pregnant. And not speaking to your husband wasn't part of it. Despite all Leon had put her through, she'd never stopped speaking to him. She saw Leon puffing up the path from the lake.

"Come to the lake this afternoon after Theo gets out of school," Frances said. She'd be back from her once-a-week stint serving the homeless lunch, a duty she did as part of St. Paul's women's group. She didn't have to mention that Leon would still be at the Elks Club with his buddies. She hung up the phone just as he reached the back porch steps.

❧

Frances bustled into the Rescue Mission's kitchen to check on her tuna casseroles.

"I'm glad you're here," Esther Hilburn said. "Jodi Trout and Bev Buckley are talking, not getting a thing done." She adjusted the hem of her flowered polyester dress. "Like magpies, those two. And I have no idea what that Sanfilipo girl is doing here. She hasn't been in church more than three times this year."

"I've been upstairs. Scouring the damn bathrooms. Yuck." Frances rolled her eyes. "Do men ever take aim?"

Esther laughed.

The fishy smell of tuna wafted through the air. Frances removed warm buttered bread wrapped in aluminum foil from the oven and set it beside huge bowls of salad sitting on the counter beside the refrigerator.

"I don't know what we'd do without you. You and Grace. All those costumes she designs and sews for the Sunday school plays." Esther picked up a sponge. "I'm going to do a quick wipe-down of the tables."

Frances snatched her cell phone from her purse and tried Grace the second Esther left the kitchen. No answer. She bit into one of the Saltines inside a plastic bag she'd tucked into her skirt pocket.

Mary Sanfilipo sauntered into the room. Her denim skirt was too short. Her strappy heels too high. And that hair. A sprayed rat's nest. "Salad dressing?" Mary said. "Did anyone bring salad dressing?"

The girl's gum chewing set Frances's teeth on edge. "Not me," she said. "I brought three tuna casseroles. Homemade. The large ones."

"La-di-da." Mary leaned on the counter close to Frances. "So, Frances, what's new with you?"

"Mrs. Thayer," Frances said.

Mary laughed. "Don't you think Grace and I are getting a little old for the Mr. and Mrs. routine?"

"What did you bring?" Frances asked.

"Paper plates."

"Why aren't you at work?"

"Wal-Mart's open twenty-four seven." Mary shrugged. "I'm on the night shift this week." She smiled at Frances. "They're hiring right now. Grace ought to put in an application. She'd get a discount on all that material she buys."

Frances bent down, opened the oven door, and pulled out one of the casseroles. She grabbed a big wooden spoon from a drawer and began stirring. "Grace is busy with Theo and Jonathan." She couldn't resist adding, "Besides, she doesn't need the money."

"That's not what I heard."

"You don't know what you're talking about," Frances said, and swirled the spoon around the tuna. She bit her tongue to keep from asking just what it was Mary had heard.

Mary snapped her gum. "Whatever you say." She leaned closer. "Grace is OK, isn't she?"

Frances slammed down the wooden spoon. "There's nothing wrong with Grace." She bit into a second Saltine.

"Leon." Mary dragged out the word so that it practically sounded as if she were speaking French. "Why don't you get him to help with the homeless? I thought he might be here today. He's retired like you, isn't he? Lots of time on his hands."

The town clock boomed twelve o'clock noon, and Frances yanked another casserole from the oven. She placed two more dishes inside, lasagnas that Janet Roper had made. "Let's get serving." It was none of Mary's business what Leon did or didn't do.

"Mr. Thayer to you," Frances said.

"The salad dressing?" Mary put her hand on her hip, jutted out her leg. Her skirt rode up even higher. The girl wore no stockings. A butterfly tattoo showed on her thigh.

Frances felt like slapping her. "Look in the refrigerator. There's probably some left from last time." Frances headed to the main room. Already twenty, thirty men stood by the door waiting for the go ahead from Pastor Ginny. After saying grace, the men shuffled past her, heads down, mumbling, "Thank you, ma'am, thank you."

Mary emerged from the kitchen, holding up half a bottle of Thousand Island dressing. She did a little dance step, and one of the men whistled. Frances reached into her pocket for another cracker.

Mary grinned at her. "Ta ta," she said, and waggled her fingers. "Give my best to Grace and Leon, Mrs. Thayer." She said Leon and Mrs. Thayer really loudly. Carol and Esther turned to look at Frances. The horrible flush of rosacea spread from her neck to her hairline. The hot rash burned her face.

Mary moseyed out the side entrance.

Frances motioned to Jodi to take her place. Her face burned. She went into the kitchen and hit redial on her cell phone. No answer. She took her bag of crackers and sat at the kitchen table. She felt like crying. Frances snatched up a handful of Mary Sanfilipo's paper plates and tore them in two. She crushed them in her hand and stuffed them into the recycling bin.

꙰

When Grace didn't show up that afternoon, Frances telephoned her daughter four more times, left three messages. She didn't call Jonathan because she didn't want to worry him. Grace was known not to answer her telephone. Frances almost drove into town to check on her, but by then Leon had returned from the Elks Club for cocktail hour at the cottage. Cocktail hour, the only time Leon seemed truly with her.

They sat on the cottage porch, a screened-in wrap-around veranda. She put the tray with their drinks and Saltines on the wrought-iron table between their wicker chairs. She smoothed her pink suit, a light linen she had bought at Frugal Fannie's. She glanced at Leon, touched her hair. Would he notice the ash-blonde rinse she'd used on her tidy pageboy, a color that masked the gray completely, or the neat leather pumps on her feet? They'd reached a point, finally, where they sometimes talked a little. Oh, not about themselves, not their shared memories, but maybe about an article in her *Wall Street Journal* or maybe Leon would ask her to help him with the *USA Today* crossword puzzle.

Frances looked at her watch. Five-fifteen. She bit her lip, worried, but as awful as it might sound, glad that it was too late for Grace to show up, that she wasn't here to interfere with her time with Leon. It was these moments during cocktail hour that gave her hope that one day they might find happiness together again. They had been happy, hadn't they? Before Baby Nathan died seven long years before Grace was born? Before they ran into problems with the business? She didn't allow herself to form the thought before the *incidents*.

And yet there one was. Oh for heaven's sake. An *incident*. Miss Davies, Katharine Davies, Grace's first-grade teacher, a girl fresh out of college. Who Frances had no idea was bringing Grace home after school and occasionally meeting Leon right in the ranch house. Her and Leon's ranch house, a house in a nice neighborhood. Small, but they owned it, didn't they? It had a lovely yard and plenty of privacy—her dream come true thanks to her hard work running their insurance company. And where was Grace while Katharine and Leon were getting to know each other? Yes, that's how she preferred to think about their meetings. Not as two naked bodies thrusting themselves at each other, hot and sweaty, in her bed. No. She wasn't going there. She wasn't. And there's Katharine, sweet, simpering, oh-Leon-you're-so-great-Katharine, and she's what? Slipping off her dress? Leon's unzipped it, she's sliding out of it, she's pulled off her underpants, tiny black bikinis, how could she, an elementary-school teacher? Bikini underpants no bigger than a Kotex pad. Black bra a sliver of lace. Had she fallen to her knees then? Put Leon's penis in her mouth? The act Frances refuses? Is that it? But why then panties left in the bed, tucked down into the sheets where only toes can touch and so it's not until Frances yanks off the sheets to change them, that out comes the black frippery. You don't need a bed to suck a man's penis. She picked them up, sniffed them, that's true, she did, that womanly smell overcoming her, making her dizzy, with what? Jealousy? Hatred? Fear? *Don't leave me*. Oh, Leon, how could you? In our bed? The soft cushy mattress she had bought from J.C. Penney, bought with her dreams? And Leon's singing in the shower and what is she to do? She goes into the bathroom, and tosses the panties over the shower rod. Do they land on his head? On the slippery porcelain in front of him? He gets out of the steamy shower, that's what she knows. He leaves the water running, their water bill reaching sky high and she stands on the bathmat in white cotton. You wouldn't give me oral sex, he tells her. A man needs that. *Yes*. He's naked, only a towel wrapped around his waist, and she pulls it off, kneels on the tiles now, off the bathmat, he's on that, and she takes his penis into her mouth and sucks him. She's on her knees, cold, hard tiles stapling her skin. He puts his hand on her head, fools with her hair. She gags. What happened *then*?

Frances put out her hand, touched the reality of the smooth glass holding her wine. She sniffed the lake air and ran a hand over the front page of the *Wall Street Journal*, black ink coming off on her fingers. They go into the bedroom, that's what happened then, and Leon is caressing her and pulling off her white cotton underpants, unhooking her padded bra, whispering, "I love you, Frances, I do," and she lets him do whatever and she tries to feel, but what she feels is sorrow and a longing too great for words and she shudders, knowing that Leon thinks she's climaxed.

Frances sipped her wine. She used her foot to set her porch rocker to swaying. Nineteen years ago. No use crying over spilt milk. She looked at Leon, scribbling in *USA Today*, his knitting bag at his side. Without thinking, she slid her hand inside her blouse, ran her finger lightly over the lump.

"Leon?" She put a tentative hand on his leg.

He smiled at her and shook his bourbon tumbler, rattling the ice. "Help me with this will you?" he said. "What's another word for ghost? Seven letters."

Leon turned away, squinting, peering down the front lawn toward the shady place they parked their car. The big old evergreen standing beside what Frances realized was Grace's van looked like a stage prop, its dark blue-green needles phony against the pale blue of the sky. Frances's hand fell away from Leon's leg. Grace moved up the stone-filled drive toward them, shoulders hunched like an old woman's. If anything really *were* wrong, Frances would never forgive herself for not driving into town. Theo ran alongside his mom. He wore thick black glasses, a short-sleeved, button-down shirt, a dark tie, and bright red shorts. "Grammy!" he yelled. "Grampy Lion!"

Leon set aside his crossword puzzle and stood up to wave. Grace kept coming toward them. She didn't look like Grace to Frances. But only Grace would wear such a baggy dress, a clumsy plaid jumper of a dress with a slit up the side, a big velveteen pocket splashed across the front like a kangaroo pouch, and a low-cut top, a top that showed her black bra straps and a safety pin, too. And she was barefoot, of all things. Frances was sure she could make out a hint of pink nipple. She felt like screaming.

Grace reached the bottom step of the porch. It wasn't a nipple peeking out of that dress, but pink lace. It might as well have been a nipple. There was something about Grace Frances preferred not to think about, something hot and sensual, something that invited both male and female attention. Frances glanced up at Leon, back at Grace. For once, her daughter's wild blonde hair was slicked into a tight braid.

Theo tugged on Grace's hand. "C'mon," he said.

"What in heaven is he wearing?" Frances said.

"Can't you see he's Clark Kent?" Leon said.

Theo pulled on Grace again. "Let's go."

"We've got our routine," Grace said. Leon nodded. Frances reached for a Saltine.

Grace and Theo headed to the rear of the cottage, toward the water. Frances left Leon to his crossword and walked to the back herself. She peered from the side of the cottage. Theo took off his glasses, his shirt and tie, folded them into a pile on the ground. Grace stuck her hand into that big pocket on her ridiculous dress and pulled out a bundle of red. What on earth? She snapped it to Theo's Superman T-shirt. Aha. Superman's cape. Then her daughter and grandson climbed onto the wide wooden swing hanging from the maple tree. Theo liked to stand on the swing and have Grace stand on it, too, facing him. They'd criss-cross their feet, put both hands on the ropes, use their knees and legs to get the swing going. Theo's cape flew out behind him. "More powerful than a steaming locomotive," Frances heard him say.

It's not so different from that time when she and Leon put up the swing, Leon climbing one rope hand-over-hand like Tarzan to the branch and wrapping it around, laughing, his blonde hair blowing in the May breeze. Yes, it's May, like now, only not so warm, almost chilly with the breezes blowing up from the lake. Grace is where? Oh, maybe off with Mary Sanfilipo, that wretched girl, who's visiting the cottage with them, off in the woods with their Barbies, and she and Leon are alone and then the swing is in place and they're side by side and there's nothing about Leon that doesn't make her happy in that moment. She's sold a big insurance policy to a large company on the outskirts of New York, and they've rented a new office in town at last. Leon laces his fingers with hers and they sit on the swing, and he says, "Hold on," and she does. He uses his foot to get the swing going, and he pumps hard and it swings high into the air, and Frances squeals with fear and pleasure. Leon grasps her fingers tighter, then tighter, and he says, "I do love you, Frances, I do." And even as her heart soars into the sky with the swing, she holds something back, something inside her, something that is her, something that needs protecting, but she laughs, anyway, and squeezes his hand against hers, and to her amazement Leon starts to cry, the tears dribble down his face, and he says, "Charlie and I used to swing, we put up a wooden swing near the caves, and we'd swing just like this." Ah, Charlie. Leon's big brother who hiked the mountains with him and found two graves, graves with tombstones that read Emma and Baby and Charlie made up stories to go with the engravings. Emma died in childbirth. Emma had the baby out of wedlock, killed it, then herself. The favorite story? That her husband killed the baby and then her because he didn't want her or the baby. And then Charlie had gone missing, and he, Leon, her poor husband, had found his brother's body three days later, lying cold and lonely in the misty rain. Some careless hunter loose on the mountain, spraying his brother with buckshot. A murderer on the loose, that's what Leon always said. Still. Frances takes hold of her husband's hand and says, "It's OK," and deep, deep within her she thinks of Baby Nathan, but she bites her lip to keep from saying his name. She thinks about his nursery, the way she keeps it exactly the way it was the day he died, how it smells of baby no matter how many years go by.

And when Grace and bratty Mary show up, flushed and dirty, Barbie dolls' clothes muddy, Grace laughs and laughs at her parents in the swing. "Like couples in a movie," she says between giggles, and Mary stands beside Grace staring at them, but Grace can't stop laughing, the laughs spiraling out of control, turning to tears. Silly Grace.

"I love you, Theo," Frances heard Grace say now. The swing slowed. Theo leaped into the air, cape sailing out behind him. Grace clapped from her standing perch on the swing, arms laced around the ropes for balance. Frances waited to see if Grace would jump, she was always saying she would, but she never did. "Theo, come help me," she called out, and Theo ran to the swing, held onto his mom's ankle as she sat down and then took both her hands to help her to the ground. "You need to take a risk," he said. Grace put her hands on his cheeks, bent down, and kissed him smack on the mouth. "Mom," Theo said, and used the back of his hand to wipe off the kiss.

Theo ran to the kitchen terrace and grabbed a heavy orange life jacket, and Grace bundled him into it. She pulled his baby monitor from the big pocket on the front of her dress and shoved it into his hand. She clasped the other monitor. Theo ran toward the lake. Frances hurried to the front veranda and told Leon to bring their drinks, they'd be sitting out back.

By the time they got the snacks set up on the rear porch, Grace, too, was down by the lake. She headed slowly up the path toward them. She turned around once and called out, "Be careful, sweetie. Stay where I can see you," and Frances saw a flash of orange life jacket. Leon stood up, started down the stairs, but Frances put her hand on his arm. "Wait." She tried to take hold of his hand, but he moved away.

"Everything OK?" Leon called out.

"Sorry I'm so late. I forgot about a first-grade open house this afternoon." Grace chewed on her pinky nail. "I don't know what's happening to me, it's like

I'm basted together."

"Basted," Frances said. "Don't be ridiculous. What are you, a turkey?"

"A basted stitch. Loose. Temporary."

"You could have told me you'd be late," Frances said.

"Late?" Leon sounded gravelly. "For what?"

With her hair pulled back tight that way, Grace's face looked bleak and empty. Something awful *has* happened. Oh, please, God, not another *episode*. No, that couldn't be, Grace was here at the cottage, not home lighting candles for Jesus. Had Jonathan turned the tables on Grace for once?

"Jonathan," Frances said. "Did he decide not to speak to you?" She was both furious and pleased, furious because Jonathan had no business hurting her daughter and pleased because maybe Miss Me, Me, Voluptuous Me was going to have to learn life wasn't all about her. Frances pushed away that thought in a hurry, not wanting to accept for one second that she had even thought it. Mothers didn't resent their daughters, did they? She, too, stood up.

Grace lowered her head, pulled up her ratty dress to wipe away what had to be tears.

Leon hurried down the stairs, stumbled just like he always did under pressure, those weak ankles of his, put his arms around Grace. He pressed Grace's face to his shoulder, smoothed her already smooth hair. Frances wanted to rush down the steps and enfold both of them in her arms, but all she could think of was what if they pushed her away? Her rosacea smeared across her cheeks, her nose, her forehead. Oh, why did she have to feel so out of place, so unwanted? She thrust Leon's iced tumbler against her hot cheeks. Neither Grace nor Leon looked up. Frances reached for her wineglass and took a quick gulp. She took another and then poured another glass. She maneuvered a third rocker beside hers and Leon's.

At last Leon led Grace up the cottage steps, pinkies linked in their time-honored fashion. The three of them sat in chairs beneath the porch roof. Late afternoon humidity hung in the air, thick and close, ghostly. Grace set her monitor in her lap.

"Specter," Frances said. "The seven-letter word for ghost is specter."

"I tried to call you back," Grace said. "No answer."

"I had the Rescue Mission today. You could have left a message," Frances said, but she knew Grace always just hung up and tried again.

"Why didn't you tell me Grace was coming?" Leon said.

Over the rim of her wineglass Frances said, "You were jogging when Grace and I talked." She turned to Grace. "Is this about Jonathan?"

"Why would it be?" Leon asked.

Grace gave Frances a look of inexplicable anger, an unreadable anger that Frances didn't understand.

"It's about me, Mom."

"No need to get huffy," Frances said. "Everything's not about you, Hon." To Leon she said, "Maybe you should go down to the lake?"

"Theo's fine." Leon moved his chair closer to his daughter's, pointed to the monitor she'd set on the table.

Frances took hold of her daughter's hands. Grace gently pulled her hands from her mother's. She tugged at her bra strap. Frances felt Grace's eyes on her as she stretched out a hand for her wineglass. Leon sipped Jack Daniels, three ice cubes, same as usual. Not that Grace ever said one word about Leon's drinking. She leaned toward Grace. "You're being silly. Overreacting. Jonathan says you're not speaking to him."

"You talked to him?"

Leon patted Grace's knee. "That's a great dress," he said. "Unique."

"He called me, Hon."

"When?"

"Last night."

"Of course I'm speaking to him. I got up with him this morning. Made him breakfast. I was upset last night." She gave her mother a look Frances couldn't read, a look of scorn maybe, or worse, pity. "Don't you ever get mad at Daddy?" Grace said.

Frances watched her husband and daughter look at each other. Her flush deepened. Something was happening here on their cottage porch in which she had no part. "Don't use that tone of voice with me." She pressed her cool wineglass to her cheeks, her forehead. "I thought you were going to tell me that you're pregnant."

"I don't want another baby."

Leon cleared his throat, a dreadful ratchety sound. Grace chewed her nail. The rumble of Theo talking to himself came through the monitor.

Frances said, "Jonathan's worried about you, that's all. And no wonder. Not wanting a baby."

Leon fiddled with his knitting bag. Out came the red scarf again. Strands of yarn spilled across his lap. "It's unraveling," he said.

"I wish he wouldn't call you like that. Without me knowing."

"Don't make a mountain out of a molehill. You're lucky he cares so much," she said. "Look at Keith. He won't even marry Minette."

"Minette doesn't want to get married," Grace said.

A curious silence hovered over the porch, heavy and gray. Frances grabbed her wineglass and drank from it. Leon gulped his bourbon. Grace simply sat in her chair. Leon cleared his throat again. Frances felt the dampness of the lake stretching to their porch. She saw Leon's tumbler slide in his hand. She took hold of the glass and set it on the table.

Leon made a great show of going to freshen his drink. He stuffed the scarf back into the bag. "More ice," he said, and vanished inside.

Grace tilted her head to the side, looked at Frances. "I always feel like Jonathan's holding something back from me."

"Let's get down to brass tacks," Frances said. "He works all the time. He's tired." So all that was bothering Grace was lack of attention. Too bad. From the time Frances was a little girl, she had had to notice herself if she wanted to be noticed.

Leon returned, sat in his rocker.

"I don't know what's wrong with me," Grace said.

"Nothing's wrong with you," Frances said.

"I'm not happy." Grace looked down at her lap, touched her finger to her velveteen pocket.

"Yes you are." Frances' voice rose.

"I'm going to go join Theo," Leon's voice rasped in the hush. That's right, thought Frances. Disappear when the going gets tough. Still, he didn't move. He cleared his throat again.

Of course Grace was happy. *And if she wasn't, it was her own fault.* Was it possible other mothers felt the faintest flutters of pleasure under such circumstances? Maybe Grace would have to find out the true meaning of marriage now, of life. Maybe Grace would have to suffer the way she, Frances, had. Immediately Frances thought, *Please, Lord, forgive me.*

"Where is Jonathan, Gracie?" Frances heard Leon say. "Maybe we should get him out here. All have a talk."

Oh, God, things had to be serious for Leon to suggest something like that. What was it that Leon understood that she didn't? *Help me, Lord.*

"He's working. Supporting his family," Frances answered. Her linen jacket felt damp, her feet slick inside their leather.

Leon ran his index finger up and down the crease in his right pant leg. Frances watched him until she couldn't stand it a second longer. "Stop it," she said, and pushed his hand off his leg. She had to put an end to this, this *scene*.

"I dusted Baby Nathan's crib last week." Frances's mouth was dry, foul tasting. "And his dresser."

Grace's shoulders slumped. She reached out a hand to her mother. "Poor Mama," she said.

Oh, my. Grace hadn't called her Mama in years. It frightened Frances.

"I've got to check on Theo." Grace pushed the monitor into her pocket and hurried down the steps, her bare feet a slap, slap against the wood.

Leon hurried after Grace, limping, caught up with her halfway down the path to the lake. The maple tree off to the side of the house stood watch, a blur against the grayness all around, its swing hanging still, the empty picnic table beside it, forlorn. Frances saw Leon speak, then Grace.

And there it was. Another *incident.* Oh, how she wanted these memories buried. But no, there was Leon, right here at this cottage, on his knees in the living room. He's on his knees in front of Frances who sits on the couch in her pink quilted bathrobe. And where is Grace? Oh, she's down at the lake, maybe sunning on the raft or drawing in that sketchbook of hers, those silly little draw-ings she does, Minette beside her, the way Frances has always yearned for Leon to keep her company. She reaches out a hand, touches Leon's hair, runs her finger up and down his whiskery cheek. Hasn't he shaved? Leon always shaves, even on vacation. He's crying. She presses his head to her bosom, wishes she had Grace's chest, oh, God, just for one day she'd like to have cleavage, that soft, smushy pillow that even she, Frances, longs to touch just to know what it feels like. It's all she can do not to reach out and put her hand on Grace's breasts whenever she walks by. Oh, how she'd like to wear something low cut, sprinkle lavender co-logne between her own big breasts and feel Leon's mouth warm against them. Or dust them with sugar and let him lick it off. She's never gotten into bed without a shirt to hide her small breasts, she only lets him touch them in the dark and she moans, his mouth on her nipples sets her on fire, his finger twirling around them, electric, her nipples as a direct line to her toodle. Oh, God, oh, God, what's Leon saying? She can't hear him even though his mouth is against her chest, right in front of her, her ears aren't working, but oh, her heart is, he's saying, Please, Frances, please, let me go. And it's right then that Katharine Davies knocks on the cottage door and walks straight into the living room like she owns the place, like she's been there a million times before, a little boy holding her hand, a boy who has Leon's golden hair, his blue eyes. The pain is so great, Frances can't breathe, she's staring at this woman and boy over Leon's head, her hand so tight in his hair that if he pulls away from her a tuft of hair will be left in her hand, leaving a blank bald spot in its place.

"She's here?" Katharine's voice is high and wavy the way Grace's gets when she's upset. She's wearing a halter top, breasts spewing from it, lush hips filling out blue-jean shorts, navel showing, and God, her legs long and tan, not a single freckle, oh, no, smooth and tan.

Leon tries to pull away, tries so hard Frances's fingernails dig into his scalp. At last she lets go, and he stands up, faces Katharine and that boy. The boy says nothing, looks at the three of them.

Frances smells nothing but cottage, fusty, damp air, and then the other odor reaches her, the Katharine odor, she knows that's what it is, a scent she's smelled on Leon more times than she's ever let herself know. She thinks this can't be happening, she's walked into a bad dream, that's all it is, a nightmare, and she'll wake up and Katharine will be nothing but a ghost of her subconscious, a faded figure, nothing.

Now Frances touched her flushed face. She finished her wine, poured another glass, and drank it. She did her best to focus on her husband and daughter, standing on the path to the lake. Grace was nearly as tall as her father. Leon appeared bent, old. Why hadn't she noticed that before? Eight, ten years earlier, he hadn't been gray, oh, no, his hair is blonde in her fingers, blonde as he gets off his knees, blonde as he looks first at Katharine, then at her, blonde as he covers his face with his hands. And Frances slowly unties the belt on her bathrobe and lets it drop to the floor, a slow swirl of pink puddling onto the pinewood floor, and she stands, a tall thin woman in white underpants and padded bra, and she doesn't care about the boy or Katharine, she looks Leon straight in the eye, she reaches behind her back, unhooks her bra and lets it flop to the floor, and then she's reaching for her underpants, and Leon's saying, "No, stop it, no, there's a child here, a child, Frances," and Katharine is stumbling to the door, she's got the boy by the arm and she's yanking him outside, and clump, clump, clump, they're down the steps. Now it's she and Leon alone and she knows he's half in and half out that door and so she steps out of her underpants, says, "Follow me," and walks toward the bedroom, naked, rotating her ass in slow undulations, oh, she knows it's her best feature. He follows her, she knew he would, she had only to speak in a certain tone, that tone that said, "You killed my baby," because always, always that lies between them. Leon was at home with Baby Nathan when he died, but they never, ever speak the words, the suspicion that lies in her soul. The doctors said it was SIDS but she knows in her heart her baby wouldn't have died if she had been the one home and so she can't stop asking herself, why did I go out for Kotex that day, oh yes, that's exactly where she had gone, the drugstore, Leon too embarrassed to buy her feminine products, so she left him with the napping baby and came home to a baby who wouldn't wake up and now Leon would follow her into the bedroom and for the first and only time in her life she straddled him, fucked him hard, her own fingers on her nipples, she spit on them first, then whirled them around, she fucked him, then sat on his face, saying, Is this what she does, is this it? Is fur pie, oh, yes, she said those words, fur pie, words she'd never used before or after, words she didn't know she knew, words that flew out of her mouth that day like vomit, fur pie in your face what she does? Is that it? You like the smell? The taste? Is that it? And Leon? Oh, Leon is lapping away, he's got his hands on her hips, he's holding her to him long after she wants to get away, roll over, hide beneath the blankets, he won't let go, a punishment, he's leaving marks on her hips, yellow bruises that last for weeks, and she's crying now, please, please, Leon, please, no, enough, but he won't stop, and when he does, she slips off the bed and gets on her knees, hands clasped on the bed, *Help me, God, help me, I love him* and there's no answer but the sound of Leon crying.

Frances took a long, deep breath and watched Leon take Grace's hands in his. She refilled her wineglass. Had he held her own hands in the last year? Two years? Five? On their twentieth wedding anniversary? It didn't matter. She drank more wine. She pressed the cool glass to her face. Leon would come back to her and send Grace to her, too. He always did. She saw him drop their daughter's hands, put his own on her cheeks, kiss her on the forehead, nose, lips. Now she heard him say, "Go on, Gracie, sit with your mom. She needs you. I'll look after Theo."

Leon touched Grace's shoulder, said something else that Frances couldn't hear, and walked off down the trail. Grace stopped at the empty swing and gave it a fierce push. She stood on the grassy lawn, watching the swing dance back and forth as if she were contemplating climbing onto it, pumping higher and higher into the sky, and then taking a wild jump into the air. But no. Grace headed toward the porch. She went inside the cottage, coming back with a damp towel. She pressed the towel to her mother's hot cheeks. Frances closed her eyes, enjoyed the cooling sensation, the closeness of her daughter. Vanilla bean. Grace's scent. *Thank you, God, for nothing being wrong with Grace.*

"Why don't we have a picnic?" Frances said. "All five of us? Here at the lake tonight? We'll have brownies, guacamole, chicken on the grill."

Grace's face took on that odd shuttered look of hers, the look she got that made Frances want to knock her head hard and say, "Hello, anybody home?"

"Call him," Frances said. "He's worried about you. And here you are fine, just fine."

Grace stood up, that look still on her face. She disappeared inside the cottage.

Frances picked up her wineglass, ran her index finger along its rim until it sang, a faint whistle in the gloom.

ॐ

The smoked hickory odor of marinade lingered around the grill. The sky had gone pink, and the air seemed more dusky than dark. From where she sat at the wooden picnic table beneath the shade of the ancient maple tree, its swing unmoving, Frances could make out Theo's orange life preserver as he knelt at the edge of the lake. His hand glided across the silver surface, sending out little rippled sprays. "You'll be safe, Wonder Woman, I'll take care of you" came over the monitor, now lying on the picnic table. She heard what was probably the slap of a stone hitting water.

Grace gathered the paper plates, stacked them in a pile. She reached toward the plate of brownies, but Leon put his hand over hers. "Let them set awhile." He handed her the ketchup. She carried the plates and bottle inside the cottage.

"Lucky little kid, isn't he?" Jonathan said. "He's playing baseball this summer. Grace tell you that?"

Leon nodded. "I played as a boy, too."

Frances glanced up to see Grace heading toward the table. The bluing mountains looked like a backdrop to a stage set, Grace, of course, the star. It was beginning to cool off. Why didn't she get a sweater to put on over that low-cut dress?

Leon helped himself to another Tostitos chip and dipped it into the guacamole Grace had made. Grace sat beside her father, leaning her arms on the table. Frances feared her breasts would fall out of that outlandish dress. The safety pin on her bra was unclasped. Frances reached across the table and touched it. "Better do that up," she said.

"Let me," Jonathan said, and everybody laughed except Grace.

"Help me, will you?" Frances motioned toward her linen jacket lying on the bench between her and Jonathan. He slid it around her shoulders. She smiled at Leon. "Such a gentleman." A bullfrog croaked somewhere nearby.

Grace's and her father's hands met in the Tostitos bowl. "I found my Maternity Medley last night," she said.

"Your what?" Frances swung one leg over the bench, then the other, skimming them past Jonathan. She remembered Grace's Maternity Medley just fine. It won her a scholarship to that ritzy designing school. Frances would like to have hated herself for begrudging Grace a college opportunity, but she didn't. Why should Grace have something she didn't? And for a maternity collection she'd designed when she wasn't even pregnant. What on earth would Frances's friends at St. Paul have thought? It was bad enough, wasn't it, that Grace had gone and gotten herself pregnant a month later? Oh, no. Frances had nothing to feel guilty about. She had never stopped her daughter from sewing and wearing those silly clothes of hers, now had she?

"Coffee?" Frances said. Did Jonathan notice that she wore no stockings, that her bare legs were smooth, that Flash Bronzer had done its work? An instant prayer formed in her heart: *Forgive me, Lord.* She glanced at her daughter, but nothing showed in Grace's face. Her face appeared blank, pale gray in the dusk, as if that yanked-back hair of hers had erased her expression.

"I'll get it." Grace stood up across from her at the table.

"Isn't that the collection you did in high school?" Leon asked.

Grace leaned against the maple tree. "Yeah," she said. Frances didn't know what she had to act so miserable about. Those old drawings of hers? What kind of sense did that make?

"The coffee?" Frances said.

Her daughter climbed the slope to the cottage. Frances pulled her legs back over the bench beside her son-in-law and squeezed his arm. Nothing in that. A harmless gesture.

Grace came out with the coffee on a tray and moved toward one of the old wooden lawn chairs. A little sprinkle of paint chips fluttered to the grass as Grace sat down in the chair closest to the picnic table, a chair facing the lake.

Jonathan pulled a chair close to Grace. He handed Frances and Leon their coffee and settled beside Grace. They placed their coffee cups on the wide armrests. Jonathan had a steak knife in his hand.

Leon bit into a brownie, and Frances frowned at him. "You're not a kid anymore. You have to watch what you eat."

"There's chocolate chips in these," Leon said.

"I put them in the batter for you, Daddy."

"That's my Gracie."

Frances watched her husband stuff yet another one of Grace's brownies into his mouth. Heat crept up her neck, her face. She slid off the end of the picnic bench and went over to the other side and slipped in beside Leon.

"That collection is so dated," Grace said. "It's not any good."

"Isn't that the one Ms. Povolo raved about?" Jonathan ran the knife up and down the edge of the armrest.

"It's been a long time," Leon said.

"Too long," Grace said. "My sketches looked so imitative. Nothing like the way I remembered them." Her voice was high, annoyingly young. "I might begin a new collection."

Grace and her little clothes drawings. Why on earth were Leon and Jonathan acting like they mattered? Grace had been making them since she could hold a crayon, but Frances had never seen the point. She knew better than anyone that you can't live off dreams and little drawings. Design school? Ridiculous.

"Seems silly to me to care at this point." Frances watched Leon take yet another brownie. "Don't you need some milk to wash those down?" she said.

"I'll get more milk." Now Grace's voice had that irritating tired quality.

"Go ahead and draw if you want to," Frances said. "Far be it from me to rain on your parade."

Grace headed toward the cottage. Jonathan joined her, the knife in his hand. Frances turned so she could watch them walk up the lawn in the evening shadows. Oh my, Frances thought, glancing at Leon slouched beside her, skin pale and wrinkled, thin hair exposing his pink scalp, and then at Jonathan's erect back as he moved up the slight incline. Such broad shoulders. Not a bad waistline, either. When Jonathan took hold of Grace's hand, Frances's heart constricted. Her hot red rash deepened.

"She thinks finding her Maternity Medley last night is a sign," Leon said.

"Sign? That's the silliest thing I ever heard. Sign of what?"

"I don't know," Leon said. "Lost dreams?"

"In a pig's eye Grace has lost dreams. Please. What that girl needs is another baby." Lost dreams, thought Frances. How can he have sympathy for Grace and her lost dreams and not for me? As if it were yesterday, that afternoon with Katharine and her boy are back in her heart. Lost dreams, that's what Frances had and that night after Leon left the house yet again, how many times had he left her, she couldn't even count, left her alone in the house with Grace, and this was one night she couldn't stand it, no she couldn't, and she wraps up in that faded pink robe, wraps it tight around her, and she slides on high heels, grabs her wineglass and a bottle and heads down the path to the lake. Is Grace with her? Frances no longer remembers, all she remembers is the shimmering lake, her pale pink robe somehow turned yellow in the glimmering moonlight, and she remembers knowing that it's over, her dreams are dead. She puts her foot into water and doesn't feel its chill, she feels nothing, and she keeps going, she never learned to swim, no, her childhood wasn't one with swimming lessons, oh, no, no lessons for Frances. Grace is the one who gets lessons. And now she's walking into the lake by herself. Has she ever not been alone? She doesn't even have the dream that Leon loves her and she keeps moving forward, moving, swaying to a music swelling in her brain and then she's underwater and her bathrobe puffs out over her head like a thick pouf of yellowy cloud and the pain is fading, she can feel the numbness now of nothingness. Oh, God, thank you for that, she gave thanksgiving, offering herself to God and then, who was there? Leon. Leon is in the water beside her, his arms around her. He's pulling her to safety and somewhere there's screaming, and Leon is saying, It's over, Frannie, it's over, I give you my word, he's never called her Frannie before, only one time, when they first made love, oh, so many years before, when they accidentally conceived Baby Nathan, he told her again and again that he loved her, always and forever, that he'd never felt like this before, that he never would again, and all Frances can hear is Frannie, he's calling her Frannie, and then he's saying, I'll never see her again, not anyone else again, and she hasn't smelled Katharine again, she knows she hasn't, she's not lying to herself anymore, and he's saying, Hush, Gracie, hush Gracie, and Frances doesn't know who Gracie is, not at that moment, she just wants whoever she is to disappear, to leave her alone with her Leon. At the hospital, yes, Leon takes her to the hospital, it's all a mistake, she fell out of a boat, and Grace's eyes are wide and Frances knows who she is.

Frances sat up straight at the picnic table. The sky was a dull yellow glaze now resting just above the mountains. She watched her daughter. Grace looked up at Jonathan, said something. Jonathan leaned down, kissed her right above the ear. Grace pulled her hand from his, moved a step ahead. The steak knife gleamed dully in his hand. Frances wanted to run up the lawn, grab her daughter and shake her hard enough to rattle her teeth. How could she rebuff someone who so clearly loved her? How *dare* she? What was *wrong* with her?

Jonathan moved closer to Grace, put his arm around her waist. Grace pushed him away. He ran the edge of the knife across the tip of his finger.

Frances stood up and tried to wiggle out from the picnic bench. Leon put his hand on her rear end and squeezed. "Stay put," he said.

A thrill ran through Frances. "Someone has to knock some sense into that girl," she managed to say.

"Least said, soonest mended."

Frances stared at Leon. Those were words she might have used. He patted the bench. "Sit down." She did.

"Leave your daughter and her husband alone."

Frances took a deep breath. Her legs felt like Jell-O. Oh, for another bottle of wine. Her flush deepened. "Let's go down to the lake," she said.

"The milk?" Leon dipped into the Tostitos once again.

"They'll bring it down."

"My ankles hurt."

Frances's face burned. She wanted to go inside and hide her hurt. Almost on its own, her hand slipped inside her blouse and bra and touched her lump. She snatched Leon's tumbler, held it to her left cheek, her right, her forehead.

"Listen, Lex Luthor," came from the monitor, "you don't stand a chance against Superman."

Frances glanced toward Grace and Jonathan. Grace's whole body sagged. She rubbed her finger across her velveteen pocket. She twisted a strand of her hair around the index finger on her other hand, the same way she had as a little girl. Jonathan pressed the knife against his finger again. *Don't let there be anything wrong with her. I couldn't stand it if she had to go back to the Psych Institute.* St. Paul's would never stop talking. *Forgive my selfishness, Lord. Please don't let there be anything wrong with Grace.*

Grace suddenly left Jonathan and hurried down to the picnic table. She faced her father, head tilted to the side. She opened her mouth as if to say something, but she didn't, just linked her pinky with his. Leon nodded as if he understood something. Frances had no idea what Grace meant. She felt distanced from her family, as if a mist had settled around them, separating them, one from the other. If only she could grasp Grace's meaning, the tilt of her head, then maybe she could somehow be part of their relationship, she, too, could link pinkies with them, but if she said anything her words might hang in the air, unheard, adding to the fog, making it denser. Still, she took a deep breath. Just for a moment she was ready to risk speaking, to say, "What is it, Gracie? Let me help you," but she happened to look up at Jonathan, see the cottage outlined behind him. It looked scary, a dark, ragged-edged shape against the evening sky. Frances gave an inadvertent shiver. A goose walking over my grave, she thought. She pressed her lips together.

"Let's get the milk," Jonathan called.

Grace patted Leon on the shoulder and walked back toward the cottage.

Frances stood, taking hold of both Leon's hands. "C'mon, let's go down to the lake." She tugged at him, hard. At first he didn't budge from the picnic bench. "C'mon," Frances said, and she used that certain tone of voice, willing him to do what she wanted.

"Okay. We'll go down to the lake." Leon let Frances pull him to his feet.

Relief and something that might have been gratitude spread through Frances. When Leon gave her a gentle shove toward the path to the lake, she moved her hip toward his with a little rhythmic movement. He pressed her shoulder. Maybe tonight, thought Frances.

Mary Kay Zuravleff

# Hold Your Breath and Count to Ten

MARY KAY ZURAVLEFF is the author of *The Frequency of Souls* (Farrar, Straus, Giroux, 1996) and the upcoming *The Bowl Is Already Broken* (Farrar, Straus, Giroux, 2005). She lives in Washington, D.C., with her husband and two children.

Al nudged me awake at five-fifteen Thursday morning. I pawed the nightstand for my glasses so I could read the clock. Now that basketball season was over, band practice was back in the gym. As I made my way down the hall to Juliet's room, I remember toying with how hours are counted in base twelve but minutes are base sixty. Five-fifteen is actually a complicated notion.

We have always had to coax Juliet from a deep, drooling trance. When I used to obsess during her afternoon naps, my mother's pale skin and my husband's thick lips on her sleeping face made me fear she would be a slow child. But Thursday morning she was nothing. It was as if I had thermographic vision and could see the shape her warmth had left in the bed. She was missing. I pushed my hands into her fluffy quilt, but of course she wasn't under the folded-back corner. "Al, Al, Al," I cried out, as I searched beneath the lacy bedskirt, clearing a nest of socks and bras away. Her window was locked from the inside; her closet was too messy to hide in.

When I looked up, Al was in the doorway, rubbing his eyes. "That's weird," he said. "She can't be far, she's just on foot." I tried to imagine reasons why my sixteen-year-old would be out at dawn. I followed Al to the kitchen, where he started making coffee and poaching an egg for himself. I knew his form of hysterics was to stick to the routine; whereas, on a normal morning, I might leap into the air if I heard a cricket.

"Someone's taken her," I sobbed. "You know what it's like to get her up—she's been taken." Al shook salt into the pan. "You're cooking," I yelled.

My husband tucked me into the crook of his elbow, holding me against his chest with one strong hand while he coddled his egg with the other. "Barbara Ann," he said. "Baby, it's just breakfast."

I was glad he did not like his eggs hard-boiled. The smell of vinegar in the egg water reminded me of Easter eggs. While Al ate, I slit open two brown grocery bags and found a few felt-tip pens that had managed to keep their caps on. I drew our house as the origin of concentric circles, each ring representing a mile-wide step away from Harrison Street. Juliet-specific landmarks were next: school, Courtney's house, Mazza Gallerie and its thirty-two shops of convenience, Georgetown. The backyard floodlight shone through the kitchen window; when the timer switched it off, I flinched. I could usually hear Juliet's hair dryer when the beam turned dark, and I would start boiling water for oatmeal.

Al grabbed my shoulder and held it like a ledge. "I checked on her after sports."

"What did she say?"

"I asked her what time you should wake her up, and she said five-fifteen." His blonde beard made his rounded chin look like a cactus.

I chanted, "Five-fifteen, five-fifteen, five-fifteen." As Al stood behind me, soaking up his yolk with his toast, I rotated the numbers. Five is a factor of fifteen. Five times one is five, $5 \times 1 = 5$. My brother's birthday is May fifteenth, 5/15. I knew there was no code in Juliet saying the time, but I couldn't stop trying to find a pattern. Before I realized Al had left the kitchen, he was standing in front of me, fully dressed and shaved. He picked up his briefcase, which was my signal that we could leave. We'd lost six or seven minutes to his egg.

"You driving?" I asked.

"You want to?" Al offered me the Honda keys, the built-in transmitter a cruel bobble in light of Juliet's absence. Why couldn't I push a button and locate her with a beep? Why wasn't she alarmed?

"No, you drive." He always gravitated to the driver's seat. I only drove when he or I asked, as if it were a special occasion. This was how my parents behaved and my grandparents and great-aunts and -uncles. Tradition always confused me at times of crisis. How had this pattern established itself? And what if it changed? You know, if the earth were tilted just one degree more on its axis either way the planet would be unfit for human life. I knew I was obsessing in an effort to stave off fear. There was no evidence that she'd been abducted, which didn't mean she hadn't, because there was certainly no good reason for her to have walked out of the house before five-fifteen. I concentrated on drawing more circles around the house on my bag map. I wanted to surround Juliet; even in this schematic rendering, I was desperate not to leave her outside. I shaded certain bands where I thought we would most likely find her. Then I started hyperventilating. "If we believe she's on foot," I panted, "we should search within the red bend." My map was spread out and flapping.

"Breathe normally," Al said. "In a second, you'll need that bag over your head."

I begged him to say something comforting.

Al reached under my hair; his fingers got caught in the red swarm of curls when he tried to pull his hand back. "Just because Juliet wasn't in bed this morning doesn't mean she's in danger."

"It's dangerous out here!" I screamed.

"I know," he said, "but she might just be sleeping at a friend's house. None of the doors was tampered with; someone would have to have roofing ladders to get to her room."

So he had checked the doors, thought about the distance from the ground to the second story.

"Honey," he said. "Whenever you hear thunder, you imagine bombers strafing the house. Worse, I step into the shower with you, and you scream. Who do you think it is every morning?"

I did not actually think it was someone other than Al in the shower, but most mornings I did yelp. "It's pretty easy to picture the worst in a case like this."

We stopped at a light that I would have ignored. The bank sign flashed 5:42 in turn with "Ask us about college savings." Tears dropped onto my cheeks, although I hadn't even known I was crying. Waiting to cross the street, a perky brown-and-white spaniel was tugging at a leash held by a yawning woman. I longed to be in her shoes, bored with morning family habits. If Al weren't with me, I might have rolled down the window and counseled her, "Don't take that dog for granted."

Al stroked my thigh. "The only places Juliet goes on her own are Georgetown and the malls."

I tried to imagine her involved in some prank so I could be mad instead of frightened. "Maybe she and Courtney are up to something."

"That's better," Al said. "If Juliet gets a fever, you suspect meningitis."

"She's the only daughter we have," I said.

"I just think the mathematician should be the one talking about logical explanations."

I said, "Your father's the craziest person we know, and he's a psychiatrist." Then I was so embarrassed that I paid attention to my map for the rest of the ride.

As I imagine it, the circle was more discovered than invented, more experienced than discovered. Our ancestors saw the moon, that glowing orb, above them each evening. They witnessed its roundness and experienced the cycle of its changing shape. The snow and ice came after so many round moons, but the earth warmed after a predictable number of round moons, too. On the heels of fire, people next discovered that the warmest and safest arrangement for a group was in a circle around the flame. You might be warmest in front of your own blaze, but you could be picked off the easiest that way as well.

So I told myself the circle was cycles and it was protection. I expected this thought to be comforting, some sort of geometric shield. But when I looked at my map—shaded bands radiating from a red blob—our house looked like the bull's eye of a target, and I couldn't help thinking we had been chosen for disaster. Don't you eventually pay for the happiness of previous years?

Al had turned west off Wisconsin Avenue. "Where are you going?" I asked.

"The police station," he said. "Let's get them on the case, even if she's just messing around."

There was a metal detector as we entered the police station, and this made my head spin. Of course, the police had to worry about their security; however, they're armed to the teeth *and* they're the police. If there were people who would bring a gun in here, how vulnerable were the rest of us? To make matters worse, they asked us to wait.

"Should we?" I asked Al. "Every minute we're here, we could be looking."

"We need their help," Al said. "It won't be long—they're not busy."

I thought about last Saturday, when Juliet and I had been a normal mother and daughter bickering at Hecht's. Juliet picked out a band concert dress that was so low we would have to buy her a special bra. "The dress is not supposed to upstage the music," I'd told her.

"I can't believe we're making a big deal over this. I'm like sixth or seventh chair and we're playing stuff that doesn't even feature my section. I think Mr. Bradhue wrote in the flute music."

"Sweetpea, without the flute section, the orchestra is heavy, constipated."

"Mom!" She'd acted shocked that I would say "constipated" in a mall, though I had heard her say worse on the phone to her friends. She had taken up flute just the year before, because she heard that Mr. Bradhue was arranging a summer trip to Barcelona for the orchestra.

Juliet traded the V-neck for a thin silk dress from the rack; this one had a mandarin collar and a peplum. The only thing wrong with this dress was that it showed off her voluptuous figure to its full advantage. Juliet's thick lips had taken on a pouty, foreign model look when she was in ninth grade, which went with her ropey red hair. Al says she gets her looks from me, but I remember being barely presentable before I turned twenty. Her body was still just an idea to her, and she waved it under people's noses to study their reactions. My job was to safeguard this raw data until she knew how to read it.

"It's twenty percent off," I'd said. "What would that make it?"

"Ninety minus eighteen would be seventy-two. OK?" Juliet hated buying dresses on sale, and she hated performing math tricks for me.

When we came home with the peplum dress on Saturday, we were both cagey but satisfied. Now, I felt I'd overplayed my authority; if I could, I would have lined the road between us with low-cut dresses. I would have tied lures of silk scarves and dangly earrings, set traps with lasagna and chocolate-covered graham crackers.

Officer Maynard gazed at my husband. "Right this way," the cop said, as if he were showing us to the honeymoon suite. He looked porterish, with young puffy skin and a uniform that was too long in the sleeves. I smoothed out my map on the card table in the little room. The small-boned officer smirked with pity.

"Please, Mrs. Kittridge, we have maps."

I said, "Your maps are not centered around our house. This map is color-coded to Juliet's habits. This map has probability fields—"

"Whoa," Officer Maynard reigned me in.

Al said, "Barbara Ann's a mathematician."

I'm not sure Al could be heard over my panting. Maynard spoke loudly to me. "Mrs. Kittridge," he said. "Take it easy. Hold your breath and count to ten."

I gulped some air. I was probably going to faint.

"We need to start with the basics," Maynard said. "Has Juliet left home before?"

"Never," Al said. "She's a great kid, good grades, the works. I spoke to her last night between eleven and eleven-thirty. She was already in bed."

I stared at the way Maynard's gum-chewing elongated and compressed his square jaw until he lifted his notebook like a screen between us. "Go ahead," he said to Al.

Al said, "I asked her when we should wake her up and she said five-fifteen."

"Is that normal?" Maynard asked.

"Band practice starts at six-thirty," I explained. "They're getting ready for the spring concert. Her flute is still on the living room floor. What if she's there now, waiting to explain?"

"Take it easy," Al said. "Don't pass out on me." As if I were already in a straightjacket, Al folded my arms across my chest. He was trying to contain me, but I wasn't going anywhere. At most, my anxiety might melt me into a puddle at their feet.

Officer Maynard put his pencil down. "So, you're a homemaker?" he asked.

"I work at home. I write math books."

He looked me up and down. "I hate math," he said.

That brought me back faster than ten deep breaths. Any other day, I would have comforted him. There, there, I know. Bad teachers, rote memorization, no applications. I had an inkling that Al and my publisher might be right about my new math book for people who hated math. But I was not at the police station to teach Officer Maynard percents.

Maynard was trained to respond to unpredictability rather than to deductive reasoning. What Maynard did not understand was that Juliet was still too naïve to be unpredictable. To my knowledge, she had no boyfriend and took no drugs— once she came home from a basketball game and threw up beer. She loved Spanish to the degree that she could be lured like a stray cat by a bowl full of anything related to Spain. Sure, she surprised and delighted and angered us in ways we never could have imagined, but not in ways unlike other sixteen-year-olds. "You think your Laura's bad," we might say. "Juliet completely forgot to call home when she got to Courtney's on Tuesday."

Maynard was trying to tell me that if Juliet crossed his path, he would bring her home. Meanwhile, the petite cop doted on Al, who performed like a circus dog. "Around five-foot-three or -four," he said. "Red hair, a mole on her left ear."

"Left ear?" Maynard asked. He looked at me for affirmation. "Parents get that wrong all the time; their left, the kid's left, they can't seem to distinguish…"

I told him she had the constellation Cassiopeia in freckles across the bridge of her nose. "Her eyes dart back and forth when she looks at you; I don't think it's intentional but she looks at your left eye then your right then back again." She was more than what could fit on Maynard's form. She was a supplementary page; she was indescribable. "Her hair skirts her eyelashes. And it is not red," I said, resorting to the colors in Juliet's teen clothing catalogues. "Her hair is yam puree, mango popsicle." Maynard asked to speak to Al alone.

Ten minutes later, Al and Officer Maynard came out of the room, each holding a cream doughnut. In the car, Al said, "Maynard's a golfer."

Another spray of tears covered my cheeks, like the periodic misting of the lettuce at the grocery store. "You're not even rattled." My voice sounded like a howl. "You're eating a doughnut and talking about golf."

We passed the bank sign again; now it flashed 6:07. Al said, "I'm a golfer, too. And I'll bet that playing golf with Maynard will get me farther than any of your probability theories."

I crumpled into the bucket seat. At the next red light, Al hugged me as best he could.

He said, "We are going to get the Sweetpea back."

As if we had performed missing child drills, we began immediately dealing with Juliet's absence. We called her teachers and arranged to pick up assignments. That night, I prepared two essays for her, which shows my desperation more than anything else, because we were never parents who did her work. I wrote a book report on *A Tale of Two Cities* and three paragraphs on the merits of grouping ninth graders with junior- rather than senior-high students. I held my daughter inside me, just as I had when we first discovered she was alive.

Friday afternoon I watched old cartoons on television, but they reminded me more of my childhood than Juliet's. Though she had a terrific sense of humor, Juliet never thought cartoons were funny. "That's dynamite!" she would yell when Bugs offered up a cigar, and I remembered she would hiccup, which she did when she was overly excited.

During the days, I tried to work on my book or even a reason to write my book. In the beginning, math is either zero or one. There is only one right answer at this stage, and I believe that when some people say they hate math, they are still stinging from the frustration of unmistakably wrong answers. It reminded me of the day Juliet threw her flute down on the couch, bored with the hours of winded exercises required to blow a simple tune. "I hate scales," she cried. "The flute is stupid." Her disgust clarified my mission, and I told her, "Scales are not music. Don't stop learning because you don't like scales."

The math beyond arithmetic exists between zero and one; in this realm, you could be right with a good argument, two plus two may not equal four, the model we previously accepted might be flawed. I wanted to give my readers a glimpse into this world, even if they didn't choose to dwell there.

The truth is I prefer the zero-or-one world. My daughter, for example, is missing. She is not threatening to leave. She is not getting moody at the dinner table, decrying our choice of veal as an entrée. She was one, sometimes two, scallopini slices at dinner—now she is zero. Unfortunately, the in-between world will not always take no for an answer. Divorced friends have reminded me of this, forced as they are to live among the fractions.

Saturday morning, when a lanky boy was sitting at Juliet's breakfast spot, I felt my own accordion of uncertainty being pulled apart.

"Morning," Al greeted me. "Matthew and I were just saying that it's nearly golf weather."

"Don't choke on your oatmeal, Mom," this Matthew said, "but can I have a little trig help after breakfast? I want to start my problem set before Sunday night."

"Why do you call me Mom?" I asked.

"Because you're not the kind of Mom who likes to be called Barbara Ann."

True enough. I used to hate it when Juliet's friends said, "Sharon could drive us to the game." Or "Ralph snores constantly." He was a different kind of kid from Juliet and her friends. Shaggy hair, rips in his clothes from actual use, a T-shirt with "Stoned Lizards" printed on it. Juliet's crowd acted like vain, giggly adults. They polished their shoes, waxed their eyebrows, had their hair cut every six weeks. This child was refreshingly teenagerish.

I asked him, "What exactly are you doing in my kitchen?"

"Eating a rhombus or two of toast and a cylinder of milk."

"No," I said.

"A trapezoid of toast?" he asked.

"No. What are *you* doing *here*?"

"What's with the cross examination?" Matthew asked, and he looked to Al. "Dad."

"Barbara Ann," Al spoke as if I were the troublemaker. "Is this one of your logic games?"

I made a note to save Al's reaction for a discussion on the difference between existence and uniqueness. A child at the breakfast table was not enough for me.

When I was finally alone with Al, he said Matthew was in the kitchen calling him Dad just moments before I came in.

"You answered to it?" I asked. "I thought I was the nut in this house. How did he get in? A strange, scruffy boy Juliet's age is sitting in your house and you don't investigate? You don't call Officer Maynard?"

"He was using one of the cereal bowls, and he also knew where you keep the sugar."

"So he looked around," I said, though finding the sugar in the peanut-butter jar above the sink may have meant he'd been peeping through the windows. I was crying again and I was scared. "I want to make toast for Juliet. And cook her watery oatmeal with half of a banana."

"You didn't see it," Al said. "He took a paper towel and wiped off the edge of the butter dish just the way you like. If this kid wants to call me Dad, I'll go along with it. Eventually, he's going to let slip who sent him. I'll bet he knows where Juliet is."

چو

Once when Juliet was in sixth grade, she came home from school in a snit. I was in the kitchen lining up spices on the counter. Juliet ground her front teeth while she watched me measure out paprika, salt, parsley flakes for dinner.

Angrily, she asked, "What if you only had a teaspoon of salt and the recipe said two teaspoons?"

I thought she was just acting peeved, so I pretended the answer was difficult. "I guess that I would have a negative teaspoon of salt."

"No!" she yelled. "You can't have a negative amount of something. You and Mr. Morgan are wrong."

"I could say I need a teaspoon of salt or that I still owe our dinner a teaspoon of salt."

"You and Mr. Morgan are wrong," she insisted, and she jerked her head with a hiccup. "Last year Miss Shields said, 'I can't give you a dollar if I'm broke.'" Then she took a breath and held it.

"Last year," I said, "we didn't let you stay out past seven. That didn't mean Washington did not exist for other people past seven. Last year you weren't ready for the fact that I really could give you a dollar if I was broke—I could borrow it, write you a bad check, steal it—"

Juliet exhaled. "You have wigged out. Why can't you just say you're wrong?"

So we teach our children one thing—numbers start with one, three is not divisible by two, you can't take the square root of a negative number—and one semester later, we say HA! and snap the tablecloth out from under them, sending their waxy milk cartons flying.

Of course, I felt tricked now, with Matthew rooting around Juliet's dresser, requesting his boxer shorts. I tried ignoring him, but he was needy and amusing and annoying in turns. When he asked for a ride to the music store, I said, "Don't you have a bicycle?"

"Buy me a bike and I'll have a bike," he said. And then he began that throaty laugh, which I guess boys his age can't help.

After dinner, as I was folding towels and Al was sorting his socks, Matthew sat down and studied us.

"How did you two meet?" he asked.

"I was parallel parking in Georgetown," Al began, "and your mother was sitting in her car wearing a pink and orange halter top, blasting the radio."

"I was killing time before class," I said curtly. I didn't want to play along; I wanted to shake this kid upside down until whatever Juliet bits he had fell from his pockets.

Al was a convincing actor, probably no surprise to the many juries he had entertained. He was in his element telling Matthew his favorite story.

"She was singing at the top of her lungs, throwing her hair around, using her lipstick as a microphone. Her father's vintage Mustang was rocking back and forth. I was backing up, but I couldn't stop staring at this wild woman..." Al looked me up and down, the same way Officer Maynard had at the police station but without the contempt. I silently counted the beats of Al's timing, its rhythm established after years of retelling this tale. "And then I ran over her rear bumper."

With our tale of car wrecks, loud music, and the hot pants Al would soon mention, we had Matthew's complete attention. He probably thought we had met in a bank line.

Al said, "Barbara Ann leapt out of her car and started ranting in this razor-sharp pitch." He slowed his voice with reverence. "She was wearing just the hint of a pair of shorts."

I chipped in for Al, for Juliet. I said, "I must have babbled for five minutes. 'What are you, an idiot? My father is going to kill me, and then he'll probably kill you.' Al let me wind down, then he took my hand and said, 'If I tell you you have a great body, will you hold it against me?'"

Matthew laughed. It was kind of fun telling him the story for the first time. He chucked Al on the shoulder. "You're lucky she didn't deck you."

"Ah, but she did," Al said, and they both snorted and guffawed.

He wasn't a bad kid—a little smart-mouthed—but he was not mine.

The next morning I was working on a simple proof to explain the behavior of negative numbers, but I kept imagining Juliet's voice asking "Who cares?" It was a welcome relief for me to focus on her prissy side, because thinking about her wonderful attributes sent me into an afternoon of guilt and hysteria. For the first time since starting my book, I saw why people might not care about proving things already known. The truth is that things that matter are unresolved.

Besides, people who hate math won't respect a mathematical proof as evidence of anything. Why is a negative number times a negative number a positive number? Juliet seemed a good analogy, although most questions I asked myself these days had Juliet in the answer.

You have a child at great negative risk to your body. When Juliet was born, she and I both went into shock. From the start, she was expensive and demanded we figure out her quirks (Al had to bare one breast when he rocked her or she would scream until she ran out of oxygen). Yet when that bundle of shared genes focused her hazel eyes on her crib mobile, we were positively moved. My theory breaks down here in that the negatives are not necessarily groupable two by two, but I can remember them multiplying on and on and doubting anything good would come of our lack of sleep or the stains on all the shoulders of my blouses or our new debt.

Now, Juliet's absence seemed such a huge negative that no other negative could rescue it from the left of zero. And just who was this replacement child?

By Tuesday, I had mostly cried myself out. Officer Maynard had no news, except that he promised he'd call Al if he heard something. Matthew kept the noise at a teenager-in-the-house level, for which I was grateful. He and Al had a tussle over sweeping out the garage on Monday.

"He's got to learn to do some work around here," Al said.

Afraid to lose him, too, I squeakily defended Matthew. "He washed both cars yesterday."

Matthew was embarrassed by my high-pitched defense. That's when it occurred to me that people can explain anything, even an instant son. They can rationalize blows they have been dealt, or worse yet, forget about them. I felt disloyal to Juliet trying to hold on to Matthew. Maybe if he left, she would return.

When Al and I were getting married, it seemed appropriate, perfect even, that only eight weeks earlier, I had been singing away—"Would you like me to dance? Take a ch-ch-ch-chance"—on the side of the road when he'd nearly run me down. What could be less coincidental? My parents talked about pacing and breakneck speed as if I were a racehorse, but I used momentum and the logic of inexperience to wear them down. With a Ph.D. in mathematical theory at twenty-five, was I the kind of girl who thought a pickup line excused reckless driving? Certainly not. Therefore, Al and I were meant to be together.

And so on with getting turned down for tenure, not crying every Christmas after my mother died, or even the lucky breaks, like Al's continuing handsomeness and his distaste for television football, and, until last week, Juliet. No logic comforted me in Juliet's absence. Better to be perpetually depressed than to be strong enough to withstand the loss of my daughter. And when I became conscious of one moment when I had not been thinking of her, I believed that I deserved to have her taken from me.

Wednesday I went to the library for stimulation, somehow forgetting that the place would be filled with kids, slouched in their seats and reading in bad light. When I came home around three, there was a police car in the driveway. I snuck cautiously into the house, not wanting to scare Maynard off.

Officer Maynard was sitting at the kitchen table with Al. "If they're so upset," Al said, "why did they wait a week to report him missing? Barbara Ann and I immediately came to the police."

He'd left out the poached egg.

With the same smirk of pity he'd shown my map, Maynard looked at my husband. "He's not such a great kid, Al."

"Save your stories," Al said. "I know what you're after."

"He's not your boy. His parents are in fairly often. They've got some temper problems. Mr. drinks a few scotches too many, throws a glass or barks at the kid, and Matthew takes off."

"Jesus," Al said. "You can't throw stuff at a kid."

"Al, you can't keep him just because Juliet is gone. These people miss their boy."

"Well, here he goes to class and comes home at a reasonable time and cleans the garage and doesn't have to duck during cocktail hour. His parents don't know where the hell he is, they can just wait."

I retreated to the car and drove around the block a few times until the squad car was gone. When I came in, Al did not mention that Maynard had been by. Because I wanted Matthew to stay with us, I couldn't bring up the subject. How could I argue that his parents deserved this?

Matthew had dropped no hints that he knew Juliet. Some of their friends had the same names; for example, he knew a Nathan and a Lawrence. But in his circle they were Nato and Law. He played music I'd never heard before, and he called girls who reminded me of Juliet "mall rats." The girls who called him had boys' names: Alex, Sam, Benton. Their voices were not familiar.

Then, during dinner Thursday night, Matthew asked Al, "Can you drop me at school?"

"Matthew," Al prompted, "I thought we agreed that your mother and I were going, too."

I looked around me as if Matthew's mother were nearby, but Matthew thought I was joking. For a second I felt bad. If he were my son, I would not treat him this way.

"I have to be there early to tune my tympani."

"There's no need to make two trips," Al said and pushed away from the table. He rubbed my shoulders. "Your mother and I can visit with the other parents." Then he left the kitchen.

"You don't have to come," Matthew said. "I just need to be there early for one more run-through. I can't practice at home, like the other kids." My hand was flat on the table; Matthew started tracing it with his spoon.

"You can practice here," I said.

"I'm not allowed to take the tympani home, Mom." He lowered his voice. "We're playing with St. Agnes, you know." I kept my hand perfectly still, as if he were throwing knives around it. "Juliet will be there."

"Juliet?" I asked. "My Juliet?"

"She goes to St. Agnes," Matthew said. "Second chair flute."

"Is she all right? Is she safe?"

"I think she's fine," he said. I could see he already regretted bringing her up. He said, "She didn't want to leave here."

Tears ran along the frames of my glasses. I was furious at Matthew, the ragged punk, for keeping this information to himself until now, but I also recognized the generosity in his sharing it. I wondered if Matthew's mother were crying right now; how could my heart have been so hardened to her? "She's living with another family?"

Matthew nodded. "It's not her fault. Blame the phone chain."

I was stunned. "The phone chain? The phone chain is for snow days and carpools."

"We were reassigned. No one really knows who started it."

"I'll get dressed," I said.

I careened through my closet, looking for a gentle, motherly, smart dress, one that would woo my daughter home. My child, who could argue for an hour about who had the right to tell her to eat her parsnips, left home because of one phone call? She couldn't be happy at St. Agnes, with only other girls and nuns for company. What would she wear tonight? Her peplum dress was still in her closet.

I ran back to the kitchen in my pantyhose and slip. "Matthew," I said. "Your real mother and father miss you."

"I suppose," he said, with what seemed to me great relief.

Together, I felt, we had cracked some wartime code. I kissed him on the cheek. "Ah, shucks, ma'am," he said in a western twang.

Where was she living? Did they know about her delicate stomach? Would someone put a barrette in her hair so she could concentrate on her flute? I let my own ringlets down and struggled with contact lenses for the first time in weeks.

Al came into the bedroom and patted me on the rear. "I'm happy to see you paying attention to Matthew," he said. He stroked me, and I went along with it. Maybe Al was part of my excitement, the idea that we could be a family again, Al and I cavorting in the bedroom on Saturday morning knowing our talented daughter—not slow at all—was sleeping like a lump down the hall. I couldn't say what Matthew had told me. Superstition had suddenly taken on all the glamour of logic: if I spoke the words, she wouldn't be there or Al would say Matthew was "shamming" me.

In Juliet's bedroom, I looked through her orderly desk for the book report. Matthew came in just as I was turning a drawer upside down.

"I'm looking for something," I said.

"Dickens?" Matthew asked. "You got a B. The teacher only assigned a two-pager. And she did not buy your description of the Parisian streets as 'slimed remains beneath a sink of dishwater.'"

"Matthew, that was not for you." And what exactly had I planned to do with it? In my dresser, I'd been hoarding little gifts for Juliet: a CD by some teenage heartthrobs from Madrid and peace-sign earrings I'd saved from the seventies. I would not see her with an empty purse.

We drove to the school, Matthew pounding out some rhythm, perhaps his tympani part, on the back of my seat. He was nervous about the concert, or maybe he was nervous about something else. I didn't have to tell him not to talk about Juliet in front of Al; I think he was regretting he had mentioned it at all.

At Juliet's old school, Al visited with parents. I unblinkingly watched the stage until my eyes were dry with strain. "Spacey," I heard Al say. "She's been working on that book again." Who knows what he said when I wasn't around?

When the curtain closed and reopened, it was Matthew I spotted first. Of course, that was because he stood out at the only tympani in the joined orchestras. But then I found the flutes and thanked God for Juliet's flag of hair. She was wearing a flattering black dress that I had had no hand in. In a perverse way, it was no relief to see her safe and beautiful apart from Al and me. I had spent even the space between moments worrying about her, when she was apparently well-fed, well-dressed, and unconcerned about her parents.

"It's her," I pointed. "It's her," I said to Al.

He followed my point. "She's breathtaking," he whispered.

Juliet did indeed take my breath away. My chest hurt with heavy inhalations, breaths that threatened to bring up my heart as well. Juliet played a duet with the first chair flutist; she had never played such a complex piece or with such technique. Even though I knew it was inappropriate, I applauded the duet, and a few people followed my lead. If Matthew pretended Al and I were his parents, Juliet had probably been calling some strangers Mom and Dad all week. Perhaps they were the other people clapping. Intermission actually arrived without my stopping the show.

When I found her backstage, Juliet was talking to Courtney, her best friend since grade school. "Hola," I said. I should have tucked her into my purse and taken off for the car, but for some reason I could only think of annoying mother things to say. "You have an orthodontist appointment on Monday." My voice was low and even, the sound of the possessed.

Juliet's eyes darted from left to right. "My new orthodontist gets cable in his waiting room."

"Dr. Pullman tightens your bands, and then we go to Bob's where you drink a shake laced with crushed-up aspirins. You have to miss English once a month. That's the plan."

"There is no plan anymore," my only daughter said. She ground her silver-banded teeth and tipped up her head with rhythmic hiccups. "You can describe our old routine in the minutest, but it won't help."

"Sweetpea," I said. "We miss you so much. Why did you leave?"

"It wasn't my idea," she said. Her white, white skin flushed, and the constellation across her nose faded against her self-consciousness. "Courtney went to the Hendersons'. Now she has two brothers who will drive her anywhere."

I touched her dress. "This is beautiful," I said, and we both felt the electricity. "You can tell me about it at home."

"Don't," she pleaded. "I was just getting used to this and now…"

"Getting used to this?" I blurted out. My cheeks burned as if she'd slapped me. "This is an aberration, a glitch. Nobody's getting used to this."

Juliet's body shook in little gasps. "It's so random. You play the flute like a retard, then you pick it up overnight. You have one mother, then the phone rings."

I took her into my arms; she was shuddering with hiccups.

She said, "Remember that story about how you met Daddy?"

"Blind luck," I said. "Hold your breath and count to ten."

She stood apart from me and took a breath. We watched each other anxiously. I saw that it was the surprise rather than the violence of the cartoon dynamite that bothered her as a child. I thought of sage Officer Maynard, who'd scoffed at my grocery-bag map and my belief that I could sniff out my child with reason.

Al was struggling upstream to us. He waved timidly, but when he reached Juliet, he lifted her off the ground with a hug.

"Sweetpea. It never occurred to us you were in the neighborhood. What a pleasant surprise."

Al put her back on the ground, and Juliet blew out her breath. We listened to see if she was cured. Schools of students dodged us on their way back to the stage.

"Mom," she asked me, "how do you live with random?"

I took her hand, which was colder than mine, and squeezed it. As much as I relished hearing her call me Mom, I wished she'd addressed Al—men are good at shrugging off hard questions.

Al jumped into the silence. He said, "Sometimes you can go your whole life without a jet crashing through your bedroom window."

Or without losing your daughter, I thought.

Al swung his little girl up in the air again. Her hair flew out in a circle, a wide, curly halo around her grinning face. "Daddy," she said, "put me down. I have to go back out there." When she touched the floor, she asked, "What about Matthew?"

Al said, "He has his own family."

"Maybe," Juliet said, "but he likes you guys better." She smoothed her clingy dress down her flat stomach. "This is truly rambunctious. I have like a six-measure solo in the Stravinsky piece."

I dug into my purse for the peace-sign earrings. "Look what I brought you." I was a little dizzy.

"Don't faint, Mom," she said. "Just sit out there and be my proud parents and figure out what you're going to say to Mrs. Lowell. I don't know if you'll like her."

Al said, "We like anyone who's been good to you."

"Not you," Juliet said. She turned to me. "She told me to call her Elizabeth and she can't even figure out how to double a recipe."

"That's not what matters," I said. I kissed the mole on her left ear.

"Take your flute," Al coached, "and play for us."

We all waved bravely as she walked back out on stage. Matthew kept up a steady beat on the tympani. In the audience of parents, I waited for Juliet's six measures. I should have answered her question; I wouldn't have been as glib as Al. "My little Sweetpea," I should have said, "you don't have any choice but to live with random. But give me the chance, and I will show you a glimpse of beauty in the arc of a curve, lovingly integrated."

For here was an auditorium full of people appreciating short bursts of order. Although any one of them might say they had no use, saw no beauty, possessed no comprehension for mathematical patterns, what were notes on a page but that? No doubt many of them found comfort in hearing a familiar melody, though knowing the intended notes at a high school concert can make you a nervous wreck. I listened for the single strand of flute that would be my daughter's sigh. And then Juliet breathed a melody that Stravinsky had created out of pure possibility, a pattern contrived to match a tune in his head.

I breathed a hymn to my daughter in time to those six measures. Even if Juliet were in her bed the next thousand mornings in a row, I might wake with a stitch in my side and run down the hall to check. Likewise, I wanted a chance to explain to her that in every penciled proof there are shadows of partially erased doubt.

RICHARD PEABODY wears many literary hats. He is editor of *Gargoyle Magazine* (founded in 1976) and has published a novella, two books of short stories, six books of poems, plus an ebook, and has co-edited six anthologies with Lucinda Ebersole including *Mondo Barbie, Mondo Elvis, Mondo Marilyn, Mondo James Dean, Coming to Terms: A Literary Response to Abortion*, and *Conversations with Gore Vidal* (forthcoming 2005). He also edited *A Different Beat: Writings by Women of the Beat Generation* for Serpent's Tail in 1997. Peabody teaches fiction writing for the Johns Hopkins Advanced Studies Program. He lives in Arlington, Virginia, with his wife and two daughters. You can find out more about him at gargoylemagazine.com.